Hope you enjoy b

COMMENTS FROM READERS

"One of the best books I have ever read. This book had you hooked on the first page." Eillien Smith

"I have not enjoyed a book as much as I have enjoyed this one for a very long time. Thank you for this amazing gift." Peggy Goddard

"An excellent book and I give it 10 stars out of 5. Waiting for her next book to come out." Rosemary Albert Sanders

"I'm reading it now. Love it. Can't wait to pick it up every chance I get to read. Buy it. You will be glad you did." Pat Tracy McKinnon-Larocca

"I read your book in two days. I loved it. It was hard to put down. You captured the reader from the beginning and connected all the dots to make a satisfying ending." Brenda Munro

"Just finished your book. I couldn't put it down. Fantastic book." Diane Leard

"Didn't want to stop reading last night ....Awake at 4:30 and back to reading." Rosemary Albert Sanders

"Finished reading your book last week – couldn't put it down! Congratulations on a riveting story!" Mayumi Bailey

"I didn't want this book to end." Frances Carrick

"I thoroughly enjoyed this book....Great read, would highly recommend it to anyone." Anne McGowan

"Just finished it. I am sorry it came to an end. I enjoyed every moment of it! I will definitely read it again!" Gabrielle McTavish

“This was by far one of my most favourite reads in a while. I felt like I was living it. I absolutely loved this book.” Kim Galbraith

“I loved it... such a good story and reminder of what is important in life.” Teresa Fenwick

“ I love it. I bought 2 books Saturday and am halfway through mine. Thinking about buying another for someone else. Great read for both young and old!” Sheila Wood

“Couldn’t put it down. Brilliant!” Christine Woodman

“I just finished your book. It was so touching and real I felt like I was friends with Isabel. It was so well written and such a delightful read.” Janet Shaw

“Excellent read. The author has a unique voice that grabs the reader’s attention until the very end.” Ann C. (Amazon rating)

“I bought your book and enjoyed it so much! Passed it to my 88 year old Mom and she could not put it down and her friend Betty loved it too! Thank you for writing this book!”
Angela Walker Duncan

“What a wonderful book.... Finished it this morning and enjoyed every minute. Thanks for the lovely read.” Charlene Crandall

“Bought this for my friend... She absolutely loved this book and storyline... She said it was one of the best books and enjoyed it thoroughly. Thank you for writing such an awesome story and helping me give a gift of such enjoyment.” Debi Cowgill

“I have just finished reading your wonderful book. I have been reading it out loud to my husband and we both enjoyed it immensely.... We could not wait until the next reading.”
Jack and Marilyn Groom

BEHIND THE PICKLE JAR

By Wendy McQuaig

Horse & Carriage Publishing
ISBN # 978-1-7380582-0-4 (Paperback)
ISBN # 978-1-7380582-1-1 (Ebook)

**This book is a work of fiction. All the characters and stories in this novel are imaginary. Any resemblance to an actual person or circumstance is coincidental. Some creative liberties have been taken with the descriptions of Orillia and area in 1900. The pictures in this book are random photos of people from another century. Unfortunately, no diary was ever found in the cellar.

www.behindthepicklejar.com

goodreads.com/ Wendy McQuaig

facebook.com/ Wendy McQuaig Author

instagram.com/ @wmcquaigauthor

This book is dedicated to my wonderful husband Fred: my soul mate and best friend. Thanks always for your enduring kindness and encouragement!

This book is also dedicated to my three favourite children Jay, Jennie and Murray. Thanks to each of you for your endless support and inspiration. I am lucky to have such great kids!
You are all irreplaceable.

One last thing.... A very special thank you to Lois, my loving mother-in-law who was my avid literary fan and cheerleader throughout. Unfortunately, she did not live to see this book in print. She is greatly missed.

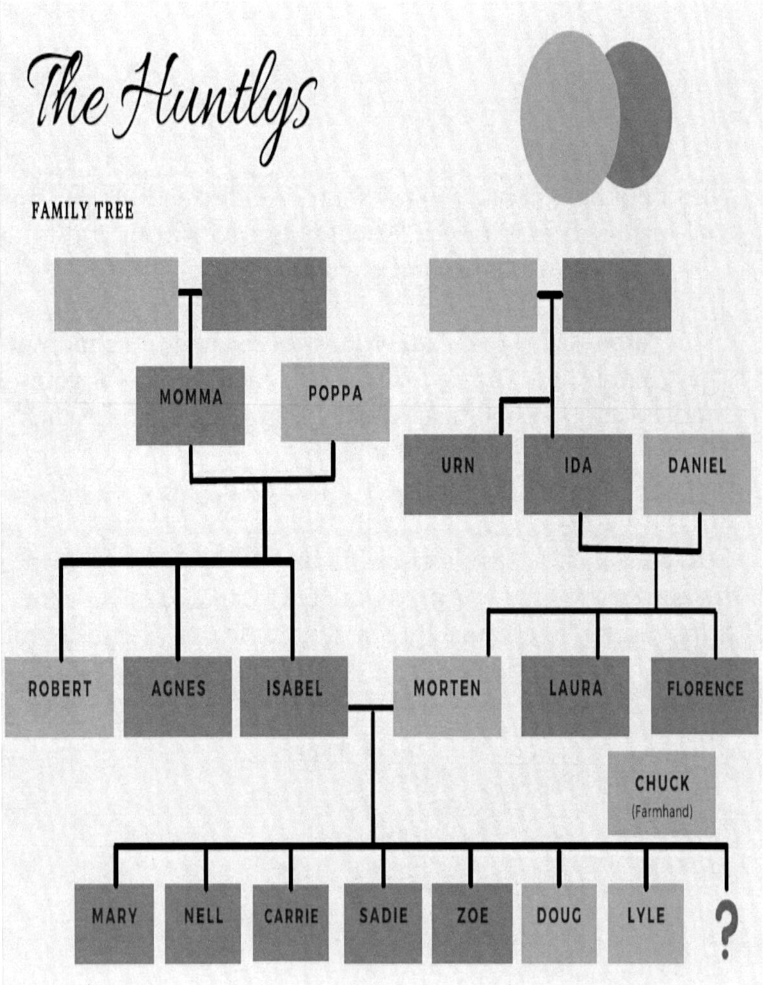
The Huntlys
FAMILY TREE
MOMMA
POPPA
URN
IDA
DANIEL
ROBERT
AGNES
ISABEL
MORTEN
LAURA
FLORENCE
CHUCK
(Farmhand)
MARY
NELL
CARRIE
SADIE
ZOE
DOUG
LYLE
?

CHAPTER ONE

At 142 years old, I've seen a lot of things, some good, some bad, but nothing compared to what I worry I may see in the years ahead. I'm not as attractive as I once was. Some people say I have character. My bricks are slipping, I'm leaking here and there, and my porch needs repair. Some want to fix me up, even renovate me but most just want to tear me down and forget I was ever here. Despite all that, I believe I still have something to offer. I'm wiser than I was when they built me back in 1875. I was just a kid then. At that time, life from my vantage point seemed so simple and carefree, but as I age things are becoming more complex and confusing, often even worrisome.

My first family was the Huntlys. They lived within my walls for years. I loved them all and I felt so proud to provide a home for them. Eventually they left my shelter and I shed a tear for every one of them as they went. Life has changed so much over the years. Now, over a century later, I have the Hewstons. I don't know them very well yet, but I do worry about their little family. They seem so alone in the world. Maybe I can help them.

Perhaps, if you have some time to listen to an old house prattle on about yesteryear and some of the changes I've seen since then, you might enjoy this tale. It involves both the families who have lived within my walls and how they became connected by what was found behind the pickle jar.

2017

It's hard to breathe. My heart is pounding like a jackhammer, my hands are trembling. Something terrible is about to happen, I can just feel it. What's the matter with me? These bloody panic attacks are controlling my life. Take a break, move around, get my mind elsewhere. That's what my therapist tells me to do when it starts to build. Sometimes it works, usually it doesn't.

I shut my laptop, pry myself loose from my big mahogany desk, and begin pacing restlessly around my lavish corner office. I glance out the floor-to-ceiling window and take in the sea of office buildings below. 'Breathe, Amy breathe', I chant to myself as I strut back and forth in the spacious expanse. Imagine a big, beautiful sandy beach with the water lapping onto the shore, I tell myself. Think about the sun beating down on me and Matt as we walk aimlessly on the white sand, surrounded by palms. Think about anything that takes me away from this ongoing flood of emails, decisions, phone calls and responsibilities that never end here in the central office of Ultra Luscious Relaxation Spas. Eventually, my breathing begins to slow slightly as my mind veers temporarily from the tasks at hand.

The phone rings and I'm jolted from my reverie. I pick it up and answer sweetly, "Amy here, what can I do for you?" the superficial tone barely plausible. "Melissa, what's the matter?" I ask, "Yes, come right in."

My administrative assistant is a tall, attractive young woman who has recently been jilted by her cheating husband. Devastated by his sudden departure, it has unexpectedly left her a single parent. Melissa barges through the door in tears. "Amy, I'm so sorry. Can I leave early?"

"What's happened? Are you okay?" I query, taking in her blotchy face and puffy eyes.

"The daycare just called, and Lily has a really high temperature. I've texted Adam but he never responds. I tried my mom, but she's out of town. I know I've left early so many times this month, but I don't know what to do," she explains between sobs.

"Go Melissa. Lily needs you. Don't worry, I'll cope here. I hope she's okay." I say, already overwhelmed at the thought of the empty reception desk.

"Thanks so much Amy. I owe you one...again," she says as she darts from the office.

With Melissa gone, the phone is ringing off the hook. I can't even locate a pen on this cluttered, disorganized desk. The afternoon is a long one. One minute I'm assistant manager of Ultra Luscious Relaxation Spas, a national, rapidly expanding chain of high-end spas and the next I'm playing secretary to a phone that doesn't stop. My anxiety begins percolating again as the delivery guy appears at the door.

"Delivery for Amy Hewston, Assistant Manager. Please sign here." He drops the heavy parcel on the reception desk as I produce my signature.

I rip into it only to find someone has messed up royally. These soaps aren't lavender. In fact, they're dark blue musk, not at all what I ordered. The odour is enough to infuriate me. I distinctly recall wanting the peaceful lavender. The invoice shows a shipment of 10,000 of the musk soaps have been delivered to our warehouse. My hyperventilating returns with a vengeance. I want to scream but I just sit down and cry.

The phone rings. I can't bring myself to answer it until I see Matt's name on the call display. I grab it quickly.

"Amy is that you? Where's Melissa, your efficient screening service?" he chuckles at his own joke.

"I sent her home Matt, Lily's sick again," I manage to explain before I break down completely.

"Amy, you're going to be okay. Don't worry if you can't get it all done. Just do what you can," he says calmly, having read my tone of voice.

"I'll see you at Megan's concert at 7:00. She's so excited," he gently reminds me. "I'll get the kids dinner and meet you there. Hang in. You'll get through it. Tonight, I'll pour you a big glass of wine and you can tell me all about it," he reassures.

Sam, the 30's something owner and CEO of Luscious Relaxation Spas happens to be sauntering by my office. A handsome, lanky, type B sort of fellow, he casually pops his head in the door.

"Oh, hi Amy, I was expecting to see Melissa but I'm glad I've caught you. I wonder if you could drop by my office tonight before you leave. Just something I want to discuss with you. Are you okay? You look a little stressed."

"No, I'm fine Sam. Just my allergies. Sure. I'll be there at 4:30." My heart falls at the thought of trying to fit this in before Megan's concert.

I spend the rest of the afternoon frantic about what this could possibly be about. A thousand possibilities run through my brain. Has he heard about the mistaken soap order? Have we lost a key client? Am I going to be fired? Every possibility becomes more catastrophic than the last. When the digits on my desk clock read 4:30, I head to Sam's office. Mindful of Megan's concert at 7:00, I must leave by 5:00 at the very latest.

"Please have a seat Amy," he directs me calmly to the big leather chair in his office, with a relaxed heart rate of 68 bpm. I don't know how he gets anything done. He lights a joint and sits back in his easy chair, his wavy brown hair falling over his eyes as he puts his feet up on the desk. "Want one?" he offers kindly. "No thank you." I decline politely, hoping, beyond all odds, that he'd just skip to the point. When he turns to get a document from the shelf behind him, I check my watch. I can just hear Megan holler, "Mom, I can't believe you missed my solo. Where were you?"

Twenty-five minutes later, I was relieved to finally hear Sam's concern, which I could have summarized in a sentence. He'd like to add turquoise to the water in the hot tubs and serve the clients ice water in real coconuts to give the feel of a tropical island.

"Great idea Sam. I like it. I really must fly as Megan's in a school concert," I explain.

"You like it? What about if we added a palm tree in the middle of the pool?" he continues.

"Sam, I really have to go, or my daughter will never forgive me," I say as I stand to leave.

"No worries, Amy. You should have told me you were on a timetable."

My whole life is on a timetable. I dart from his office, grab the elevator to the ground floor and sprint to the subway. On route, Bernard, a local homeless man, looks up as I rush by. "Hey Amy, got any change?" I always have a toonie for him when I pass. I quickly scramble in my messy purse. Damn, nothing. No change. I fish around the bottom of my bag, hoping for a toonie, a loonie, a few quarters... something. Who carries cash anymore anyway. I'm horrified to see that all I've got is a twenty. I take in his makeshift newspaper bed, his paper cup, his scrawny, hungry looking build. He's overjoyed when I hand him the twenty.

I cram into a subway car and push in way too close for comfort among the throng of people. A seat is not even in the realm of possibility, and I am simply grateful to be on a train rocketing towards the commuter parking. Finally in my car, I inch north on the highway, in a desperate effort to get there for Megan's Grade 8 concert. When the 6:30 news update comes on the car radio, I know I'm really cutting it close. The mother guilt sets in full force. 'I cannot miss this.' By 6:45, the texts are pinging in my purse, ... probably Matt. At 6:55, my cell is ringing but I can't answer it as I'm trying to catch this yellow light, three blocks from the school, despite the slow poke in front of me. The weather report prior to the 7:00 news is just coming on as I squeal into the parking lot. I sprint the 200 meters to the gym door in my heels and produce my crumpled ticket from my purse. I hurry to the seat beside Matt, just as the lights begin to go down. I feel like I'm going to pass out.

"You're here," he smiles.

January 1900

Alone in the dark parlour, Isabel stares at the flames in the fireplace. It is a cold night outside with the temperature well below zero. It is the wind that really makes the night air chill. Outside my brick walls, the winds are howling, and the branches of the maple tree are scraping relentlessly against the windows with every strong gust. As Isabel rocks quietly back and forth in her rocker, she listens to the steady ticking of the big clock on the wall. It comforts her to hear its patient rhythm as she relaxes in her chair.

Isabel is a quiet woman, and she looks forward to some solitude at the end of a full day. It has been a busy season, with Christmas just past, followed by a festive New Years and plenty of company, some of whom are still visiting. She sighs in exhaustion just thinking of it. After all, Isabel is no longer a young woman. At 39, and already the mother of seven children, she is deeply troubled by her suspicion that another may be on the way. A tear rolls down her cheek as she wonders how she will ever get through it. She can't imagine raising another child at her age. Depleted and drained, she prays that her worst fear won't come true. How will she find the energy to face yet another pregnancy, not to mention the years of childrearing that inevitably follow. As she reflects by the fire, the house is thankfully quiet except for the sounds of sleeping children overhead and some snoring from her exhausted husband upstairs. The cat is curled in a chair nearby, paying her no heed whatsoever.

Mary, her eldest, is seventeen now, very fair and quite clever. She always excelled at her schoolwork and is hoping to become a teacher, since she got her matriculation a few years ago. Nell, who just turned fifteen, is quieter and less self-assured than her older sister. Lately, she has seemed sluggish and uninspired. This worries Isabel as she reflects in the dark room by the fire. No doubt her thoughts move to fourteen-year-old Carrie and Sadie, her little sister by a year. They are the best of friends and will always have each other to shoulder whatever life may hold. She's comforted by the thought of cheery little Zoe who's only ten. Zoe's whole life revolves around trying to keep up with her big sisters. Four-year-old Doug is another matter; he is Isabel and Morten's first boy. He just seems to be into everything, whether it is digging in the vegetable patch or scaring the chickens. He's a mischievous little thing. Lyle, at eleven months, needs constant supervision as of course is always the case at this age. He has a little twinkle in his eye and loves to laugh. Isabel loves them all dearly. In her own quiet way, she is a devoted and consistent mother. But even for Isabel the thought of another child is too much to bear. The tears begin to flow more freely as she contemplates the possibility.

Eventually, Isabel is roused from her thoughts by the cooling temperature in the room, and the fading embers. She has been here a long while, perhaps over an hour. The clock gongs ten o'clock. She should really turn in and join her husband upstairs as the morning

will be here before long. The cock crows early on the farm and she needs all the sleep she can get these days. She puts another log on the fire, pats the sleeping cat and turns out the oil lamp.

-2-

Matt's comforting hand rests on mine, which is about the only thing I remember of the concert. There are so many things flooding my brain, the barrage of people I have to call, the emails yet to answer and the endless tasks that need my attention. On top of it all, I find myself trying to string together a few thoughts for my presentation tomorrow, despite my racing pulse. I don't suppose they serve wine at this school concert. Naturally, I tune in for a few minutes to hear Megan's solo, which was absolutely wonderful. I'm so proud of her. Matt tells me she's been working on it for weeks.

By the time the three of us get home, we've talked all about the concert, and how amazing she was. Delighted with herself, Megan disappears to her room to text her friends. Tyler, on the other hand, has probably never left his room or video games all evening. I know because Wilbur, our big hairy sheepdog, is going berserk on the back porch and probably hasn't been walked in hours. At 16, Tyler's delighted to have the house to himself. I don't understand the fascination with these online games. When I was his age, my parents couldn't keep me home.

Dropping my brief case by the front door I head to the porch to let Wilbur out. I round the corner to the kitchen and am horrified to see the colossal mess that greets me. Dishes in the sink, cooking ingredients spread all over the counter, dinner plates still on the table. How is it humanly possible to make this much mess just to make dinner?

"Matt!" I shout.

He saunters in. "What's going on?" he says, puzzled.

"Look at the place," I say exasperated.

"We were in a rush, Amy. Don't worry about it. I'll clean up. You sit down here at the counter and I'm going to pour you a big glass of wine, while I do the dishes and let the dog out." He always knows just what to say.

I drink, I vent, he cleans. He's the perfect husband and I'm a less-than-perfect wife.

"I don't know how much longer I can take this." I rant. "That spa is driving me crazy, and Sam is the icing on the cake. His pace is like a sedated turtle."

"Amy, do you think you're going too hard? I'm worried about you."

"What do you mean? What choice do I have? I'm the assistant manager Matt. Ultra Luscious Relaxation Spa is counting on me. I can't exactly put my feet up."

January 1900

As Isabel rouses, she hears her husband already downstairs, preparing for the day. Mary is up and is waking the children, as is her job. Gradually, the scamper of feet fills the farmhouse, and the day begins. The sun is not yet up, just the rooster and the family. Life starts early on the farm as there is much to be done. The stoves need to be stoked, the horses fed and watered, the eggs collected, the cows milked, the pig trough filled, the breakfast begun. Luckily, there are many hands to help with the load. There are thirteen here, counting the farmhand, Chuck. There are the children, seven in all. The girls are in the large bedroom, three in one big bed, two in the other. The boys are in the small room. The parents are in the master bedroom and the grandparents are downstairs in the room nearest the outhouse. Morten's parents come with the farm. Laura, Morten's younger widowed sister is upstairs across the hall. She is still visiting from Peterborough. Laura has been here for a few months now and it is undetermined how long she will be staying. Chuck, the farmhand, gets the small, makeshift room off the kitchen. The Huntlys would be lost without him! He is an invaluable help to Morten, as Doug and Lyle are of little assistance at this stage. It is no wonder Morten always longed for boys. A hundred acres is impossible to manage alone, even with four excellent horses. Chuck has been with the family for years and hopefully will stay on until Doug and Lyle can be useful in the fields, but that is a long way off. Morten's father Daniel is a wonderful man. However, at 63 his strenuous workdays on the farm are behind him.

Ida, Isabel's mother-in-law, is always the first in the kitchen in the morning. She is the one to open the shutters and light the oil lamp, as the sun is never as prompt as she is. There is too much to do for anyone to be idle. She already has the tea on the woodstove as Morten and Chuck like hot tea before heading to the barn on a cold winter's morning. Soon Sadie marches in with the eggs from the hen house. Within minutes, Grandma has them on the grill in preparation for a hearty breakfast before the workday begins. At that moment, Carrie bursts through the door griping about the cold as she dumps some wood by the stove. Her body is fully covered with the clothes of winter and the frost on her scarf supports her statement,

"God, it's cold out there." Grandma turns to Carrie with a shocked and scolding scowl on her face.

"Never use the Lord's name in vain, dear girl. If I hear it again, you will go to school without breakfast." The sentiment is seconded by Isabel who is appalled that her daughter would utter such blasphemy. She

knows better than that. The threat of going without breakfast is enough to stifle Carrie.

"I'm very sorry," she says remorsefully which is enough to regain her right to sustenance.

She takes off her snow-covered coat and hat and hangs them on her hook on the wall. Meanwhile Isabel, still perturbed, lifts Lyle into his highchair, as she has lifted all her children before him into the same piece of furniture. Mary gently coaxes Doug to the table and attaches his bib. Her seat is beside his as, at four years old, he requires supervision. Nell gathers the toast from the stove, careful not to burn herself while Zoe completes laying the table.

Aunt Laura, who says little in the morning, or ever for that matter, carefully pours a glass of milk for each setting at the table. Laura's countenance is cloaked in grief. She conducts her life as if under a gloomy cloud that never blows away. It is understandable, no doubt. This past year has been hard, being widowed at 34 years old. She and her husband were very well suited, and his sudden drowning last year was a devastating loss. As is her misfortune, they did not have children, so there is little to compel Laura forward. She lives with her husband's kin, on their family farm in Peterborough and has done so for some time. However, now that he is gone it is different. A lost soul, she does not seem to know where she belongs anymore. Ida thought it would be best if she were to come home and stay for a spell until she is feeling herself again. Losing her husband has taken a toll. To be 34, and a childless, single woman, is hardly an enviable lot in life. Quite honestly, it is both a blessing and a sadness for Laura to be here amid this busy family. But here she is, and here she will stay until she feels ready to return to Peterborough.

All is ready and the family are eager to eat. The family bows their heads as Daniel offers grace from the head of the table. Once completed, the family instantaneously bursts into dialogue, or better put, dialogues. With thirteen gathered, there is much to be said. The lively family comes to life around the table not long after the sun has reached the horizon.

Grandpa, of course, is a favourite of the children. He is a patient, kind man who seems to understand all struggles innately. It seems it is from him that little Lyle gets his sense of humour and Zoe her cheery disposition.

"Well, what's Miss Walker got on the classroom agenda for this morning?" he asks the girls.

Sadie and Carrie offer a long-winded account of a play the class is working on. Obviously upset by their enthusiastic conversation, Zoe begins to chime in that she doesn't even have a speaking part in the play. Grandpa can see the tears welling up and is sensitive to her distress.

"Sometimes the greatest treasures are the last discovered," he comforts her with a smile. "What part do you play Zoe?" he asks. Carrie rolls her eyes, as though bored by such a trivial review.

"I'm only a tree," sobs Zoe. "I don't say a single thing."

"You are the prettiest tree in the forest," Grandpa offers to which Grandma agrees.

"Nell, you are quiet this morning," remarks Isabel.

"Probably thinking about that handsome David on the next concession," quips Grandpa. Nell blushes and shakes her head in adamant denial.

Doug, bored with conversation, is already halfway out of his chair and has knocked over his glass of milk.

And so, the meal continues: a mixture of chaos, communication, and camaraderie. There is a warm feeling in the kitchen despite the frosty winter morning.

The breakfast consumed, the girls clear and help their grandmother with the dishes. The water on the stove has boiled and is ready for the task. Meanwhile Isabel takes Doug to the outhouse while Daniel heads outside to ready the horses and sleigh for the trip to school.

Daniel has a way with horses. He seems to instinctively understand them, and they appreciate his patient way and comforting hand. Daniel has had Scarlet since she was just a foal. He trained her to pull a cart and sleigh and she does it as well as any in the countryside, if not better. Barney, a sturdy bay horse, was purchased from the next farm in exchange for several sacks of oats. He is strong and more spirited than Scarlet. Munching on hay, Scarlet and Barney, now long-time friends, look up in expectation of a carrot as Daniel enters the barn. Creatures of habit as they are, the other animals continue eating, as they know he has not come for them. It is the morning routine. School starts at 8:30 and the children need a ride in the winter. The road is long, and the weather is cold. Not until spring returns will they have to make the trip on foot. Scarlet and Barney look forward to the morning jaunt they have been doing with Daniel for years.

In minutes, Daniel has them harnessed. He backs Scarlet gently into the drive shed. Despite his cold fingers, he deftly attaches her to the sleigh alongside Barney. What Scarlet lacks in speed she makes up for in dependability and co-operation. Barney is enthusiastic in the cold morning air and is restless to begin the trip. His nostrils flare as his breath rises into the air. Soon Daniel and his pair are at the front door, awaiting their cargo. Within moments, the girls grudgingly emerge from the house and climb into the sleigh. Always there is the disagreement about who has to sit in the front seat. Obviously, it is more exposed to the elements than the back. Grandpa reminds the quibbling girls that there are two fur blankets, and everyone will be sufficiently covered. Grandma has also heated some bricks on the stove and placed them on the floor of the sleigh to keep their feet warm.

Grandma hollers from the doorway, "Daniel, the weather looks ominous so right home after. No visiting at the neighbours."

"Oh, that never stops Scarlet, right old girl," he quips. "I was referring to the horse," he states in jest to his scolding wife.

With a little whistle, they are off and the sleigh glides through the fresh blanket of snow, on route to the carriageway at the end of the lane. The girls huddle in tightly as it is well below zero. In the back seat, Sadie and Carrie chatter about the play while in the front Zoe tells Grandpa about her friend Meg and how they get to sit beside each other at school. Grandpa appears fascinated by these mundane details of daily life, which inspires little Zoe to fill him in on all the highlights of what the day will hold.

The snow continues to fall lightly, as Scarlet and Barney trot along unconcerned. There are some winter birds and squirrels in the trees but otherwise the morning is generally quiet as the sleigh glides along silently. Occasional 'hellos' ring out as cutters pass in the opposite direction. Nevertheless, with the air so bitter, not many are in a talkative mood.

Nell's stomach churns as the family sleigh rounds the last corner towards the schoolhouse, her graduation still months away. There is a boy at school, Billy, whom Nell doesn't care for much. In fact, he downright terrifies her. Billy is 16 and not very smart. He's the only one still in the schoolhouse at his age. She feels his eyes are constantly on her and recently he has become much more forward in his advances. Yesterday, he approached her at the lunch break, and she felt quite uncomfortable. While Mary would have told a boy like this to 'go jump in the lake', Nell just could not find the words or the voice to make such a statement. Only a quarter mile out now, Grandpa can see the smoke rising from the tiny schoolhouse up ahead. Sleighs descend from several directions as the children begin to gather for the school day. Miss Walker will have a roaring fire in the woodstove and the schoolhouse will be comfortably warm by now.

Grandpa reins in the horses and the sleigh comes to a halt by the gate. The girls climb out, laughing, giggling, or worrying, whatever their state of mind might be. While Meg bounds up to the sleigh to greet Zoe, Nell is acutely conscious of Billy's eyes following her every move as Grandpa, oblivious to the onlooker, helps her down.

"Goodbye girls. Have a good day. We'll be back at 3:00. Remember you're the prettiest tree in the forest," he winks at Zoe.

"Goodbye Grandpa. See you this afternoon," they call as they hurry towards the schoolhouse.

After a brief visit with others delivering their children to school, Daniel directs the sleigh towards home. "Let's make haste, you two," he shouts to his team. "This weather isn't fit for any of us."

-3-

It's now 3:00 a.m. and I'm still not asleep. Instead, I'm mulling over possible comments to include in my speech while I recite it repeatedly from my pillow. Should I get up and practice it or should I keep trying to get some rest so I'm fresh for tomorrow's meeting? After another hour of tossing and turning, I climb from my bed and head downstairs. I step over our slumbering watchdog Wilbur, pour myself a big glass of wine and head to the living room to rehearse my presentation.

Having felt my absence, Matt eventually locates me downstairs. "What's going on Amy?" he utters, shielding his eyes from the light.

"I can't sleep. I'm sorry I woke you. I'm so stressed about this stupid speech, and the volume of work coming at me every day." I explain in a semi-hysterical voice.

"Amy," he comes over to the couch and puts his arms around me. "This is too much. I'm getting really worried about you. This has been going on for almost two years now and it's not getting any better. You're always on overdrive, your anxiety is out of control, you're hardly spending any time with the kids, and it has been destroying your sleep."

By this point, the wine has kicked in. My resolve and drive are finally waning a notch and my emotions are growing uncontainable.

"Matt, I've worked my whole career to get this far. I am the most experienced person to run Ultra Luscious

Relaxation Spas." I insist as I wipe my nose on the sleeve of my nighty. "If it weren't for me, Sam would be lost. You know he's been talking about promoting me to national manager."

"Listen Amy. Maybe you need to take a little time away, just to get some perspective. I'm worried you're going to crash. I don't mean leave 'Relaxation', I just mean take a break from it for a month or two," he pleads. My marketing job could support us. We could make it work. We would be tight, but if it weren't for too long, it would be okay," he suggests cautiously.

"What are you saying? You think I can't do this?" I shout defensively.

"No that's not what I'm saying at all," his voice raised a notch. "I'm saying I'm worried that all this stress is too much."

I can't even imagine a few days off work, let alone a month. He's out of his mind.

When my sobbing finally subsides, and the fatigue takes hold, we go upstairs and return to bed.

Despite my semi-delirious state, I triple check the alarm as my head hits the pillow.

January 1900

It being Friday, Grandma and Isabel now turn their attention to laundry. Laura sits in the big chair by the window and helps with the mending. While Isabel is busy with the washing, even Doug gets into the act. He dumps the clothing out of the hampers for sorting. Eventually, a large mound of clothing rests in a pile in the kitchen. Of course, what is most rewarding for Doug is jumping in the pile and throwing clothes at Lyle, who inevitably giggles. Isabel tosses a few clothes on top of the pair, burying them in whites. The water on the stove has boiled and together

the women pour it into the tub. Isabel is delighted that Morten splurged on the new, two tub with wringer, laundry washer. It is so efficient to be able to wash, soak, and wring the clothing all in one contraption. It is unthinkable that he indulged and spent such a sum on an unnecessary extravagance when money is in short supply at the Huntly household. A washboard and stirring stick had done the trick for years. Nevertheless, she and Ida are overjoyed with this new purchase as it makes the tedium of all day laundry, much easier and more convenient. Doug picks an item, hands it to his mother who puts it first into the washtub and churns it around, then lifts it into the soak tub to de-soap. Grandma is on wringing this morning. She carefully feeds each item through the wringer as she cranks the handle. Then she lays it in the pile for hanging…underthings, petty coats, sheets and Morten and Daniel's church shirts. Once they're almost dry, she can apply the iron. The boys do more playing than helping and generally they enjoy laundry day for opportunity it provides to jump in a big pile of clothes. Later the farmhand Chuck, will take Doug to the barn to help him milk Tulip. Doug always brings Tulip an apple from the basket in the cellar.

Grandma, glanced out at the barn, keeping a watchful eye for Daniel and his team, "I don't see any sign of that sleigh," she grumbles. "Where would he be?"

"I'm sure he's fine Momma. You know how he likes to visit," offers Laura.

"But the temperatures are not conducive for that dear," she replies emphatically.

"Perhaps, he stayed at the school for a spell, to help bring in wood for the stove," suggests Isabel.

As time wore on, Grandma grew increasingly uneasy. "I don't like the feel of this. We have been here for the better part of the morning, and I don't see any sign of him."

After several tubs of hot water, the whites were finally completed.

"I'm worried about him," Grandma insisted to Isabel. "He should have been back long ago."

"I'll walk over to the barn to see if Morten might know where he is." Isabel bundled up and trudged through the blowing snow towards the barnyard.

-4-
6 Months Later....
2018

The next six months haven't been much different. Sam has been away on another holiday in South America, all the hot tubs have been converted to turquoise blue, our clients are sipping water out of coconuts as they sit beneath palm trees, and I'm closing in on a nervous breakdown. The phone keeps ringing, the emails continue to pour in, and Melissa's absentee rate is escalating.

Matt and I haven't had a date night in months, Megan is almost finished grade 8 and I have no clue who she's hanging out with. I don't believe Tyler ever did emerge from his room.

"Amy, what's wrong?" Matt asks, his toothbrush in his mouth, the clock showing well past 6:00 a.m.

"I can't face it." I whisper, tears rolling down my cheeks and into my pillow.

"What are you talking about? You're going to be late Amy, it's almost 6:30. You slept in. The traffic will be brutal," he implores.

"I can't do it Matt. I don't know what's wrong with me. I just can't face the spa today." My chest is heaving in an effort to catch my breath. I am beside myself and I feel like every last spark of energy has drained from my body.

"It's okay Amy," he says now sitting down beside me on the bed. "You're going to be okay, but this is getting ridiculous. He strokes my hand. "You need a break. I'm calling Sam to tell him you're sick today and you won't be in."

Inwardly, I am both profoundly grateful but terrified what it will do to my growing workload. By this point, however, I am too out of it to care.

....

After forty-five minutes waiting in the examination room, Dr. Neal finally whisks in the door. Looking a little frazzled himself, he gives a terse greeting to Matt and me, and heads directly for his computer. With his eyes never straying far from his Mac, he asks me curtly what the problem is. I explain my symptoms but find myself tearing up as I begin to describe the level of stress I've been under lately. At this point Matt kicks in, explaining how I can barely get out of bed these days, and that I seem to have hit some kind of cranial short circuit. By the time we emerge eleven minutes later, Dr Neal has recommended a six week leave of absence from work and prescribed a beginning dose of anti-anxiety medication, with a little something extra for my panic attacks.

I'm numb with disbelief. Six weeks away from work? How will Sam feel about this? What will this do to my career? My thoughts are running wild.

On the ride home, Matt expresses his relief. "This is exactly what you need – a good break," he confidently reassures. "You have some coverage for sick leave. Your salary will be reduced but we'll get by. Don't worry about the money."

I hadn't even thought about the money. Now I'm extremely stressed.

Within the week, Matt had arranged a 'work at home' agreement for his marketing position. Provided he shows up to the office for the weekly team meeting, all is good.

January 1900

Daniel pointed the sleigh towards home. The winds had picked up slightly, causing the snow to sweep across the fields. Even dependable Scarlet found this unsettling. The snow impaired her vision so badly, that with the blinders on, she likely could not see beyond a foot in front of her. The team began to balk and whinny and protest the conditions. In his many years of driving, Daniel had rarely experienced horses reacting to the weather but occasionally it did happen, especially in a storm such as this. The snow was relentless, and it continued to fall. Worst of all, it was now blowing. Daniel took the hills cautiously despite the cold. It would be better to go slow and steady rather than rush and risk slipping. A thought crossed Daniel's mind after leaving the schoolhouse. As the roads were getting so blowy and the vision so limited in the whiteouts, he considered taking the short cut through the woods. With the cover of forest, the visibility and wind protection were bound to be better, an appealing thought in these frost-bitten temperatures. Even Ida might understand on this rare occasion. She was always one to be overly concerned with safety. There would be no bears at this time of year as they were wisely sleeping through the winter months.

"What do you think guys, right or straight?" Grandpa shouted to his team over the gusts of wind.

"Right it is you two, into the woods and out of this darn snowstorm." He reined the horses to the right, and they carefully descended the hill towards the

welcome shelter of the trees ahead. Upon entering the forest, it was an instant reprieve. The world became silent and peaceful and both man and beast could once again see unencumbered. "That's better," he said comfortingly to his team as they trotted along through the fresh blanket of snow, their sleigh bells ringing through the wood. They were obviously delighted with the new route.

Despite the heavy snowfall overhead, the forest teemed with life. Winter birds populated the branches and watched from above as the two-horse team and sleigh calmly made its way through the peaceful forest. Deer tracks were everywhere. They weren't far off but the sound of the sleigh bells no doubt pushed the deer further back into the woods. Occasionally a hare scooted by in the snow. The cold persisted but the wind did not. A welcome respite for all of them.

As he glided along, Daniel's mind wandered from his cold fingers to his plans for the rest of the day. When he got home, he had a lot to do. There were a few trees that needed to be felled for wood, there was a board in the barn that required repair, especially in this weather. Morten would need help fixing the equipment and Daniel had to return to pick up the children by 3:00. The day ahead was full.

There was no traffic on the winter trail today. As the team approached the bridge, he slowed them to a walk. Despite the frozen world all around, the creek was full of life as the water rushed over the stones, creating some substantial, yet shallow rapids. It was the one part of the river that never froze. The water wasn't deep, but it was fast, and in summer the pool below made it a favourite fishing spot for many around. On a lovely day in June, Miss Walker lost half her class to this restful spot. Scarlet and Barney lazily lumbered across the narrow bridge as Daniel steered *them carefully. Suddenly, out of nowhere, Scarlet was down, having slipped on a patch of black ice, her front right leg went out from under her. As she fell, the weight of her body veered to the right. Barney, spooked by the unexpected movement, reared up and whinnied. The entire sleigh was thrown off balance. Suddenly, Scarlet plunged through the wooden railing and off the sturdy little bridge into the water a few feet below. The sleigh toppled from the bridge and landed on its side. Barney, clearly beside himself, was forced off the bridge and into the water as well. Both horses were frantic. Dumbfounded, Daniel suddenly found himself hip deep in the ice-cold creek. In his panicked state, he managed to wiggle free of the semi submerged sleigh. He reassured himself that although he was drenched, he was largely unharmed, save for a few cuts, some shattered nerves and very cold legs. He regained his composure as fast as one could and tried to settle the panicking horses. Barney's struggle to break free of the sleigh only made things worse. Daniel shouted at him to 'whoa'. Scarlet's nostrils flared and the whites of her eyes showed an unmistakable panic. She appeared unable to move. It was not clear whether she was simply shocked or seriously injured. It wasn't long before Daniel could see that she was both. Her leg appeared crushed beneath her as she whinnied in pain at each tug and pull Barney made in his effort to free himself. Daniel's adrenaline pumping, he quickly leapt to his feet to grab the knife from his bag. Despite Barney's hysteria, Daniel was able to cut the harness, allowing the panicking horse to free itself. Barney burst from the wild little creek and took off at a gallop through the woods, complete with a remaining rein and his damaged harness dragging from his side. Daniel feared that the ending might not be so liberating for Scarlet. He could see she was badly injured as she lay on her side, her weight resting on the harness. She had a wild, crazed look. She whinnied in pain as she lay immobilized. Daniel, himself soaking wet, tried to calm her and help her, but to no avail. He cut her loose from the sleigh, but still she refused to get up despite his ceaseless efforts to rouse her. Daniel knew in his heart what this meant.*

He berated himself for taking the short-cut. He should have known. How stupid could he be to risk such a passage in the dead of winter. He stood motionless, overrun with guilt for having endangered the life of his faithful companion. He debated whether he should stay and try to assist the struggling horse, or abandon her to seek help from the closest farm. Drenched, he only now noticed his uncontrollable shivering and numbness from the cold. Nevertheless, it was unthinkable to abandon Scarlet here in such a state, and a state that he had brought on through a foolish decision. Surely, some passerby would find Barney running franticly down the road, discern what had happened, and come to his aid.

After what seemed an eternity, it was clear he could be of no help to Scarlet. She was seriously wounded. He tried in vain to coax her to her feet. Having untethered the tack as completely as possible, he commanded her to stand. All to no avail. In a state of desperation, he grabbed the whip from the cart and cracked it furiously. Although her eyes flared wildly, she remained immobilized. He knew it then. She could not move even if she wanted to. There was no point harassing her further. He had to save himself. It felt far worse to abandon her than to put her out of her painful misery. He climbed into the rushing stream and spoke calmly to her as he stroked her neck. She struggled helplessly as she snorted in pain. How could he leave her in such despair? He grew increasingly aware of his own discomfort. The wetness soaked through his clothes, and he trembled in the cold, as did the horse. He had to go, but he couldn't go. If only he had a pistol. Then the thought crossed his mind. The knife. He should slit her throat, but he could not bring himself to do that to his dear friend. At that moment, he decided to run for help, both to save himself as well as the horse. He stroked her one last time and reassured her he'd be back, as she lay there half submerged in the rushing, frigid stream. He threw a blanket over her and wrapped the other around himself. As he left her, he was gripped with guilt. Nevertheless, as the cold and wet settled into his bones, he knew he had to flee.

-5-

"What are you talking about Matt? I don't need to get away to a country retreat." I insist from my side of the bed.

He brushes the hair away from my eyes. "Amy, I've been thinking about this for awhile. It is exactly what you need – a little time away, a change of environment. In fact, I think it would be good for our whole family. It would give you a chance to unwind, Tyler could leave his room, Megan could re-connect with us, and I could get some time away from my computer. We could be a couple and a family again," he pleads, propped up in bed.

"The only one who's going to like that idea is Wilbur," I respond.

"Let me show you this." He points his computer toward me. A real estate listing is up on his screen. "You see this farmhouse... well, it's for rent. The price is right," he said with excited puppy dog eyes, teeming with enthusiasm.

"Are you crazy? We don't know a thing about farms," I say, extremely apprehensive at this sudden turn of events.

"I talked to the realtor on the phone," he confides. "He says it's a beautiful little country property – 30 acres with an older farmhouse and barn. The rental price is amazing and it's only two hours north of the city. I could get back to the office as needed, the kids could have a fun summer there and you could relax and get back on track," he announced, excited about the limitless possibilities he foresaw.

"I don't know Matt," I say, leaning in to take a closer look at the photo. It looks like a pretty old place, and we've never lived in the country before, my doubts multiplying by the minute.

"Amy, I've arranged for us to look at it tomorrow," he explains sheepishly. "I had to make a snap decision because the realtor said we might lose it to someone else if we waited until the weekend. Come on, it will be fun. If you don't like it, we'll just drive away."

I know this is something Matt's always wanted – to have a rural get away property where he can go to decompress. The trouble is he has a wife who has been chained to her career and two teen kids who are so entrenched in their social lives and computers that they wouldn't spend a weekend with their parents if their lives were at stake. The guilt envelops me.

"Just come and look at it," he begs. "What do we have to lose?"

"OK, but just to look." I hear myself saying, already regretful of my compliance.

-6-

No wonder the price is right. After a two-hour drive north through plenty of traffic, I realize that all Matt has found is a dilapidated old farmhouse in need of a complete overhaul. The FOR RENT sign out front has probably been swinging in the breeze for some time now. It's a forlorn old relic, badly in need of major brick repair. It has three big maples out front at the end of a long driveway, off a dirt road in the middle of nowhere. It's at least 150 years old and looks like the owners may have long since died. The front porch desperately needs fortifying and the oil tank on the back porch is not exactly eye candy. Curb appeal 'zero'. As I look inside the door, I decide to keep my shoes on. The kitchen floor is on a slant and the appliances, and the kitchen cabinets look like something out of a museum. The living room has fake panelling ... and the flies... I've never seen so many flies in all my life. It is clearly some kind of breeding ground. Obviously, they are the only form of life that gravitate to this lifestyle. The furniture is badly outdated. To top it all off, everything is painted a depressing grey, likely a garage sale purchase. The worn-out carpeting in the living room has likely been there since the house was built in the late 1800's. The place could use some staging. The bedrooms are puny and the larger one over the kitchen looks like it might harbour something with red eyes and a tail. Meanwhile, the realtor chatters on about the original pine floors, the historic character and the majestic views. I can't help thinking that he and his wife live in something a little more upscale than this.

The realtor points over towards an old barn and drones on about the impressive 'mortise and tenon' construction of barns at the turn of the century. He emphasizes that the location is so convenient they're building many new homes in the field across the road. Matt enthusiastically raves about the beautiful trees, the spacious lawns and the numerous fields, while I am in disbelief that he is actually considering this.

I'm not sure country living is for me. I think I'd go crazy here. What would we do all day?

The realtor explained that the elderly woman who lived here, has recently moved to a senior's home. However, she was very unsure about the move, so she wanted to try it for the summer. As a result, the rental comes with some inclusions: dated furniture, a couple of horses and a big, overweight cat. All you have to do is take care of them during your stay. In addition, you are welcome to redecorate or do small home improvements to make it more liveable, given its current state.

I must admit, the old place does have a little charm.

What the hell is she talking about, "Curb Appeal O!" That's a bit harsh. I have damn nice gingerbread trim and good shutters too. I may not be modern and sleek like she's used to, but I'm loving and dependable and they would enjoy their stay with me.

January 1900

Morten and Chuck had one of the other horses harnessed immediately. They set off towards the school. By this time, a full winter storm had descended on the area, and they did not pass a single sleigh on the road. It was about a mile along the way, when they caught sight of the dark apparition hurtling towards them. Reins were dragging along behind, and it was travelling as fast as a steam engine despite the depth of the snow. Morten pulled the cutter to a halt. Chuck jumped out to intercept Barney. "Whoa fella, calm down," Barney slowed his pace as he heard the familiar voice ahead. He broke to a trot and Chuck was able to grab one of the dragging reins as he came within a few feet of them. "Settle down boy," he said to him softly as he pulled the rein into himself. The horse eventually slowed to a stop. Nostrils flaring, sweat and steam were pouring from his body and small, thin icicles hung from the coat on his belly. The men could tell he had run quite a way, perhaps a mile or so. This was not good. Chuck took Barney back to the farm while Morten hurried on in the small sleigh, inwardly terrified of what he might find. As he made haste along the concession, not a single horse, nor person came into view. Morten was puzzled. Where could his father be? He had almost reached the schoolhouse and there wasn't a trace. The snow was falling so heavily now, even Barney's hoof prints from moments ago, were practically erased. With no track to follow, he made his way toward the schoolhouse. All looked in order from what he could see from the bend in the road, but visibility was bad. He abruptly stopped the cutter by the front of the schoolhouse and tied the horse to the post. He burst through the door. He must have been a sight to behold as the children gasped at his sudden arrival. Miss Walker was taken aback,

"Mr. Huntly, what's wrong? You look vexed."

Morten immediately took in that all his girls were present. Greatly relieved, he blurted out his concern.

"My father and his sleigh have gone missing. He must have made it here this morning, as I see he has delivered the girls. Yet on the road, I can't find a sign of him," he announced.

The teacher gasped as she took in the scene through the snow-covered window. The children were silent and fearful. Then Zoe shouted.

"The shortcut. He always wants to take that shortcut that Grandma won't let him." She ran to get her coat and boots.

"No Zoe, stay here. I only have the cutter," he said not wanting to frighten her about what he feared he might find.

Jeffrey, one of the older boys in the class was on his feet in a flash. "I will get my dad and uncle. You may need help." He tore out of the room before Miss Walker could protest. He threw on his coat and boots, bridled his horse and left the stable at a canter to fetch his father from the neighbouring farm. Before much time had passed, four of the neighbourhood men had gathered with their horses and sleighs and were ready to set off in search of Daniel. The children stayed behind in the safety of the warm building, all but Zoe. She insisted on coming to find her grandfather and adamantly hopped up alongside her father.

Sure enough, Zoe was correct. A mound of relatively fresh manure was barely visible near the entrance to the woods. Encouraged by the sign, the entourage entered the forest at a swift clip, calling out as they went. The woods remained calm and peaceful and portrayed no sign of crisis. The men called out repeatedly, only to be met with an eerie silence. It wasn't long before they came to the babbling brook and took in the horrific scene. The horse lay shivering in the water with a broken sleigh beside her. There was no sign of Daniel. Zoe gasped at the sight of Scarlet lying there in agony. She lay on her side and her twisted leg was stretched at an odd angle. One of the men dismounted and walked over to her. No one said a word. He took a revolver from his pack, patted the struggling beast, put the gun to the middle of her forehead and pulled the trigger. Zoe cried out and her father put his arm around her comfortingly. Scarlet let out a last groan as her upper body slumped back into the frigid water of the rushing creek. Everyone looked away as the creek turned crimson and the life of the faithful horse drained away. There was no time to waste as Daniel could be badly injured or lost. Thankfully he did not appear to be in the creek or pinned under the sleigh. The men continued through the clearing, shouting his name.

After some time tramping through the snowy forest, they heard his muffled cry up ahead.

"Here, I'm here," he called.

There was Daniel, soaked and frozen, having stumbled along the path towards home. He wept with delight when he saw them. Morten jumped out of the cutter and came to his aid.

"Dad, are you okay? What happened?" he called as he ran to him.

"I'm okay." He shivered as he spoke. "I was so stupid. I took the shortcut because of the weather, and she slipped on the bridge. Scarlet is in bad shape. She needs help." No one said anything.

They all dismounted and helped the trembling man into the cutter. Another warm, fur throw was wrapped around him as he shivered uncontrollably. Zoe flung h,er arms about him crying "Grandpa, you're okay," she said weeping. "I was so scared."

"I was starting to get scared too dear, but I knew someone would come."

Morten turned to the others, "I'll take my father home if you fellas could tend to Scarlet." They all agreed and expressed their delight at finding Daniel in one piece.

"If there's anything you need Morten, let us know. Do you want us to fetch the doctor as a precaution?"

"No, I think we'll be fine now. I'll take him right home and get a warm cup of soup into him."

And so, the eventful episode ended, the sleighs and horses parted ways. Only one life had been lost, and luckily it had not been Daniel's.

-7-

Let's just say the kids were less than enthusiastic about Matt's 'family rescue plan'. As we pulled in the driveway of our rural, summer destination, there was some very unsavory language! Megan was furious and not shy about expressing her disapproval.

"Daddy, do you know what you've done to my life," she bellowed from the backseat, cell in hand. "I won't be able to see my friends all summer since I'm stuck up here in the middle of nowhere. Look at the place. I don't want to stay overnight here. What am I going to do all day?" she demanded, echoing my own thoughts.

Tyler was equally dismayed, although more inward in his disapproval. He looked up from his laptop, glanced out the van window, shook his head and simply returned to his game.

Clearly, fixing up the house wasn't going to be the only challenge ahead.

Wilbur was overjoyed and couldn't bound from the van fast enough. He immediately claimed a bush in the front yard as his own, in the way that dogs do. His tail wagging, he darted enthusiastically around the yard as though he had just been released from prison.

"Megan let's go see the horses," I interjected, kind of curious to meet the herd.

This seemed to strike a chord and we made our way toward the barn, Tyler still refusing to emerge from the van and engage in human life.

Megan loves horses and Matt is desperately hoping this will take her mind off being away from her friends for a prolonged period. In fact, the lure of two horses was the only thing that had convinced her to get in the van in the first place.

"The realtor said they'd be in the field. Apparently, the boy who's looking after them will come by to show us how to take care of them," Matt explained. That's reassuring because we know absolutely nothing about equine care.

After some searching, we located the pair out grazing behind the barn. Despite my profound lack of knowledge about horses, it seemed to me with my untrained eye, that these animals were possibly as old as the house. The big brown one's back sagged prominently creating the appearance of a rocking horse. Its hip bones jutted out, and its eyes were opaque. "I guess this rules out riding," I smiled at Matt.

Megan was visibly disappointed, but nevertheless intrigued and went over to the old fella to pat his neck. He seemed friendly enough and was delighted when Megan produced a carrot from her pocket and pressed it against his droopy lip. It wasn't long before the other horse hobbled over for a snack as well. Although she seemed to have better vision, she walked with a decided limp. What a pair, one blind, one lame, a kind of palliative care barn. These seemed more like hungry lawn ornaments than functional animals. Nevertheless, a few carrots later, some solid friendships had been established.

After meeting Zippy and Bolt, we wandered into the old barn to look around....and we thought our accommodation was bad. I hadn't been in a barn in some time, which would be the understatement of the year. This was not some state of the art, airtight, spanking clean, new barn that you might find at an upscale horseback riding establishment. However, it did have an historic, awe-inspiring quality about it. The first floor was lined with a solid stone foundation which appeared to have been there for years. The floor itself was covered in a mixture of straw and cement. There were some large stalls that hadn't been cleaned in a while, a water pump jutting out of the ground and the beams that held up the ceiling were immense tree trunks, literally. There were bird nests tucked in the rafters and the scent of fresh manure permeated the air. Birds flew in and out of the open doorway. This place certainly had personality. The rickety old stairs led to a second-floor hayloft which stretched twenty meters to the tin roof overhead. The space was cathedral like in its silence. There were hundreds of old bales of hay or straw on one side, a couple of huge ropes hanging from one rafter and built in, wooden ladders all the way up either side. If this didn't inspire our kids to put down their cell phones, I'm not sure what would. The sun poured in through countless cracks between the barn board and illuminated an old granary, as well as millions of spectacles of dust floating in the air. It had an abandoned yet engaging feel to it. This definitely had some barn party potential.

-8-

The house, well that's another story. For now, Matt and I will just enjoy a beer on the dilapidated old front porch in the lovely June weather. As we gaze out onto the lawn, there is a tree that has a mesmerizing quality as it basks in the sunlight. It is a smaller tree, covered in beautiful, white blooms, as though adorned in a bridal gown. It stands majestically in front of a pastural view down the valley.

Despite the peacefulness around me, I am haunted by this gnawing feeling that I should be getting something done. It just doesn't feel right having all this free time. For no reason at all, my anxiety is building. Probably just habit. We pull a few folding chairs out of the trunk and make ourselves at home. Have we taken on too much of a project, we both wonder? Just as we are sipping our beers and reflecting on this disturbing question, a pick-up truck turns into our driveway from the concession road a quarter of a kilometre away. That's odd, I didn't order anything, and I sure don't know anyone in this part of the world. Matt and I look at each other puzzled. Do you think they're coming to rob the place? They'll probably leave a donation when they see the inside.

The truck comes to a halt by our front porch and out climbs a woman from the driver's seat. Her young son and daughter emerge from the other side of the vehicle looking mildly curious. She is dressed in jeans and a sweatshirt, with her hair in a ponytail. "Hi", she says with a friendly smile. "We're the Findlays. I'm Joanne and this is my son Mark and my daughter Hailey. We live just up the road. We heard you had rented the place and just thought we'd stop by to say 'welcome'." She produces a jar of homemade honey from the truck.

"Here, this is for you."

"Thank you so much," I say, taken aback by this unprovoked act of kindness and generosity. "I'm Amy and this is Matt. It's nice to meet you. It's such a beautiful area." I reply, searching my brain for what I can give in return. "Have you lived here long?" I ask.

"My husband's family goes back generations, but I just moved here when we married. I heard you were from the city."

"Yes, we're from Toronto. We're just here for the summer."

We chat for about ten minutes before she departs.

In all the eighteen years we've lived in our home in Toronto, no neighbour has ever pulled into our driveway to introduce themselves. I must admit, I am strangely touched that they took the time to stop by to say hello.

Not forty minutes after Joanne Findlay's departure, another car pulls in. By this time, we are starting a second beer. An older, casually dressed woman climbs out of her car and introduces herself, Phyllis, from down the road. She has a carton of eggs with her. As she presents them to me, she explains that they have "ten laying hens and more eggs than they know what to do with." She wanted to drop some by as a 'welcome to the neighbourhood'. I thank her profusely, unsure how to react to this unexpected generosity. Within one hour of arriving, we are feeling very welcomed to our new neighbourhood.

With Megan and Tyler out patting the horses and Matt examining the relic of a tractor in the driveshed, I find myself with a few minutes to explore this antiquated house. Uneasy about the enormity of the redecorating task, I sit down on the living room couch and take in the overwhelming job that lies ahead. My feet now resting comfortably on the scuffed wood coffee table, I contemplate how I can make this extremely outdated room liveable for the next few months. Looking around the dusty room, I notice the forlorn, old wall clock that hangs in the corner. It looks like a grandfather clock but is only a fraction of the size. It's inert pendulum hanging in the middle, it appears broken and archaic like the rest of the house. Upon closer inspection I can see that its face is hand painted and it has been done by someone with a slightly unsteady hand. I gently open the little cabinet surrounding the pendulum. My goodness, an old slug of a key. Surely this unusual looking thing does not have any relevant function. I pick it up and scour the old wood for an entry point. Evidently, this odd-looking key is for the purpose of winding the clock, which I proceed to do for almost a minute. I can't recall a clock that didn't require either a battery or an electrical plug. I step back and much to my amazement I hear the old relic tick into motion. It is like stepping into yesteryear. It keeps a nice steady beat and has a haunting, hollow 'tick tock', that is unanticipatedly soothing. When it reaches the top of the hour it actually gongs, which initially makes me jump. Remarkable! This clock probably hasn't been wound in years... but it just keeps going. I wonder how long it has hung on this wall and what those gongs would have signified back in the day? Milking time? Time to light the candles? Time to quilt? It certainly didn't mean time to watch Netflix or check your email.

Don't worry Amy, the kids will enjoy it here, once they settle in. When they put their phones down, it's amazing what they'll see. You too. It's so nice having

a family within my walls again. It's been kind of lonesome here lately.

January 1900

"Sakes alive, what happened?" Grandma asked frantically as she helped Morten get Daniel through the front door.

"You're frozen. Let me fetch another blanket. Sit him by the fire, Morten." Ida directed in a frenzied tone. She scurried around anxiously, searching for towels and blankets, as Morten peeled off Daniel's wet clothes.

It wasn't long before Daniel was seated by the hearth in warm, dry attire, but still his teeth chattered, and he could not seem to stop shivering. Zoe climbed on his lap and hugged him.

"Grandpa we're so glad you're okay," she exclaimed.

It was a happy yet anxious reunion around the fireplace that afternoon. The news was not long in coming that Scarlet had to be shot. Daniel wept when he heard what he feared would be her fate.

"There, there dear. You couldn't have known that the bridge would be so slippery or that she would lose her footing. The main thing is you're okay." Ida said reassuringly as she held his hand.

Her well intended words brought little comfort to Daniel.

Chuck and Morten soon had to face the snowstorm again to fetch the girls from school. With only one cutter in the barn, and the big sleigh in the brook, it would be impossible to fit them all. No doubt their neighbour, Andrew Findlay, would help out. The girls and the whole school for that matter, would be eager to learn that Grandpa was found unharmed. Word would have reached the school earlier today when the men returned that there had been an accident and a horse had to be shot. The girls would have been on pins and needles all day, anxious for more news.

Grandma brewed a warm soup and Grandpa, Morten, Isabel, Laura, Doug and Lyle all sat around the fire, eager to hear the tale, but mostly glad it didn't come to a more serious ending. Although costly and essential, horses could be replaced, and sleighs could be repaired.

As anticipated, there was an eager reunion when the girls got home. Much commotion ensued and Grandpa was hugged and scolded a million times over. When the family gathered around the dinner table that night, they bowed their heads in prayer, thankful to have their grandfather among them. Scarlet's passing was noted with deep sadness.

Zoe sat by her grandfather as the dinner table talk continued about other, less pressing events of the day and the women moved about the table getting the meal in place. Nell seemed quieter than usual, and Carrie and Sadie updated the family on the details of the upcoming play, in an attempt to lighten the somber mood.

As Daniel climbed into bed that night, his shivering had abated only slightly. He couldn't seem to get warm. Ida was growing concerned at his bluish lips and his continuing chill. "Do you think we should send for the doctor Daniel?" she asked, her tone worried.

"Don't be silly Ida, this will pass. I just have a bit of a chill. We don't need another expense, especially after today," he insisted.

In the night, Daniel awoke feeling hot and sweaty. A far cry from the way he was when he started off the evening. Ida immediately felt his forehead and was alarmed to feel the heat radiating from it.

"Daniel, you're burning up!" she exclaimed. The moonlight streamed in through the windowpane, illuminating the small room. Ida scrambled out of bed to light the lamp.

"You don't look well Daniel. I'm sending for Doctor Moffat, whether you like it or not. I don't care what it costs. You have a fever, and I don't like the feel of this," she announced in a decided tone.

Uncharacteristically, Daniel put up no argument. He lay there passively as Ida ran upstairs to rouse Morten and Isabel. The couple awoke in a flash. Morten immediately got dressed to prepare for a late-night journey to the doctor's house, about six miles off. He wakened Chuck, as it wasn't wise to travel alone on a frigid night such as this. Although the snow and blowing had abated, the temperatures dipped well below zero. Barney would not relish being roused from his comfortable straw at this hour. He was still restless not knowing Scarlet's whereabouts. The sleigh and horse harnessed, the oil lamp hung on the side, Chuck and Morten set forth.

Isabel fetched water from the pump in the kitchen as well as some cloths. Still dressed in nightclothes, she lugged the pail to Daniel and Ida's room. Her normally jolly father-in-law looked pale and drawn. She dipped a rag in the cool water, then wrung it out and passed it to Ida. Isabel and Ida patiently applied cloth after cloth to the old man's forehead. The clock in the sitting room gonged twice, alerting them to the hour. The cat jumped on the bed, sensing some new activity.

"It's a cold night for Morten and Chuck to go out. I hope they don't meet with any difficulties," mumbled Ida preoccupied.

"It's critical they bring the doctor," was Isabel's worried reply.

The women waited. Still no sign of the sleigh or the men. The clock gonged again three times. The time that passed seemed an eternity. Finally, they arrived. They helped Dr. Moffat in the door with his bag and assisted him off with his snow-covered coat and boots. After some brief and somber greetings, they led him directly to Daniel's room.

Now in his mid-forties, Dr. Moffat was not a young man himself. He was likely thinking how he would have preferred to remain in his own warm bed this frigid, moonlit eve, rather than risk his own health travelling the hills and dales of the countryside in the middle of the night. Nevertheless, no one had ever heard him complain of such unwelcome intrusions and he did his job as cheerily as though it were noon. His wife Margaret was a supportive woman and always helped to get him out the door at these ungodly hours. The Moffats were a well-loved pair in the community as they served everybody so generously.

Dr. Moffat took a seat on the side of Daniel's bed. "Daniel, word has it you've been swimming in the creek in January," he teased.

Daniel smiled slightly and nodded while Ida filled in the details. Dr. Moffat felt Daniel's head and took his temperature. He instructed the women to continue with the cool cloths on his forehead. He praised their efforts and told them their timely intervention would likely make a positive difference to the prognosis. "If the chills return, give him hot tea. The doctor gave him a tonic, to help break the fever. He was to have a spoonful three times a day, despite the undesirable taste. He also gave him some of the new aspirins that were apparently good for controlling fever. He took Ida to the other side of the room and explained, the fever would likely lift by morning. Dr. Moffat said he would be back to check on him tomorrow, to see how he was getting on. He explained that this was a

common after effect of a chill but nevertheless, very important to monitor so that it doesn't worsen. Dr. Moffat wouldn't accept any payment for the visit, despite Ida's insistence.

"We'll worry about this later, Ida. In the meantime, you take good care of him."

Ida gave him a jar of pickles and chili sauce to take back to Margaret and she thanked him profusely. Morten and Chuck readied the horse and sleigh for his return.

-9-

"What do you mean, there's no internet!" I exclaim, too loudly for the family dinner table. "How could that be?" panic rising in my chest. I put my fork down and take a big sip of my wine.

Matt attempts to comfort me by explaining, "It's okay Amy. We just have to go into town tomorrow to get an internet hub. Apparently, the internet isn't too bad on this concession road," Matt reassures calmly as he continues to eat his dinner.

"What's that mean 'not too bad'?" I bark.

"I don't think it's a big deal. The guy at the store said it might be a little intermittent due to the distance from the tower." He explained rather matter of fact.

Suddenly Tyler was paying attention, his eyes wide with disbelief. The thought of not being able to go online to his heart's content was a dynamic he had never considered. The idea that there might be lots of idle time began to loom large. With just the four of us around the dinner table, it felt a little ominous. He stopped eating and took a sip of water.

"Isn't this nice to just sit down to dinner together, even if it's just a frozen pizza. We haven't done this in a long time," Matt offered, trying to lighten the now tense mood. "Megan, how did it go when you told Sarah about your summer adventure?" Matt asked innocently.

"Not good Dad!" Megan snapped. "She said she felt really bad for me but would post pictures of everything I'm missing." Megan sobbed, clearly upset about where her life was heading. She darted from the table and out the back door.

"I'm sorry sweetheart," he called after her, but to no avail. "She must be going out to look at the horses," he said to the rest of us. Nobly, he tried again with Tyler.

"Isn't it nice to be up here in the fresh air Tyler. What did you think of the barnyard?"

"Dad, could I stay in the city on my own? I promise I won't do anything bad," he pleaded.

"Not a chance Ty. Come on, give it a try. You've only been here a few hours."

He looked at me for parental support, but I was coming up a little short. I know Matt's heart is in the right place and he's mainly doing this for me. I'm just not sure this is going to help. My body and mind have blown some sort of circuit and being away from my beehive of activity feels very uncomfortable and strange. It's as though I was speeding down a racetrack at two hundred kilometres an hour and someone slammed on the brakes, bringing myself and my family to a sudden halt and hurling us into this bizarre situation, a long way from home. We are still trying to get our bearings and to be honest, I'm missing my stimulation fix.

It is so weird spending the night in this old farmhouse. Usually, I love the end of the day when I finally get a few minutes to myself. But it's so quiet here and everyone is asleep, except me and this big, jumbo cat. According to the note left by the realtor, the cat's name is Brutus, and he comes with the house. What was the old lady feeding this thing? He must weigh forty pounds. The note said to just feed him the kibble left on the counter, but he looks like an absolute tank. That kibble must have steroids in it or he's having some kind of supplement. I think we better get him a smaller bowl. Even Wilbur was a little uneasy around him. Brutus is obviously accustomed to sleeping in our room, because he's currently parked himself beside me as I read on this loveseat near our bed. His purring sounds like an idling motor, but at least he's content. I cautiously pat his back and enjoy his softness. In the distance, I can hear the old clock ticking steadily in the living room below. Maybe staying here for the summer won't be so bad. With a glass of chardonnay in hand, I feel myself beginning to relax for the first time in a long while.

Life is too busy. I never seem to be able to keep up. Ultra Luscious Relaxation Spa is playing on my mind constantly as I feel I left so many things undone. I just abandoned my job and ceased to return, and I don't know how Sam is going to cope without me. As much as I can't face it, I'm not sure I can leave it alone. I've been feeling my phone vibrate all day, with texts, emails and calls trying to get at me. However, I promised Matt I would stay away from office issues for one full weekend before I looked at my cell. It's taken everything in me to set it aside. I'll be honest, it's been hell.

And now there's this farmhouse to deal with. Not to mention that when I wake up in the morning, I'm going to have to get groceries and the bathroom and kitchen will require a good cleaning, as well as some redecorating. It's constant. Even though Matt shares the load of household jobs, there's always way too much to do. It just seems that between managing a huge network of spas, commuting, running a household, parenting two teens, and looking after my aging parents, I always feel incredibly stretched. It has become a way of life.

To calm my racing thoughts, my therapist tells me to breathe deeply while visualizing my version of a perfect day. As I inhale, my fantasy goes something like this: ....

'I do exactly what I want from beginning to end - a day where I'm not responsible for anyone, or anything and yet somehow it all gets done. This is what women really fantasize about, at least when they get to middle age. No wonder so many couples have sexual troubles. Anyway, back to my fantasy... First, I sleep in in the morning as late as I want. When I wake up, the kids have co-operatively got themselves up and organized for school. Matt and I lie in bed and read our page-turners until noon. Then we go out for a late breakfast at a diner that serves an all-day breakfast menu for a discount. Following that we find some terrific garage sales and get some unbelievable deals on things we don't really need. Then we go for a relaxing walk in the park, never disagreeing about anything. When we come back home, I look in the mirror and think 'wow I look fantastic' (remember this is a fantasy). In my fantasy, it's a beautiful day so I sit in the back yard and continue reading a great novel. The kids are out this evening having dinner and overnight at reputable friends' houses, so Matt and I have a glass of wine together on the back verandah and watch the sunset. Then we go out for dinner and to a really good movie. After, we catch the news and some late-night comedy on TV and then we go to sleep.' That is my perfect day. Matt's perfect day ends differently.

Oh my God.... a mouse! It just darted across the room and immediately I leap on the bed to get as high off the floor as humanly possible. My blood curdling scream jolts Matt awake. My heart rate is now up to a million. So much for relaxing fantasies. Brutus instantly kicks into action like some kind of ruthless panther. Everyone is up now and rushing to my aid, trying to make sense of my sudden emergency. Then Brutus emerges from underneath the bed, his prey wiggling in his mouth, he trots from the room to consume the hapless rodent. The supplement mystery is solved. Clearly, there isn't enough Chardonnay on earth that could ever make this farmhouse work for me now.

All my old friends are collapsing from neglect. It's heartbreaking to watch. I used to have a close friend

across the street. She had shapely lines and lovely gingerbread trim. She's gone now, taken out by a heartless wrecking ball and now I'm all alone. I miss her most at sunrise, as I look across and see the faceless housing development going in where she once stood. They're planning to level that old maple woodlot and put up 150 houses on that property. How ghastly. I'm glad she's not here to see it. Where will all the wildlife go, the birds, the squirrels, the animals? They can come over to my side while I'm still around but who knows how long I have left. Only a few of us old timers are still standing on this stretch of concession road. I don't know which one of us will be next. Our barns are crumbling too. Don't they understand we hold their history. No one seems much interested in that anymore.

January 1900

Carrie and Sadie tried to concentrate on their chess game while Nell practiced the piano incessantly. Zoe distracted herself quietly with her dolls as Mary read a story to Doug. When Lyle wakes up from his nap, it's Zoe's job to mind that he doesn't get near the fireplace. The women are gathered in the kitchen mending and having tea while talking in hushed voices. Ida is in with Daniel when Dr. Moffat arrives for his anticipated visit.

"Well, how's he doing?" Dr. Moffat questioned as Isabel greeted him at the door.

"I'm afraid he isn't much better," Isabel took the doctor's coat and led him to Daniel's room. Daniel seemed less responsive than he had last night.

"Ida, you look tired, take a rest. Don't wear yourself out. He will need you again this evening," he advised.

Despite the best nursing care a person could wish for, Daniel grew more despondent and delirious as the day wore on. The children were restless and demanded to see him, especially Zoe.

"Not now children," Isabel stated firmly. "Let him regain some strength before he has visitors. Perhaps tomorrow."

The clock gonged 5:00 as Dr. Moffat made his way out the door. Some of the neighbourhood women had come over to prepare supper. Morten returned from the barn chores and asked after his father. Isabel shushed him as he entered the bedroom, where Daniel was sleeping. Morten came over and felt his forehead. "This doesn't look good Issy. Where's Mother?"

"She's resting. She's exhausted from being up all night with him." Suddenly Isabel felt overwhelmed with nausea and ran for the chamber pot. She wretched repeatedly. Morten rushed to her side, puzzled about what was happening.

"Issy, are you sick too?" He got her a damp cloth and reached for her forehead.

Isabel began to weep. Ida opened the door, mildly refreshed from her nap and anxious to see how Daniel was. "Oh no, has he been sick?"

"No Mom. It's Issy," Morten explained.

"Are you sick dear?" Ida queried.

"No, I'm fine. Perhaps I ate something that didn't agree with me."

Morten helped her to her feet and up to her bed.

That evening was a long one. The cool sponges were clearly not working. The children insisted on seeing Grandpa before bed and Ida, fearing the worst, eventually granted their wish. They all filed in and gathered around the bedside, taking turns comforting him and holding his hand. He smiled faintly to acknowledge their presence but said nothing. Lyle climbed up beside him and pulled at his beard but even that didn't get much of a response.

"Grandpa," Zoe sobbed, trembling by his bedside. "Please get better."

He reached out his warm hand and held her sweaty little palm. He managed a slight smile at her despite his weakened condition. The tears flowed down Zoe's cheeks, as she sensed what might follow. After all, could she think of anyone who had made it through a serious fever?

Her mother whisked the children out of the room, and they gathered in the hallway, shaken and upset. "I know it's hard to see your grandfather so weak, but we must let him rest now. We will all pray that he regains his strength soon. Let's try not to make a commotion for Grandma right now. Do your chores and I will keep you posted about his condition."

"Momma," Zoe whispered through her tears, "is Grandpa going to die?"

"We hope not honey, but he may. That's why he needs your prayers. It's comforting for him to know that you are all here with him." Isabel explained supportively, her eyes welling up.

"Oh Momma, this is terrible," Carrie blurted out as Sadie sobbed quietly. Even restless Doug was silenced by the solemn feel amongst his siblings.

"Now girls, your grandfather is still in the land of the living. It doesn't help for us to stand around crying. Let's continue with our responsibilities and I will call you if there's a change," she urged.

Zoe threw on her coat and fled to the barn. Despite the cold temperature, she needed to get away from the house. There was only one being who could make her feel better at such a time and that was her donkey. Gaby had been on the farm since Zoe was an infant. Over the years, Zoe had developed an affinity for this lovable, affectionate animal. Often while the men did the barn chores, Zoe would play with Gaby. She loved climbing on her as Gaby lay in the straw. She would braid her mane, hug her, brush her. Gaby took it all in stride. She seemed to understand that this was just a child, so she needed to be gentle. However, if a coyote entered the barnyard, it was not a pretty sight. Gaby's hind end could take out a predator crippling it beyond repair in a matter of seconds, yet with Zoe she was as gentle as a kitten. As Zoe aged, they became fast friends. Zoe often brought carrots from the garden to further cement Gaby's affection.

Tonight, Zoe needed her. Gaby seemed to sense it as she too was uneasy with Scarlet's absence. When Zoe got to the barn, it was dark and warm inside and Gaby was lying in the straw by the far wall. Zoe knelt down and flung her arms around Gaby and sobbed. Gaby, with her inexplicable wisdom, absorbed her embrace patiently as her big white ears stood alert. Eventually, Zoe cried herself out and feeling safe and comforted, fell asleep in the straw beside her faithful friend.

-10-

I don't like the cellar much. The entrance is through a large trap door in the pine floor. Luckily as you climb down the rickety, wooden staircase there is a switch for the single bulb fixture halfway down. When I first saw the cellar, it was covered in a few inches of water. The realtor had explained it was seasonal, as if that should be comforting. Although we currently seem to be at low tide, I wear boots as the ground still looks moist. However, moisture is not my primary concern. It is the rodents and other species that might call the cellar home that totally freak me out. I haven't seen any mice since the incident in our bedroom last week, but I know they're still around. I've seen Matt going downstairs with traps and boxes of warfarin.

I climb down the cellar staircase cautiously while deliberately making lots of noise. I am also armed with an immense flashlight despite the overhead bulb illuminating the dingy little 'cave' below. The musty smell is overwhelming. I am on high alert for anything that moves.

"Hi Matt," I call down to him. "Any sightings? Is it safe to come down?"

"Nothing at all. I've been down here for an hour repairing this basement window. It's fine." Matt is a trustworthy guy, but he doesn't want to worry me. He wouldn't lie but he might not have noticed being so fixated on his project.

"What are you doing?" I ask, while scanning the floor for movement or eyes.

"Replacing this broken basement window," Matt says looking over his shoulders, a hammer in one hand while supporting a window frame with the other.

"Any critters?" I enquire cautiously as I continue to glance around.

"Don't be silly, there's nothing down here. Can you hand me that level?"

"So that box of warfarin is just for show, is it?" I clarify.

"Oh, that's just... in case. More of a deterrent. By the way, I want to show you this shelf I found. You won't believe it." Matt says excitedly as he eventually puts his handful down. "Come over here and look at this."

I reluctantly follow him into the other cellar room, equally dank but darker and even less inviting. On the side wall, underneath the kitchen, is a series of shelves. They are covered with a thick layer of grime and dust, now illuminated by my jumbo flashlight. Beneath the dust are some badly outdated jars of pickles.

"Oh gross, what do you figure the vintage is on those?" I remark squeamishly.

Matt picks up a jar with his gloved hand and dusts it off. "Still looks pretty good," he says as he examines the glass jar.

"Maybe there's some bootleg wine down here," I add hopefully.

Matt suggests that we bring the pickles upstairs. I suggest that we leave them there for another hundred years for the next lucky renter.

As Matt and I cautiously take them down from their resting place, I notice something behind the last jar on the shelf. It is small and rectangular, wrapped in a cloth and covered in a layer of thick dust.

"What is that?" I point to the object.

Matt reaches behind the jar and picks it up. "It's a book of some kind." He unwraps the cloth. It is filled with handwriting. "It looks like a diary."

"Let me see that," my curiosity now peeked. I leaf through it, fascinated by the find.

"Who would stash their journal down here? Is there a date on it?" I ask, my eyes squinting in the dim light. "This is coming upstairs!" I insist.

My heart pumping with excitement and curiosity, I am upstairs in no time. Matt is right behind me with a jar of dated pickles in hand.

We examine the unique treasure in the brightness of the kitchen.

"Does that say 1900? This is incredible. The inside cover says 'Happy Birthday to my dear Isabel. Love always, Morten." I flip through it. Almost every page is written on.

"There are hundreds of entries. Amazing! It's probably written by someone who lived in this house almost 120 years ago." I declare in astonishment.

"The handwriting is beautiful, and the diary is in remarkably good shape for something that has been in that disgusting cellar for so long." It smells a little rough, but overall, it is readable.

Listen to this..." I say as I flip randomly through the pages.

January 6th, 1900. I am afraid the sleigh has taken an awful beating and may not be salvageable. What shall we do if Chuck can't fix it? We'll have to rely on the cutter alone. That won't do. How could this happen? Of course, I'm far more concerned about Daniel. Dr. Moffat has been sent for but it's a bad night out and who knows what time they will return or even if the horse can make it through those drifts.

I am stunned. "Can you believe this?" I say to Matt, shivers running up my spine. "This is amazing. What an archive. I can't wait to read this. Who do you think this belonged to? Who is Isabel?" I'm so excited my thoughts are all over the place.

Matt looks at the diary and is equally amazed, but far more ethical than me.

"Do you think we should read that? It is someone's diary, and it has clearly been hidden," he implores.

"Don't be silly. Of course we should read it." I insist unflinchingly. "She's not coming back for it. Maybe she would be honoured to know she has left a piece of history," I say to justify my actions.

"Maybe we should give it to a museum," Matt suggests.

"Not a chance. It belongs to the house!" I insist, clutching the diary to my chest.

Matt puts on coffee as I look over the newfound treasure.

Sitting in the living room beneath the steady ticking clock, the musty smell of the diary makes me sneeze uncontrollably.

Meanwhile, we carefully wipe the dust and grit from the well aged journal and begin to look over its pages. Before long we discover an old photo of a young woman stashed inside. The woman's face seems content, somewhat pensive and serious. I'd guess she's about mid-thirties. "I wonder if this is Isabel?" I say, passing the photograph to Matt.

"I think we should turn this over to an historical society or something," Matt pleads again in an uneasy tone.

"Don't be ridiculous," I retort decidedly.

After a more thorough examination and three cups of coffee later, we determine that the diary begins in Dec. 1899 and is kept throughout the year of 1900, at the turn of the 20th century. It appears to have belonged to an Isabel Huntly, who had impeccable handwriting. Clearly, no one knew about this journal being in the cellar. It was behind the pickles and those jars hadn't been disturbed in years.

After pouring over the journal for some time, Matt returned to the cellar to resume work on the window. I went upstairs and put the diary beside the loveseat in our room. I will definitely have Brutus by my side this evening as I dive into some serious diary reading.

-11-

I'm going stir crazy and my mind just won't stop. I need to get something done. The truth is, I'd rather prepare my tax return than go grocery shopping, but that's the most pressing thing in my day now. Regardless, my goal is to get in and out of the store as quickly as possible.

Due to my temporary away from work, financially reduced state, I head to the local 'nameless' grocery store in the nearby town. I enter the predominately yellow store and begin in the produce aisle. It is hard not to notice that sometimes the produce has had a lengthy journey to its destination. There are vegetables from the U.S., fruits from Mexico, even Africa. Without a doubt, there will be some long distant transportation involved in the ingredients of tonight's salad. However, the price is right. It is so convenient, and being on a budget and a timeframe, it is the best I can do. My conscience argues with the practical side of my brain. I should be shopping locally, especially now that I'm on a farm for the next few months. I should plant a garden; I make a mental note to myself as I push my cart through the aisles.

I have learned over the years that it's important to read labels. My goal is to keep the sodium content low, the fat content even lower and the price the lowest. I'll admit I'm not the best cook, so those dinners in a box are always very tempting, even though they break the rules in all my above listed goal areas. Of course, they are laced with sodium and trans fat, so I try to limit it to one instant meal a week although sometimes I cheat a little. The convenience is just so tempting. I used to call before I'd leave work, tell one of the kids to heat up the oven, take the plastic off the lasagne that's in the box and place it on the middle rack. I've since heard my kids say they "know how to make lasagne". Everyone loves it, I'm less stressed but we all gain a few pounds each time I do that. It's a no win. I can do about six meals really well, but that's the extent of my repertoire. So, I shuffle around the same six meals, mix in the odd box dinner, Matt cooks sometimes and everyone gets by. Now I roll my overflowing cart to the checkout line by the magazine rack and catch up on the latest news from Hollywood. I pay, I bag, I give to the food bank. Done for another week. Now I just have to load, unload, cook, clean up... and so it goes.

Throughout my day, I find my curiosity retreating to whatever happened to Daniel. For some reason, this simple diary has a grip on my psyche.

As the evening eventually draws to a close, Tyler is holed up in his room on the computer and Megan is texting all her friends to beef about her current plight of rural living. I retreat to our room to wind down before bed. Matt is snoring softly but otherwise the house is quiet. Brutus and I settle in on the loveseat with Isabel's diary, my feet well off the floor in case of rodents and my glass of chardonnay in hand. I open it to page one.

THE DIARY

Dear Diary: *December 1899*

What a festive night we have had. The Christmas carol sing is always such fun. This afternoon we had about forty family and neighbours for songs and supper. Nell played my favourites... Deck the Halls, Oh Come all ye Faithful, and Joy to the World. Our new choir master from the church was here and had us all divided up in sections of soprano, alto, tenor and bass. It was beautiful with the harmonies. Carrie played her fiddle and with Nell at the piano, it sounded so pretty. My little Sadie has such a lovely voice so she and her friend from down the road sang a mesmerizing rendition of 'It Came Upon a Midnight Clear'. When we all sang Silent Night, I found myself moved to tears. All the family were there and so many from the concession were able to come as well. It was a merry event. Poor Mr. Jack is practically tone deaf, but he always sings so loudly, just like at church. It is quite comical, but everyone tries not to laugh. The children find it hilarious, but Morten and I have warned them to be polite. Even his wife calls him a big bullfrog, but he doesn't seem to care. After at least an hour of singing and everyone shouting out their favourite carol to do next, we retired to the kitchen for the potluck meal.

What a spread before us. There was hardly space to move around but it was festive and warm, nonetheless. There were casseroles, buns, jellied salads, a wide array of Christmas baking and several desserts. Our home smelled delicious with the scent of apple cider on the stove drifting through the house. No one went away hungry. The children were all in fine spirits and filled with excitement for what the coming days would bring.

Mr. McNaughton recounted a cute tale that happened to his son Bill a few nights back. Everyone around these parts knows that Bill has been courting Elizabeth Murray for some time. Apparently, Bill has taken it upon himself to take her out for frequent evening drives in the cutter. Seeing as the Murrays' farm is the next concession over from Bill's, I guess the horse was getting accustomed to making the trip. One night, after Bill had delivered his sweetheart back to the door and was returning home, he apparently drifted off to sleep while driving home. The horse, being well used to the nightly visits to Miss Murray's home, had become quite familiar with the route. Apparently, Bill eventually woke up later that night to find himself still seated in the sleigh but parked safely in his own barn with the horse still harnessed and munching on some hay. Everyone roared with laughter, and someone commented that he was lucky the horse didn't have a girlfriend of its own several concessions away.

We ended the afternoon with sleigh rides and races across the field, which is always a fun activity. It was so nice hearing the sleigh bells in the field. By the time it was over, I must admit I felt exhausted. Luckily, we have a house full of relatives to help with the cleanup. Morten's tedious sister Laura is still here, and Momma and Poppa have come for a few weeks over Christmas. The house is filled to capacity, in fact it is overflowing, and it will be somewhat of a relief when life returns to normal in the coming days. It will all feel so quiet when the season ends and no doubt it will be a little lonesome. I must turn in now as I am quite played out. Time to blow out the taper and turn in as before long the sun will be rising.

December 31, 1899.

What a wonderful New Year's celebration we had this evening. Of course, it was a big event as we are welcoming in a new century. As the calendar turns from the 1800's to the 1900's, it seems like tremendous transition is in the wind. The world is changing so rapidly with electricity, indoor plumbing and now even talk of horseless carriages. I understand they are starting to appear in the big city. Imagine that.

We had a wonderful celebration. The whole family was here, and we had quite a little party. There was singing and square dancing and story telling. What a time we had! Who knows what this year will bring.

Friday, January 5, 1900

I'm feeling very out of sorts tonight. My stomach has been terribly nauseas, and I can't seem to keep anything down. Morten isn't back yet, and I can't sleep so here I sit, in the flicker of this candlelight noting my uninteresting thoughts. It was a busy day as laundry day always is. Doug is tiring me out, as four-year-old do. He's so full of energy and I seem to be the opposite these days. Mary has been such a help, minding him when I am helping Ida with the household chores. Lyle is such a cute, chubby little fellow and good natured too. He's just into everything now that he has found his feet. He's always on the go and with a little twinkle in his eye.

I can't bear the thought of what may lie ahead. Maybe I should tell Morten. Soon but not yet, not until I'm sure. I don't need to burden him with that right now. I'm so hoping I'm wrong, but with each passing day, it is harder to deny. After being through it so many times, it's not hard to know when I'm expecting.

What a day it has been. It was so exhausting yet what relief we all felt when Daniel came through the door. Ida was overjoyed. Life is precious and we take it for granted. However, now I wonder if he'll make it. I know Morten is thinking the same thing. I heard the women talking in the kitchen before dinner, all telling stories of their own experiences. Some were hopeful and some not, but I'm relieved the doctor has been sent for. Thank God, I hear the sleigh bells coming up the hill telling me Morten and Chuck are near home. My prayers have been answered. There is nothing but snow on the sill, but I can hear them a short distance off. I must blow out my taper now.

Mesmerized, I put down the diary. Did she write that right here in this house and by candlelight? I wonder what room she was in. Where was Daniel and what happened to him? Surely, he didn't die here in this bedroom. I look over at Matt snoring in the bed and feel that maybe this is all a little too close for comfort. I close my eyes and imagine the sound of sleigh bells coming across the field on a snowy night. It seems surreal, especially in June.

My goodness, forty people in this house! How did they all fit? A carol sing – that sounds like fun. However, I cannot imagine multiple family members moving in for weeks at a time and over Christmas. What a nightmare! On that unsettling note, I blow out the 'taper' and go to bed.

Saturday, January 6th, 1900, 4:15 a.m.

Daniel is currently down with a fever after a mid-winter spill in the brook. I know Ida is worried sick.

I share her fears. It is always a worrisome thing to have a fever. On the other matter, nothing yet. Surely it can't be. We have been so careful to only be together occasionally. I don't know how I can face it. I feel so tired all the time. Lyle is still up in the night and Doug is such a handful. Laura is dragging down my spirits. She is so melancholy I can't stand to be around her. Fortunately, Ida and the girls are very helpful, especially Mary. Even though Morten will welcome another little bundle into the fold, he'll be worried how we will make ends meet. At least the farm will always feed us. And... what if it's another girl?

Daniel is no better. In fact, he's worse. It is a good thing it's Saturday as the girls are here to help. To add to the troubles, our main sleigh is out of commission. Some of the neighbourhood men had their workhorses drag it back to the farm. It is badly in need of repair. Word has quickly spread around the community that Daniel has taken ill. Reverend Mactavish has promptly paid us a visit as he is concerned about his good friend of many years. Many of the neighbourhood women have come by to relieve Ida of the household chores so she can tend to Daniel. There is a noticeable hush in our home despite it being filled to capacity. All are fearful of what this fever could bring.

8:30 p.m., Jan. 6th

This evening as the girls were preparing for bed, getting in their nightclothes, and brushing their hair, Sadie asked if I had seen Zoe. With such a busy household and so much going on with Grandpa, Zoe's absence had gone unnoticed until now.

Mary told me she had searched downstairs in Grandpa's room, fully expecting to find Zoe cuddled in beside him. She had knocked gently on the door and peeked inside. She said she saw Grandma holding Grandpa's hand and talking to him quietly as she wept. Not wanting to intrude, Mary quietly closed the door and retreated. Meanwhile, Nell checked the outhouse, no Zoe. Sadie found me by the fireplace, pensively writing in my journal beneath the oil lamp. She was fretful that Zoe was nowhere to be found. Immediately I thought of Gaby.

I hastily pulled on my coat and boots and trudged to the barn. It was a snowy, cold, clear night and the sky was filled with stars. The moon was beautiful and bright, illuminating the snowy fields. I said a prayer as I made my way to the barnyard. As I opened the large wooden, door, the moonlight spilled in, casting light upon the weary livestock. The warmth of their bodies and the scent of their hides filled the barn with an unmistakable aroma and warmth. The horses stirred in their stalls and Barney was restless, still on the alert for the return of Scarlet. The cows were lying down and off by the north wall of the barn I could make out the donkey's ears. Snuggled in beside her was the small, fragile figure of little Zoe, sound asleep. I tread gently towards Gaby, talking quietly to her as I approached. I patted her warm neck when I got to her side. Gaby nuzzled me in hopes of a carrot that never materialized. I nudged Zoe's shoulder gently to rouse her and whispered in her ear. "Zoe, it's time to get up. You've fallen asleep in the barn."

She came to, confused about her whereabouts. then anxiously asked if Grandpa was okay. After some reassurance, we made our way back through the snow on the cold, moonlit night. Exhausted, Zoe returned to her sisters and climbed into bed alongside them, greeted by many questions as to where she had been. I returned to the rocker and once again have taken up my pen by the oil lamp.

I fear it will not be long now. Daniel does not seem to be recovering and our home is cloaked in sadness for what seems inevitable. Reverend Mactavish and Dr. Moffat have both visited our house regularly these last few days. Morten is beside himself as is little Zoe. I will say more prayers for Daniel tonight. I too fear the worse about my own situation, as there has been no blood to speak of. I suppose I should tell Morten, but now does not seem the time. He has so much on his mind.

Laura's sadness is so heavy. I secretly wish she'd return to her home but that is unlikely. I fear she's here to stay. What has she to return to? Her husband is gone and there are no children to care for. She mopes around the house all day and I know Ida is growing more concerned about her. She never did seem to inherit that 'joie de vivre' that her father exudes. Tomorrow I must find a safe spot to tuck this journal out of sight. It would be so hurtful to Laura if she read this.

Ida, Laura, Mary and I have pressed all the Sunday clothes for church. Morten is in with Daniel now and will call me if there's a change. The Findlays are sending an extra sleigh for the girls in the morning and Morten and I will go to church in the cutter. I know Ida won't be convinced to leave Daniel's side. Laura will likely stay home to be with her father as she shies away from all society.

Thank goodness for church. These long winter months sometimes feel so isolating. It will be nice to get out. I know there will be countless questions as to Daniel's health. No doubt the many prayers will be an advantage to Daniel and Ida. It will be comforting to be surrounded by so many who care.

I must go and check in on Morten and Daniel now. It is my turn to sit with him for the next few hours.

-12-

Matt felt it might be good for me to have a distraction as I've been so anxious lately. Now that we've been here a week, he invited his sister and her family up for a barbeque. It is nice for the kids to have their cousins around on this beautiful June evening. Given the growing mosquito population, we decided to move inside for the meal. Matt is on the barbeque, I set the table and my sister-in-law Liz, is putting out the salad and condiments.

The kids begrudgingly put down their cell phones when they arrive at the kitchen table. Dinner is served and we all load up our burgers. It's shaping up to be quite a fun time. Then, suddenly out of the blue, my nephew Thomas starts spitting out his burger all over the table. The kids erupt in shocked laughter, but the parents are horrified. Typically, Thomas is a well-mannered boy, so this is very out of character.

"Thomas what's going on?" Liz demands.

In utter disgust he blurts out, "The pickle is really mushy" and he continues ridding his mouth of the remainder of it.

"What are you talking about?" I inquire.

He knocks back some water and emphatically insists the pickles are very soft and mushy!!

"But I just opened them," his mother responds.

Horror struck as it dawns on me what has happened. Hoping it's not true, I turn and glance at the jar of pickles on the shelf that Matt stubbornly rescued from the cellar. I feel sickened to see the half empty jar on the counter.

Liz looks puzzled.

Immediately I took the pickles from the table and threw them out. Despite my threatening eye contact, Matt now realizing what has happened, proceeds to explain why they might be mushy. Well, the kids roared with laughter although Thomas dashed from the table. I felt terrible. Anyway, we now know there is a shelf life on pickles in a jar.

Thomas gradually recovered from the trauma and luckily suffered no other ill effects. I don't believe he will ever eat another pickle, certainly not at our house anyway.

Sunday, January 7th, 1900

Last night proved to be a long, fretful night filled with the sounds of Daniel's relentless coughing and gasping for breath, but he got through it. We all did, but not without the emotional and physical toll it takes to watch a loved one's demise. Otherwise, Sunday morning was as it always is. After Henry's crow at sunrise, the chores done, the breakfast eaten –

we donned our Sunday best. Looking the elegant family that we are once a week, we paraded into Daniel and Ida's room to say goodbye before leaving for church. This was perhaps the first time in as long as I can remember that Daniel missed the Sunday service. As an elder in our church, he is as reliable as Henry's morning wake-up call. Zoe suggested we sing him a hymn before leaving for the service. Sadie led us in, "O God, our help in ages past, our hope for years to come…," Daniel's lips curled upwards as he laid there weakly, absorbing it all.

When we arrived at our little Presbyterian church at the end of the road, numerous sleighs and blanketed horses were tethered in the shelter. The church was toasty warm. All eyes were on us as we entered the sanctuary, immediately taking in Daniel and Ida's absence. Of course, they all knew about the accident as some of the men had been there to recover the sleigh. Word gets around despite the temperature. Morten, in his friendly, affable manner immediately reassured the curious congregation that his father was still with us, although quite weak from fever. He explained that Daniel was not able to attend the service today and that Ida and Laura had stayed home to tend to him. Reverend Mactavish offered up a lengthy, heartfelt prayer for Daniel's recovery. As we sat in the Huntly pew, it felt strange to see the empty spaces.

Of all times to feel nauseous. I thought I would have to zip out in the middle of the scripture reading. Mary wondered at my sudden agitation. The younger children played restlessly, and Lyle even got down on the floor and crawled away. How mortifying. The Barclay boy never does that. Evelyn's son is so well behaved, while my son crawls all over the place when least convenient. Zoe was quiet and pensive. I know she is profoundly worried as she has always had a special friendship with Grandpa. Doug sat uncomfortably in his lace up boots, knickers and button up shirt. He looked so mature for such a busy little fellow.

Several long dreary hymns later, it was finally children's time. I thought it would never arrive. Zoe led the smaller ones to the front and then accompanied them to Sunday School. Nell, Sadie and Carrie are now old enough to stay and follow the service, although Sadie and Carrie are forever exchanging glances that cause them to break into untimely giggles. No doubt they are admiring the Findlay lad who has grown into quite a handsome young man over the past year. They could hardly fail to notice him as the Findlay's pew is only one pew

up and across the aisle from our own. Nell of course, took no part in this silliness but uneasily scanned the congregation. I have no idea what is troubling her, but clearly something is.

After the service, we gathered for tea in the fellowship room. The ladies were busy arranging a schedule to help at our home. That is such a relief, especially since I've been feeling so depleted lately. Everyone imparted their concerns and plans to come by with a casserole. It's funny how a congregation of such humble resources can produce so much comfort and food to share in a time of need. Then there are the Gillies, who don't go to church. I know the minister has visited their home occasionally, but they continue to convey disinterest. For the life of me, I cannot understand it. Imagine choosing to be disconnected from the community. I sometimes wonder if Adam isn't good to Grace and so doesn't permit her to interact with neighbours. It's the only thing I can think of to explain it.

Thankfully it's Sunday and finally a day of rest. After our noon dinner I eagerly await our family time in the sitting room when I can just sit and relax until the evening service. I know the children get bored with letter writing and singsongs, but the adults need the break. I will write Momma and Poppa in Bond Head and let them know about Daniel. By the time the post reaches them, he may have passed. Nell plays so beautifully it always picks up my spirits. Oh darn, I have got to go again. It seems it's all I ever do these days. I hope someone remembered to hang the toilet seat by the woodstove. There's nothing less inviting than an icy cold seat in January!

I have decided where I will hide this journal. There is a small shelf behind the jams and pickles where there are no prying eyes. Who would think to look behind the last row of pickles when there are multiple jars in front. I could tuck it in my apron at night and place it back in the fruit cellar the following morning, completely unnoticed. Must dash to the loo again.

-13-

It's now 11:30 p.m. Brutus and I are settling in on the loveseat for our evening reading. It is hard to hold back my tears as I read of Daniel's illness. Why am I upset about a man I've never met who probably died over 120 years ago? Did people actually die of pneumonia, despite Dr. Moffat's compassionate care and late night, horse drawn, house calls? There were no nursing homes or around the clock medical staff to care for him, just his closest loved ones, his wife, son, daughter, and daughter-in-law to hold his hand in those final hours. There were also countless grandchildren, neighbours and community supporters to help with all his needs and the needs of his grieving family. More impressively, he could die peacefully and swiftly and the whole community could come over to say goodbye to him right here in his own home.

It makes me think of my own father, who is now 92 years old. I've been told I was a 'surprise addition to the family' late in the game. He used to say I was the best 'mistake' they ever made. My siblings often disagree. I realize Dad is almost as old as this house. However, unfortunately he's not in as good shape. In fact, he's recently become a great concern on my growing pile of worries.

It's hard for me to think of Dad as ill. Having always been such a fun loving, health-oriented person, it seems surreal to see him in a sickbed. I keep thinking he's going to wake up tomorrow morning and stretch and say, "I feel much better today." However, that day has not arrived and likely won't, given his advanced years and the number of weeks he's been in bed. It's a hard thing to accept. It was only weeks ago he was going for one of his daily, three walks around the block, chatting with neighbours, flirting with the bank teller and going out for dinner at the local restaurant with Mom.

It all changed when he fell out of bed one night - an unusual turn of events in adulthood. We're not quite sure how it happened, and he can't remember. Mom being hard of hearing, slept through the whole thing and was surprised to find him on the floor in the morning. This unexpected situation brought on Dad's downfall, despite his 91 and a half years of previous robust health and vigilant self-care.

One by one, my siblings arrived to visit and offer support. A day or two went by with Dad immobilized and having difficulty swallowing. Despite many calls, it took the doctor several days to arrive. It seemed his (600 horsepower) Mercedes was not as fast as Dr. Moffat's (one horsepower) sleigh. The truth is, he didn't usually make house calls, so we were delighted when he arrived.

He felt Dad had likely had a small stroke. However, Dad refused to go to the ER fearing he might pick up a bug, which is an understandable concern at 92. The doctor wisely explained to all of us (my father included), that sometimes falls or medical events happen to elderly people and sometimes it's better not to intervene too aggressively but let nature take its course. Usually it is a very peaceful, gradual, and painless way to end one's days. Unfortunately, dad slept through 90% of this conversation and the rest of us weren't emotionally prepared to accept this reality. We were all at various stages of acceptance or denial of what lay ahead. Should we intervene and force Dad to the hospital against his will or simply let him gradually slip away in his own bed? Little did we know that this was only the first complicated question of many to follow.

One of us insisted he must go to the hospital as this whole situation might be resolved more easily than the doctor suggested. Mom agreed and roused Dad, "Glen, you're going to die if you don't go to the hospital." One sibling was undecided. One sib never showed up. Another felt we should let Dad make the choice. And so the family dynamics were activated. Given this 'life or death' situation, Dad eventually decided on the hospital.

After a lengthy wait we were taken into the emergency area. The nurse came around the curtain to take some information, while Mom, Emily, Allan and I stood around the hospital bed.

"Mr. Morrison when did you start feeling sick?" she questioned loudly for all to hear, even those beyond the sound barrier of the thin cotton curtain. "What are you experiencing?" She made some notes on her clip board, barely looking up. "What medications are you on? None?!" The nurse paused. Suddenly, there was eye contact. "Are you sure Mr. Morrison?" She repeated the question in a louder, slower voice. "You're not on any medications?" She confirmed this astounding information with my aging mother and then with the three of us, thinking that he was likely just confused and forgetful of his medication. We confirmed his sanity on this fact. Puzzled and surprised, she recorded this in her notes.

"I am on some vitamins," Dad piped up, "a multivitamin, some fish oil and some brewers yeast," he clarified. I'm not quite sure what all those things do but they seemed to be working for him up until yesterday.

Eventually, Dad was admitted to the hospital. He had not eaten in almost two days, following some difficulty swallowing. In addition to his medical care, we felt he would need someone with him during his hospitalization. We were going to need extra help.

All of us being busy professionals (or off on sick leave), none of us were available to take on the role of caregiver. Not knowing where to turn, I phoned a private senior's care service and explained our needs. ($ca-ching$!) The fellow on the other end agreed to meet with us and assign a caregiver to Dad's hospital room. We all knew it would cost, but this seemed outrageously expensive. However, there were no options. None of us were available and Mom practically needs a caregiver herself. Besides, we are trying to discourage her use of the car so getting to the hospital on her own would be problematic. We would have to hire someone.

That afternoon, we met Bill, aptly named as he was good at giving those. Bill arrived with Sharon to meet my mother and the 'kids' first. We had a lengthy discussion about my father's medical history. Then my 88-year-old mother signed a contract hiring Bill to organize care and Sharon to provide it. For this service, Sharon was paid $15 an hour and Bill was paid $35 hourly. This didn't feel quite right but we were in a desperate position and Dad needed someone fast. Mom signed, Sharon began working and Bill began receiving kickbacks. Daniel and Ida never had to deal with these sorts of middlemen.

Things went downhill quickly, but somehow Dad managed to hang on. Despite his weakening state, his mind was somewhat clear although this oscillated randomly. What he was consistent about however, was that he wanted to live. For whatever reason he could not manage to swallow, but you can't live without food. Decisions had to be made. It had now been days since he had ingested anything. The head doctor explained that with a surgical procedure they could insert a permanent tube in his stomach to feed him. At 92, did he want this somewhat aggressive measure? In one of Dad's lucid moments, we explained the situation to him. Admittedly, we half expected a 'just let me go' response. Much to our delight Dad, who has been hospital phobic throughout his entire 92 years, decided "yes" he would like the surgical implant.

Dad sailed through the procedure and was wheeled back to his room later that day. Within days, he was feeling somewhat perky, and we could see glimpses of his former self.

Then, one day, he announced that he was 'ready to check out of his room and could Allan call the front desk and have them send a cab'. Eventually he was discharged by another doctor whom we hadn't met before, however Dad attempted to tip him well upon 'check out'.

Bill and his team went into full throttle providing around the clock care for my rapidly aging father. Mom was overwhelmed and not sure she wanted this 24/7 intrusion of caregivers. She was quite used to her private life with the cat and her elderly spouse. However, her options were diminishing. If Dad wanted to be home, and he did, he would now need a nursing bed downstairs. Life had suddenly become more complicated.

Wednesday, January 10th, 1900.

As I write this, I am a weepy mess. Daniel's time has come. He has just passed. It happened a few minutes before the clock gonged 3:00 a.m. Ida, Morten, Laura and I were all with him. It was a peaceful death. First there were deep breaths in that seemed to go nowhere. For over an hour we held his hand as the breathing grew more unusual, ...the breaths in with no exhale. Eventually it came, the final deep inhale, a strained gargle in the base of his throat, and then the final letting go of life. We all knew. I could almost feel him pass through me. Although comforting to witness a peaceful death, it is heartbreaking to lose one you love. Ida kissed him and wept as we all did. It is all so sudden, in the midst of life. How we will miss that kindly man. He looked so peaceful as we observed him lying there in the moments that followed.

Reverend Mactavish will come in the morning. I dread breaking the news to Zoe and the others. Here I sit, pouring out my sorrows on paper, to ease my pain. It has not yet sunk in. Only a few days ago Daniel was so vibrant and alive, and now life will never be the same. Damn that stupid bridge and the blasted short cut. Here comes Morten back from the outhouse. His eyes are red and puffy. I know he has been crying.

In the morning, it didn't take long before the news seeped through the household. First, I started in the girls' room, and they knew from my face as soon as I walked in. Zoe shouted, "he's gone isn't he. Grandpa died," she screeched. I nodded and cried, and the news permeated through the house like a cold chill. It was a painful, mournful morning and no one ate much breakfast. Everyone hugged Grandma and wept. She tried to carry on without too much fuss, but it was impossible to hide her heartbreak.

Morten and Chuck went out in the cutter to get the undertaker so Daniel could be prepared for the parlour. The children all filed into his room to give him a goodbye kiss. The word spread quickly throughout the community. The children stayed home from school and assisted with the preparation of sandwiches for the mourners. It was a quiet, solemn day.

Within the next two days, it seems every neighbour, church member and friend, whom any of us has ever known, has paid a visit to say so long to dear, old Daniel. Ida has a lot of support to help her deal with the days ahead but right now she's growing weary. It's gradually sinking in, like water trickling through the soil. The sad reality and the permanence of it all will gradually absorb into her soul. The service will be in a few days and his body will be placed in the crypt, awaiting burial in the family plot in spring.

That was a dark day for all of us. My tears are overflowing in my gutter. I will never forget him.

Monday, January 15th, 1900

What would Zoe do without Gaby? She is such a great listener with those big ears. Zoe spends more time out there with that donkey than she does doing her chores.

We have been cloaked in sadness for days now. Such an unexpected and deeply felt loss for us all. Morten does not talk about it. He keeps it all in. He tries to keep busy out in the barn with Chuck, but I feel he needs to unload. Why is that with men? They keep everything in as if to express emotions were a weakness.

The service will be this afternoon and I'm dreading it. The funeral carriage will arrive soon and then we will follow the casket to the church for our final farewell. Poor little Zoe has not spoken all day and her eyes are weary and red. Here come the big black horses pulling the casket coach. They are just turning into the drive now. Must go.

-14-

Dad continues to hang on, yet it has been hard watching his gradual decline. It should be noted, there have been complicating factors. First, Dad has a 'female friend'. For years, we have all known Barb. She lives around the corner from my parents and has done some book-keeping for my father in the past. When he turned about 80, he found it harder to get to his office. Dad loved his work and as a self-employed entrepreneur he didn't want to give it up, despite his age. It made him feel young, purposeful and alive therefore retirement was still on the back burner. By the time he was 80, he was going into his office for one hour a day. However, the daily subway ride was getting beyond him. Instead, he decided he would hire this nice, young neighbour to retrieve his documents from the office and they would meet at her home so he could review and sign them. That way, he would still get out each day on business, but the business would come to him instead.

Surprisingly, Mom was in support of this plan. She felt it was good for Dad to maintain his interests and get out for a regular walk. Also, I believe she liked her space. These business outings became the highlight of Dad's day. The cute, young neighbour was now almost middle age, but still a fraction of Dad's age. Mom used to tease him and of course we all knew it was harmless. However, after twelve years of meetings, I imagine you discuss a lot of things with that person, and you develop quite a 'friendship'. It seemed Barb knew all Dad's worries and helped him with all his decisions, (including financial). It was getting a little creepy. They continued their meetings when Dad was flat on his back at home on a bed in the living room. The content was getting pretty thin: "Glen do you want to renew this magazine? Glen, shall we pay the hydro bill today?" Nevertheless, it seemed to help Dad's morale which was the important thing. Gradually, this emotional attachment and the frequency of Barb's visits at the house, began to grate on Mom (finally). Growing increasingly uncomfortable with the arrangement, Mom asked us to speak to Barb about it.

Despite our best intentions, it did not turn out well. We invited Barb over. As we were going through household expenses together, it came to Barb's salary. We soon learned that she was no volunteer! In fact, she was pulling quite a salary for her very part time hours. Barb could see we were taken aback, and she quickly jumped in with explanations. Evidently there were a lot of magazines to renew, and it was pressing business.

That sure gave us our 'in' to discuss Mom's concerns about her frequent visits to the house. We started with "Barb you have been a great friend to our father over the years. He values your visits, and we hope you will continue that. However, given that there is no further 'work to be done', we are no longer able to pay for your visits."

Well, that was enough for Barb. She left abruptly before we even got to the part about Mom. However, she didn't slink away quietly as one might anticipate. Instead, she immediately barged in to see Dad in the living room. Mom was there and greeted her pleasantly. Then, out of the blue, Barb leaned over and planted a deep, long kiss on Dad's father's mouth. There was tongue involved, slobber, loose dentures and spousal shock and trauma. The smooch went on for at least a minute before Mom grabbed her cane and whacked her. With that, Barb disappeared forever, and Dad remained in the living room with a big smile on his face.

Monday, January 15, 1900.

It was a cold, grey, depressing afternoon and the church was packed to capacity. There was a sea of people, all clad in black and with somber faces.

When Reverend Mactavish took his place at the pulpit, you could have heard a pin drop. Aside from the occasional sniffle, there wasn't a sound.

"On this somber day, we are gathered here dear friends, to remember the colourful life of our beloved friend Daniel Huntly".... Zoe buried her head in my sleeve, and I could feel her little body convulse with sobs. Trying to contain my own overflowing emotions, I fixed my gaze on the stain glassed window hoping for a sense of momentary escape. Rev. Mactavish gave a powerful and touching remembrance of Daniel's existence.

"Difficult as the days ahead will be, we will not be alone. Not only is God by our side holding us up, but we also have each other." He went on to say that "in this community of friends and family, we will gather around Ida, Morten and Laura and all their kin and be with them in our time of grief. Nothing can lighten the heart like a true friend in our moment of need."

Sadness blanketed the grieving congregation. Morten and Laura supported their mother as they followed Daniel's casket from the church for the very last time. Ida looked as white as a ghost in her black garb.

Our family filed out, with wet eyes and heads downcast. The procession of devastated family members followed each other to the snow-covered churchyard where the weather was reminiscent of the day of the accident. The men lifted Daniel's humble coffin into the crypt where it will rest until the earth thaws in spring. At that time, we will gather again for the burial.

Afterwards countless friends congregated in the fellowship room for tea. Daniel would have hated to miss this. He loved a gathering.

It has been a draining day. Death leaves a deep scar that fades with time, but never disappears.

-15-

Most people crave time off work but I'm just not able to function. I'm not accustomed to it. I'm used to firing on all cylinders, multi-tasking and managing numerous projects at once. My brain is struggling to adjust to this new, relaxed pace. I keep feeling I should be achieving more. I'm worried about the spa and no matter how hard I try; I can't seem to let go of that. Sure, I have the kids to focus on, and my parents' care, and Matt, but I feel as though I'm dropping a ball, and that I'm headed towards career failure. Nevertheless, I can't bear the thought of returning to work. I'm a restless mess.

Matt is on me to reduce my screen time, so I've turned to reading to cope instead. It is quickly becoming my second favourite escape. I must admit, I crave to look at my phone. However, I'm finding there's nothing like a good book to lose yourself in. Imagine many nights of entertainment for only $4.99, now that I shop at the second-hand bookstore.

Electronic readers are so impersonal. I know it's the way of the future. Generations now grow up being introduced to the computer from birth. Computers and electronics are second nature to them. My grandchildren will probably say "what is cursive writing Grandma? Can you write something for me so I can show my friends. They don't believe it." "You mean you used to cut down a tree to make paper? How did that work?" Are books destined to become relics from the past? Some day we may see libraries in museums and books may become nostalgic antiques.

What will happen to the concept of cuddling up by the fire with a good book? It will soon be cuddling up with your e-reader beside the electric fire replica. What about the cost of electronic readers? What kind of waste does it leave behind? I wonder what all those electronics do to our minds and bodies? We often rush ahead before considering the drawbacks. We seem ever so smart but never so unwise. Maybe change is not always progress. We seem to be living in a cult of change. Maybe we should consider how to retain the good aspects of something before pressing delete on the previous method.

I realize I like holding something concrete in my hand. I want to see how long the story is and where I am at in it. I like to carry it in my purse. When I look at a book, I remember where I was when I read it and what was going on in my life. It has some depth, some character. It's like an old friend. I see it again and I remember that slice of my life. An electronic download doesn't speak to me the same way. It's just a faceless thing. I will neither treasure it nor hang on to it with any kind of lasting sentiment. I will not file it alphabetically on the shelf under E nor loan it to anyone so they can enjoy it too.

And letters, there's a concept that's gone the way of the dinosaur. I remember when I was a girl, I used to write my grandmother a letter every week and she would do the same. I still have them in a shoebox somewhere and when I read them, I remember her. As a teen, I recall the incredible excitement of seeing a letter come through the mail slot of the front door from some boyfriend away for the summer. Not long ago, Mom gave me a package of old letters I sent home from camp. Emails and text messages just don't have the same longevity. Will I save an email my daughter sent me from camp and re-send it to her 35 years later? Doubtful. My guess is the technology will have changed a few thousand times in that duration. What window would I have into the past if Isabel never wrote down her thoughts? There's a certain permanence to the written word. Are we losing a beautiful part of our history? What about Christmas cards, postcards and wedding invitations? Maybe some things are worth holding on to...literally.

Tuesday, February 6, 1900.

Several weeks have passed since I've written. Although our home is still cloaked in grief, life must go on. Without a doubt I am in the family way. I will tell Morten soon, as he needs something to look forward to. Mary is growing concerned, always asking if she can get me a cup of tea. She seems to sense it. Daughters are so perceptive.

I am worried about Nell. She has just turned fifteen and is becoming a young woman. It should be such a fun time of life for her. No husband or children yet, no responsibilities except her daily chores, she's almost completed her schooling, ... yet she seems so distant and sad. Carrie and Nell don't get along. They never have. Carrie has outshone her older sister throughout her life, not a shy, self-conscious bone in her body. She would do well to have a little of Nell's humility. Nell, on the other hand, has never seemed sure of herself. She has always been painfully shy and had trouble making friends. I remember when she was just a young girl and some of the neighbourhood women were over with their children. The girls went off to have a little tea party and I later found Nell on her own, in the parlour looking at a picture book. She had tears in her eyes and said Carrie wouldn't let her play. She would have been about seven and Carrie only six. You can be sure I had quite a little talk with Carrie and Nell was quickly allotted a teacup. However, without my ongoing intervention, this alienation seems to have been the theme throughout Nell's life. I have talked with her 'til the cows come home about being friendly and joining in. It makes no difference. Carrie has become slightly more inclusive when I am looking, but

I imagine this kindness is not extended at school. No doubt Carrie, with her unfailing charm and her adoring little sister Sadie, has the whole schoolyard eating out of her hands. I thought it best to approach Zoe to gain some understanding of what is happening at the schoolhouse.

Astute little Zoe was very insightful, even at ten. She explained that Carrie rarely includes Nell with the other girls. The girls often walk about the yard flirting with the boys, who generally kick a ball around and mostly try to ignore them. Some of the boys, however, are starting to pay more attention. Nell is not part of this. She has one friend, Helen, but apparently, they both are somewhat reclusive. Often, they read at the break, or stoke the fire in the schoolhouse. Helen has been away a lot lately as her mother is sick and so she is needed at home. That leaves Nell pretty much on her own. Zoe tells me there is an older boy at school (Billy), a young man really, as he is almost seventeen. He's not very smart and there are no other students his age. He often tries to talk to Nell, but she does not seem to like him around. She moves away whenever he comes near.

I must talk to her. She would have no experience in this area. However, beyond some social difficulties, which Nell is no stranger to, she seems listless. Before, she used to practice the piano before school, do her lessons in the evening and never needed reminding about chores. She appears weary for a girl her age. I will make sure she is getting some cod liver oil.

Doug has taken to hitting his little brother lately. Lyle is adorable and everyone wants to tickle him to hear him giggle. This, of course, gets Doug extremely jealous. I will make a point to tickle Doug tomorrow and let him help me with the chickens.

Laura is driving me around the bend. I'm sorry God, I know it's not Christian of me, but it's the truth. I am trying to be patient with her but she's just so morose. Everything is gloomy. I cannot wait 'til the weather warms up and we can get outside. There are too many people in this house and too much sadness. We all miss Daniel and his sense of humour and light heartedness.

When Nell arrived at the schoolhouse, there was no sign of Helen and her spirits fell. Not another friendless day amongst all these students. Miss Walker had just rung the bell and the children were beginning to file into the toasty, little schoolhouse on this cold but sunny February day. There were about twenty in total today. Attendance fluctuated depending on the season. During planting, or haying season, there were few boys as they were needed on the farm. The girls were the ones who usually attended more regularly but of course that depended on weather or family illness. Today Nell counted exactly eighteen present. She was relieved Billy wasn't there.

Miss Walker was such a nice teacher but not much older than Mary – 19 or 20 maybe. She boards with the Baxters, at the farm across the street. Billy is by far the oldest student - almost the same age as Miss Walker. Nell wondered if that made it hard for her. Did she ever feel nervous or uneasy like Nell did? No doubt, the fact that students ranged in age, sometimes made discipline a complicated issue. However, Miss Walker was the teacher, and few challenged a teacher. If they did, she could snap the palms of their hands with that little switch that teachers had. But that only happened when it was really needed. Nell had never seen this happen to an older boy and she wondered what would happen if Billy spoke back.

Nell sat in her desk, which was near the back on the left, on the girl's side. She brought out her slate as did the others. As Miss Walker was beginning this morning's lesson, Billy walked in late and took his seat. He sat down loudly and wiped his runny nose on his sleeve. A chill went up Nell's spine. He was frequently staring at her. Nell wanted as much distance between her and him as possible. Should she talk to Miss Walker about it? What would she say, "he stares at me?" What could Miss Walker do anyway? If she was moved to a different row, he would know she said something to the teacher, and he would be angry. She felt her anxiety growing. At the lunch break, she decided to stay in. Helen was still away, and she wanted to avoid Billy. However, Miss Walker insisted that they all go outside today to get some fresh air. It was a beautiful winter day, and the crisp air would do them all good.

Although Zoe was engaged in play with her numerous friends, she noticed Nell alone near the maple tree. Zoe ran over to her. Of course, Nell would not want to play with her young friends, but Zoe decided to stay a few minutes just to cheer her up. Maybe she was missing Grandpa.

Before long, Zoe ran off to re-join her friends. Billy had been watching Nell from the step and realized she was alone. He made his way over to her through the snowy yard. Nell froze when she saw him coming. What was it about this boy that made her cringe? He smiled at her, exposing his brown teeth with a space in the upper right jaw, where several more teeth should have been. He looked disheveled and it was common schoolyard knowledge that Billy always smelled of body odour. He did not come from a very nice home and his family were known to be equally unkempt.

"Where's your friend today?" he asked. Nell ignored the question and looked away, quivering inside.

"What's a pretty girl like you doing standing here all alone, don't you have no friends?" Nell glared at him, and he laughed. He sneezed in her direction without so much as an 'excuse me'.

"How'd you like to help me with my homework after school today?" He smiled and touched her arm.

Nell was growing more uneasy. "Can't, I'm busy. My momma needs me at home," she retorted as she jerked her arm away.

"Aww, tell your momma that you have a date with a boy, and you can't make it," he chuckled.

By this point, Nell had a mixture of fear and fury churning around inside her. What right did this uncouth young man have to approach her while she was alone, touch her arm and then suggest that she avoid her mother for a 'date' with him. Nell's blood was boiling and somewhere from deep in her gut she shouted, "get lost Billy."

Zoe, who was playing nearby, heard her sister and stopped in her tracks. She came running over. She wasn't about to let that big, smelly oaf Billy, intimidate Nell.

"Are you okay Nell?" she panted out of breath.

"Here's your little sister to the rescue. Maybe tomorrow then." He smiled sinisterly at her, then turned and walked away, coughing and spitting as he went, never once thinking to cover his mouth. His manners were as deplorable as his countenance.

"What was that all about?" asked Zoe.

"I don't know, but I can't stand him," said Nell. "Thanks for coming over."

"I think you should tell Momma about him," Zoe said emphatically.

"I will," Nell responded unconvincingly.

Chuck was whistling in the barn as he mucked out stalls and laid down fresh straw. It was dull work, but Chuck didn't seem to mind it. He was a happy soul with an uncomplicated mind. He chatted with the horses and cows as he adeptly manoeuvred around them. They loved Chuck. Barney had stopped waiting for Scarlet to return and he finally seemed more settled, although quite lost.

Chuck climbed the stairs to the second floor of the barn and entered the hay loft. Only six months earlier, the family had been busy tossing countless pitchforks of hay and straw into either side of the loft. Chuck, Morten and a few of the neighbourhood boys had filled it almost to capacity. Chuck clamoured over multiple obstacles and made his way to a large pile of straw. He climbed the wooden ladder that was built into the

side of the barn. He was at the top of the pile sending down straw when he heard something. He stopped and looked around but didn't see anything. Maybe it was his imagination. Sure enough the sound continued softly. Was it a cat giving birth? a barn owl? a racoon? It sounded like a muffled whimper or cry. That was odd. He climbed down and listened again. The noise was coming from the granary. He crept to the door and listened. With closer attention, it sounded like sobbing. He gently opened the door and peeked in. To his surprise, there was Nell, sitting on a sack of feed, with her hands in her head, convulsing in tears.

"Nell," he whispered, "what's the matter?"

Nell looked up with a start. She hadn't expected anyone was nearby. With her splotchy face and red eyes, she was clearly surprised. Tears trickled down her cheeks and her voice came out in a high-pitched whimper.

"I'm sorry, I didn't know anyone was here."

"What's the matter, Nell? Are you okay?"

Nell continued to weep and was clearly beside herself. Chuck sat down beside her and put an old horse blanket around her shoulders. "What's the matter Nell?" he inquired gently. "Are you missing your grandfather?"

Eventually, Nell found her voice. "Yes." She debated whether to say more, then stopped herself.

Chuck seemed to sense that this wasn't the whole issue. "Is there something else upsetting you?" he asked protectively.

She ceased her crying and looked at him. "I'm fine. I'm just upset about Grandpa," she lied.

"If there is anything I can do to help, you let me know." He took her hand supportively and she sobbed a little more. He pulled out an old handkerchief that smelled like hay and dabbed her cheeks and eyes.

"Thank you Chuck," she said self-consciously.

-16-

What could possibly be behind these living room walls that grey paneling is an improvement?

After an afternoon of tearing down outdated panelling, Matt and I discover some kind of bumpy stucco covered with multiple layers of a hideous floral wallpaper. Grey panelling actually is an improvement. The faded, ripped wallpaper is held in place by lath and plaster, which is mixed with horsehair (probably compliments of Barney). As we continue to peel off the wallpaper, a layer of faded, old newspaper appears underneath.

"Wow", I exclaim to Matt. "What era is this from?"

What a historic adventure. Before the afternoon is out, we have about half the wallpaper off and nearly six pages of legible newspaper laid out on the floor. My heart is pounding rapidly when we discover a date - 1900! 'Interpretation of Dreams, published by Austrian Neurologist Sigmund Freud!', reads one headline. The paper, quite faded and cracked, made reference to a term called 'the unconscious'. Under other wallpaper, 'Devastating Hurricane in Texas, Kills Thousands...President McKinley Expresses Deep Sadness for the Citizens of Galveston'. And behind the couch.... 'Carrie Chapman Catt named the New President of the American National Suffrage Association'. Next to the TV, 'The Montreal Shamrocks Capture the Stanley Cup for the second year in a row - March 1900'. There is a lengthy article about Wilfred Laurier's Liberals winning another majority. Our living room is an historic mess. 'Queen Victoria struggles with the Croup', 'Kodak Introduces the 1$ Brownie Camera'. Near the fireplace, an excerpt of what seemed to be an ongoing fictional story as though from a book. Then there appears to be some local papers used in the insulation of this house 'Horse Thief Caught on Line 4', 'Judy McKinlop's sister visits from Lindsay', 'Town Hall meeting on Tuesday March 9th (Topic: road improvements)'. There are countless advertisements for women's clothes, boots, kitchen stoves, kettles. These newspapers, although not all from the same day or week, all appear to be from the same year.

It reminds me of Isabel's diary, which has become my nightly bedtime reading. Her life was so radically different from my own even though it was lived within these same four walls. In some ways her life was much richer, in other ways it was significantly more deprived. I'm becoming strangely obsessed with life at the turn of the century. It keeps popping up and I am starting to feel some sort of connection to it.

Friday, February 16, 1900

I told Morten. I have never seen his face light up so much as it did with my news of yet another pregnancy. If only I could feel the same way. He was delighted but worried. Worried about money, about me and my advanced age for childbirth, yet excited for the joy of having yet another newborn. He said, "it is just what we all need after losing Dad last month." Nevertheless, I hate to put this on him. No matter how you look at it, it's another little mouth to feed and we don't have a lot of extra right now. I explained it was early on, so for now we won't tell the children.

I am ashamed to say, but I am not excited about this baby at all. I have seven beautiful children, what do I need with another? Lyle is almost out of babyhood, and I could see a little glimmer of freedom on the horizon. I am tired of sharing my body. Why did I consent that night? I should have insisted Morten leave me alone, but he was so persistent.

Zoe is beginning to recover some of her zeal. Spending time with that silly donkey somehow seems to help her. She spends her life brushing it or feeding it our few remaining carrots from the cellar. Chuck told me the other day he heard her singing to it. We all laughed at that. Isn't she sweet.

Ida is acting stoic. Her staunch Presbyterian, Scottish background leaves her little choice. I know she is hurting inside. She never seems fully there. When she is doing her baking, she has a faraway look. I know Morten and Laura are missing their father too, as we all are.

Something is troubling Nell. She won't let on, but I know. It is hard to get her alone for a talk as there are so many people in this farmhouse. How I long for spring and the opening of windows and doors and a little elbow room. What could be on that girl's mind?

Zoe hoped Helen was back, but she knew that was unlikely. The weather was a little warmer today, so the children gathered outside and played in the yard. Nell watched for Helen's sleigh, but it didn't come. Billy was on the far side of the yard whittling a stick. Nell tried to stay near the others, but it wasn't her nature to join in. Nevertheless, she stayed in their midst.

Miss Walker came to the door of the schoolhouse and rang the bell. The children gravitated chaotically towards the door, ran up the steps and filed into the little building. Nell took up the rear of the crowd and she could see Billy approaching from the corner of her eye.

"Good morning Nelly," he grinned. "I seen you looking at me. Meet me behind the schoolhouse after *lunch and we can spend some time together." Almost as an afterthought he added, "Your little sister is so cute. You wouldn't want anything to happen to her."*

Nell was dumbfounded. What did he mean by that? Was that some kind of threat? Would he hurt Zoe if she didn't show up? How did this get so out of control? Was she mistakenly giving him signs that she was interested in him? Nell kept her eyes fixed on the schoolhouse and refused to look at him as she followed up the steps behind the others and nervously took her seat on the girls' side of the classroom.

Miss Walker greeted the class and began with a prayer as always. Nell stared at her slate but could still feel Billy's eyes on her. His irritating cough was getting worse. Clearly, he had been smoking. The morning lagged on, what should she do? Miss Walker had been insisting they go outside at lunch and today would be no exception because the sun was out, and it was a beautiful day. If she didn't meet him behind the schoolhouse, was she putting Zoe at risk? If she did go, what would happen?

Nell couldn't concentrate. She thought she might be sick. At break time, Miss Walker rang the bell and the children raced for their coats and boots and burst through the door. Billy looked over at Nell and smiled.

She was an anxious wreck all break, but she didn't go behind the schoolhouse. Instead, she stayed uncharacteristically close to Zoe so she could keep an eye on her. The break passed incredibly slowly, and Nell pined to go home. She used to love school.

Billy started following her at a distance and he looked angry. Every chance he got he tried to approach her, and he was getting bolder with each passing day. Her anxiety was growing. His eyes seemed to follow her everywhere and that grin that had made her so uncomfortable had turned to a hardened glare. As he watched her talking to Zoe in the yard, her blood ran cold. She had to do something.

The day came when it was her turn to bring wood in for the schoolhouse stove. She slipped into the shed when no one was paying attention, to hastily gather a few logs. As she was loading them into her arms, she heard the shed door creak behind her. Too terrified to turn around, she saw a shadow on the wall in front of her. She froze as she felt a hand on her shoulder,

She turned and glared at Billy, "Leave me alone," she growled.

"Just one little kiss," he leaned in close to her.

She pushed him back, but he grabbed her and pinned her against the shed wall. She tried to scream but before she could he pressed his lips against hers and thrust his disgusting tongue inside her mouth. His breath was repulsive, and Nell was in a panic. It all happened so fast, and he seemed to have incredible strength. The 'kiss' seemed to go on forever. She could feel him against her as she tried with all her might to struggle free. He was clearly aroused and wanting more of her as he held her face and continued forcing his tongue in her mouth. She had never experienced this in her life, and she hated it. She bit down as hard as she could on his tongue, and he lurched back and shouted. "What are you doing, you little whore!" He slapped her across her face. With strength she didn't know she had, Nell smashed him in the nose with her fist. There was a loud crack. As he cursed and stepped back, Nell fled for the door and into the school yard.

-17-

My cell is ringing. It's Mom. I debate whether to answer. However, it might be something urgent about Dad, although it is normally just toxic conversation laced with subtle criticism. Begrudgingly, I take the call. After Dad's medical update and pressing news about her cat, she nonchalantly reveals that she took the car out. What?!

"Mom, you know you are not supposed to be driving after the stroke you had last year." I say, gently reminding her of the safety precautions we discussed a few months ago.

"I know, but I still have a license," she insists.

"Mom, you know the doctor didn't advise any more driving," I reasoned.

To put this in perspective, my mother now has access to two of Dad's caregivers, who have offered to drive her around as needed. She also has a comfortable budget for cab companies. We have even offered to hire a college student a few afternoons a week to drive her wherever she wants. She has declined it all. Understandable, I guess. Who wants to lose their independence after a lifetime of doing things your own way. However, a few things have changed over that lifetime. For instance, she is almost blind in one eye, does not hear well, and has poor balance. I can't imagine her reflex response time is very efficient either. I would not want my dog on a street where she was driving, let alone my kids. In fact, I'd much rather be in a car with my teenage son at the wheel. I don't want anyone getting hurt, including Mom. I feel a nagging responsibility to keep her off the road and it is becoming increasingly difficult. I finally have some time away from work and now I have to worry about my parents. All I really want to do is read the newspaper from 120 years ago.

I email my siblings and for once we all agree. Who wants to take this project on? Of course, at the crux of our fear is that we know the wrath of our mother all too well. If she wants something, she will fight for it, even at 88. Her predictable response would be to threaten to cut us all out of her will if we get in her way. I worry she'd do it and then she'd have to drive to her lawyer's to make it happen. No doubt all monies would be re-routed to the cat.

We know we must move in on this but how? We asked her friend to talk to her about it, but she wisely declined. We could take the keys to the car but then how could the caregivers drive her around when needed? If they had the keys, she would badger them or simply fire them if they didn't hand them over. We could let the air out of the tires or somehow sabotage the car, but she would quickly arrange for it to be repaired. We could call the police if she tried to drive but technically, she isn't breaking any law and she might figure out who tipped them off. We could all show up in her living room and do an intervention, good naturedly explain how much we care about her and don't want anything to happen to her and therefore we are all taking the keys. That could collectively cost us our entire inheritance, but I simply could not live with myself if she inadvertently hurt someone. We better think of something fast.

Tuesday, February 20, 1900

Laura generally annoys me with her glum demeanour and the way she mopes around feeling sorry for herself. Today I walked into the parlour while she was doing some sewing. She was preoccupied and she didn't notice me as I looked through the shelf for a book. She was humming and she had a slight smile on her face. It seemed odd. I don't think I've ever really seen her cheery. When she became aware of my presence in the room, she immediately stopped and became self-conscious. She's so bizarre. I don't know how Morten can be related to her. He and his sister are night and day. Morten is so much like Daniel, with his jovial and easy-going nature. He loves people and seems to know how to get the best out of life. Laura, on the other hand, is the epitome of melancholy.

Zoe has told me more about the young man at the schoolhouse. Apparently, he is not a very nice fellow. I think I know the family he's attached to. He's new to this area so I don't know him personally, but his grandparents live two concessions over, and north of the side road. If it's the family I am thinking of, they are quite poorly off. There is drinking in that home and the daughter moved away suddenly many years ago. She did not come to school much so I don't remember her well, except that she was very quiet and her appearance was sloppy. This must be her boy. I have not seen her in years, and I cannot recall her name. The grandparents are not church goers, and their farm is poorly maintained. Their animals are often underfed, and their crops are always late to be brought in. I know the neighbours have helped them many times, because my good friend Rose lives up that way. She says their home is unkempt and the kitchen is disgracefully dirty. She was there to deliver some eggs and she was taken aback by the conditions. I imagine their grandson Billy has come to help them on the farm. Maybe the mother has returned too, although I have not heard of it and normally word would get around. I cannot imagine Nell would be much interested in a fellow from that home. This can't be good. I must ask her directly.

Zoe tells me he talks with her frequently at the break and that Nell is very uncomfortable whenever he comes around. I told Zoe to stay close with her sister during yard time. I will pay a visit to Miss Walker to let her know of my concerns.

-18-

The farmhouse living room is a mess. We have now removed all panelling, wallpaper, plaster and newspapers from these four, historic walls. Who would have thought so much history could have survived behind such hideous panelling.

When I wind the old wall clock each morning, I love its even tick tock...tick tock. Such a steady, comforting sound. Despite its age, the clock continues to gong even when I move it temporarily to rest on the couch, a subtle reminder that time doesn't stop. On closer inspection, I see its roman numerals are mildly faded but otherwise it's extremely well preserved for a relic from the past. I suppose the darkness of the corner has protected it over the years. It is a simple piece but as I take a closer look at it this time it appears to be constructed from several pieces of wood and nailed together with miniscule, little nails. I examine the back to discover the intricacies of the clock. Such fine little pieces, working together in perfect synchrony as if a tiny little team of golden ants were toiling together towards the common goal of documenting the minutes. In the right corner, down at the bottom, I can see someone's name is scrolled in dark ink or paint. Somebody made this by hand. I wonder if he sold it with a 120 year warranty. In fact, this clock has outlasted its maker. It's a quiet, steady heartbeat from a century ago that continues to beat in the farmhouse to this day.

As I sit on the front porch with Isabel's diary, I take in the beautiful day, filled with birds, a warm summer breeze, and the occasional mosquito. My lemonade in hand, Isabel's diary takes me back to a dark, frigid winter day sometime in February. The weather sounded brutal and so did her life. Yet, despite her burdens, she never seemed alone in her difficulties.

Imagine having seven children and suspecting you are pregnant with your eighth. And... they didn't even have anti-depressants, not to mention adequate birth control. Her life was such drudgery.. endless laundry… babies… cooking…cleaning.. and not even Netflix to help her cope. She could read and write well but I realize, from reading the newspaper discovered in our wall, that she couldn't even vote. She couldn't work outside the home unless she was unmarried and a teacher or a nurse. There was no birth control, unless her husband had access to an underground supplier and even then, it was probably just a jumbo diaphragm. With withdrawal as the only available approach, it's no wonder there were so many children.

On the other hand, she had a rich fabric of people and an intricate community in her life which seems unmatchable today. If she were on Facebook, she'd have five hundred friends, except they'd actually be present in her life. Everything was done through teamwork, just like the clock. How much she must have felt connected to other women who shared these responsibilities, especially in the same household. She had her mother-in-law, her sister-in-law, her daughters as well as countless relatives, neighbours and church friends. She was not alone. How many women today are single parents, or live in nuclear families disconnected from extended family, friends and community? How many are displaced far from family or friends, or lead nomadic lives, changing address with every new job or relationship? What ever happened to rootedness? At least Isabel didn't have to worry about her mother-in-law taking the sleigh out for a spin and running over all the neighbourhood children.

We have come so far, and yet we haven't.

Although still resistant, Megan is gradually coming to terms with her summer stay away from the pulse of her busy social life. She claims there's 'way too much family time' and 'no one around to hang out with.' However, I've noticed she's talking to us a little more which is either a sign of desperation for human contact or the beginning of enjoying her family.

I'm sorry. I can't stop laughing. That maple branch is tickling my side again. Every time the wind blows, it makes me giggle. Regardless of the relentless tickling, I love being so close to her shelter. She makes me feel protected and it's so nice being near the birds. My maple has a robin's nest just above my eave where I can watch the eggs hatch and hear that little family squawking as they come to life every morning.

Several days went by and Nell hadn't told a soul about what had happened in the shed. She had horrendous dreams, waking in the night in a deep sweat. Her sleep became so fitful that it often woke Mary, who shared her bed.

"What is going on Nell? You keep waking me," Mary groaned.

"I'm sorry, I just had a bad dream."

"You're okay. We are all here with you," Mary comforted half asleep.

In the other bed, Zoe, Carrie and Sadie slept soundly, but Nell's torment continued. She wondered whether she should tell her mother or maybe Chuck. He and Poppa would deal with Billy by paying a visit to his grandparents. But what if Billy did something to Zoe, or one of her sisters. Nell's thoughts circled in the familiar cycle for what seemed hours. Eventually, late in the night, she drifted back to sleep in the safety of the bed beside Mary.

Morning came fast. Too fast. Nell didn't relish the thought of facing another day exhausted on next to no sleep. She did not relish heading to the schoolhouse with Billy glaring at her constantly. He was downright furious with her now since she had clocked him in the nose and wounded his pride... but he had left her no choice. He had been like a hawk waiting for his prey to be in a vulnerable situation.

The Huntly sleigh arrived at school and the girls climbed out. Morten waved goodbye before he turned Barney homeward, reassuring all of them that he would stay on the main road. Nell's first order of business was to look around for Billy. He must be running late again, as there was no sign of him. The day passed and Billy never showed up. This meant relief for Nell. She felt so free and at ease, without his eyes constantly prying. Maybe he was planning his retaliation. In fact, several days went by, no Billy. She was even starting to concentrate and enjoy school again, although with an uneasy feeling hanging over her. Even Miss Walker remarked upon the difference in her demeanour. Nell mulled his absence over in her mind and decided he must be needed on the home front. This was too good to be true.

It was that night at supper when everything changed. Earlier in the day, Momma had been quilting with the women when the talk turned to the subject of Billy.

"Children I have some sad news. You know Billy Finch, the young man at your school."

Nell froze. What had he done? Had he hurt someone? Was he in trouble with the law? Had he told someone that he had kissed her and led them to believe that she had consented or even invited it?

"Doug, sit up at the table. You don't leave your seat until dinner is over," Isabel scolded.

Nell couldn't move. Zoe sensed her tension and said, "Momma, what were you saying about Billy Finch?"

"I'm sorry. I heard that unfortunately Billy has come down with tuberculosis. Dr. Moffat saw him

yesterday and confirmed it. He is in isolation at home and quite ill."

There was a stunned silence at the table. Nell secretly worried that her wishing he'd come to harm, had brought it all on. She hadn't wanted this. She had just wanted him to leave her alone. She felt awful.

Zoe was the first to respond. "Oh, that's terrible. Will he die Momma?" Morten reached out and held her hand.

Isabel continued, "He could honey. Unfortunately, consumption can be ruthless."

Carrie piped in, "where did he get it from? No one at school is sick."

"Apparently his mother died of tuberculosis in late summer and that is why he was sent to his grandparents. There is no father to speak of and his grandparents are his next of kin. Word has it that he had seemed well throughout the fall and the harvesting, so they figured he had been spared. However, I guess it was not to be and he struck quite ill just last week. The house is quarantined due to fear of spreading. As you children know, consumption is contagious, but one would have to be in close contact. Dr. Moffat felt it was highly unlikely anyone at the school would be exposed. As soon as Billy developed a cough, they kept him home from school and it wasn't until after that he developed a fever."

Nell was stunned. She couldn't move. Suddenly it all came flooding back to her, remembering all his coughing and spitting that had so disgusted her. The wiping of his runny nose on his sleeve, the sneezes in her direction, oh no,.. the kiss. What would become of her? This was beyond comprehension.

Nell was in a state of disbelief. This situation had turned from a nuisance to a fear, to an assault and now maybe to a death sentence. She had to tell someone.

Nell said nothing during dinner and barely touched her food as family life streamed around her. Isabel could see that she was clearly floored by this news and planned to talk with her after the meal. Amid sibling bickering, passing of dishes and plates, children being corrected for their table manners and further local updates, Nell sat motionless.

Once the meal was completed, Laura got the dish water off the stove in preparation for cleanup. The children cleared the plates and lined up in their usual spots either with washing or drying rags. Nell was still frozen. Isabel came over beside her and put her arm around her daughter.

-19-

Since Dad's fall, I am trying to visit my parents more regularly. I encourage the kids to come with us, but that is a losing battle. They don't have much in common with their grandparents, so it's a hard thing to enforce and not worth the conflict. I had always emphasized to the kids the need to be on their best behaviour at their grandparent's house. I remember a visit when Megan was about five. They were both dressed up and looked very presentable in their nice clean clothes. Of course, we had reviewed the rules in the car about 'please' and 'thank you' and no wrestling in the living room. They seemed to understand. On the day in question, the kids frolicked around and chatted with my parents in cute, acceptable fashion until Megan decided to try out a new word she had learned in the playground. "FUCK," she announced in a strong and forceful voice. I froze, as did everyone. Sensing her newfound power, she said it again, this time quite deliberately and in a louder, firmer voice and with a little glint in her eye. "FUCK, FUCK, FUCK," she continued boldly.

"Megan," I shouted, "stop that immediately," I exclaimed in an intolerant panic. Dad burst out laughing, quite entertained by the daring little imp. Unfortunately, this only encouraged her more. She pranced around the room uttering the obscenity until her brother tackled her to the ground, trying to solve the problem in eight-year-old fashion. Mom, disgusted, marched out of the room. Matt and I were on the situation in no time, but the damage was done. Megan had a new word which evoked attention. Mom was mad at Dad for laughing, I was furious with Megan, Matt was mortified in front of his in-laws, and he took the offending party outside for a 'talking to'. Moral: Never warn your kids to be on their best behaviour even though sometimes it is the elders who are acting the most childish.

The visits have gradually regressed from there. The kids have become more disengaged and immersed in their electronics and my parents are aging and are not trying very hard. I never need to worry about that phone scam where the person on the other line tells my parents that their grandchild is in a crisis overseas and they need money fast. I'm sure they would say, "why are you calling us, call their mother."

Today, Matt and I dutifully drove south to visit my parents on our own. The traffic was crazy, as always. What should have been a two-hour drive, was taking us over three hours. No wonder there is road rage. I consider myself a pacifist, but I could feel my blood boiling. How did I ever do this on a regular basis?

There we were, stuck in highway gridlock, due to 'volume of traffic' and a fender bender. As we sat there at a standstill, I took in the scenery. There isn't much else to do but gaze at the rows of housing, which I think have been erected since the last time I drove south a few weeks ago. There are countless kilometers of faceless townhouses and cookie cutter homes. There doesn't seem to be a tree or a park in sight - just endless housing. What if you forget what number you live at? It could be days before you find your home. I guess that's what it will eventually look like across the street from our farm. There must be 50,000 people living in this 'community' beside the highway. These aren't small homes, probably about 3000 sq. feet, with tiny little yards. These must be the homes of commuters, hence the 'volume of traffic' going the other way. No one will even let you in their lane let alone their life. Imagine the mood in that neighbourhood when everyone finally arrives home from work.

Finally, the fender bender is moved to the side, and everyone is understandably furious. People are much more interested in getting to their destination on schedule than concerning themselves with the safety of those involved. No one stops to check on the passenger or offer a hand or a cell phone. We have learned to mind our own business and continue on our way. I plan to do the same. 'They will figure it out', think the gawking drivers in the unending stream of traffic inching by. When Daniel toppled from the bridge in sub zero weather, a search party was promptly dispatched. Concerned neighbours galloped to his aid from miles around and were there within minutes. However, we have come a long way since then.

It seems our sense of community has evaporated somewhat over the last century when we all needed each other to survive. Perhaps this is a good thing that now we are more independent. We no longer rely on one another the same way. We can manage by ourselves. We each have our cell phones and computers. Our mobility is greater. We can move to a bigger home or a different town, wherever life takes us. Amid all the progress and development, it seems we've grown closer to our screens than each other.

We eventually arrive at my parents' house. Dad is in the living room which has now been converted into his bedroom. Only a short time ago, Dad was so fit. I would generally have to jog to keep up as he 'walked' around the block at a tremendous clip, during his three walks a day, even before the invention of step counting apps. He always took the stairs up from the subway, while 99.9% of people took the escalator, including me. Dad was constantly in a hurry to go somewhere or get something done. That must be where I get it from. Life was too busy to lie on your back in bed. I never really imagined a vibrant person like Dad could decline overnight, even at his age.

Mom is in the kitchen talking to the cat. The whole house reeks of cat food as she heats his 'Seafood Buffet' in the microwave while I struggle not to gag.

"Hi Mom," I interrupt her conversation with Whiskers. She smiles as she gets up.

"How was your drive? You're late!" This, even though I gave her regular updates regarding our delayed timing.

"I know. There was heavy traffic that delayed us. Sorry to keep you waiting. How's Dad?" I reply, trying not to take the bait.

"He's about the same. Come on in and say hello. He's been waiting for you."

"Hi Dad." I am immediately struck by his pale face and gaunt look, as he lies stretched out on the hospital bed in the living room.

"How are you? Great to see you both," he says grinning, clearly delighted to see us. We exchange some small talk about the weather. Dad loves to sing and has taken up singing lessons in his ninth decade. Of course, we all encouraged this hobby, despite the fact that he can't hold a note. My brother had put together a collection of golden oldies, favourites of Dad's. Matt pulls out the song book. Together we break into a chorus of 'Take me Out to the Ball Game' as I struggle with the smell of lingering cat food in the air.

We chat for a few minutes. I help Mom pay some bills at the kitchen table, then Matt and I take Mom out for lunch.

"Mom, what is this about you driving?" I ask over a chicken salad wrap, knowing full well that I need to re-visit this subject.

She smiles demurely and says, "Just a little, only over to the grocery store."

"Mom, you know you aren't supposed to drive since your stroke last year," I reluctantly remind her as I glance at Matt.

"Well, no one took my license away, so I am still licensed to drive," she insists, starting to get her back up.

"No one wants to upset you Mom, but we don't want anything to happen to you or anyone else. What would happen if a child ran out in front of you?"

'I would put my foot on the brake!" She insists gruffly, in full denial of how long it takes the message to get from her brain to her foot, on the off chance that she was able to see someone dart in front of her car. It would, of course, depend on what side the child came from because only one eye is fully functional.

"Yes Mom, but what if it were Whiskers?" Now I'm hitting below the belt. She is taken aback, clearly not having considered this before. She puts her fork down and sips her coffee.

"I leave him in the house when I go out," she counters, but is giving off visible signs of shutting down.

"How did you know I went out in the car?" her crabby, aggressive tone escalating, not recalling that she told me this on the phone.

I'm getting nowhere with this approach, so I soften a little. "What if we hire someone to take you anywhere you like a couple of afternoons a week?" She's not difficult with others, just with family.

"No!" she says with disdain, as if I am crazy for suggesting it. She stops eating and puts her napkin on the table.

"Mom, do you need groceries, is that it?" I ask naively.

"No, I do the groceries with Sharon (the caregiver) every Friday," she insists, looking about ready to leave. "How are the kids?" she abruptly changes the subject.

The matter is closed. My mother is no longer open for discussion. I suspect it is not a matter of need, but more of desire to retain her independence and have some entertainment from her relatively uneventful life. I tacitly agree to leave the subject for now, but I am far from finished with it.

Mom's been through a lot lately. One might expect she would be struggling with the declining health of her husband of over sixty years. However, she seems to enjoy his bedridden state. In fact, it has helped their marriage significantly. In an odd twist of fate, Mom and Dad have never seemed happier. To refer to their marriage and the word 'happy' in the same sentence is an oxymoron. The two terms simply don't belong together in this situation and neither do my parents for that matter. The fact that our home was surrounded by a white picket fence is just downright misleading. In fact, I remember as a kid secretly wishing they would split up. Nevertheless, they have stuck together despite their misery. I'm not sure if I am more damaged as a result of them staying together. However, Dad in his 93rd year, recently confessed to me from his hospital bed in the living room, that he has decided to 'stay with Mom'. What a relief as I wasn't sure who I would live with. Maybe he just needs some time to think about it.

He went on to assure me that he and Mom had never gotten along better. It seems all that was required to improve their marriage was for him to fall and hit his head. The whole system has changed. He seems to have forgotten the previous sixty years. Now that Barb is comfortably out of the way, my mother drops into the living room periodically throughout the day and holds his hand. He says he loves her, and Mom likes this. She feels young and beautiful, then she hops in the car and drives to the grocery store. I realize that he may actually outlive my mother with her driving record.

In all honesty, I am very happy for them. Who would have ever guessed that after sixty years of conflict, mutual disrespect, and a general distaste for each other, that there would be a passionate and compatible love at the end of the rainbow. I just hope it's not physical.

Monday, February 26, 1900

I am so troubled! Nell has disclosed to me some very upsetting news. I remember Billy's mother vaguely now. Her name was Rebecca and she kept to herself. I've come to learn that she has since died of tuberculosis and now her son is sick with the disease. Nell was stunned following this news. I know this boy has been bothering her as Zoe has kept me informed. During our talk, Nell began sobbing uncontrollably. I hugged her and held her, but she continued on for some time. Finally, she told me. Billy had grabbed her in the woodshed and begun to force himself on her, kissing her and pinning her to the wall against her will. She described him kissing her fully with his mouth and how she bit his tongue. Thank goodness she broke free when she did. She was terrified from this incident and told no one because she felt so shameful. No wonder she was so withdrawn. However, what is most concerning about this is his current state of health. I tried to comfort her and explain that, at that point, he was not exhibiting the disease, but she corrected me. She said for the past few weeks he had been coughing and sneezing everywhere. He never used a handkerchief, and he was spitting on the ground. She was inconsolable.

"Momma am I going to die?" she sobbed.

"Of course, not dear" I said as I held her, but the terror began to infect me as well. What if my sweet Nell had contracted TB? I couldn't bear to lose her, I have already lost one, although in a very different

way. What would this mean for the rest of us, and of course for the young one growing in me? It could be disastrous! I knew in my heart that we had every reason to be terrified, but I didn't want to admit that to her. This damn plague has wiped out so many in these parts over the years, but it had subsided recently. I feel so blindsided.

The implications of this are trickling into my brain as I write. My God. Should I keep Nell away from the others? She sleeps in the same bed as Mary. If I get it, it will cost two lives. This is awful. That stupid boy and his damn churchless family. How can people be so thoughtless! I wish Morten would come in from the woodshed. How much blasted wood does he need? If what Nell tells me is correct, Billy has been coughing and sneezing all around the schoolhouse for almost two weeks. This could be a crisis.

Morten will be furious and devastated to learn of this. I don't know what he'll do but we will definitely need to exercise precautions for the sake of the family. I'll have to talk with Dr. Moffat at once regarding the level of risk. Nell is beside herself and who can blame her.

Wednesday, February 28, 1900

Things have not gone well these last few days. We have kept the children home from school for their safety although I wonder if they wouldn't be safer at school. We have not shared Nell's predicament with her siblings yet as there has been no indication that she is ill, and she doesn't want the situation with Billy discussed openly. Morten has paid a visit to Miss Walker at the Baxter's farm. As a School Trustee, he will be recommending that the schoolhouse be closed temporarily so the safety of all the students is protected. Tonight, the Trustees will meet to discuss the closing. No one is prepared to put their children at risk.

The season seems to be dragging on at an unendurable length and I am afraid Laura's melancholy is beginning to infect us all. Her black garb alone is enough to make one feel low. How badly we need to get outside and inhale some spring weather, especially with this news. Oh, how I await the time I can fling the screen door open and stride into the grassy meadow. I pine for the season when the windows can be left ajar, when there are vegetables sprouting in the garden, apples on the tree and the children can play in the yard. However, that seems a distant dream as we sit here, confined to the house, that darn clock ticking away the minutes as the wind howls outside.

I am so tired of this sitting room. Perhaps I will pick a fresh wallpaper in the spring. It will depend what money we can spare and what's available at the general store. Rose said she's ordered something from a catalogue. She's going to bring it when she comes for tea next week, weather permitting. She said they have some delightful new floral wallpapers that really dress up a room. This house needs something cheery to offset our sadness following the loss of Daniel, this long, never ending winter and the deep-seated fears we're struggling with. I dare not dwell on the overwhelming cost of losing our beloved mare in January. I must think of something cheery to get my mind away from this gloom. Perhaps I will read my bible for a while before bed.

-20-

Finally back home, I have some time to peruse that newspaper from 1900. Amazing, an ad for corsets. I guess it's the same concept as my gym pants. Did women actually wear corsets every day? They hadn't yet experienced the freedom of the G-string. That might have shaken Morten up a bit. They might have ended up with ten kids. Didn't women know they could just starve themselves on some fad diet or go to the gym for an intense boot camp work out to get an impressive waistline? I guess their lifestyles were more balanced back then.

Look at this ad for 'Plough Boy'! This beautiful, sleek looking horse, prancing across the field, has stud services for sale. What mare in her right mind wouldn't be interested? I half expect there to be line below, 'sign up now with 'plenty of horses.com'. Wow, a book on Temperance. Who could resist that, I think as I reach for my jumbo glass of wine. I bet that wasn't a bestseller. It is enough to make one thankful they weren't born at the turn of the century. There's one you don't see much today – an ad for 'bells' –'church, steamboat, factory bells and all kinds of brass works'. Initially, I thought it might be something for cell or internet services.

At least they had newspapers in 1900. Now that everything is online, what will we insulate our homes with in the years to come? What can we depend on to learn the facts?

Megan has been enjoying the horses, but more importantly she's enjoying the boy who is helping take care of the horses. I think Bolt and Zippy have become background scenery in the barn and the real drawing card is Zach. The big clue was when I saw her putting on makeup to go clean the stalls. I've also noticed those horses are being fed several times a day. How often are you supposed to feed horses that spend their entire day grazing in the field? I think five times a day is too much, but according to Zach, those old nags need a lot of care.

Tyler was sitting outside yesterday. Although that sounds un-newsworthy, I was delighted to see him getting a little vitamin D. I spotted him in a lawn chair, underneath the pear tree with his iPad in hand. I took a picture for Matt just to prove it. Who would have guessed he would voluntarily emerge from his room.

After a few weeks of my reduced salary, our bank account is growing lean. I'm dying to go out for dinner or a show, but the budget no longer allows for that. I was even thinking of some clothes shopping, but that's not going to happen either. I guess it doesn't matter how I look these days anyway, as I'm out here on this farm where no one sees me. Matt assures me I look beautiful even without new clothes or any clothes for that matter. I know that isn't true but it's sweet of him to say. He has decided to make me a fancy dinner tonight to make up for our dwindling entertainment funds. I know how badly he wants this 'farm experience' to work.

How many pots does it take to boil spaghetti noodles? The answer is... it depends who's making them. For me, the answer is '1'. For Matt, the answer is 'how many pots do we have?'

Despite the state of the kitchen, we had a lovely, candlelight, spaghetti and meatball meal. Matt created a wonderful spaghetti sauce, which included copious tomatoes, some red wine, too much sugar and several jars of tomato sauce... most of which are spilled all over the counter. Matt means well, even though he rolled the meatballs on the cutting board, and then fried them on the stove in cooking oil. You can imagine the state of the stove top. Then there was a lovely, tossed salad, the remnants of which are strewn throughout the sink. While it was wonderful not to have to cook, the clean up will take the better part of a week.

I'm sweating so much these days. I don't know if it's just my age or my insulation, but I find I'm a lot warmer than I used to be. I don't remember being so hot when I was younger. I wish the hydro hadn't cut down that towering pine near the road. She and I grew up together. She was just a sapling then, but she grew into such a stately pine. She used to provide so much shade. I miss her dearly and I'm sweltering without her. My ivy is dying, and my bricks are cracking. Why is it so damn hot?

Tuesday, March 6, 1900

Margaret says it won't be long now. Billy Finch is very near death and has been in declining health ever since the news broke. That funeral won't be well attended. Not only is everyone petrified of catching his illness, but we're all furious that he was not kept home from school at the very first inkling of a cough. The school has been closed until further notice. The children have been out in the snow, building snowmen and having snowball fights. It's a relief that they are outside as the more fresh air they get the more they are protected from the illness. Nell seems fine although I'm alert for any signs of a cough. Nevertheless, we all know that consumption can lie dormant for months. There's no cough to speak of and that is an excellent sign.

It's a darn good thing that the Finch family don't go to church, otherwise the plague might have spread through the entire community.

Saturday, March 10th, 1900

It has been several days since I've written. Life has been so busy. Morten and Chuck have been down in the wood lot chopping every day. They are working hard to clear some extra farmland for the spring plant, not to mention have sufficient wood to keep the fire and stove going during this never ending, biting cold winter. Mary is great help around the house but she's growing restless. She's so keen to get into normal school to become a teacher. She thinks of little else. Lyle and Doug have been delighted to have all their sisters home as they provide additional play opportunities. Lyle has taken his first steps this week, much to the delight of everyone. Thankfully, Laura has been a little cheerier lately. Zoe was heading to the barn with a handful of carrots from the cellar, clearly intended for Gaby, and Laura allowed it. It seems the only one getting sufficient vegetables this season is that silly donkey.

Chuck has been in a lively mood lately. The other day I noticed him helping Laura hang some clothes out on the line. It's women's work and no doubt he had plenty to do around the farm without getting involved in the laundry. However, they seemed to be involved in quite a conversation when I was returning from the loo. Was Laura actually smiling and chatting with him? She seemed so at ease and eagerly participating in the conversation. What could they be talking about that would perk Laura's interest?

My bosom is so sensitive these days which just confirms my condition. The other morning, Morten was helping me with my corset, and I thought I was going to die. Morten is so excited. He has been rubbing my belly at night and beginning to think of names even though it is very early on. I reminded him not to get ahead of himself. We already have a little one buried in the field, one who never made it beyond six months gestation. I will never forget the anguish of that loss, especially as it was my first pregnancy. Luckily the season was on our side and Morten and Daniel found a pleasant spot in the meadow, so I could be near him when I walked. I felt so empty watching Morten and Chuck place the little bundle in the ground on that heartbreaking occasion. I hope to never relive that, but I am continuously haunted by the fear of that recurring. Morten held me for days on end, until I recovered my strength. Yet still he looks forward with such hopefulness to yet another delivery.

I still go down to the pasture each spring where he was laid to rest. Morten has built a beautiful stone bench for me, made from the rocks the men and horses dragged from the fields. It is such a peaceful place to sit. Last spring, Morten planted a lovely forsythia bush near the grave. Often on a summer day, I will sit there with Lyle and Doug and gaze across the beautiful view down the valley. I often wonder what our son would have been like and how our lives would have been different. My only hope is that I will not be laying another infant to rest there in the months to come. I never really consider my own health in this, but I suppose I should. After all, I'm 39 now – far too old for childbirth. No doubt some of the ladies are whispering about it. I'm not sure I even care. Now I'm starting to sound like Laura. I must be grateful for what I have. We are lucky enough to be blessed with seven wonderful children and too many extended family to count, great neighbours, a fine church, a productive piece of farmland and spring lies ahead.

My, it's cold in here. The upstairs is always so drafty despite the floor vent in our room. I must wrap another shawl around me.

Wednesday, March 14, 1900

What a lovely day. Finally, signs of spring are in the air. I have just received a letter from Momma and Poppa in Bond Head. Oh, how I wish they lived closer, but Momma wanted to move back to her family home for a time to help Nanna and Grandad. With Agnes and I both married and Robert and his wife, now in charge of their farm, it seemed fitting that they have someone to care for them in their golden years. According to Momma's post, they are all well but were very sad to hear about Daniel. The good news is they are hoping to come to see us again later this year. What a surprise they will get to see their daughter expecting her eighth child, and their fifteenth grandchild! I know their first concern will be my health.

Bond Head is a long journey from here – too much to undertake lightly. Unless we can think of some acquaintances along the way, they will have to stay at an inn and put their horse in a livery station for the night. They'll need to stay at least a few weeks to make the trip worthwhile.

There is talk of the school re-opening next week as it has been several weeks, and no one has shown any sign of consumption. The whole community has been on pins and needles.

Billy Finch passed away last week. I saw the notice in the paper and of course I heard it from Rose well before it hit the printing press. Evelyn Barclay told me that she is worried about her young son who has had a cold, but it seems nothing more. I hadn't known that the Findlays had lost a cow last week while birthing. Had it been in the warmer months we would have known at the time, as I can often hear their cows giving birth from my back porch. That is a costly loss, and I will have Morten drop in with some of our extra milk. God knows, we don't have much, but we must share what we can as they have children too.

It seems the river in Coldwater is expected to flood again this spring as there has been so much snow this past winter. All are worried about the roads being washed out again and the community being brought to a standstill for a time.

Rose has assured me that no one else up her way has come down with consumption, so I may rest assured about Nell. What a relief. Rose is coming for a visit tomorrow, and I eagerly await her carriage.

-21-

My sister Emily called. Dad had a serious stroke and is now in hospital. We all worried this day was coming. My parents seem to be aging at an alarming rate.

When Matt and I arrived at the hospital, Dad was as white as a ghost. He lay perfectly still on the hospital bed. At first glance, I thought we were too late until I saw his chest rise very slightly. We approached his bed and announced our presence. He didn't move or acknowledge us. I could see that one side of his face was droopy and his lip was turned downward. I held his hand and whispered in his ear that we were here with him and hoped he was not in any pain. Still no response. We sat with him for a long while. Mom and

Emily arrived looking exhausted. My brother Allan and his wife came in shortly after them. This was serious and we were all clear that this could be the end for poor old Dad. At one point, the nurse and an orderly came in and announced they were taking him for some tests.

The rest of us filed to the cafeteria to get coffee and await Dad's return. I realize that it doesn't matter how old your parent is, their demise still comes as a shock. We tried to make some small talk, but it was hard with the shadow of death hanging over the table.

When we returned to the room forty-five minutes later, Dad was back, looking exactly the same as when we had left. We all noticed the drool leaking out of the side of his mouth. Emily grabbed a tissue and silently wiped it. We waited and waited. Eventually the doctor arrived with the grim news. He explained, in a matter-of-fact tone, that my father had had a serious stroke. He was not expected to recover as there had been extensive damage and he would likely never get out of bed again. The silence in the room was palpable. He might regain consciousness. It was hard to know for sure. The doctor explained that my father would now require full nursing care and that the social worker would be in soon to discuss options. He asked, in a rather emotionless tone, if we had any questions. 'Is Dr. Moffat available? If you let him know we're here I'm sure he and his wife would get in their sleigh and be right over,' I found myself thinking. How did we get to this? The last thing in the whole world Dad would want is to be in a nursing home. Life can change so suddenly.

Here was a possibility we hadn't really considered – a vegetative or further cognitively impaired state. After all, we've never been through a parent's demise before. Now what? We waited for the social worker to come as we sat, gathered around Dad holding his hand and silently weeping. While waiting, the conversation meandered into random recollections of Dad in his finer days.

I told the story about when I was a little girl. I remember it clearly. With four kids and two parents gathered around the table, it made for noisy dinners. Often it was so boisterous it was hard to get yourself heard, especially as the youngest! My sister always had important opinions to express, my brother wanted to report pressing student council news, my other brother cracked jokes, and Mom had to remind us of chores to get done. There was no room for the little voice at the end of the table who couldn't get a word in edgewise. Thank God for Dad. He noticed this happening and he insisted that we were all going to be quiet for one entire minute during each dinnertime while I had my turn to talk. This was gold! I had been granted one, uninterrupted minute to talk about whatever I liked. It was unbelievable! It was like having my own TV show. Emily rolled her eyes and told me to make it quick, Allan cracked jokes about my skipping rope stories, but I had my minute and I loved it. The whole family was made to be quiet and appear interested, while I recounted numerous details about my day. It was such a powerful feeling and I nursed it to the bone. The problem is I had so much I wanted to say, and I had to squish it all into sixty seconds. Where to begin! I learned to speak fast. Eventually Dad doubled my time to two minutes, much to my sister's chagrin. I will always be thankful to Dad for the opportunity to be heard.

As the waiting around Dad's hospital bed continued, Allan told his story. He was in grade three when the teacher had just handed out the envelopes containing the report cards. Of course, everyone peeked to see what the teacher had written. It just so happened that his report card was particularly unimpressive that year. He was devastated to see mostly D's. He knew that wasn't going to be well received. He was worried sick as he walked home from public school with his buddies. They all had B's and A's and glowing comments. Allan was a nervous wreck all through dinner. Eventually he went to Dad after the meal and handed it over. Apparently,

Dad put on his glasses and looked over the report card then looked at my brother. He said, "this isn't so bad, look here's a D PLUS, and here's a C minus." My brother recollected the tremendous relief he felt that Dad seemed to be seeing the brighter side of things. Later that week, Dad hired my sister, at five cents an hour, to tutor my brother every night after dinner until the end of the school year. Emily was delighted to be receiving a regular salary. Each night she and Allan went downstairs to the rec room where she grilled him on addition, subtraction, the world map etc.. In grade 4, 5 and 6 my brother came first in his class! Given the results, Dad doubled her salary to ten cents an hour. However, at that point she became interested in boys and that was the end of the basement tutoring, despite the cash. No voice was raised, no self-esteem was damaged, my sister made almost $20 (over three years), and everyone ended up richer in the end.

Still no sign of the social worker so we continued. I remember when I was fourteen and craving to drive the car. Obviously, this was not allowed. One night when my parents were out, my friend and I stupidly decided to take the car for a little spin around the block. Luckily, being the inexperienced drivers that we were, we backed out the driveway and right into the ditch on the other side of the road. As you can imagine, we were in quite a state of distress. Our neighbour from across the street saw our plight and came racing out. He asked us what we thought we were doing. Then he helped push us out of the ditch and he drove the car back into the driveway. He was quite clear we were never to do that again and he would talk to my parents when they got home. Days went by. No one said anything to us about it. Maybe the neighbour had forgotten to mention it or changed his mind. Weeks elapsed. Maybe we were going to get off scot-free. Then one night, my parents were heading out for dinner while my friend and I were watching TV. Dad came into the room to say goodbye. As he was leaving, he turned to us and said, "No driving tonight girls." We were speechless. He knew all along. The torture of guessing whether he knew or not, was enough to keep us on our toes and never venture out again, plus he had taken the keys. He never raised his voice. When he did put his foot down you listened because he did it so rarely and for some reason, he always believed in us.

Allan, Emily and I laughed as we recalled how he used to always say to us as teens, "have fun." Those were his parting words as we headed out on a Saturday night. Who tells their teenagers to "have fun?" My friends' parents would say things like, "be careful" or "be home by midnight" or "call when you get to the party" or "where are you going?" Not Dad. He had a certain 'joie de vivre'. He wanted you to enjoy yourself but never in a foolish way. Dad trusted us, so you never wanted to let him down.

Emily reminisced about how Dad had been so health conscious throughout his life. The fridge was always stocked with a vast array of vitamins, leafy greens vegetables and fruits - everything you are supposed to eat but don't really want to. However, occasionally he liked to live it up a bit. One such occasion when he would choose to cut loose was Christmas morning. Every morning for my entire life, I remember Dad fixing himself a bowl of granola, with various healthy additions, such as wheat germ and bran, sprinkled on top. However, not on Christmas morning. Just like a little kid, on Christmas morning he would get up early with the rest of us. I remember him sitting at the breakfast table with a big bowl of chocolate almond ice cream, (without bran). It was so thrilling to see our health-conscious father having ice cream for breakfast. We were crazy with delight! Later that day, while we excitedly tore open stockings and presents, he would sip away on a coke. He might even finish off the day with a chocolate turtle. That was it, until next year. I imagine he would wake up on Dec. 26th with a sugar hangover. If he wakes up today, I'm giving him a big bowl of chocolate almond ice cream!

Mom continued with a story of her own. Your Dad was never much of a religious man, but he did have a spiritual side to him. However, that wasn't what drew him to the local church. In fact, he went there for years but he could never accept the religious teachings. What attracted him was the people. In fact, he would skip the service altogether and just go for the coffee hour. He used to say he was going for the 'cocktail party'. For the past fifteen years, Dad rarely missed a Sunday, yet he never made it to the service. Perhaps he was worried they would tell him not to eat chocolate ice cream on Christmas.

Eventually the social worker showed up. Fortunately, she was very compassionate and more emotionally astute than Dad's doctor. She talked about nursing care options and how hard it can be to put your loved one in a home. She handed us a pre-packaged handful of brochures about nursing homes and at home nursing services in the area. There was also a pamphlet on strokes and the effect on family members. She included her card and set up a time to meet with us again to talk further. She sat with us and answered some questions. Then her pager went off and she kindly said good-bye.

It's been a long, unhappy day. We decided to stay with Mom tonight so she's not on her own. It's odd sleeping in my old bedroom where I grew up, especially with Matt by my side. I was never allowed to have a boy in my bedroom.

Maybe Dad will wake up tomorrow.

Tuesday, March 20th, 1900

Rose's carriage arrived this morning in time for tea. It was so nice to just sit and talk. She lives almost six miles away, so we don't get much chance to see one another. Of course, we talk at church, but it's not the same. We can't catch up there. She brought Harry with her today. He is almost four now and Doug and Lyle were delighted to have a friend to play with. The three of them had quite a time building laundry forts and banging all Ida's cast iron pots. Thank goodness I had five girls rather than five boys. Imagine how noisy my house would have been. What would I do without the girls to help me with Doug and Lyle.

We had tea in the sitting room and thankfully, Laura left us alone. I think she was over collecting milk from the barn. Anything to be closer to Chuck, I realize. Ida minded the boys and had them bake some cookies with her. That left Rose and I a chance to catch up.

Poor Rose is so unhappy with Patrick. What a clod of a husband. I didn't dare say anything years ago when Rose was so excited about her nuptials. When she first wed and became Mrs. Patrick Reilly almost seventeen years ago, she was twenty-one. She was old enough to make her own decisions. She was so enthusiastic about Patrick. She had met him at a church picnic in Coldwater. I remember, she could not stop talking about him. He was a good-looking chap, but I always felt he was intense. I think she has grown more miserable every year since they married. He gets frustrated if Rose isn't home from the Ladies Aid meetings in time to get his supper on the table promptly. She always gets nervous if the meeting draws on past its time. Many times, I've seen her perched on the side of her horse, madly trotting down the road, once the meeting concludes. Morten never had much money, but he has always been a good-natured man. Patrick, on the other hand, is a man of comfortable means but there is no good nature to him. Their barn is extremely well maintained, and they have three hired hands to help with the milking. It is quite an operation with almost thirty head of cattle. Their fencing is impeccable. They always have the best horses, the latest Tudhope carriage and their home is lovely, yet they never entertain. I know Rose wants to have the ladies over for quilting, but Patrick won't allow it. Rose married the wrong man and we both know it. I feel so badly for her. She does not even have a kindly mother-in-law to help her. They live all alone with their four children, no extended family or in-laws to speak of.

Today, Rose really needed to talk, as she has no other females to share with. She snuck off today with Harry in tow. Patrick had gone to town to look at farm equipment and was not expected back for some time. Rose has told me countless times about how their horse hand, Edward, is so supportive of her. He harnessed up the rig and offered to drive her over today, which was very kind of him. She went on about what a gentle soul he is and how he thinks she should get out and see her friends occasionally. I know Rose has had a soft spot in her heart for him for awhile. She was quite animated as she told me about how they often share a laugh about Patrick and his crusty ways. I am glad she has an ally, but I fear she is playing with fire. She is a married woman, but she swears she will never be unfaithful to Patrick. She could never forgive herself for such indiscretion. I am impressed by her determination but question whether she is fooling herself. What woman would not understand her temptation, when stuck with a man like Patrick?

I cannot believe what she told me about him today. Well, yes actually I can. He is so intolerant with the children. It breaks Rose's heart. A few weeks ago, Elizabeth, who is only thirteen, found some kittens in the barn. She was over the moon to discover the cuddly, young treasures. I can only imagine Zoe finding such a discovery, how delighted she would be. Anyway, with school being out for weeks on end, Elizabeth would rush out to the barn each morning to give some of the cow's milk to the nursing mother cat. She had even created a little bed for them, made from some rags Rose had given her. She had named all five of the kittens. She could not wait for the day she could pick them up and play with them. What else does that poor girl have to look forward to. Her father is always criticizing her and mocking her. Those kittens probably made her life bearable through the prolonged school break and the winter isolation. Then one day Patrick lost his temper. He was furious with Elizabeth for being slow to get to her chores and instead focussing her energy on pampering a bunch of barn cats. Without any warning, he decided to put a stop to it. When Elizabeth was occupied, he put all those kittens in a burlap sack, took them down to the stream, tied a knot and tossed them in. Rose had no idea what he was up to until he came in for his noon day dinner. He recounted the morning events and Rose was incredulous. For the first time in their marriage, she found her voice and what a voice it turned out to be. She said that when he told her the story, she froze. She began to tremble with rage. She put the meal down and turned to where he was sitting and screamed, "you hard hearted, bastard of a man. Your daughter will hate you!" She ripped off her apron and stormed out of the room. She ran upstairs and broke down in tears. She considered running away and coming here. How could he be so heartless? She told me she knew she could not go anywhere because of the children. She was stuck with this brute of a man for the rest of her life. How would she ever cope? She felt so alone. Patrick did not so much as mount the stairs to talk to her. Instead, he laughed, finished his meal and returned to the barn.

I would like to give that man a piece of my mind. I would tell Patrick to smarten up and I'd refuse to cook him any more meals until he does. He's like a spoiled child having a tantrum. The trouble is tomorrow he will present her with a wooden hand carving he's made, and all will be forgotten, - again.

When Elizabeth finished her chores, she headed right for the barn to see the litter. Apparently, Rose had tried to stop her, but Elizabeth raced right out at the first chance and Rose had failed to intercept her in time. Rose knew her little heart well, so compassionate, tender and trusting. Rose heard the scream as she was bounding across the yard towards the barn. When she got there, Elizabeth was beside herself, shrieking in panic. "Where are the kittens?" she demanded wild eyed. She held Elizabeth in her arms and told her the awful truth, knowing full well if she did not, Patrick would. Her daughter moaned in horror and disbelief when she first heard the news and then convulsed in uncontainable sobs and crumpled into a ball on the barn floor. "How could he, how could he?!" she wailed in a state of agony. She could not bear to face her father again. Eventually she went to her room, collapsed on her bed and cried all night. It was torturous for Rose to see her in such pain.

When Patrick eventually returned to the house for his meal, there was no dinner waiting. Rose was downright hostile. Elizabeth was beside herself and would not leave her room and the other children did not know what had happened. Anna, being almost twelve, quickly threw together a meal with what was in the ice box in the cellar. This calmed Patrick somewhat, but Rose said his booming voice could be heard a concession away. Apparently, Elizabeth refused to go downstairs and see her father. Her devastation and betrayal felt no bounds.

What a heartbreaking story. I poured Rose more tea. "I don't know how you do it Rose. He does not deserve you."

"I'm worried about Elizabeth; she has not been the same since. That was almost two weeks ago, and she still refuses to even look at her father."

"I don't blame her," I said.

"I admire her spirit. Perhaps I have not been strong enough with him over the years," Rose reflected.

Never in my life, had I heard her acknowledge that. It was a breakthrough for her. I hope this is a turning point.

Later, I told the story to Morten, and he just shook his head. "Fool," he said. It made me even more grateful for the loving husband that I have.

Morten said the sap is starting to run which is delightful. That is always a welcome sign of spring. Soon the men will get the buckets attached and start a fire for the syrup. The days are gradually growing warmer, but the nights are bitter still. It is ideal for the syrup and rejuvenating for the soul.

This is kind of fun news. Morten has announced that as a gift for his mother we are going to have a family photograph done. I have only had my picture taken a few times before. This would be different though. This would be with the whole family. Imagine that. When Morten was in town the other day, he stopped in at the photographers. He booked a sitting for next week. He told us at dinner tonight and everyone was so pleased. Of course, he was sorry he had not thought of it earlier, before we lost Daniel. Nevertheless, Ida was delighted at the thought.

Although there are some of these new cameras available in the general store, they are expensive.

I've heard that the roll of film then has to be developed in a dark room. Imagine that, having a device that can re-create an image at the push of a button. It seems unbelievable. The world is becoming so modern in this new century. It is simply amazing.

We have a great deal of washing and sewing to do to have the whole family turned out well for the photograph. There are shoes to polish, pants to mend, I will need to sew a new outfit for Doug as he is growing like a weed. It is always easy with the girls as we have so many outfits from over the years, but the boys present a whole new challenge for me and Ida.

-22-

He woke up! To be honest, I wasn't really expecting that. The call from the hospital came first thing in the morning. My mother rushed in to wake me and at first, I was disoriented. I thought I was having a bad dream. In my haze between sleep and wakefulness, I thought I was seventeen and Mom just found me in my bedroom with someone. It took me a minute to get my bearings. Was I late for school? Oh yes, it was all coming back to me now. I rolled over in the squishy twin bed and roused Matt with the great news that Dad woke up.

I haven't slept 'at home' much since I moved out eons ago. Oddly enough nothing had changed, but everything had changed. It was like some kind of family museum. Despite my parents attempt to preserve everything as it had been, time refused to stand still.

Mom, Matt and I gathered for some breakfast before heading to the hospital. Mom was in a terrific mood, despite so little sleep. Meanwhile I felt I was struggling with some age regression, habitually sitting in the same spot at the kitchen table. The cereal was still kept in the same cupboard, and I think it may have actually been the same box that was there when I left home several decades ago. The phone rang and I automatically said, "I'll get it." This is too weird. The only difference was rather than borrowing the car, I was instead helping Mom into my own car - a bizarre feeling.

When we arrived at the hospital, Dad was so happy to see us there was a little tear trickling down the side of his face. The stroke had rendered him paralysed on the entire left side of his body and he could not speak coherently. But at least he was with us. There had been monumental damage. As the doctor had explained, it seemed he would never get out of bed again. It was hard to know if in fact Dad's recovery was 'good news'.

Now the pressing question was, where does he go upon discharge? Oddly enough, Mom felt strongly that he should go to a nursing home as did my brother Dave, while the rest of us tried to persuade her that nursing care could be continued at home. My Dad was clear his preference was to go home. This could get complicated. A line had been drawn in the family sandbox.

We all agreed that it had been a difficult day for everyone and that we would sleep on this decision and talk again tomorrow. Something tells me sleep isn't going to change anyone's mind, particularly my father's.

Now what do we do? My mother lives there, we do not. My Dad wants to go home. Mom and a brother vs. three siblings and a cognitively impaired Dad. What a stalemate.

Friday, March 30, 1900

The supplies on the shelves are thinning as spring arrives at last. The house is quiet, and I think I'll just rest here for a spell beside the fire. The men have been boiling maple syrup for the past few days. It's such a treat to have it on pancakes in the morning. The children would drink it directly from the ladle if I'd let them.

Tomorrow we go to Orillia for the family photograph. I must admit, I am excited. I have not been to town for several months as it is a good fifteen miles away. The weather is clearing, and it looks as though we may have a good day for the trip. I will be up early to get the children dressed. Ida and I have made such an adorable outfit for Doug. Ida put together the little knickers with suspenders and I made a lovely shirt with frills in the front. He will look adorable if he doesn't roll in the mud beforehand. This week, Laura, Mary and I spent our evenings getting the dresses clean, the shoes polished, the hair pieces ready and most challenging of all, locating Morten's bow tie. He hasn't worn it in so long. We finally discovered it in the very back of the cupboard in an old hat box. First thing in the morning we will don our finery and the girls will do up their hair. They are good at that sort of thing and help each other out with the latest braids and styles.

We will need two carriages if the whole family is to go as there are eleven of us in total. I spoke with Martha Findlay a few days back and asked her if anyone from her home would be going that way on Saturday. Much to Sadie and Carrie's delight, the young Findlay lad has offered to drive some of us in on his way to town. You can already guess who has volunteered to go in his carriage.

Nell seems to be coming around with the nice spring weather although her appetite has not been good. She is pleased to be back at school and no doubt it is easier for her without Billy there. No sign of a cough. Thank God. The fear seems to have passed.

Morten keeps searching my belly for signs of life. On my word, I will never allow myself to get in the family way again. Some of us were talking about it at quilting the other night when the elder ladies were in the kitchen getting the tea. There are ways to avoid pregnancy, but it would be humiliating to ask the apothecary for the paraphernalia. Imagine sitting beside him in church after that. Plus, it sounds terribly uncomfortable. Morten would try to co-operate if he thought it might save him an extra mouth to feed and guarantee him a more energized wife! I think it would be easier to just sleep on a cot but knowing Morten he would climb in with me. I am beginning to fill out. My stomach just seems to assume 'child belly' so early on now. I am growing tired of sharing my body as I just finished nursing Lyle only a few months ago.

I saw Chuck helping Laura with the milking today. I couldn't believe it. I was upstairs in the barn getting some chicken feed and I heard someone laughing.

I peered through the floorboards over the milking area. There was Laura, sitting on a stool in her black skirt, Chuck crouching behind her with his arms around her shoulder, helping her milk one of the cows. As if Laura doesn't know how to milk a cow! How ridiculous. However, she seemed to be enjoying the lesson as there was much laughter and gaiety. Clearly, she is enamoured with Chuck and he with her. I am happy for her; I just cannot imagine them as a match. She's known him for years having grown up on this farm. However, I guess she's seeing him in a new light.

We had a lovely evening tonight with games and songs. Laura played some new tunes on the piano, and we all sang along. Music does wonders to lift the spirits. I wish Rose could have been here. It would have done her a world of good. She is paying dearly for her youthful error in judgement to marry Patrick. There is not much music in her home. They don't even have a piano. Imagine that. What a shame because Rose plays so beautifully.

I can hear the girls chattering upstairs. They often talk for some time before falling asleep. They're likely excited about tomorrow's excursion to town.

Saturday, March 31, 1900

Henry was up early this morning, crowing at full volume. No one had any trouble getting out of bed. As we gathered downstairs, adjusting and fixing one another's lace collars and hairdos, I must say we looked terrific.

Morten brought the carriage around and young Tom Findlay arrived, looking as dashing as ever. He was impressed to see the girls in their fine dresses. I *have no doubt there was plenty of flirting occurring in that carriage load, especially if there were some ankles showing. The horses were frisky this morning as spring was in the air. We were at the studio in just over two hours, as the roads were muddy.*

When we arrived, there was a family ahead of us. They were beautifully turned out. It's funny to think that our image will be preserved in clothes we so rarely wear. However, it does make for a lovely picture. We eventually took our place in the portrait room and the children giggled nervously. I was so worried Lyle was going to dirty his outfit as he stumbled around the studio. Mary scolded him and was on him straight away. The last thing we needed was for Lyle to pull over the big camera and all the special equipment.

The photographer directed us all into certain chairs or positions. The three ladies were seated in the front Ida, Laura and me, with Morten standing just behind us. The children were positioned around us on various blocks of wood to give height. He even gave me a book to have in my lap so that the pose appeared natural. With this size of family, I can't think of anything more unnatural than me having a chance to read. Our biggest challenge was keeping Lyle still as he was exceptionally squirmy and wanted to explore his new environment. Eventually, I handed the book to Ida and seated little Lyle on my lap. That seemed to settle him. Finally, once we were all still, the photographer explained we were to look straight ahead and pretend we were at church listening to the sermon. Then he went behind a large box standing on three legs. "No smiling," he reminded us from behind the camera with a black cloth over his head. After a long pause, he pulled a chord and a puff of smoke emerged. Doug shrieked with delight. The photographer took another, just to be safe. The girls adjusted their hair and I put Lyle on the other knee, we stared off into space with a pensive look and puff, another photograph was taken, and we were done. All that fuss, and it was over so quickly.

After all was completed, we promised the children we would take them along the main street to look at the shops. Morten had brought along some money from our savings box to treat the children to a hot chocolate at the counter in the general store. What an afternoon we had.

The world is melting after a long winter. It was warm enough for just a heavy sweater and a pair of galoshes. The streets were thick with mud and potholes due to the spring thaw, but the boardwalks allowed us to protect our dresses. The girls had such fun looking in the shop windows and dreaming of things they couldn't have. We passed the Tudhope Carriage Company and Morten admired the lovely new coaches in the yard. We stopped at the co-op to order more animal feed. Along the way, Morten paid a visit to the bank to deposit our egg money into the account. After the teller entered the amount in the ledger, Morten was dismayed to see how small a sum we had accumulated. He's such a diligent saver. Nevertheless, our overhead is high, with feed for the animals, seed for the fields, Chuck's modest salary, carriage repairs, cloth for our clothes, and our bill for the market. It is impossible to grow everything. We need to supplement some items. Oh well. This was a day to enjoy, not to fret over what we don't have. Morten felt the same way.

After a fun meander down the main street and greeting some familiar faces, we arrived at the general store. All eyes were on us as we were decidedly overdressed for a simple hot chocolate on a Saturday afternoon.

I hadn't been to Will's General Store all winter. Will and his son James were there and greeted us warmly. We caught up on how their family had been doing over the winter months. James has turned into quite a young man now (as I believe Mary was noticing). According to Will, the store is soon to be re-named, 'Will & Son's General Store'. Will's wife Alice had ordered many new fashionable bolts of cloth. I told Will to let her know that I would be back in the future when the girls needed dresses. The children were drawn to the candy shelves like a magnet. There were peppermints, butterscotch, gumdrops, licorice... everything imaginable. Zoe was wide eyed and mesmerized. Morten had given each of the children three pennies to spend as they wished. It seemed like such an extravagance, and they were overjoyed. The girls were looking at all the latest fashions. Carrie was taken with a beautiful pair of lace up boots that unfortunately far exceeded her three-penny budget. Sadie admired the hair ribbons. Meanwhile Ida lost herself among the kitchen ware shelves while Laura secretly sniffed at the lovely smelling soaps. Eventually, we gathered at the counter and Will and his handsome young son James got us all a hot chocolate or tea, according to our preference. James and Mary sparked up quite a conversation and I have never seen Mary so lively and jovial. Morten, Ida and I watched this transaction and exchanged smiles. James is a nice young man and clearly attentive to Mary who was turning a little red with all the attention. No doubt her sisters would rib her about this on the carriage ride home. Nell seemed quiet and even declined a hot chocolate.

Will was kind enough to offer us each a biscuit 'on the house'. He explained that Alice had been feeling poorly lately so she wasn't at the store today. Her sister was at the house with her, and Will encouraged us to drop by and see her on our way out of town.

"She will be so sorry she missed you and glad of the company, if you can fit it in," he said. "Maybe it will pick up her spirits."

"We will make a point to drop in on the way home," Morten reassured him.

-23-

As soon as we drive north of the urban sprawl, I feel myself unwind. My breathing is easier, and my shoulders relax. It's nice to leave my emotional baggage geographically behind.

The next day arrives way too soon but here it is. How did I ever have time to work? After an explosive family blow out and a few disrespectful exchanges, it was decided that Dad would return home to outrageously expensive medical care. We know that he wants to be at home, so we will try to make that happen. However, it is now becoming abundantly clear that the costs of 24/7 care are staggering and who knows how long he will require it.

I will never forget visiting my grandmother in a nursing home. Once in the front door, the atrium was bright and upbeat. The sunlight shone through immense windows illuminating many of the immobilized, elderly patients seated in their wheelchairs in the lobby for some social time. It was a sight to behold. Paired with this, was the scent of urine, vaguely concealed by cleaning fluid, that met our nostrils as we entered. It was chilling to see this aging lot of humanity, some slumped over in a wheelchair and held in by a seatbelt, others drooling and looking vacantly off into space. If we dial back forty years, these people would have been in the prime of their lives, vibrant with ambitions, relationships, worries and dreams. If we dial forward forty years, where will we be?

Once we moved beyond the emotional chill of the atrium, we came to the nurses' station where the nurses worked behind a glass enclosure. I could hear one of them talking in a loud, slow, condescending voice to a woman in a wheelchair who must have been triple her age. Undoubtedly the nurse would have referred to this elderly woman as Mrs or Ms, if she had been her neighbour or teacher growing up. All that is forgotten now, this is the current reality. It must be a very demanding job to work here and an even harder job to live here. Is this the right fit for my father? I know when Dad put Nana in a nursing home, I was adamantly opposed. Now I find myself in the same decision-making position.

Unfortunately, at this point Dad is well beyond discussing it and Mom doesn't have a grasp on the finances. If all the money is spent on Dad's care, where does that leave Mom? We were becoming acutely aware that the exorbitant cost of care was seriously depleting our reserves to care for Mom's future, whatever that may hold.

It's uncanny, where large sums of money and vulnerable people co-exist, the dark side of humanity often emerges. I notice our care manager Bill has recently upgraded to a Mercedes. One of Dad's caregivers has started bringing her paroled husband over to 'visit' my parents when we aren't around. With all this stress, Mom is starting to slip as well and growing more confused and overwhelmed. It seemed just yesterday they were so 'in charge'. I realize that someday, when I least expect it, I will no longer be 'in charge' and Megan and Tyler will make decisions on my behalf. Tomorrow, I'm raising their allowance.

Frankly, this whole thing has made me scared to grow old. One day you're overwhelmed with work, family and paying the bills and the next thing, you're elderly with your health teetering on the brink. Time has a way of sneaking up on a person. I have decided I will have a talk with my kids about what I'd like if I'm lucky enough to grow old. It would go something like this, "kids, Mom and Dad want to live at home until we die (or kill each other), whichever comes first."

-24-

It's now mid-July and six weeks since I last entered the doors at Ultra Luscious Relaxation Spa. I'm starting to feel a little better. My racing thoughts are slowing slightly, I'm sleeping for longer stretches, and I can get out of bed in the morning without a knot of anxiety in my stomach. Nevertheless, I don't feel whole yet even though my doctor appointment is approaching. The thought of going back to work is overwhelming. I don't know if I can face it if he sends me back.

Meanwhile, I must have a purpose, or I'll lose my mind. It's so quiet here. Today I will sort through some boxes of old clothes. I had brought these along with the intention of cleaning out a few things while I had the time. If I don't do this before I return to work, it may be years before I get to it and then I'll have accumulated even more.

Given the beautiful weather, I lug the big box full of stuff out to my lawn chair, nestled under the pear tree. The sun warms my skin and birds flutter about in the branches overhead. I begin to weed through a box of clothes from years ago. It's depressing that none of these will fit me anymore. Who am I kidding? Am I really going to drop that 15 lbs and rock this pair of jeans from 2012? It's hard to let go of that hope, which is evident by the neatly packed box of size 8 wardrobe in front of me.

I'm easily distracted by this majestic pear tree. It's a piece of heaven growing right in the middle of the lawn, despite our horrible ineptitude for anything horticultural. In fact, we didn't even realize it was a pear tree until a few weeks ago. Having grown up in the city, the only place I've experienced food coming from is the grocery store. I decided, since moving here for the season, I would try my hand at gardening. Imagine being able to walk out on the front lawn and pick some salad fixings – a few tomatoes, maybe some carrots and a head of lettuce. A month ago, I barely even had time to make a salad, let alone grow one.

Once I am finished sorting these clothes, I'm going to meander over to the patch of garden that we planted when we arrived. I had googled how to grow tomatoes, pumpkins, cucumbers, beans and carrots. Having so much information I was overwhelmed rather than 'at one' with nature. My impatience soon took over and I bought some small plants of each variety, rather than start from scratch. My garden is about eight by five meters. This seemed like a humble beginning given that the surrounding farms have fields of crops. Clearly, the land is fertile.

It's incredible how many weeds can grow in a garden of forty square metres. I now realize what happens if you don't weed a garden regularly. Initially I felt I had quite a good growth taking root, only to find out later, that all those sprouts I had been watering were actually weeds. I'm getting stressed by the caregiving requirements of my beans and carrots, and my squash are spreading out over everything. Next time I won't plant them in the middle. I'm excited that my tomatoes are taking form. It's remarkable how many tomatoes one eight-meter row can yield. Despite the weeds, I am a tomato millionaire. My carrots, still only centimetres long, are not quite as successful and my pumpkins are downright discouraging. I've learned that the neighbours on our concession are having a pumpkin growing contest. This is something we never did in our sub-division back home. Seeing as I've never grown a pumpkin before, I'm definitely at a disadvantage. Anyway, I planted the seeds and water them daily, but nothing happens. What is really adding to my feeling of inadequacy is that the farmer across the road, beside the housing development, has an entire field of pumpkins. When I walk down the lane, which I now do regularly, I see row upon row of large, still green pumpkins peeking out from under the leaves. I cannot claim that my growing problem is the land, because fifty metres from our driveway there are at least 5,000 pumpkins thriving in the soil. Farming is harder than I thought.

The mosquitos are unbearable but if you take a day off, the weeds move in. Although there are no threatening calls from your boss or disgruntled clients or lost contracts, the weeds just strangle your garden, so you have no food. Nature is very clear.

My garden has an insatiable need to be watered and tended. Maybe I can get the kids to help me weed. I know their first question will be how much will I pay them? Regardless of the pitch I will give them about the natural freshness and health attributes of eating organic, I imagine they will gripe about why they have to eat salad in the first place. Megan, being fourteen, will undoubtedly tell me that her friends don't have to weed a garden. "What kind of abusive parent are you?" she will snipe back at me. Besides, she is not putting her hands in the dirt, especially if there are worms. If the internet is out, Tyler might agree to it briefly. I fear I may slide back to my previous habit of just buying salad in a bag.

-25-

Matt is curious about the attic. I'm not sure why, but he wants to look up there... which is evidence that men and women think differently.

"Is this really necessary?" I ask Matt. "I don't mind painting and wallpapering, I can cope with some redecorating in the living room, but the attic, that is where I draw the line! What do you think you're going to find?" I ask apprehensively.

"It's not that bad. I don't think there are any bats," he says in a genuine attempt to comfort me.

"Bats in the house! I never thought of that," I exclaim in horror.

"It won't take us long. I'll get a flashlight. It's not very big up there. I doubt you can even stand up in it," he says while adjusting the ladder.

I am starting to look forward to just returning to sorting boxes of outgrown clothes. "When was the last time someone was up there? What if we find a body?" I joke nervously, as I put on some old runners.

"Well, it would be skeletal by now," he retorts.

"Very funny. Okay let's get this over with!" I say feigning confidence.

We each don a mask, gloves and flashlights. My stomach is in knots as we inch the ladder towards the innocent looking indent in the ceiling. I had never really taken much notice of it before as the board is recessed in the ceiling of the second-floor hallway. It's not really something you notice unless you suddenly have to climb up into it.

Matt mounts the ladder and moves the ceiling piece to the side. Looming above is an ominous, gaping hole into blackness.

"I don't want to do this," I protest.

"It will be fun," Matt says as he lifts his body somewhere into the ceiling. His legs dangle from above.

"Amy you won't believe this!" he shouts down excitedly.

I begin to climb the ladder apprehensively, not wanting to look. Matt has now fully disappeared through the hole. Feeling sick to my stomach, I proceed. Reluctantly, I poke my head into the musty darkness. Matt's fading flashlight partially illuminates an attic that is small, with a slanted roof. Much to my relief it looks quite clean. He shines the light in front of me and I cautiously enter the area. I can stand up straight in the middle of the 'room'. Matt is impressed with how solid the beams look. As he knocks on the roof I look around in the dark, struggling to adjust to the absence of light and oxygen. You have to watch where you step as the visibility is poor. Matt shines the light around the entire area, and we see that there is a large, unusual item in the southeast area of the space. It is covered with a cloth of some sort. Although it does not appear particularly threatening, my heart is racing, and I do not want to investigate the curious shape. However, I know we will. Matt goes first at my insistence. Undaunted despite the dingy light, Matt marches right over and pulls back the cloth. I gasp as I take in the vague form in the shape of a person. Immediately my piercing scream sets Wilbur barking several floors below. Matt hugs me and is trying to conceal his hilarity as he reassures me it's just a sewing mannequin. Despite almost wetting my pants, I am relieved to see it is nothing gruesome. Beside the dusty old dress mannequin is a huge picture of what looks to be a family portrait. It is a beautiful old photograph of several somber looking people. They range in age from babyhood to senior citizen.

"This has got to be the family who lived here," I proclaim excitedly.

"What's that?" Matt asks, shining his light on a small trunk.

"I have no idea, you check," I insist, still recovering from the discovery of the sewing mannequin. It is hard to see in the light of a dying flashlight, but it includes some creepy dolls, a box with a bunch of letters, several dusty books and two huge, fully bound bibles.

"Incredible!" I exclaim.

Though it isn't easy, we get everything downstairs. The small trunk is full, and the mannequin cumbersome. We lug them into the living room for closer inspection. These items hadn't seen daylight for many years, but they were at least protected by a sheet. The dust is thick and both Matt and I convulse with a series of sneezes.

The portrait draws our attention first. It is in a lovely, old wooden frame with some slight gold trim around the outside. How did they make everything so tasteful back then? The faces of the people are striking. They look so grim and serious. There are several young girls in the picture, all dressed in beautiful white flowing gowns. They appear to live in a kind of pre-colour period. How did they function in their daily lives in those full-length dresses? The elderly lady is dressed in black and has a dark shawl around her shoulders. She looks about 75 but is probably closer to 50. There is another young woman who is dressed in black too, but she is much younger – maybe 35 ish. She must be Laura. There is Isabel, - no doubt the young woman with a toddler on her lap. The people in the diary are taking form before me. I'm getting to know Isabel well since I've been pouring through her journal each night. If she unpinned her hair and had a good night's sleep, she is quite an attractive young woman. Toddlers must have been more subdued back then as the little fellow on her lap (Lyle?) appeared quite mellow and contained. How could she be the mother of all these children? She looks too young for that. There is a little boy who is impeccably dressed in little knickers (obviously Doug) and there is only one man – a heavyset fellow with a sophisticated bowtie (no doubt Morten). To be honest, they all look a little glum, but they sure did not look like farmers. I count eleven people. Did all these people live in this one farmhouse? How could they possibly cope - and without plumbing! In an odd sort of way, I feel I know these people. I will hang this treasure over the mantle, near the wall clock. This must have been the mannequin they used to make those beautiful dresses. However, it and the creepy doll with the eyes that open and close, are headed for the barn.

With great anticipation, I turn my attention to the books. There are two, very large, beautifully bound and absurdly heavy bibles. Their edges are frayed from apparent use and there are a few sporadic spots of mould on the edges. On the cover of both, embossed in gold, is the name "Huntly-1815".

1815, that's even older than the house itself. Surely this trunk and its dated contents didn't travel across the ocean.

The bibles are a timeless treasure. I open one. The cover page is in a foreign language, possibly Gaelic. It has beautiful artwork with pictures of angels and people praying. There is an inscription: "Huntly Family Bible, Inverness, Scotland, 1815." Somewhere near the middle there is a leaf, pressed between the pages and perfectly preserved through the years. Although I don't recognize the leaf, I envision a unique looking tree on the Scottish shores clad in leaves of this kind.

The next book is The New Testament. The date inscribed in the front is 1899. On the first page it lists family members, dating back many years. There is a registry for births and deaths and marriages. I look for a page of divorces but there isn't one. There is even a Temperance Pledge with numerous actual signatures. There are handwritten notes and book markers tucked into several pages, citing certain verses and passages that must have been pertinent to the reader(s). This was, without a doubt, a fully utilized document in its day. There is plenty of evidence that it had not sat idly on a shelf in some forgotten corner of the parlour. There are other books in the trunk as well... a hymn book, some faded piano music, books on nature and various plants, cook-books, books on canning and pickling, a book of poems and an atlas. That should make for some interesting summer reading - an atlas from 200 years ago.

The box full of trinkets is filled with a curious mixture of items. There is an old pocket watch and a necklace, which looked exactly like the one in the picture, around Isabel's neck. There is an illustrated board game called Messenger Boy. There are some kitchen items (with a stamp of Will's General Store on the bottom), there is a thimble, a fountain pen, an empty jar of ink and some two cent stamps.

To hell with the Temperance Pledge, it's time for a glass of wine by the pear tree. I don't want to give the impression that all Matt and I do is drink wine, because sometimes we have a gin and tonic instead.

It's almost 7:00 p.m. I'm embarrassed to say what happens at dusk at the farmhouse. This is what people do when there's nowhere to go. Around 7:00 each night, bats file out from under the tin roof and fly around the yard in a crazy frenzy to eat bugs. Now let's be clear. They are not in the house, or I wouldn't be. They are actually between the attic and the metal roof top, and they get hungry for mosquitos in the early evening. Every night when the weather permits, we count the bats that zoom out into the yard. It's as though they are all lined up like airplanes on a runway, and they jet out one at a time, about three seconds apart. Our highest count is fifty-eight. If every bat eats a hundred mosquitos, that's five thousand eight hundred less mosquitos on my arm while weeding. I like that, and bats are quite beautiful to watch. Mind you I give them a wide berth and they have never come anywhere near my lawn-chair, but they bring the front lawn to life in the early evening. I'm learning that a glass of wine and the bat show is great entertainment on a summer evening.

Where have all the honeybees gone? I remember a hive that was tucked right up in the eave of my porch. Some years they'd nest in that old tree in the front yard. They moved around a lot, but they were always here somewhere, buzzing around in the flowers. The flowers sure miss them. They're on borrowed time without them. And the butterflies... they'd return every spring from who knows where. They were like clockwork despite their long journey from the south. I don't see many of them anymore. I wonder where they all went. Boy, do I need a bath. It hasn't rained in days.

Saturday, March 31, 1900

It was nice to finally shed that fancy, long dress and its itchy crinoline. I was worried that its snug bodice might draw attention to my expanding girth.

Tom was driving his carriage too darn fast for my comfort. All it takes is one spook and it's a nightmare – a surprise deer or bear. We've learned how fast accidents can happen. We had three girls in that carriage and that young lad seemed to be showing off too much for my taste. I don't know why boys need to act so recklessly when girls are onboard. I heard lots of giggling and hooting, no doubt they were egging him on. My girls can be so silly at times.

Oh dear, there's Nell's cough again. Since we returned from town this afternoon, I notice she has developed a slight cough. Ever since that incidence with Billy, I'm always wary of any little cough or sneeze. She seemed fine when we stopped in to see Alice. Here we were worried we might catch something from Alice, but I fear it could be the other way around. It's common knowledge that it's essential to burn a handkerchief if there is fear of consumption. However, Alice's distress was certainly not physical. No doubt she was struggling with melancholia, being so discouraged and low energy. Her sister kept our visit short given that Alice didn't do well with a lot of company. When I returned to get my forgotten gloves, Alice was crying. I held her in my arms. She said she didn't know what was wrong, she just felt very low. I told her I would visit again next time I was in town.

There's that darn cough again. I found Nell in the kitchen setting the table. However, I didn't think she looked well, and I told her so.

"No Momma, I'm just fine. I just have a bit of a tickle in my throat," but I knew she was terrified. She looked flushed. I put my hand on her forehead and was alarmed to feel the heat radiating from her brow.

"Nell," I said. "You must come to the other room and lie down, you're burning up," I insisted.

Her eyes were wide with fear, as she attempted to minimize her cough.

"Nell, pretending you are not sick, does not make it go away. It's probably nothing, just a little cold. Put the forks down and come with me." You can rest in the parlour where it's quiet. I'll bring your supper in here and I'll join you. We don't want everyone getting a cold," I said feeling uneasy.

When I returned to the kitchen, I instructed Ida to put the cutlery in boiling water.

I could hear Carrie provoking Sadie in the sitting room, squabbling over the Findlay boy and who he talked to the most.

"Girls, girls. Stop this nonsense," I shouted. "Nell is feeling poorly. Carrie, I need you to help your grandmother in the kitchen."

Carrie protested. "Why should I have to set when I have to clear and wash too. What about Sadie?"

"Don't be so impudent. I chose you as I heard you provoking your sister." Carrie can be so headstrong. Sometimes I worry what kind of a wife and mother she will be.

Zoe, having heard the concerns about Nell, looked worried. "Is Nell okay Momma? Should I go play cards with her?" This was the last thing I wanted to encourage as secretly the fear of consumption haunted my every thought. I desperately wanted to isolate Nell just in case her cough was something far more serious. I also worried about the little one growing inside me.

Morten would not hear of me sitting with Nell in my condition and insisted that he dine with her.

After supper, Ida and I applied some cool clothes to Nell's forehead which did help the fever briefly. Nevertheless, by the end of the evening, she was growing warm again. Morten and I decided she would sleep in the parlour tonight to err on the side of caution.

I tossed and turned all night. I repeatedly checked on her while she slept a deep and untroubled sleep. Between Nell and Lyle, I hardly got an hour's rest.

By the time Henry crowed, I was exhausted. Ida insisted I return to bed as she knew I had had a fretful night. She assured me that she and Mary would look after the children and Laura would care for Nell. What would I do without them, even Laura.

I slept until noon. It's shameful how sluggish I've been lately. When I woke up, Morten was in with Nell. Ida had called him in from the barn as she was growing concerned. Morten emerged from the parlour looking grey.

"What is it, Mort?" my voice in a panic. "Is she okay?"

"Issy... she's very warm and her nose is running constantly. She seems quite weak and a little delirious." I detected fear in his eyes.

"No," I sobbed. "I can't lose her." I buried my head in his chest as I cried uncontrollably.

"Let's not think the worst. It could be a bad cold," he reassured.

Nell's cough resumed and persisted with a vengeance all day long. Now we were all growing scared.

Chuck and Laura went to fetch Dr. Moffat. All the children were sent outside to do their chores and help in the barn. Anything to keep them away from what could be a deadly fever.

Dr. Moffat and Margaret arrived just before the noon day dinner. The neighbours had seen their carriage come up the road and were therefore alerted that something serious was happening.

As I greeted them at the door, Margaret gave me a big hug. "Don't fret Isabel, it could be just a bad cold," she said reassuringly, but we both knew you didn't call the doctor for a cold.

I offered them tea, but Dr. Moffat declined and went right to the parlour. I showed him in, but Morten immediately discouraged this. Margaret, sensing his concern, took me up on the offer of tea and we went to the kitchen. Ida already had the kettle on the woodstove and was preparing the teacups. We avoided talk of what was foremost on all our minds. Margaret, however, slipped into the conversation that consumption had not really been prevalent in the area recently, (except for Billy) and it was unlikely there was any concern. None of the children in the schoolhouse had come down with it.

Margaret, having been around to so many farms recently, updated me on all the new calves born not to mention pigs and kittens. She is such a kind and supportive person. I secretly was grateful she was not telling me the stories of still births, or women who had died in childbirth, or her neighbour's amputation following an altercation with a bull. I couldn't imagine being a doctor's wife.

Eventually Dr. Moffat emerged looking grave and serious. He explained, in his kindly way, that Nell certainly was a sick girl, but she had a lot of determination and inner strength. He could not tell at this stage whether it was consumption, but he strongly recommended isolation to be on the safe side. He looked right at me and said, "Isabel, there is no need for you to be part of her care. Leave this to the others as we don't want any other worries."

Dr. Moffat gave instructions for Nell's care: lots of fresh air, good food, plenty of fluids and aspirin for the fever. We chatted briefly over tea, but I felt my heart sinking like a stone. What they didn't know was that Billy had kissed Nell against her will with a full open mouth. I don't feel at liberty to share that as Nell would be mortified and it doesn't matter now anyway. Please God don't let her have tuberculosis. She is such a kind girl, and she doesn't deserve this. I could kill that boy if nature hadn't already done it for me.

Morten held me in his arms all night long as I wept, overcome with sadness, fear and rage. Damn that Billy and his stupid grandparents. What were they thinking?

Monday, April 2, 1900

We met around the kitchen table. It was time the children knew all that was going on, for their own safety. Morten started with the happy news (or what he felt was happy news).

"Your mother is expecting a baby." Everyone gasped and cheered, and Ida even teared up. No doubt for Ida, it was just a confirmation of what she already suspected. There was celebration around the table, and everyone talked excitedly. Questions and comments popped up from every corner. When was the little one due? Let's think of names. How long have we known? Lyle clapped his hands together *with all the excitement he sensed. Little did he know, in the months to come, he was about to be dethroned. Morten let the excitement percolate through the family for some time and then he said in a rather somber tone, "we also have some worrisome news." A nervous hush fell over the table.*

"It seems your sister may be ill." There was total silence in the room. All were conscious that Nell was not at the table and was instead resting in the parlour.

"You all know that Dr. Moffat was here, and he is worried that Nell may have TB." Then Morten's voice cracked, and he buried his head in his hands and wept. The family was stunned. This was the second time in just a few months that they had seen their father cry.

Morten composed himself and continued. "Dr. Moffat wants Nell in isolation. You are not to go in or out of the parlour for now, that includes you too Isabel. Aunt Laura, Grandma and I will care for Nell until she's better." His voice wavered again. There were sobs and objections heard from around the table, but all understood how serious this could be. Ida led us in prayer and asked that Nell be spared and given strength and courage. We all said amen and the dreadful meeting was over. The happy news was indeed overshadowed by this gloomy omen.

After supper we gathered in the sitting room as was our usual custom. No one played the piano or felt like singing. Carrie, Sadie and Zoe made a limp attempt at cards, but their hearts weren't in it. Ida and Laura continued their knitting well into the evening and Mary read aloud from the Bible.

Wednesday, April 4, 1900.

This heavy feeling just does not want to lift. When I wake in the morning, it is there. When I do my housework, it is there. When I talk with people, it is there. I just want to go back to sleep and cry. That's not like me even in pregnancy, and heaven knows I've had plenty of those. I am just not myself lately. Maybe I 'caught' Alice's melancholia. Nell is no better in fact I think she may be getting worse. I feel so useless. I can't be a mother to her, I can't even go to her as she lies possibly dying in the next room. I know she understands why, but what comfort is that to a fifteen-year-old girl who may lose her life. I can only imagine her rage against Billy now. I know mine is volcanic.

I wave to her from the window, and I write notes to her daily. Usually, I write several times a day and I have Ida read them to her. Unfortunately, she is not well enough to write back as the coughing has been taking on a whole new fury in these last few days. Morten told me she has begun to cough up blood now which is a telltale sign of consumption. Oh... how can this be happening? This stupid disease has destroyed so many households over the years. Dr. Moffat explained that the latest research shows that we must take extra care to boil everything Nell has touched, so as to prevent spreading. He says we should open the windows for some fresh air as that is the best help of all. We are doing everything we can, but it continues to worsen. There is a sanatorium on a lake several miles north of here. The cost is well beyond our means, but Dr. Moffat feels the fresh air and good food is ideal right here on the farm. Reverend Mactavish has stopped by to see us, and Ida has invited him to dinner. No doubt coming to our home reminds him of the loss of his friend Daniel only months earlier. Life is so bloody unfair.

The smell of wood fire hangs in the air and Morten tells me the maple sap is running very well. Who cares. What does it matter. Soon there may be one less of us around the table to enjoy the fruits of the season. Easter is approaching. It seems I have given up 'joy' for Lent. Although we will all be getting ready for the Easter dinner soon, we will not be having extended family over for the meal this year. We must stay apart as much as possible.

When Ida leaves the parlour for tea this afternoon, I'm going to slip in and see Nell. I cannot live with myself without holding my daughter's hand as she lies there in fear. I will put a kerchief around my nose to protect the baby, but I must go in.

...I'm back. I went in and just stayed a few brief moments. Now I am profoundly distressed. Nell was asleep but she looked gaunt - a shadow of her former self. I could see she had not eaten the food that was beside her which Laura had obviously been trying to feed her. She looked pale but peaceful. I know there is a chance she could recover but with each passing day it seems less hopeful. Why couldn't it have been Laura who got ill? She is older, she has no husband or children, and she has been downright gloomy to be around most of the time. Why does it have to be my beautiful daughter with so much life ahead? Why couldn't it have been me? I would rather suffer than stand by and watch my daughter die. What is God thinking? Does He really want to take another family member from us? I honestly never thought I would question my faith. I feel like smashing this teacup on the wall.

Morten has just come in with some maple syrup from the fire. I hear muffled voices downstairs that do not sound optimistic. The children will be home from school before long and I just can't face it. I must go to bed. Sometimes I don't care if I wake up.

Thursday, April 5, 1900

Nell coughed all night. There is little doubt it is TB. It's such a wretched sound and all of us could hear her. Little Zoe came running into bed with us. She was beside herself. Dr. Moffat had been here again yesterday evening but obviously whatever he gave her was of little assistance. Morten spent half the night in the parlour with Nell, alternating shifts with Ida and Laura. All had their mouths, noses and hands covered. Neighbours have already begun doing countless thoughtful tasks for us, at no small sacrifice to themselves. Coming into this house poses some risk yet that doesn't seem to stop them. I am profoundly grateful to all of them for their support. Reverend Mactavish has become a regular fixture in our home these past weeks. It is as though he has read my mind and reassured me to have faith, that God is with Nell and all of us. Perhaps so, but it doesn't seem to stop the pain of it all.

Morten has tried to cheer me with several bottles of maple syrup. The smell of fresh baked bread is wafting through the house. Mary has been up early helping with the morning meal preparation. The normal pre-school chaos ensues, but the happiness has gone out of it. The girls are off to school and as they go, they call their good-byes through the door to Nell. There is only a soft moan in response. I see them at the window, knocking and waving to their dying sister. What comfort can there be in that, for either side. When Chuck leaves to drive the carriage to school, I feel nothing but relief. Before long they will be walking to school as the road will soon be dry, then they will leave even earlier. I love my children, but I lack the energy to be around people and commotion right now. I am grateful when the carriage disappears over the hill.

Despite the alluring smell of freshly baked bread, I feel no drive to eat, or even arise for that matter. I'm continuing my journaling here in the sitting room where it is warmer by the fire and the ticking clock is soothing. As I gaze upon our portrait, I think how much life has changed in just a few weeks.

Ironically, as Nell lies dying the outside world is coming to life. Spring is in the air. It is normally a time when one feels renewed and hopeful. I can hear birds returning to the trees and see them flitting about. Green shoots are starting to peek tentatively out of the soil, buds are appearing on the bushes. It's the time of year of promise and inspiration, yet I feel so hopeless. I can't stop my tears. I must pull myself together.

As I walk in the garden, the air is warm and inviting which has helped to lift my mood somewhat. I can see Laura in the distance, with Doug running ahead of her and little Lyle tagging along behind. It seems to be cheering Laura, to spend time with the children.

When I peered through the window, Nell was asleep as I might have guessed. The poor girl must be exhausted after the night she had. I say a silent prayer as I lean against the glass, gazing upon my baby. Fifteen years has evaporated and who knew that would be all I would have of her. Through the windowpane I can see her laboured breathing and hear the wall clock counting out the minutes from the other room. I hope my sobbing doesn't wake her.

My poor, dear Isabel. I am with you. I wish I could help.

-26-

The cost of Dad's 24 hour nursing care is approximately $150,000 a year. How did this happen? How will we ever finance this? At least Ida, Morten and Laura weren't charging by the hour.

I wonder how long Dad will live and how will we finance this level of care for the rest of his life? How will we pay for my mother's care in time? Will there be anything left in his bank account in the end? Who wants to be in a position where they are waiting in anticipation of the inevitable. All I want to do is hold Dad's hand and tell him I love him. Instead, we are all an anxious wreck worried about hurtling over the financial cliff. What if we're left with an estate in a deficit position rather than an inheritance?

My father has always been a private man and has never discussed his financial situation. I know he has done well in business and that he and my mother live comfortably in a nice home in a middle-class area. At 92, I assume his mortgage is paid off. However, I'm not sure mine will be by then. Regardless of his comfortable status, I doubt he could foot the bill of $150,000 a year while lying on his back in the living room. Did my 88-year-old mother sign a contract she can't afford? It is interesting how shadowy characters suddenly appear when there is money, old age, and an estate hanging in the balance – a dangerous combo.

The dynamics created by the dwindling funds created some rapidly escalating tension amongst us siblings. As our family sat in the kitchen 'discussing' the situation, Mom was more fixated on who will be staying for dinner. The air was filled with a tangled web of apprehension, greed and financial desperation that makes that warm fuzzy feeling of family fly out the window at breakneck speed.

This experience makes one think a lot about wills and inheritance. I guess it's a tug of war. As an elderly person, one wants to retain an element of control over his or her life. One does not know how long s/he will live or how much money will be needed for medical care and other expenses. This becomes even more critical at a time of life when you feel your power slipping away. What a helpless feeling to become both physically and financially dependent.

Do we need to die to pass on our wealth? It truly makes one question whether this is a good way to design our 'end of days' arrangement. The cash incentive at the end of a lifespan adds an exciting prize to a devastating loss... intense sadness, mixed with economic relief. Do I want my kids relieved or rejoicing when my time comes, or do I want them to miss me as an active part of their lives? I guess the answer lies somewhere in the sharing while you are alive, both financially and emotionally. What gratitude that would evoke for the beneficiary and what warmth for the benefactor. It becomes more of a 'sharing' than an empty, end of life donation. A gift of money seems less heartfelt from one who cannot use it anymore. My goal is to die on the poor side, yet not to live that way. I have decided I will share my money as I go. It is a catch though. If I get to live to an old age, it's unlikely I'll have much income at that point. If I sell any investments I acquire, I will no longer have income from them so what will I live off? What if a pension is insufficient to support adequate medical care - you don't want to be a financial burden to your children. These are tough conundrums. I hope I will have ample time to figure out a solution. Nevertheless, I will strive to err on the side of generosity and sharing as opposed to hoarding and relinquishing.

I'm worrying about our own financial situation with my reduced salary and the mountain of bills accumulating. Things are growing fiscally tight. As much as I was relieved when Dr. Neal signed me off work for another eight weeks, I'm really hoping we can afford my reduced salary.

The thought of returning to the demands of work is less appealing by the day. Matt and I recently spotted a cute little storefront in downtown Orillia. Its beautiful hardwood floors, spectacular high ceilings and floor to ceiling bookshelves would make a perfect spot for that piano bar we've often dreamed of opening. It's not really a viable economic option, but it certainly is an inviting reverie.

Monday, April 23, 1900

Weeks have gone by, and I haven't felt like writing but today I must. So much has happened. We lost Nell a few days ago. I collapsed when Morten told me she was gone. I'm now almost five months pregnant and I think that is the only thing that makes me continue. My grief is bottomless, but I must get up, for the baby inside me and for my children. I must eat and I must drink, regardless of how I feel about my own life. Morten is constantly looking out for me, and Laura and Mary have done everything. I have so little to offer right now.

Neighbours have started coming by to pay their respects and Nell is laid out in the parlour. She looks like an angel, so peaceful and content. If only I could feel that way too. The undertaker has done a fine job of making her look beautiful and happy. Morten and I were in with her earlier. I held her cold hand, only regretful that I couldn't hold it more in life in the last few weeks.

Once again, our home has a cloud of death hanging over it. Zoe is beside herself and out with her donkey. The girls are so glum, and Ida is trying to appear strong despite everything. This loss, so soon on the heels of Daniel's death, is just too much to bear. The service is tomorrow and once again we will make our way to our little church on the hillside to bid farewell to another family member. Each Sunday, as our carriage turns up the laneway towards the chapel, it will be a constant reminder of our losses.

There have been many happy times in our church. It's where all the children have been christened. It's where I find strength and courage to carry on. It's a place of community and fellowship where I always feel welcome and at home. It's a place where my children feel belonging and rootedness, from their ancestors who rest in the churchyard to the extended family and community who surround them in the sanctuary twice each Sunday. I must remind myself of that in these dark times.

I have been trying to focus more on the baby. I have begun to feel some fluttering and movement. Morten is very much hoping for a third boy to balance out the family.

I must say this little one has given us all something hopeful to think of after the shocking loss of Nell. In fact, I am beginning to wonder what we would have done without this distraction.

Ida and Laura have invited the women over to work on a quilt for the baby. Thankfully, there will be something to talk about other than our losses.

Rose has been with me through it all, despite her own situation. She has confessed to me that when Patrick takes a drink (or two or three) at the tavern, he returns in a foul mood. Her recent bruised arm confirms that it brings out the worst in him.

-27-

What a relief to have eight more weeks in this beautiful setting. I'm beginning to settle into farm life. The relaxed pace is growing on me and I'm gradually feeling like I can breathe again.

What also makes today memorable is the dead chipmunk I found in Wilbur's water bowl. No wonder Wilbur was drinking out of the toilet again. I will never understand our dog's disgusting need to drink out of the toilet. Even without the chipmunk, he gravitates to the toilet to quench his thirst. If there is the slightest foreign object in his bowl; a leaf has blown in, a small insect swims about, Wilbur won't touch it. Is he aware what goes into the toilet? Some smart entrepreneur should develop a dog water bowl in the shape of a toilet.

I just got off the phone with my friend Sue in Vancouver. Having been friends since grade one, I knew I would be Maid of Honour at her wedding. It's hard to forget what an ordeal that was. The fancy upscale hotel was so elaborate. I recall how fastidious she was regarding all the intricate details. She drove me crazy insisting on the finest of everything. The floral arrangements were magnificent, the meal was superb, and her gown was outrageously pricey and ornate. The event was like a coronation. However, I was never convinced the couple were really meant for each other.

Who would have ever predicted such a nasty break-up. Sue had told me she thought he'd been cheating but she had no evidence. She was downright tormented trying to figure out if it was all in her head. He insisted she was 'over analyzing' everything and there was absolutely nothing going on. Then one day, he accidentally left his phone unlocked. Torn whether to snoop through his private messages, she quickly resolved her guilt and began reading the texts. It turns out he had been exchanging intimate messages with a woman at his office for almost a year, complete with photographic backup! Blindsided and devasted don't fully capture her reaction and of course there was little Caitlin to think of. Sue confronted him when he came home that night. Bob tried denying it, but she had the evidence. He moved out and is now living with his 'colleague'. Sue has never fully recovered and of course it has been life altering for little Caitlin. Caitlin is all Sue's got and she isn't about to share her lightly.

The custody battle has dragged on for months. I know she's been drinking again, and I'm plagued with the fear she might try to hurt herself like she did in university. She has no family in Vancouver. Her mother died of cancer a few years ago and her Dad re-married and moved to Manitoba. She can't stand his new wife. Her brother and his partner live in Montreal. Sue hates her job at the accounting firm and finds her position there mind numbing. She needs support and she doesn't have a lot out there. I should visit but I just don't have the money right now and I can't get away.

Amy and Matt stare at a big, black rectangle every night. I don't know why. I hate that thing. At 10:00 each evening it starts telling all these sad stories about people dying all around the world, earthquakes, floods, starvation, war, car accidents, fires, even people without homes. It shows pictures of what's happening and people in the rectangle talk about it over and over again. I find myself weeping so much I can't sleep. Amy and Matt go to bed and I'm up all night looking at the stars thinking about all the pain in the world. What would I do without the stars and the moon to help me keep things in perspective.

Sunday, April 29, 1900

The table is laid for Easter dinner. It seems the family was together just days ago for Nell's service, but in fact that was over a week ago now. As I rest here in the sitting room, beneath the ticking of the clock, I try to muster some strength to face the day ahead.

After the service we will gather around the table as we always have. Last Easter we had Daniel and Nell with us. How empty it will feel without them.

The Easter service was very moving, and Rev. Mactavish said a heartfelt prayer for our family. He spoke of death as the 'portal' to the next world, which comforted me somewhat. After the service, we had a walk in the churchyard as we often do. Her grave has not yet been dug but we placed flowers for both Nell and Daniel where they will rest. The churchyard was full of families doing the same thing this Easter morning.

When we returned to the farm the house smelled of Mary's cinnamon bread baking in the oven. It was warm enough to sit on the porch so that is where we began with a glass of iced tea. Morten's youngest sister Florence was able to make the trip from Coldwater as was Ida's brother Urn and his wife Clara. I'm so thankful that my sister Agnes and her family had travelled all the way from Brechin to be with us. Such a kind gesture. They left their farm at 6:00 a.m. this morning to travel the twenty-five miles to make the service on time. It makes for a full house with a little cheer again. It's so comforting to be surrounded by family.

The meal was fine indeed despite the dwindling of the cellar supplies in springtime. The beets, pickles, carrots and Ida's delicious chili sauce were marvellous. There was a fresh ham, although I was sorry Oliver had to sacrifice his life for the occasion. Mary's bread was delicious and with the homemade jam it was outstanding. It was a tremendous feast and I believe it helped me regain my appetite slightly. The company was uplifting. We took our tea and dessert in the sitting room followed by a game of charades. Zoe was such a character. It was nice to see her giggle again with her cousins. Laura played the piano, and we sang along for the better part of an hour. It was a lovely afternoon, despite our heavy hearts. After everyone left, Morten and I sat alone on the porch with our tea. He held me in his arms as I wept for my poor, dear Nell. With the windows opened for spring, I could hear the clock ticking in the sitting room. The company cheered us both a little, reminding us that life will go on - difficult as it feels.

-28-

I feel so badly for Isabel. How deep the pain must have been, to lose a child.

The summer is almost over now. Why is it the winter months proceed so slowly? The days are gradually growing shorter, and the birds are filing out of town in V-shape formation. "No, please come back," I want to shout.

We only have a few weeks left at the farm. It's a hard realization to accept. The office seems a world away. How can I possibly face returning? I'm not ready. I would have never dreamt I'd find it challenging to return to the city.

I find myself inexplicably drawn towards that empty corner storefront in town – across from the Opera House. I can just see a fantastic piano bar there, with art on the wall, candles on tabletops and floor to ceiling bookshelves everywhere. It would be fun to operate a friendly little tavern with Matt, in a town a sliver the size of the big city. I can envision a lively little spot where people come to relax and socialize after a play or at the end of a workday. I wonder if we could make any money at it?.... and my reverie continues.

Back to school ads have been littering the mailbox for weeks. In fact, it is the only mail we get. The kids are anticipating their return home to school and friends. It is hard to believe Megan will be starting high school and Tyler is going into Grade 11. Like many grade 9 s, Megan has been insisting she 'needs' new clothes, despite being unable to close her overstuffed drawers.

The other half of her wardrobe is strewn all over her floor. She has so many clothes she can hardly slam her door at night when she is furious with us. Nevertheless, she 'has nothing to wear'. The only thing she really needs is a little more gratitude. Tyler has grown four inches over the summer and has outgrown nearly everything he owns, which isn't much. He couldn't care less about clothes or style. It's that time of year again when every parent and their growing children head to faceless box stores to quench the need for back-to-school clothing.

For my son, the goal seems to be to 'get it over with'. He perceives it as a necessary evil that would be better if it didn't have to occur at all. Firstly, my son walks several paces ahead so as not to be seen with 'his mother', even though he doesn't know anyone in the area. However, once we are in the store, he relies heavily on me for sizes. "Mom, what size is my waist?" "What length of pant do I need?" For boys it seems to be nothing more than an equation and then pulling the appropriate combination of waist X length off the shelf. I insist he try it on to confirm it fits. "What's to fit? Those are my measurements so that will work," he reassures.

Megan on the other hand, takes ten pairs of pants into the change room. She is limited only by the maximum number allowed. I have to painstakingly see her in them all and give an opinion on which ones make her look the best. "Do you like this style?" "Is this colour okay on me?" "Do these make me look fat?" "Can I buy both?" By the time Megan has eventually emerged from the change room, Tyler has completed his shopping, checked out the electronics section, leafed through some questionable magazines in the book department, had some fries at the food court and is waiting in the car ready to leave.

Meanwhile, Megan is determined to get the 'right' running shoes, as if there is such a thing. Imagine the expense of taking two kids, with growing feet to a sport store to upgrade their shoe supply. How badly do we need runners, cross trainers, walking shoes, dress shoes and sandals, ...when they barely leave the couch? How about we find one pair of shoes that covers all gaits and events. Four boxes of shoes later, I reach the discouraging conclusion that it cannot be done. However, they now have both gym shoes and walking shoes, so that they can sit in front of a computer in maximum comfort. At least there was a 'back-to-school' deal, buy one and get the second pair only slightly overpriced.

Where I refuse to give generously is the insatiable need to keep up with whatever pricey garment 'all' the girls in Megan's friend group are sporting. With their young and shapely physiques the brand names should be paying them to wear their products. They expect the consumer (or more accurately, the consumer's parent) to pay a ridiculous price only for their shapely customer to sport the brand name publicly and boldly across her chest or rear end. A phenomenal marketing ploy. Megan's only concern at this age is to fit in and be accepted and according to her, the box stores don't sell 'socially acceptable clothes'. Therefore, I have kindly agreed that Megan can have her allotted money from the budget to buy what she needs wherever she likes. This too will cut down on the amount of clothes in her room, as she will only be able to afford one item. She tells me I'm a 'cruel parent' because I won't finance her obsession with overpriced clothes. She claims I set her up to be a 'social misfit' clad in clothes outside of the acceptable names. I tell her that she is helping to create a teenage world that more kids can feel a part of. Sadly, she is unimpressed with my logic.

Just when you think you are done with the shopping you are reminded about the pressing need for school supplies. How many funky pens and flashy binders does one require to excel in school? But this is nothing compared to the electronic requirements to learn these days. One must have a computer, a printer, printer ink and computer cases. I remember when the school board just issued students a few colourless notebooks and some pens and pencils. Nevertheless, I hate to discourage excitement about school and learning, so I tend to give generously in this area.

On the drive back home, the kids retreat to their cell phones. I am enjoying a few minutes of peacefulness as we return to the farm. I'm secretly feeling proud that they have achieved a moment of harmony they rarely experience. Tyler in the front seat and Megan in the back, they seem uncharacteristically content. Just as I'm feeling wistful to think of them growing up so fast, Megan suddenly shrieks from the back, almost causing me to veer off the road. Recovering my equilibrium and trying to keep the car in the correct lane, I scream "what the hell is going on?" in a very non-parental tone.

"Tyler said I look like a hippo in my new jeans!" she accused.

"What are you talking about? He hasn't said anything." I look over at Tyler who is sitting angelically in the front seat, looking equally confused.

As I have been calmly reflecting, sweet little Tyler has been texting a series of horrendous insults to Megan. So much for harmony.

The binders are purchased, the clothes are chosen, the knapsacks are organized, and in a few weeks, they will head out the door in new directions.

-29-

It's odd we haven't had any mail in weeks. I check the box daily and nothing. Usually there's a bill or two. I enjoy my amble down the long driveway on an August afternoon, Wilbur following at my heels. It's nice to not have much more on my mind than whether there's mail. I'm dreading September and all the commotion it brings. It's actually going to be hard to leave this farm.

Megan and Zach, the horse feeder, are now officially 'an item'. They don't seem to care so much about the horses anymore as they do about each other. From what I know, Zach seems like a nice young man. I'm not sure he would fit in with Megan's regular friend group, who enjoy following fashion trends and hanging out at the mall. Zach seems more down to earth. He usually sports a tee shirt, a pair of jeans and a plaid baseball hat. He lives on a farm and is currently busy helping his Dad with the haying, something I had never heard of before. Regardless, he seems quite taken with Megan and appears to be fitting her into his schedule despite his long hours in the field. This evening he came by in a tractor to pick her up. Tyler thought it was hilarious until he realized he had to feed the horses himself.

While Megan and Zach were out for a spin around the field, Tyler and I headed to the barn to manage the livestock. Neither of us had a clue what we were doing. Bolt and Zippy meandered into the barn after us. Motivated by oats, they dutifully filed into their stalls to await their portion. There's nothing to this. What had been taking Megan and Zach so long with each feeding? Tyler was in Zippy's stall, gently patting her neck and pulling some burrs from her mane. He chatted with her amiably as she powered through her oats. Zippy soon turned to nuzzle him for a carrot which he promptly produced from his pocket. How nice to see him laugh as she rubbed her nose against him, eager for more. Imagine being that excited to consume vegetables. Bolt whinnied for his portion and Tyler soon did the same for him. Tyler's such a gentle soul, I'm not surprised the animals take to him easily. It was refreshing to pry him away from his electronics and spend a little time with him, even if it was in a barn full of manure.

When we returned to the house, I downloaded the pictures of Megan on the tractor and Tyler brushing the horses. They would be ideal for my next Facebook post. As I scrolled through my feed, I noticed a few new posts from someone I didn't recognize. Who is this 'friend' who has been liking so many of my comments and pictures? I was puzzled that we had several mutual friends. Her recent post said that she was "off sick for two more weeks". I don't know who she is or when I accepted her friend request. She doesn't look familiar.

When I was in town, I stopped by the post office to inquire about our mail. "We haven't had any for a while," I explained to the bored looking woman behind the counter.

"What concession line are you on?" she asked without looking up.

When I told her, she replied nonchalantly.

"You're on Kathy's route. She's been away sick with a burst appendix, but she should be back soon," she explained, totally unconcerned with medical privacy or my postal rights.

Dumbfounded, I simply responded, "I hope she's feeling better." I was stunned to think our mail was being held while the postal worker recovered. Surely, they have back up. This would never happen in Toronto. The worker behind the counter handed me our pile of bills. It was then it dawned on me, 'Kathy Ellis' that's her, my Facebook friend who's been sick. She must have added me when we moved in for the summer. Poor Kathy. I'll have to leave a card for her in the mailbox when she returns. I wouldn't have thought to do that a few months ago.

It's so smoky. I'm having a lot of trouble breathing these days. I wonder if those racoons are in my chimney again?

Sunday, May 6, 1900

We've decided to have a memorial planting at the end of the laneway. One maple tree for Daniel and one for Nell, standing across from each other at the entrance to the farm. That way we will always have a pleasant memory of them standing there together, greeting us as we enter.

This afternoon, after the Sunday noon dinner the family made a rather sad procession along the lane to the carriageway. Rev. Mactavish had come with his wife and children as had many neighbours from the concession. It was a drizzly, cool, overcast afternoon as we gathered for the tribute. The birds were out but thankfully the bugs were not in season yet. Morten and Chuck dug the holes, and the saplings were planted. The girls huddled together as we all bowed our heads for a prayer of remembrance. Rev. Mactavish offered a blessing,

"God, we pray that these fine maples live a cherished life just as the two, fine souls they represent. May all who pass beneath their branches be reminded of the lives of Daniel and Nell."

"Amen," we all echoed in unison followed by each of us shovelling a little dirt on the trees. The memorial over, Ida, Laura, Morten and I lingered to take in the scene. It has all been so sudden. I'm glad we have an enduring reminder of them. Each time I pass here, I will think of them both.

So far, no one else seems to be stricken with this ruthless disease, but that fear is never far from our minds.

Nell will never meet her baby sister or brother, who is currently tumbling about in my belly. Someday soon, Ida, Laura, the boys and I will make a trip to town to see what wallpapers the general store has to offer. I am hoping for a floral pattern for the sitting room and maybe, if cost permits, for our room. After all, the baby will need something cheery to look at. I realize the more I lounge the worse I feel, I must keep busy, or I may never get up. I know it is an extravagance to spend hard-earned money on wallpaper, but Morten insists it is needed. I will make a point to stop by and see Alice too. Mary is wanting to come as well. No doubt she 'requires' some items at the store, such as 'a handsome young man to court'. Perhaps it would be a nice diversion for her.

I received a lengthy post from Rose this morning. She is ecstatic to find that she's inherited a piano from her neighbour. Rose is delighted about this as she has not been able to play in years, since her old piano gave out and Patrick refused to replace it. In fact, she used to go over to the neighbour's to practice. The old gal loved Rose's music and often invited her to play for her, while Rose was over delivering eggs. It was the highpoint of Rose's life, and probably the neighbour's too. They struck up quite a friendship. When she passed, Rose learned, much to her delight, that the piano had been left to her. Apparently, it will be lifted over next week by the woman's sons and placed in Rose's parlour, despite Patrick's disapproval. He wanted it in the barn! Imagine that, beautiful classical music for the cows. What a lump-head, not to say what the winter weather would do to the instrument. I don't know how Rose won the battle, but she did. She must have finally put her foot down. Anyway, she has invited me to tea once it's in place and says she will play me a 'concert'. New wallpaper, a piano concert, the baby is lively... perhaps life will begin to improve.

-30-

August is quickly disappearing and soon September chaos will be in full swing. What really makes September chaotic however, is the unending barrage of activities that re-commence. Gone are the long summer evenings sipping wine on the lawn. Instead, the days grow shorter and bring an explosion of commitments. As always, this will require an elaborate schedule of driving to make it all happen. The big question is of course, where will we be?

Matt and I like it here and the doctor has recently extended my leave another six weeks. In an attempt to avoid conflict, we haven't yet told the kids that we are considering staying longer at the farm. This would mean they would do their first term of school locally. Imagine the outrage!

We're still undecided as the busyness of returning home is about to begin. I crave extra coffee and additional iron supplements just to get through it all. No doubt we will quickly revert to boxes of frozen meals laced with way too much salt and fat and convenience, which we worked so hard to avoid all summer. More importantly, it means gearing up for life again. I'm just not there yet despite the increased dose of anti-anxiety medication.

Matt and I have always said to the kids that they must have one activity (to keep them engaged in life). To put that in perspective, that is 2 kids X 1 activity = 2 commitments during the week and usually X2 if you include weekend games or performances = sometimes 4 commitments per week and then if Matt and I want to do one thing each, such as a book club, or hockey, add 2 more = 6 commitments beyond school, homework and the office. Just doing the math weighs me down.

It is hard to forget those blow out arguments we'd overhear at our next-door neighbours in Toronto. Sitting on the back patio on a spring evening we were constantly reminded how stressed Jill and Mike were with their young family. Jill's work as a nurse was exhausting with the 12 hour shifts, alternating days and nights. As a police officer, Mike could relate to the stress of a fluctuating schedule and the accompanying fatigue. Their conflicting work schedules made it challenging finding daycare for their children, not to mention sleep or couple time. This does not even take into account Jill's three kids from her previous marriage. Her 9- and 12-year-old live with them. Her oldest daughter lives with her dad an hour away, and visits Mom occasionally. Mike has two teens with his ex. They are supposed to visit every second weekend. One would need a colour coded calendar to map this schedule. Despite hearing these blowouts nightly, we're still confused who visits when.

Mike's sons' rep hockey includes practices, games, tournaments and travel time and then there's the daughter's competitive dance schedule. Jill and Mike's four-year-old loves her swimming lessons, so that can't be missed. Their toddler goes to daycare across town because there isn't yet a space for him at the school daycare where his sister attends. I'm hyperventilating just listening to it all.

Jill despises her ex because he never pays child support on time. He's usually over an hour late when the kids visit, leaving her stranded at the mid-point doughnut store parking lot with an impatient two-year-old. Mike's kids don't want to visit anymore. The fifteen-year-old has his own life now and avoids Mike and the new 'siblings'. Jill's nine-year-old girl struggles with social anxiety. According to Mike's full volume complaint, she has significant difficulty leaving her mother's side and remaining in her own bed at night. Jill's oldest daughter, who resides with Dad, is a rebel. Her marks are slipping because she has been known to ditch school and hang out at the mall. There is suspicion that she has been smoking (various substances) and was spotted holding hands with a boy who looked about 18. When she tried living with her mother, Mom could not 'contain' her defiant behaviour. She frequently swore at Mike in the presence of her younger half siblings. Bio Dad apparently did nothing but sabotage Mom's efforts at limit-setting, so Mom eventually said, "Fine, you take her." Her younger brother is a sweet boy who struggles with ADD/ADHD. He has difficulty keeping up in school and even remaining at his desk. Mom feels they should follow through with the paediatrician's prescription that would 'help him focus' but Dad refuses, so that is on hold for now.

The tension between Mike and his son can be heard down the block. His younger sister is a perfectionist who tries to please everyone. I almost forgot about her, which I think happens at home too. However, there is mounting concern about a possible eating disorder, although she denies it.

Mike dislikes his job. He is feeling increasingly frustrated at home as intimacy is non-existent and fun, lighthearted times are scarce. Jill is overwhelmed at work due to continuous cutbacks and workplace politics. Teetering on the brink of depression, she constantly worries about those attractive mothers hovering around the arena at the rep hockey tournaments. Life is far from simple. In fact, it is quite complicated at times, and the schedule is only part of it. These are our city neighbours to our left. You should hear the couple on the right.

I realize there are neighbourhoods and cities full of people living similar scenarios. At times, life has become nothing more than mere survival. Addiction, affairs, suicide, gambling start to look pretty inviting to escape the tedium. It almost makes one envy Isabel and Morten's family and their simple life on the farm, with little money and few distractions. Maybe that's part of why I'm considering staying a little longer.

Stay as long as you like Amy. It's nice to have you here. I'm enjoying watching your young family come to life.

Tuesday, May 8, 1900

It's been a very difficult week. The evenings are the worst. We gather in the sitting room and try to play games, but it is just too heavy a feel. The only one who seems to be in a brighter mood, oddly, is Laura. I would have thought the death of her father would have put her over the edge. Instead, she seems to be improving. The only sense I can make of that is that perhaps Chuck's attention is brightening her spirits. Surely, she can't be seriously enamored with him. Of course, he's a decent fellow but I would have thought a bit simple for Laura. Laura enjoys a book, reads plenty of scripture and is musical as well. I'm not even sure Chuck is able to read. Chuck is a reliable and good-natured person, perhaps he could make a workable husband. Certainly, he's better than that scoundrel Patrick.

Rose has invited me over for a recital, which I'm very much looking forward to. I desperately need a change of atmosphere. Farm work is relentless. It seems impossible to steal away for even a few moments, let alone an afternoon.

As I write this, the oil in my lamp is burning low, and I may lose the light. Nevertheless, I must tell about how pleased Mary is to be coming along for the wallpaper outing tomorrow. All the women know why she is so cheery but none of us would mention it. After all, love is a sensitive topic and I know she would be mortified if she knew we were all exchanging knowing smiles behind her back. I just hope he doesn't break her heart. He's a fine young man. I imagine he has many suitors.

Apparently, his mother Alice hasn't been able to do any cooking or cleaning and the house is in quite a state. The neighbours are helping but it is an ongoing project. They are starting to talk though because Alice doesn't appear to be trying to help herself. Instead, she just sits there weepy, withdrawn and feeling sorry for herself. I must admit, it is hard to understand what ails her.

I can hear the girls chattering away in their room. I don't know how they ever get any rest. There are times I hear them arguing but then they are sisters. It must feel very different in that bedroom knowing Nell will never return to it.

Friday, May 11th, 1900

Henry has just alerted us that day has dawned. And what a beautiful day it is, lovely and warm with the sun rising into a cloudless sky. The birds are just arising themselves and we can hear their banter outside our open window. For the first time in a while, I feel grateful for life. Morten is pleased to see his growing wife more energetic, something I guess he hasn't seen much recently. "My what wonders a little wallpaper will do," he teased. "Chuck will take you ladies in after breakfast, but please get back before supper."

"I will Morten. I know exactly what I'm looking for – and so does Mary."

"Well, if you come back with some wallpaper and a son in law, it will surely have been a worthwhile trip," he quipped.

Ida is staying home to prepare the noon day meal for the men but is sending me with one of her strawberry pies for Alice. It's bound to cheer her.

Mary has done her hair in a lovely braid and has a spring dress on. I notice Laura has begun to 'lighten' the colour of her wardrobe, suggesting that she is emerging from her period of mourning. How ironic. Now I am the one grieving and melancholy. As Chuck offers us each his hand to help us into the carriage, I notice he manages to hold Laura's just a little longer than is necessary. Clearly there is some fire between them. Laura sits up front with Chuck while Mary, Lyle, Doug and I are in the back. What a beautiful day for a carriage ride. I have my purse with the money that Morten has counted out and Mary and I tuck it into a safe place between us. Once we reach the end of the concession, there is some traffic on the carriageway. We pass by a few buggies and riders. The roads are pleasantly dry today as it hasn't rained in days. I notice the Connollys have a new horse in their field which looks extremely fast and spirited. I don't know how they can afford such extravagances, but I know they travel to town regularly so no doubt the extra speed is helpful. Barney trots along at a steady pace. His legs are sound and that is what's important, especially now that Scarlet is gone.

The town is bustling with activity. Everyone is out and about, preparing to plant their vegetable gardens. People in town are so nicely dressed, I must admit I feel a little shabby. Chuck stopped at the livery downtown. Little Lyle and Doug are overwhelmed with all the excitement. As Lyle is young still, his walking cannot be depended upon and so we three women will be his cart horses. Doug takes Mary's hand very agreeably. He's given to dart off when he sees something that catches his eye thereby creating a handful for Mary who's trying hard not to mess her hair. Chuck stays behind to tend to the horse, while the five of us meander down the street. Laura has a permanent smile on her face announcing to all that the woman in half mourning garb is

shamelessly courting. Mary, on the other hand, is noticeably anxious and distracted as she holds Doug's hand tightly, much to his disapproval. Her eyes scan the busy road for a sighting of her beloved. She adjusts her dress and fixes her hair. "You look terrific," I tell her. She shoots me a scowl that suggests I'm not to have noticed her preoccupation with her appearance.

We arrived at the general store and made our way toward the housewares to locate the wallpaper. Oh my, they were beautiful. I eventually picked a large floral pattern that was bright and cheery, with lovely multi coloured gladioli and chrysanthemums throughout. It is the latest style so we will be fashionable and current as we begin the new century.

The store was busy with lots of people coming and going. As I wandered along the aisles, a gentleman asked if I could assist him. He introduced himself as Stephen and we chatted briefly. He explained that he was trying to pick a present for his fiancé, Beatrix. He wondered which scent of perfume did I think would make the best gift. He was such a good humoured and intelligent fellow. Isn't it sad that Rose couldn't have met a fine man like him.

Mary's eyes darted about nervously, and it wasn't long before James appeared to serve us. He was delighted to see Mary and he greeted her warmly. Mary, though blushing, feigned surprise and returned his attention, with a slightly flirtatious air. It was hard to get his attention back on the wallpaper and let us not forget, that was the true purpose of our trip. Finally, he lifted the additional wallpaper rolls down from the top shelf while Mary furtively looked on. James topped the experience off by giving Doug and Lyle some peppermints, thereby securing his favour with the boys, not to mention Mary.

"How's your mother, James?" I asked.

"She's about the same Mrs. Huntly. Thanks for asking," he replied.

"We will be sure to visit her on the way home," I assured.

Mary was overjoyed when James asked if he could escort her on a picnic with his family. She asked my permission and of course I consented, knowing Morten would be agreeable. Much flirtation and smiling ensued from both sides and finally we emerged from the general store with a bundle of wallpaper, not to mention everything else we had come for.

We returned to the livery where Chuck had Barney watered and ready. Lyle was being an absolute handful and was long overdue for a nap, as we turned down Cowbell Lane to pay a visit to Alice.

When we stopped at the MacNally homestead, it appeared no one was home. The curtains were drawn, the garden was overgrown, and the porch looked as though it hadn't been swept in weeks. I entered the porch uneasily and rapped on the door. No one came. I called through the screen and eventually I heard Alice reply from within. I let myself in and there she was in the dark, stuffy parlour, lying on the couch and having a rest in the middle of the day.

"Alice, how are you?" I enquired, but I could see that she was not well. She attempted a weary smile and held out her hand. As I took it, I tried to think of some encouraging words.

"I brought you one of Ida's pies. I thought you might like it."

"Thank you," was all she managed with a half-smile.

She looked gaunt and pale, and it was clear she needed more than a strawberry pie to lift her spirits. I told her about our encounter with her son James just now. I was desperate for subjects to discuss, and I thought that might cheer her. However, she didn't appear to care. I held her hand as we exchanged pleasantries. To be honest, I didn't really know how to reach her. I reassured her that I would pray for her as would our congregation. Just as I was leaving after our short visit, Will came in from the back garden and greeted me. He was delighted to see me and thanked me for dropping by. Regards to Morten and the family, he called out as we departed in the carriage. We exchanged a friendly wave, but I had a bad feel about the situation.

Melancholia is a strange thing. Alice used to be such a cheery person. I don't know what has befallen her. Morten's sister Florence said that she had heard that Alice had lost a pregnancy, but who knows. I can't imagine where Florence gets such news from. Poor Alice. She has only one child, James, despite their marriage of many years. I know she always wanted more. I can't imagine the pain she would feel at losing one now. However, she's getting on in years. Who will look after them as they age? Who will continue her parents' farm after the sudden death of her brother last summer? Will her family name die out and the farm be sold? Alice must feel such disappointment. Thank goodness I had a shawl around me concealing my own condition of five months gestation. Now I feel such shame that I have so dreaded this next addition to our plentiful family,

It was a peaceful ride home, everyone escaping to their own thoughts of the day. Laura seemed to be sitting closer to Chuck as he navigated the horse around the bumps and ruts on the carriageway. Thankfully, Lyle has fallen off to sleep and Doug is consumed with his peppermints. Mary is gazing off in the distance, no doubt dreaming of the upcoming picnic. My own thoughts are filled with guilt that I have not been more thankful for this new life growing inside me. My daydreams are consumed with a mixture of floral wallpaper and the death of my sweet daughter, soon to be buried in the churchyard. No amount of spritely wallpaper can make me forget my Nell.

Monday, May 14, 1900

The rain is teeming down. I do hope Rose will make the trip anyway, despite the inclement weather. It's just Ida, Doug, Lyle and I here by the hearth. Ida is working on a blanket for the baby. I've had two cups of tea and several trips to the outhouse and still no Rose. Lyle is amusing himself with Ida's wool and Doug has been busy with some building blocks that Chuck made him from some spare wood in the barn. Chuck is a kind soul. His thoughtful construction grants much peace to us ladies who must entertain a busy little boy day in and day out.

Ah... finally. The sound of hooves trotting in the lane. My spirits are lifted. I'd know her mare a mile away. It is pure black with a big white blaze down its face and long white socks to match. The rain is coming down in buckets now. It's great weather for the garden.

We had a wonderful day together. I was delighted to see her again and I thought she looked well. Perhaps the piano is agreeing with her. Edward, Rose's farm hand, was very attentive to her as always and I could see that they have become devoted friends. I invited him in, but he would not hear of it (thankfully). Instead, he headed to the barn to get a dry stall for the mare and catch up with Chuck. Perhaps those two have much in common.

We talked in the sitting room where the children were engrossed in building a fort with cushions, which left Rose and I some time to catch up. Apparently, Patrick has been drinking more lately. Not much of a surprise! Clearly when Patrick stays too late at the tavern, Rose has found another shoulder to lean on. I'm torn and I told her so. I want her to be happy, but I do worry that she is straying into dangerous territory. She assures me there is no need to worry, that she and Edward are merely friends. Personally, I think she is playing with fire.

Perhaps I'm naïve. After all, I've never had to worry about that. Morten and I met in school when we were just kids, and our families had known each other for years. I took a liking to him right away. Back then he was slim and athletic and always kind to the younger children. I will never forget my first day of school. I was shyly standing off to the side, watching the kids play tag. He came over, dressed in his beaten-up overalls, and said, "do you want to play?" Being painfully bashful, I said "no thank you." That didn't stop Morten, he smiled and said, "you mean you'd rather stand here by this tree stump all by yourself, than join us?" He was pleasantly insistent that the tree stump was not the place for me, and he was right. If left to my own devices, I'd probably be standing there still. From that point on, I had a soft spot in my heart for Morten.

I can't imagine what it would be like to be married to someone who was unkind and who didn't seem to have your best interests in mind, so how can I judge Rose? I'm glad she has Edward to keep her company. Perhaps even the Good Lord can understand her dilemma.

I've known her all my life and I know something is off. Her countenance is a strange mix of elation and preoccupation, but I don't want to meddle. Over tea we talk about everything. The conversation inevitably leads to Nell and how I am faring. As I tearfully relate my struggles, she is supportive as always. We discuss wallpapers, the trip to town, Mary and James, my pregnancy, Evelyn Barclay and her nauseatingly perfect children, my suspicions of Laura's growing admiration for Chuck, but we steer clear of the untouchable subject of her fixation with Edward. Finally, I can't stand it anymore. "Rose what are you doing? I can see how you feel about Edward. Be careful," I plead.

"Issy, you know me. I won't do anything stupid. I just get so lonely, and he is always such a good friend to me. It is hard to resist friendship when Patrick is

so unkind. I know I have a little soft spot for Ed. I won't let it go anywhere, but I can't let go of it, otherwise I have nothing. Finally, my life has a little glimmer of meaning, I have the children, and good friends like you and Ed and now I even have the piano. These are my reasons to continue."

Life with Patrick must be hell. He is such a fool. I can hardly blame her for her 'extra-curricular' interests, but I'm nervous for her all the same. I believe she's kidding herself regarding the depth of her connection to Edward.

After a lovely afternoon together, Edward takes her hand to help her into the carriage. I can see the sparkle in her eye and I'm secretly happy for her. It must be tiresome being alone. I imagine some marriages make you feel even more alone than if you were unwed.

-31-

The lightning flashed and the thunder cracked in almost intertwined succession. The rain was pouring down on the tin farmhouse roof and Wilbur was shaking like a leaf, nestled securely under my arm. Megan huddled a little closer as the three of us snuggled on the couch under a blanket. The power of those crashes made us all feel vulnerable. Tyler emerged from his bedroom, annoyed that his internet had abruptly cut out along with all the lights in his room.

"What's going on with the power?" he shouted from the top of the stairs.

"It's a black out," I hollered over the thunder.

He was down the stairs in a flash. The rain was pelting down in torrents and the wind was magnificent. You could hear the tree branches brushing against the window. We sat on the couch, watching the powerful storm in the dark. Finally, Megan located a candle and some matches.

"How long will this storm last?" she asked, clearly shaken by the crashing bangs of the world outside. There were split seconds when the entire lawn was illuminated with a flash of eerie, bluish light. It was breathtaking to feel the power of nature right outside the living room window. The eye of the storm passed within a few minutes, but the power remained out for hours. Even the water and plumbing were off. Through it all, the old clock ticked along methodically. To pass the time, Megan told us about one of her friends who had been texting some snobby messages to her. Tyler vented his irritation about being stuck at a discouraging level in his video game. I shared how much I enjoyed walking Wilbur down a country road, without doggie bags. We all laughed. Why did I never do this before? I guess the lights had to go out before I could see what I normally don't.

-32-

I've recently learned the pear tree is over a hundred years old. When I first saw it in late spring, it looked like a scruffy, short tree in the middle of the lawn. By the time we moved here, it was covered in pretty, white blooms. With my limited horticultural knowledge, I had no idea what beautiful pears it could produce. As time went on, Matt and I noticed the tiny pear shaped 'bulbs' growing on the branches. By mid-September, I've been told the tree will be covered with the tastiest pears around. Imagine having perpetual fruit and all we've done to the tree is admire it.

The vegetation on this farm is beautiful and abundant despite our lack of gardening abilities. The previous family must have truly understood the land. The crop of perennials remind us that there were people on this farm before us. How much change those towering maples at the end of the driveway must have seen in their lifetime.

With their expansive width and height, their branches stretch over the yard providing welcome shade on a hot summer day. They are lots of fun to climb or hang a swing from, and the host of birds and squirrels they are home to, is lengthy in number and variety. I have come to enjoy reading in the hammock under these majestic maples. In early spring their sap runs, in summer, they provide shade and when fall arrives, their radiant leaves will be spectacular.

You can imagine my horror this morning when a township truck pulled up with a team of men, clad in orange vests and began marking 'X's' on random maples up and down the road. God forbid, those beautiful maple trees sporting big florescent 'X's' in the middle of their stately trunks!

Ditching my morning coffee, I raced out the door clad only in my slippers and housecoat. "What is going on here?" I demanded of the men.

"These trees are on town land ma'am, and they are going to have to come out for the road widening and paving next spring," he said as he took in my housecoat.

"What are you talking about? What widening and paving? These trees are on private property," feeling suddenly protective of our rental farm.

"Well, no ma'am, those three at the end of the driveway are actually on township land. They are going to have to come out as this road will be widened six metres on each side for the new housing development," he responded indifferently while turning back to his task.

I felt sick to my stomach. These trees were planted in memory of Daniel and Nell. Although I will have returned to the city long before the road improvements occur, I found myself mourning the eventual loss. I considered how the corduroy roads kept fools from racing down the concession at breakneck speed. One can drive down paved roads anywhere, but only in the country can you find a genuine and charming dirt road. The traffic is light to begin with, so the thought of increasing its width seemed ludicrous. I guess the housing development will change all that. This paving became even more offensive as it involved not only lopping down beautiful, shade giving branches but entire maple trees that had stood on this site long before these workmen were born, probably before their parents were born. Surely, we wouldn't chop down our history just for a smoother ride.

The maples that stand at the end of our driveway, reminders of the cherished lives of Daniel and Nell, now sport a big orange X. In a world that is striving to be more 'environmentally friendly', surely we can grant some compassion and appreciation for a few hundred year old maple trees which produce the very leaf featured on our flag. If I waste a few pieces of paper or fail to recycle an envelope,

I am riddled with guilt for not being more green. However, if a township truck drives down the road and heartlessly levels a row of century old maples, no one bats an eye. Both are crimes against the environment but surely one is a greater injustice than the other.

I've been watching those 'homes' go in across the road. They throw those kids up in a few weeks. From what I can see, they don't seem like they're built from much. I don't understand how they will stay standing on those flimsy foundations? Where are their stone cellars and their heavy timbers? How will they breathe so close together? Where will their families plant a garden or even a tree? There's no way they'll last 142 years, like me. Poor kids. They don't stand a chance out here on this windswept ridge. One of them has a crack in his foundation already.

-33-

I'm so tired of trying to lose weight. Maybe it would be easier to just get rid of all my mirrors. If I thought that would do the trick, I would do it. However, I will still be reminded when my pants are too tight or I step on the scale (which I avoid). It's not fair. I'm very careful with my diet. I go to the gym regularly, even when I don't feel like it. I should look shapely, but I certainly don't. It seems so unjust. I didn't used to be heavy but over the last twenty years my weight has crept up. I must have put on twenty pounds since university. At a pound a year, what will I look like by eighty?

How did this happen? I feel a pressing need to destroy all pictures of myself. I always try to portray my most flattering angle, which I have yet to find. Despite my caution, the pounds creep on. My cell is loaded with my favourite tunes which carry me through forty-five minutes of mindless workouts on the cross trainer and the treadmill. I don't have much more time or inclination to devote to my physique and it shows. I fall mid-way between two-hour intense gym workouts and a total couch potato.

I think I'm reasonable in my approach but clearly, I need to do more. It scares me to admit this, but maybe I should cut out wine. That's a big price to pay just to wear a bathing suit a couple of times a year. Perhaps I can live with the extra twenty pounds. Life without alcohol, seems like an oxymoron. I don't drink much but I do enjoy a glass of wine from time to time. It really takes the edge off. However, that has got to be a few hundred calories a day. Multiply that by thirty days in a month and that's a few pounds right there - but an immensely satisfying few pounds I might add. Damn. I'll have to think about this. One of my friends told me that she cut out wine and dropped fifteen pounds in four months. That's both inspirational and depressing. I will sip this glass slowly as it might be my last for a while.

Saturday, May 19, 1900

Today Mary had her 'date' with James. From the moment she awoke she has been a bundle of excitement, racing through her morning chores, preparing some sandwiches to contribute to the picnic basket, brushing her hair endlessly. Ida and I have been watching this morning's preparations with delight. I hope all goes well.

The MacNally carriage arrived right on time. Their large bay gelding was beautifully turned out and his coat glowed as though James had groomed him for hours, in order to make a noticeable impression. In his hand was a lovely bouquet of freshly picked wildflowers, encircled with a ribbon. Mary was quite the young lady receiving this treasure and her cheeks turned a shade of crimson upon being presented with his gift. James stepped into the house and awkwardly greeted Ida and me. We gingerly waived to Will and Alice from the porch, not wanting to indulge in a full visit which might cramp the style of the two young suitors. It was good to see Alice out for a little change of environment. James is a nice boy and from a good home. We had a brief visit with him at the door as Mary gathered her things. One could feel their nervous anticipation as he helped her into the buggy. I'm sure they'll have a lovely time.

I thought of them often throughout the afternoon. As any mother, I was beginning to worry a little that perhaps I hadn't prepared Mary enough for how to conduct herself in the presence of a young man. Ida rested her hand on my shoulder as we later awaited their return on the porch. "They will be fine," she reassured me. "I have no doubt James will be a perfect gentleman. Besides Will and Alice are there to chaperone," Ida reminded me.

We sipped our tea on the front porch and eventually the carriage rounded the corner with the young couple in front. Both were glowing and had an empty picnic basket beside them. As James walked her to the porch, it was clear there was a volt of electricity between them.

"Where did you picnic?" I inquired.

"By the willow tree at the end of Mossy Stonecrop Trail," James responded.

"The creek is lovely there and the trilliums are countless," he continued.

Apparently, the picnic had been a great success. Of course, Mary had many interested sisters peering out the front window who will no doubt be pressing for more details.

Mary is becoming quite a young lady. Morten and I need to prepare ourselves for suitors and her eventual departure from our home in the next few years. She is almost eighteen and sooner or later, this is bound to happen. She has a good head on her shoulders, and I hope that she finds a husband with a kind heart. I sure don't want her ending up with someone like Patrick.

Nevertheless, Nell inevitably dominates my thoughts. How does a mother proceed? It takes so much energy to keep my mind busy, but it keeps reverting back to Nell the second my thoughts are idle. I'm hoping the new baby will take my mind to cheerier places. I'm so sad that 'he' will never meet his big sister. The whole thing seems surreal. Here I go feeling sorry for myself again, but I can't help it. When you've carried a child inside you and then spend fifteen years caring and nurturing her, to see her wiped out by disease is devastating. Why couldn't it have been me instead? My pillow is wet with tears.

-34-

I've reflected about the wine and decided to stick with the twenty pounds.

Despite our seriously depleted bank account, I was so relieved when Dr Neal renewed my leave for eight more weeks. Matt will be relieved that we can prolong our stay. In fact, he had already called the realtor to check to see if we could extend the rental beyond the summer. The family was agreeable as their elderly mother was experiencing some indecision about the retirement home. Now that it's nearing the end of August we really need to have a talk with the kids. I'm not looking forward to this.

Wilbur and I set off for our daily walk down the concession road. Walking Wilbur used to be such a chore, especially the pick-up. At first this was puzzling to Wilbur. After doing his business, he would wait politely while I cleaned up after him. Since moving to the farm for the summer, he no longer expects this kind of service and I'm happy not to provide it. I don't recommend walking in the bushes on the far side of the ditch, but then there aren't pedestrians there anyway.

In fact, the only bag I carry is a canvas grocery bag. There is a fantastic roadside stand that the local farmer has which is filled with fresh produce. Everything I can't grow is thriving on his acreage a few doors down. You know it's a trustworthy neighbourhood when he can leave his cash box in the centre of the table and expect it to be there when he returns. You simply put your cash in the box, make whatever change you need and take your goods. Imagine trying that at a busy, downtown intersection in the city.

When Wilbur and I walk, the road is usually empty. However, on this particular day, I catch sight of a disheveled looking fellow strolling along the road towards me. Immediately, my inner, urban radar swings into high alert. I can't see him well from a distance, and I wonder where he's headed. Maybe for the cash box on the farm table? Should I turn around? He hasn't posed any threat to me. Would that be rude? ...especially as he's the only other person on this isolated road. I decided to stay the course. The closer I got, the more I questioned my choice. Wilbur however, was ecstatic to meet some company walking along the concession. He bounded toward the fellow, and before I knew it, was chaotically jumping up and licking him. This is out of character for Wilbur who has been well schooled in stranger danger. Despite Wilbur's immense size, he is a total coward. This is a dog who cowers under our bed with the slightest rumble of thunder. If we hear a coyote in the night, he's immediately in bed between us, shaking like a leaf. Why would he have such uncalled-for positive regard for this stranger?

I pulled Wilbur down and apologized profusely. The man was very gracious and forgiving and took the whole thing in stride. We got to talking briefly, and it turns out he operates the pig farm down the road and was on route to the corn stand for his dinner fixings for tonight. No doubt the scent of swine was wildly exciting to Wilbur's sensitive nose, hence his unruly behaviour. I had never seen Wilbur quite so animated, and it wasn't long before he escaped my grasp and was hurtling down the road towards the field of pigs. I hollered at him but to no avail. They obviously didn't train for this in dog school. It was then that the kindly pig farmer took off at a sprint and eventually captured him for me. I thanked him abundantly for retrieving Wilbur. I was ashamed to think that moments earlier, I was considering dodging this man altogether simply because he was clad in his farming clothes.

Since moving to this farm, my eyes have been opened. Fancy lavender soaps and fine attire aren't everything. I've come to learn that one can have 'fragrance of swine' on the outside but have a very kind heart on the inside, which is most important of all.

-35-

I'm in a coffee line up when my cell phone rings. I let it go to voicemail. It rings again, I glance at the number and realize it's my brother and it may be important. I have him on speed dial since Dad's decline.

"Allan, what's going on? Is everything okay?" My medium with milk now in hand, I step outside.

"Amy, he died about thirty minutes ago. Sharon (the caregiver) said he had been sitting up in bed looking out the window, then he smiled, closed his eyes, gasped a few times and was gone."

"Oh my God. That's unbelievable. Are you there now?" I responded in a panic.

"I just got here. Mom is pretty shaken up. She's with him and I've called the funeral home."

"I can't believe it," I hear myself saying. The man was 92 and in failing health. What did I think was going to happen? Why am I so shocked?

It seems that's the way death is. You think you are all prepared for it and then it just slips up and nips you from behind and you are caught in a state of disbelief. It's just, he's never died before.

Allan and I talk for several minutes. I talk to Mom. I call Matt... I call my sister. We are all crying. My cell battery is running low. Eventually, I remember I must dash over and pick up Tyler at the computer store. I tell him the news as soon as he gets in the car. Tyler is shaken. Once the initial information sinks in, his eventual question is whether he will have to go to the funeral. "Yes," I respond emphatically. It speaks volumes as to the relationship my father had nurtured with his grandson.

It's been a long day. I was glad to get home to a big, reassuring hug from Matt. I realize all we really have is each other - our friends, our family, our loved ones. Having someone to hold you when you're upset is pretty darn nice.

Tuesday, May 22, 1900

Chores, chores, chores... Is that all there is to life? I wake in the morning to Henry's call at dawn and I'm on the go all day until the sun sets. Every morning, the same exhausting routine of getting the children organized for school, then helping with breakfast and dishes. Thank goodness I have lots of helpers. In addition to minding Doug - Ida, Laura and I have all the household jobs: tending the fire, mending, washing, cleaning, collecting eggs, baking bread, preparing meals, weeding the garden, assisting with homework. It is never ending. By the time we gather around the fire in the evening I can barely keep my eyes open. However, my quiet time with the children is my favourite part of day. I love hearing Mary read from the bible or Laura play the piano as Ida knits and the girls play cards. Evenings are just nice to be together. Now that the days are growing longer, we can sit out on the porch.

It seems like just yesterday when little Nell arrived, right here, both conceived and delivered in this very bed. She was my second born and I remember it well. The delivery was lengthy and painful as always, but I had Ida and Rose to help. Nell's birth was a good seven hours, but it felt like forever. I remember it was not until after midnight when it began and then the sun was up when she arrived because I recall the rooster. I remember worrying that Mary would awaken soon, and I couldn't go to her in my state. Nell cooed so softly as Ida wrapped her in a little blanket and put her on my chest. To lose one in pregnancy is hard enough, but to lose a daughter fifteen years into her vibrant young life is another thing altogether. I hope I did enough by her. I feel I abandoned her when I couldn't hold her in her final days.

Morten and I decided we'll have the internment in early June. By then the soil will be dug and we don't need to delay the sad task any longer than we must.

I know Morten is worried about money. He has so many mouths to feed and children to clothe and no one to help him now that Daniel has gone so suddenly. Chuck is tremendous but he's not a brother or a son. One of our milking cows is sick so that is another financial worry to Morten. I have reassured him I will tighten up on kitchen supplies to help make ends meet. We can make do with less flour and sugar if need be. I wonder if the wallpaper was too much for right now. I wouldn't know because Morten would never tell me but then again, he would never have permitted the purchase if it meant going short on an essential.

There is a church meeting later this week about prohibition. Rev Mactavish feels we really ought to come out and support this important cause. It is disgraceful how those loggers over imbibe. Apparently, the downtown is a rowdy place in the evenings making it unfit for families or couples to walk about. Ruth, from the Women's Auxiliary, lives in the house beside the tavern in Coldwater. Apparently, every night once the sun sets and the logging tools are put down for the evening, the men begin their antics. She told Ida that she hears hooting, and cursing well into the night, which is often followed by a fight. She has even seen some women there, but she will not repeat names. I'm not sure I believe that - the part about 'she will not repeat names'! I'm sure there has been plenty of discussion during the Ladies Aid meetings, names and all.

We will definitely attend Rev. Mactavish's meeting as drinking can lead to no good outcome. We would never have alcohol in this house, except in the medicine cabinet. We do have a small bottle of whiskey for pain relief if we had an emergency surgery or dental extraction or a serious farm accident. I know Evelyn once told me her father was kicked by a horse and the doctor had to set the bone.

She said she will never forget him screaming in pain. Her mother insisted he drink the whiskey from their medicine cabinet. Once he did it eventually dulled the pain, which was a blessing. I suppose there's a good use for alcohol in moments like that. She said her father was so sick the next day he spent the entire day recovering from the painkiller, not to mention the broken bone.

Saturday, May 26, 1900

My paperhanging arrived at the store and James delivered it to the house in person. Mary was quite taken aback at the surprise as she was in her chore skirt. Nevertheless, she looked beautiful as always and James was delighted to see her. I suggested the two of them walk out in the field to retrieve the goat that had broken through the fence. That would give them a little time to talk on their own while still in plain view, without a host of sisters descending on their conversation.

Ida was delighted with the wallpaper. I'm so glad as it really is her home. Eventually it will be Morten's, but I don't want to be presumptuous with the decorating.

I'm hoping the wallpaper will give the 'pick me up' that is needed in this home. While moving the couches to prepare, we disrupted some mice. What a nuisance. We'll have to bring in another hungry barn cat.

As it was Saturday, the girls were home to help. The main job was to keep Doug and Lyle entertained during the wallpapering. By the end of the afternoon the smell of vinegar, molasses, potash and lye permeated the air. The room sure didn't smell like flowers, but it looked like a field of them. We were all in great admiration at the transformation before our eyes.

This evening as we took our tea before the fire, (despite the odour) we all commented on the makeover. Mary had a rosy glow and didn't say much, her thoughts elsewhere. My little Zoe seems to gradually be recovering some of her zeal. With the fading light, I decided to turn in early. This baby is tiring me so.

It's a funny thing but as I lie in bed at night, I sometimes hear sounds by the back porch. It may be an animal but I've yet to find any evidence of any creature. For the life of me I don't know what it is. Tonight, if I hear it again, I'm going to sneak downstairs and discover what kind of critter is out there. Morten thinks it's a racoon, but it sounds bigger than that. I don't like to rouse him in the night as he needs his sleep. Maybe I'll recruit Mary to join me.

Sunday, May 27th, 1900

What egg I have on my face after last evening. The 'racoon' was back last night. I could hear it rustling around on the back porch. Mary had told me to wake her if it came again so I took her at her word. I turned the oil lamp out so as not to scare the critter off. We crept down the stairs careful not to wake anyone. Butch looked up and wagged his tail and then returned to his slumber. The only sound was the ticking of the clock. We gingerly stepped into the kitchen, nervous as to what we might find. I half expected a bear rummaging for food. Never in a million years had I expected the sight before us. As

Mary and I cautiously peeked out the window to the back porch, we could see two people in the moonlight, locked in a passionate embrace. Mary gasped. Luckily, they were so engrossed in each other they did not take notice of our presence. Laura and Chuck had their arms wrapped around each other and were exchanging a long and intimate kiss.

We looked on in astonishment. There it was right in front of us, confirmation of their involvement. This certainly explains the song in Laura's heart of late, but what can come of courting a farmhand? What life could possibly lie ahead for her? What is she doing?

Mary and I looked at each other in a mutual state of disbelief which soon collapsed into muffled giggles. Once we tiptoed back upstairs, Mary whispered to me that she had actually suspected something was alight between the two, as had I. It's hard to hide love even when you try.

This is, of course, what concerns me about Rose and Edward. I hate to think what would transpire if Patrick ever discovered her feelings for him.

As I slipped back into bed, Morten roused slightly and muttered a question, "so what was it?"

"You were right dear, it was a racoon," I couldn't be honest. He might put a stop to it if he knew the farmhand was taking up with his vulnerable, grieving sister. I thought it best to keep it to myself. Obviously, Laura and Chuck have chosen to keep this between them.

Morten seems troubled these days. The money is getting low as often happens in spring. There is the expense of buying seed but there is no crop to sell yet. I so wish I had been able to give Morten a son earlier on. What a help it would be today, to have an eighteen-year-old boy around to help. The regrets of losing our son haunt me daily. I know it troubles

Morten too, but we never speak of it. We both love our five beautiful daughters but imagine that, five daughters and living on a farm. In ten or twelve years Doug and Lyle will be a great help but that's a long time to wait, especially with Daniel gone.

I feel I failed Morten in losing that pregnancy. Perhaps if I had not worked so hard while I was with child, things would have been different. However, we were newlyweds, and I was eager to impress Morten. I wanted to show him what a capable wife he had married, even though I didn't feel so capable. Perhaps it was all those pots of water I lifted, or insufficient rest. Dr. Moffat assured me it was nothing I did, but then he is such a kind man. He wouldn't tell me. Margaret explained there were countless women across the township who had lost babies and that it is not uncommon.

Since losing Nell, the emptiness inside me burns a hole in my heart. The Good Lord has blessed me greatly with many wonderful children, both female and male. But surely there is more to life than having babies. I feel a restlessness in my soul. I have been raising children since I was twenty-one and I'm now almost forty. Silly as it sounds, I crave a passion beyond motherhood. I wonder what Evelyn Barclay would think of that!

Momma used to tease me that I was such a bookworm, and that I really should get out and be more sociable. I guess Nell got her shyness from me. Momma used to say, "How are you ever going to meet a husband and make something of your life?" Although I knew she was right, some part of me couldn't relinquish the inner stirrings of my soul. Momma would scold me for wasting so much ink recording my thoughts. It's still true, but I can't help myself.

Little Zoe seems to be recuperating gradually but she misses her grandfather and sister dearly. They cannot be replaced by a donkey. The other day as Ida and I went to add some sugar to our tea, we found the bowl had been entirely emptied. That donkey is cleaning out what is left of our supplies. It's absurd how much Zoe spoils her. I guess whatever helps her little heart mend is a good thing. Morten finds it comical. The other day Zoe, and her little friend Katherine, attempted to take Gaby for a walk along the road. You can imagine how that went. Anyone who has ever tried to walk a donkey knows they are eight hundred pounds of dead weight when they chose not to co-operate. Zoe and Katherine got that animal out to the road where Gaby promptly found a patch of fresh spring grass. Do you think they could get that animal home? It took them hours and cost me the entire contents of my sugar dish for only a few feet of movement. Eventually, Gaby headed back to the barn on her own volition, when it was feeding time. Gaby remains the apple of Zoe's eye and it keeps her mind off her sadness. For that I am truly thankful.

Saturday, June 2, 1900

The internment was today. I didn't want to go as it makes it all so final. Having them both in the crypt meant they were still with us in a way. When I awoke in the morning, there was such a heaviness in my heart, I could barely rise from the bed. The darkness has hit me full force. Regardless, I had to get up. Morten came in and we held each other for several minutes.

The atmosphere in the house was somber, which is so unlike our busy home in the morning. We gathered around the breakfast table and Morten offered a prayer. As we bowed our heads, there were many sniffles, and the meal was noticeably quiet. Lyle worked hard to make me giggle, but he wasn't having any luck. Amazing how children sense things even though they are too young to really understand. Doug began to act up and get down from the table, almost in a dual effort with his brother, to pry me from the depths of despair.

It was a grey day but thankfully warmer. When Chuck brought the carriage around, I was numb. Morten took my arm and helped me up. The children filed in behind, all of us dressed in our black grieving clothes. The Findlays had arrived to escort Laura and Ida in the carriage behind us. We made a sad entourage, through the drizzling rain, towards the churchyard on the hill. It was a long, silent, joyless ride. The only audible sound was the rhythmic clip clop of the horses' hooves. By the time we arrived a small crowd had assembled in the churchyard.

A host of close friends and family had gathered around the family plot, despite the rain. Rev. Mactavish said a few words. To be honest, I don't even remember his message. Undoubtedly it was hard for him too as he and Daniel had been close friends. In fact, their friendship stretched back to when he first arrived here taking up a new charge with three churches on his circuit. No doubt the reverend felt this loss deeply. It's a wonder he was able to conduct the service. My anguish really took hold when the pall bearers emerged from the crypt carrying the casket – first Daniel's and then Nell's. I could not contain myself and the grief flooded over me like a wave. The two deaths were inextricably intertwined in my soul, and I could not seem to emotionally disentangle them. When I thought of one loss, the other crowded in, similarly if I thought of the other. Both were locked forever together in time. I hardly recall the service. All I remember is the black hole inside me as Daniel was lowered into the ground – a man who had been like a father to me for so many years. He was such a wonderful father to Morten and grandfather to our children. He was a kindly, gentle soul who was adored even by his animals. He had a soft spot for Zoe, who was beside herself. She cuddled into her grandmother as both supported each other. Next, Nell's casket was carried to the graveside. I couldn't look. When they placed my daughter in the ground and the dirt was thrown upon her grave, Morten and I held each other and we both wept, myself uncontrollably. Rose hugged me repeatedly. Lots of friends offered me their kind-hearted condolences as we made our way from the churchyard. I thought I might collapse. Ida was not faring much better.

I couldn't wait for the whole thing to be over. Life will never be the same. Oh sure, we will move on. There will be new adventures, new children, multiple distractions, and I will get through. However, there will always be a hole in my life which my daughter once filled. She is not replaceable, and the scar is indelible. Grief is heavy. I know it will lighten in time, but it will never be gone. My life is changed.

So here I sit, in the early evening having endured a horrible day, a day I wish on no parent. What would I do without family to pull me through? Morten holds my hand and reminds me they are at rest now. We will pretend to move on and perhaps in pretending we will help to make it so.

I'm haunted by the senselessness of their deaths, Daniel due to a cart of all things, with horses he knew and trained since they were mere foals. One slip on a bit of hidden ice and one's entire life comes crashing down. And my little Nell, slobbered on by some ill begotten, young man who had no business coming anywhere near my beautiful, sweet girl. I can't think of it, or I will live in constant rage. My anger consumes me. I try to tell myself that God is with me to help me endure, and I will get through this. Tomorrow is a new day.

-36-

Poor little Zoe and her lovely donkey Gaby. What a beautiful way for that little girl to grieve – to pour her love and sadness into a patient, old, kindly donkey. How will my children grieve their grandfather's passing, or will they even have time? Between computer games, dance lessons, homework, social media, texting, how would they have the space in their day to retreat to a barn and befriend an animal? Life has become so busy we can barely fit our emotions into it. They are often swept aside, buried under a host of activities and commitments. Then, one day years later, interned in the depths of our heart when our mind is briefly unoccupied, we inexplicably feel down and cannot pinpoint why. Our emotions don't evaporate when they are shelved or re-directed. I'm learning that the more we ignore emotional pain, the more we need stronger remedies to numb it when it rears its head. There are anti-depressants, alcohol, pot and a host of stronger legal and illegal antidotes. The pharmaceuticals are constantly creating better, more effective ways to soothe our troubled emotions, but often the answer lies in just feeling and accepting them, as excruciating as that may be. It's so easy to submerge painful experiences in a lifetime of busyness, instead of facing them deliberately in the here and now. Little Zoe had the right idea. Hug that donkey all you need to and weep into its neck, because that is the only way the pain eventually gets more manageable.

As I sit here listening to the old clock ticking in the living room, I can hear Tyler in the kitchen talking to Wilbur.

"Ok Buddy, you can have one cookie. I'll walk you after. I can't go right now because I'm playing online with some friends." He's such a sweet, shy kid. I wish he'd come out of his room more often. How can he possibly be online with 'friends'? He rarely leaves the room. Wilbur follows him around all the time but even Wilbur needs to go out occasionally. Megan is chatting with Zach on the phone. Things seem to be heating up there, which might help my cause when Matt and I reveal our plan to stay here a little longer. Zach seems to be a nice young man. He always addresses Matt and me as Mr. and Mrs. Yesterday he offered to help bring the groceries in. Imagine that, an adolescent offering to help. Even Megan participated and pretended she did that all the time.

....

Now that Dad is gone, there is the issue of the will. There is nothing that divides a family faster than a poorly designed will. So much for all those nice birthday cards and Christmas dinners, the gloves are off. I am finding that the quickest way for a family to unravel is for a parent to die.

It is hard to believe Dad is gone. I am happy he is at peace but I'm still a little frozen with disbelief. It's all so permanent. That is the part that is so hard to accept. Now the second guessing begins. Did we do enough for him? Was he in any pain at the end? ...

And then there are all those after death things that one never thinks of. Where do we send the body? These are things one avoids contemplating when their loved one is still breathing. Will he be cremated or buried and if so what type of urn or casket would be best? Where will we have the service and how many are we expecting? Who will plan it? Who will give the eulogy? Will there be a reception and what will be served? ...And the newspaper announcement, what shall we say and who will write it and what picture will we use? Suddenly we are thrown from complete numbness into event planning. Now this is all assuming that the rest of your life goes on hold. What about all those other issues such as parenting, paying bills, Matt missing critical work meetings, getting the car fixed, doing the laundry and the groceries and all the other countless mundane tasks that are required of a human being during the course of a day. Who has time for crippling emotions? Too bad we didn't think to consider some of these details in the 91.5 years preceding this event.

I realize this represents not just the end of my father but the end of an era. As one more integral heart ceases to beat, I have inadvertently slid another rung up the ladder of generations. That buffer zone is eroding between me and the afterlife.

When I next saw Dad, he looked happy and peaceful. Maybe death is a wonderful transition rather than a morbid finality. It would explain the contented look he had in the end. I will miss him, but I am happy for him. Life was no longer enjoyable, and he was declining. Perhaps there comes a time when the best thing one can do is 'let go'.

As I read Isabel's diary each night, I realize life in 1900 was simpler in many ways but it wasn't necessarily better. Thankfully, medical treatment has progressed significantly. However, if you're nearing the end, it can become harder to actually die. If you haven't signed a DNR, you may have to fall apart one piece at a time before the central engine is finally able to quit. In Daniel's day, it was a matter of days, maybe a week, but generally speaking, the end was around the next corner. Dad gets sick (a good 35 years beyond Daniel's age) and he is rushed to hospital in a fully equipped ambulance, rocketing down the road at 150 kilometers an hour. Without a DNR, he is x-rayed with state-of-the-art equipment, medicated with the newest intravenous antibiotics and monitored by machines day and night until his condition is better. Then he is discharged until the next wheel comes off the bus. It may be a month or two, but eventually the next dilemma occurs. Perhaps it is something different, at which point he is given medication until his condition stabilizes. The poor guy was running out of ways to die. If medical science kept replacing his parts, how long could he continue?

Although it is difficult to face, we are all going to die. Ready or not, eventually our time will come. Perhaps the important question is 'how well can we die?' Can we die painlessly, quickly, peacefully, surrounded by our loved ones? Will we linger so long that we lose our minds, our bladder and bowel control, our memories, our dignity? Maybe nature has a kinder exit plan. Maybe death isn't the enemy. Perhaps instead the enemy is the ever-lengthening road to death and how damn bumpy it gets in those final kilometres. Where it once was only a few potholes that signified the end, it is now a veritable endless highway littered with sink holes, until finally your engine just falls right out. Meanwhile, everyone has had one hell of a tough ride.

It was an awkward funeral. Barb never did show up. We were all profoundly sad to lose Dad. An empty crater has been left in our family where our kind and engaging father once was. No matter how prepared you think you are for an inevitable loss, it is still a shock to the system.

The churchyard seems to be a thing of the past. There was a time one could wander amid the stones and remember their loved ones. Now people are often sprinkled rather than buried. Is there more permanence in having one's remains interned in the ground, in the family plot with one's name engraved in stone, born this date, died this date? Perhaps it's a testimony that you existed and are remembered and hold an important link in the chain to the next generation? When I stand on my great grandmother's gravesite, I have a sense of where I came from and who I came from. It brings a certain centering and connection to those who came before us. Now we are sprinkled here and there or reside on some loved one's mantel, or our ashes are dismembered into bits for all to share. Even our family members, let alone future generations, couldn't locate us if they tried. What does that do to rootedness and identity? Does it erase the previous generation without so much as a reminder that they once existed?

When I was in Scotland, I stood on the grave of my great, great grandparents. Will my great, great, grandchild be able to stand on my grave someday and experience the same sense of connectedness that I once did? Although it was only a moment, it opened up a different dimension of my awareness. Maybe we're losing our link with the past or maybe we just can't bear to spend eternity stuck beside our family members.

We have gained incredible technology, instant global communications, mass efficient transportation but somewhere along the line, we've diminished our sense of identity and connectedness. What are we missing in this throw away world? If we lose connection with our past, maybe we lose a sense of ourselves as well.

Monday, June 4, 1900

Our spirits are lifting slowly as summer creeps in. The lilacs smell lovely, although I have hardly noticed them. There has been a stream of buggies going by the house. The post has just arrived, and I see there is a note from Rose.

The laundry hung out, Ida, Laura and I sit on the porch for some afternoon tea as we await the return of the children.

According to Rose's letter, she 's thoroughly enjoying her new piano and wonders if I might come within the week to hear her play. There's a cryptic message about Patrick suggesting that the two have had another quarrel. Her message is subtle as perhaps she worries he'll read it as he takes it to post. It doesn't appear to have been opened. She reminds me that the church picnic is at the end of June – as though I could forget. It's all the girls have been talking about. The Findlay boy will be there and some of the other handsome young lads from the vicinity. Mary was delighted to learn that both the Orillia and the Coldwater Presbyterian Churches have been invited to the event for this turn of the century celebration.

Next week there's a picnic meeting of the Ladies Aid to get the planning underway. I'm on the games committee and am trying to think of something more original than the usual three-legged race and tug of war which we always have. We need some fresh ideas now that we are in 1900. We want to set the church in the direction of a lively start to the next century.

I just had a wonderful idea for a game - 'which team has the sharpest senses'. Each contestant would be blindfolded. We could begin with a flower test where one must identify the type of flower by its smell. We could follow it with a hearing test where a bird call is made and the species is named, then a taste test, where a unique herb is selected, and the participant must identify if. Then by feel while blindfolded, one must identify their own horse. Finally, a sight test, who can spot the camouflaged owl? I think the ladies will like it.

I know Ida's main concern is that she doesn't want to weigh anyone down with her sadness and she works hard not to let it pull her down too. She's had her share of losses. She lost her own daughter 'Nellie' long before my Nell had ever been born. Morten says he still remembers the day so vividly when his little sister drowned. He would have only been about five. They were down by the frog pond when little Nellie was mesmerized by the bullfrogs, which were plentiful. Apparently, while the others had their attention diverted preparing a picnic, Nellie charged into the water in pursuit of a frog. Immediately she was in over her head in the murky pool. Daniel raced after her, but the muddy pond made it impossible to get to her quickly. Hearing the commotion, the men, and even some of the women, promptly jumped in after her, few being able to swim themselves. Morten remembers his mother shrieking uncontrollably as the group spread out in the water, laden with their spring clothes and boots. Some time passed by the time Nellie was retrieved. It was a horrific day that has been seared into Morten's memory forever. He says he'll never forget the terror in his mother's eyes and the shrill of her screams.

A carriage has pulled into our lane. I can't see who it is only that there appears to be several ladies aboard. It turns out it is a collection of representatives from the Women's Christian Temperance Movement proclaiming the merits of prohibition. They couldn't have found a more supportive destination than right here on the Huntly homestead. In fact, I felt ashamed that I hadn't volunteered to become more involved when Rev. Mactavish had first reminded us of this important cause. We invited the ladies up to the porch for tea and there were a number of familiar faces, Evelyn Barclay being among them. She just seems to find time for everything that woman. We had a little visit and shared some of Ida's freshly made cakes. Meanwhile, they explained how we must close the local taverns as they are such a disgrace to our communities. Now if women could vote, drinking never would have been permitted in the first place. Ida, Laura and I gladly signed their petition and expressed our gratitude for their fine work. Laura trotted over to the barn to get the men, who are supporters of this cause too. Morten even made a very generous one dollar donation. The women left us a Household Temperance Pledge that we can review as a family and put our signatures to. It can be placed in the front of the family bible as an ongoing reminder of our commitment.

After a nice visit, the group continued their journey down the road. It is important work for the welfare of our communities. It won't do to have intoxicated men stumbling about, fighting with one another. I hope they pay a visit to Patrick's farm.

Thursday, June 7, 1900

Little kicks nudge my insides. The baby is so active in the morning. Morten is so proud and always feeling my belly for the daily progress. The children are starting to get excited too - all but Doug. He is not at all keen on the idea of another 'brother'. In fact, he would just as soon return the one he has. Zoe was lying on my lap the other day and found it comical to hear the gurgles and activity taking place beneath her ear. She has expressed her definite wish for a little sister.

Patrick has finally allowed Rose to have the piano in the house. It would have been ravished by mice had it spent a summer in the barn. One would think it would be situated in the sitting room where it rightly belongs but not a chance. Rose was told, in no uncertain terms, it was to go in the summer kitchen. What an unfeeling clod. Imagine an instrument of that calibre being relegated to a summer kitchen, which gets darn cold in the winter! Nevertheless, Rose was delighted that he had even allowed it into the house.

I was able to sneak away for a visit this afternoon. With great excitement, she presented her new pride and joy. I was happy for her as she passionately brought the piano to life with some familiar, old tunes. She played a few hymns and some fireside songs, and I could see she was in her element as she lost herself in the music. We had tea around the piano, and she went on about it all morning. She's a beautiful player. I'm happy she has some 'escape' on this cold-hearted farm.

It's dreary here with Patrick. You can feel the tension when he's around. As soon as he enters, a part of her shuts down. She seems silently infuriated with him. Those poor children. Elizabeth is a beautiful young girl, but she is unhappy inside and so unsure of herself. I suppose that is the result of having a father who is consistently critical, particularly of the girls. Meanwhile, Patrick turns a blind eye to Robbie's horridly disrespectful behaviour. Rose constantly tries to correct Robbie's misdemeanours. However, when Patrick tells her to 'leave the lad alone' right in front of Robbie and returns the item his mother has just confiscated, what does that say to him? He does the same with little Harry. Myself, I would throttle the man. To be honest, I think Rose finds it easier when Patrick is off drinking. At least he's away from the house and out of her hair temporarily.

Saturday, June 9th, 1900

I love bath day, especially now that I go first, being with child. I feel so fresh and clean and it's always well worth the work it takes to heat the water.

We had the Ladies Aid meeting yesterday to put some finishing touches on the church picnic. They loved my Senses Game Relay. As always, it's potluck and there will be such a fine array of dishes. No one leaves hungry. Ida and I will prepare a casserole, while Laura and Mary will bake buns.

The children are getting restless for school to end. I don't envy their poor teacher having to keep them all contained. Mind you many of the boys are already away for planting season. Given the warmer weather, the children can all walk or ride to school now. Thankfully, Mary is here to help with the *boys. Sometimes I think Lyle gets confused and almost thinks Mary is his mother. She is keen to take her teacher training at the normal school in Toronto. She seems so young to become a teacher. I keep forgetting she will be eighteen in July. It hardly seems possible.*

Rose isn't herself lately. She is nervous and on edge and frankly, she looks tired. It's tough not to notice these things when you have been best friends for as many years as we have. After the Ladies Aid meeting, during tea, she told me Patrick is getting progressively harder to live with. Sometimes he comes home very late, and extremely inebriated. She went on about how awful he smells, reeking of scotch and tobacco. She can't stand to share a bed with him. If she tries to slip out into one of the children's beds, he gets angry with her. She explained that he has quite a temper when he comes home drunk, and it is growing worse. She described her gratefulness that the children are in bed at this hour. We talked some more as we dried dishes, but one has to be careful of prying ears in the church kitchen. I'm worried about her. He is such a brute of a man. I am thankful she has her piano, not to mention the longwinded letters she gets from me. She also explained that Patrick has taken to reading our correspondence lately, which I find extremely intrusive. It's absolutely none of his business what Rose and I talk about in our exchanges. Imagine the gall. Likely he's worried that Rose is telling me the truth about his antics. He doesn't deserve a fine woman like her!

-37-

Living in a small town, rush 'minute' hardly qualifies as traffic. It's such a refreshing change from the big city. Nevertheless, there are a couple of stop lights between the grocery store and the farm. I head towards 'home' at slightly over the speed limit. Wild turkeys or grouse meandering by the road are a common sight in the area. One grouse has taken it upon himself to stroll out on the pavement. Now Matt has previously assured me that I never need to worry about grouse on the road as "one couldn't hit them if they tried". To back this up, I do recall a time we were driving along, and the grouse did in fact flee as we approached. Given this reassurance, I was confident this one would also dart out of the way. Nevertheless, I slowed down to the actual speed limit, giving the grouse a chance to take off. As my car got closer and closer, I was puzzled. What's going on with this bird? Doesn't he know the rules of nature? I lay on my horn to get it moving. The grouse looked around stunned. However, I knew "you couldn't hit a grouse if you tried". I was confident it would flee, and I was in a hurry to get home. SMACK! Feathers flew everywhere. It looked like a pillow had exploded in the road. I felt almost as awful as the grouse. Shaken, I pulled over in a state of horror and disbelief. I thought that wasn't possible! There, crushed in the middle of the road, was remnants of grouse. The moral of the story is 'drive slowly, grouse are stupid' and 'never listen to your husband'.

Rattled, and my front grill covered in feathers, I finally arrived at the farmhouse. Wilbur, who usually greets me with a big slurpy kiss, was instead fascinated with the carnage on my front fender. I was extremely upset as I stepped inside the house. Tyler and Megan were glued to some rerun of 'Big Bang Theory'.

"Hi guys, I'm home." I announced, putting the groceries down.

No response.

"You wouldn't believe what just happened on the drive home!" I exclaimed, my voice shaking.

Someone grunted quietly.

"Hello, is anyone here?" I snapped, my hands now on my hips.

Tyler turned to me sharply and said, "Quiet Mom, we're watching."

Eventually an ad came on and I adamantly stepped in front of the set to announce my presence. "Oh, hi Mom," Megan said. "What's the matter?"

I told them what happened, and they were fascinated until the show resumed. That was it. Greetings and support that lasted as long as the commercial. They would notice if dinner wasn't served or if the groceries weren't purchased or if the cell bill wasn't paid, but if their Mom is in distress, having an emotional melt down, it could go unnoticed until an ad. If I were to push the power button on the remote, I am confident there would be vehement rebellion. It's tough to get acknowledgement during a rerun of 'Big Bang Theory'.

I must admit, most of the time I like this. It allows me to slip in unnoticed and put my things down before I become a parent again. But today it is not working for me. Finally, Matt arrives, and I relay the story. He is both supportive and apologetic and admits that he has never actually put his theory to the test. The verdict is in, his premise is false, and my husband is in trouble.

-38-

In an attempt to make some friends in the area, I decided to join a book club. I've been a couple of times and it's quite fun. I've met a few of the local women and they seem very nice although they are much better gardeners than myself.

The truth is, I am enjoying book club provided it is at someone else's house.

However, now it is my turn to host, a task I'm not looking forward to. The first issue is that you have to clean your house – a chore I dislike immensely. In my attempt to make a good impression on my newfound friends, I shift into overdrive.

The first stop is the grocery store which brings me directly to the second issue. Money. How many countless bottles of wine and elaborate cheese trays do I need to purchase to be an appropriate book club hostess? There seems to be a subtle competition to have incredibly good snack food and a collection of fine wines to accompany the elaborate finger foods. I stop at a high-end grocery store for this important occasion. I have bypassed my regular favourites (the green and yellow grocery stores). I head directly to the fancy cheese section, which is totally out of bounds now that I'm off work. I load up my cart like some kind of hungry millionaire. I select a lovely brie, some swiss, and a nicely aged cheddar. Next is to the cracker section, where I chose a few special delicacies. Then I move onto the grapes, olives and the raw materials for an impressive veggie and dip tray. It should be called an eating club because that is a big part of our focus. I can't even remember what we're reading. I don't even attempt to participate in the home baked competition that exists among some of the overachievers in the group.

Eighty dollars later I head to the LCBO where I will need a cart to satisfy our thirsty membership. Now it is important to have a suitable collection because someone might want a red or a blush wine. Then there are those who prefer Pinot Grigio to Chardonnay. I proceed to clean out my account.

Now I must rush home through those three annoying traffic lights to clean up the messy old farmhouse. The kids have been warned to be on their best behaviour, but we know how that has worked in the past. The last thing I want is for Megan and Tyler to break into a sibling melt down in front of company.

Now for the overwhelming job of clean up. I only have to do the downstairs. My cleanup consists of running large loads of laundry upstairs out of eyesight, shoving baskets full of random papers into the hall cupboard, and tossing multiple pairs of shoes onto the back-porch. I'm counting this as my workout for the day. Then the floor needs to be vacuumed, the bathroom needs cleaning, the kitchen floor requires scrubbing and all because I enjoy reading. Two and a half hours later, the downstairs looks phenomenal! The upstairs looks like hell.

It is 6:30 and they arrive at 7:00. I still have to prepare the veggie and cheese trays. I am in the middle of slicing carrots in high gear when the dog darts in from outside, right across my freshly cleaned floor.

"Hi honey. The place looks great. The kids and I are off for pizza," calls Matt innocently from the side door. Meanwhile there are jumbo paw marks throughout the house and slobber all over the couch. You can't live, parent and enjoy hosting book club. Those variables don't co-exist for me. How did Isabel and Ida ever pull off those huge carol sings?

Despite all odds, the evening is a great success. In fact, the only stressful point occurs when the conversation turns to that dead grouse that everyone saw in the middle of the road. We have a very fun night filled with lots of wine and lively book analysis. Regardless of how self-conscious I feel about the state of the house and the substandard décor, I pull it off flawlessly and make it look easy – thereby raising the bar for the next hapless book club member. The only real flaw in the whole event was when Wilbur came bounding into the living room at the end of the evening. His huge tail wagging with delight at all the company, he managed to clear the coffee table of all eight wine glasses with a single swish of his tail.

My fantasy book club would be called the 'No Stress Book Club', where everyone's house is poorly decorated and a complete mess, where you only host every five years, where we all enjoy the same reading list, and it is not the quality of the wine but the quantity that matters. That is my kind of book club. That said, I love reading and the great people I'm meeting. I will miss this group when I return to the city.

Please turn off the rectangle Amy. I can't watch any more. The cruelty and pain are heart-wrenching. How can they be so ruthless with each other? It just breeds more hatred. Can't they learn to get along? Maybe they should let the mothers take over because mothers don't want their children hurt and mothers know their children need a world to grow up in.

Friday, June 15, 1900

As Rose was reaching for some music, I saw the dark, purple bruise on her arm. When I asked her about it, she immediately covered it and explained she had just bumped it on the dresser- an unlikely story. When we got around to discussing Patrick, she admitted he was getting worse. She became tearful as she talked about the alcohol and how uneasy she was when he came home late. She practically came apart at the seams when I hugged her. The poor thing is a nervous wreck. Apparently, he's at the tavern almost every night now despite her working so hard to please him.

"Don't be ridiculous," I exclaimed. "There's no pleasing a drunkard. It doesn't matter what you do, he's still going to be outrageous and unruly."

Rose seemed uncharacteristically nervous.

"Rose, this isn't like you. Perhaps this is too much."

"No, no," she insisted. "The children... I'd never leave the children with him because he can be so cruel with his words. And I can't leave with them."

"They can come to our place. I know Morten wouldn't mind." I offered, despite wondering to myself what I was getting into.

"Think how humiliating that would be for them. What sort of light would that cast them in?" She countered.

"Don't be silly. If your personal safety or the children's is at stake, then it's not a choice it's a necessity." I insisted.

"No, I can manage him. So far, he's never hurt the children and I intend to keep it that way."

"But Rose, he's clearly hurting you. Look at your arm," I said.

"I told you that was a dresser," she said defensively.

I stared at her in disbelief. "Well, I'm here if you need me."

"So is Ed. He's here if I need him. He helps me with everything from bringing in the firewood to fixing my piano stool."

"Perhaps that is what is keeping you here," I suggested.

"No that isn't it although Ed does make it bearable. I don't want to lose my children. The law does not look favourably upon women who leave their husband Issy, and you know it. How would I have any money to feed or clothe them? I try to tuck away the odd coin in my apron, but it doesn't add up to much. Patrick keeps such a close eye on the money it's nearly impossible to pocket any of it.

I held her as she broke down and convulsed in a spasm of tears, but still she found no room for reason. No matter how clear and well-intended my arguments, she remained steadfast that she was staying.

"If I had money Rose, I would give it all to you. I can't stand to see you here with this beast."

Then the discussion turned to Edward. "I know you care for him. I've seen you around him Rose and I can feel the electricity. Surely Patrick feels it too."

"Ed rarely comes around when Patrick is nearby. Ed has told me he wants to throttle Patrick for the way he has been treating me."

"Well, Patrick must sense something. He may not be bright but he's not blind."

"Eddy and I are good friends, but I must confess, my feelings for him grow deeper by the day. I know it's wrong, but I can't help it. He's so kind and caring and I feel safe when he's around."

I didn't know what to say. What an awkward dilemma for Rose. If I were married to a cruel man like Patrick with no way out, and Morten worked on the farm and came to my side every time I shed a tear, wouldn't I want to be with Morten?... and shouldn't I be if he treats me right? Sometimes the rules that are supposed to be so clear just don't seem to fit. All I know is that Rose is my friend and I love her. I would help her in a heartbeat and I'm happy she has someone looking out for her. Surely God can understand this. Heaven knows that Rose has tried to please this fool for years and to no avail. It seems so unfair that she should be chained to him for life due to a youthful promise of long ago.

I suggested she talk with Rev. Mactavish. She said she'd think on it but in the meantime, I was not to breathe a word to anyone or put anything in my letters about our conversation. If Patrick ever heard of this, he'd be furious.

We walked in the garden and picked some flowers for the table as we continued talking. I said hello to *the children when they came home from school but for the first time, I felt relieved to say good-bye. Rose's children looked tired and disillusioned. I detest leaving her there, but she insists she won't go, and I don't know how to convince her. I was so delighted when our buggy arrived in the laneway. Maybe Morten will know what to do.*

Saturday, June 16th, 1900

This pregnancy feels like an eternity. I relish the time when my body will once again be my own and my swollen feet return to their normal state. Soon, my body will expand to the size of a barn, and I don't relish the horrendous pain of childbirth. I don't care what Evelyn Barclay says about how her breathing made the whole experience a pleasure. I cannot imagine ever finding it so. She's only had five children and her last one was so small it hardly counted as a true delivery. She should keep her thoughts to herself, in my opinion. Anyway, I'm off on a non-Christian tangent.... After a night of unliveable torture and screaming, the little one will arrive. Then, however, that bundle of joy wakes on and off all night for the next six months and requires my breast to be produced at a moment's notice. It means constant nappy changing and the inevitable washing that goes with it. It means a body that is once again stretched out of shape. It means fatigue and exhaustion for several years to come as it suckles, teethes, walks, runs, and grows. Oh stop, Issy. These thoughts are not leading anywhere good. I must remember the joy of that warm tiny brow, the soft little bundle and how it gazes into your eyes with utter adoration. I must remember that it is our newest family member and a part of Morten and I. Stop thinking about yourself and remember your job is to carry on the family and be a loving mother. Why do I feel so empty? I do hope the baby can't feel my sadness. God knows I try hard to hide it.

The girls are chattering constantly about the upcoming church picnic. The farmers are predicting lovely weather, so I do hope they are correct. There is levity in the air as the warm evening breezes remind us that school is almost finished for summer. Being the busy season on the farm, Morten and Chuck have been in the fields from daybreak to sunset, planting crops and tending to animals. The only one who has a more demanding schedule than that is the life of a mother with a newborn, who has no division between night and day.

I can hear much ruckus down below in the kitchen. There's all sorts of shrieking and laughter. I shall waddle down and see what's going on.

Arriving in the kitchen, I quickly learned what the driving force was behind all the commotion. There in the middle of the kitchen floor was the cat with a little present in his mouth. Well, gracious sakes - a mangled snake. The poor thing was still trying to escape. No doubt the snake was in a state of shock, especially given all the shrieking. Chuck came running in with a rifle over his shoulder. Clearly, he was expecting more than a helpless garden snake, now lying prostrate on the kitchen floor with the cat guarding it possessively. As he took in the scene, his face melted into a smile.

"Ladies, what have we here? A tortured snake and a mischievous cat." Morten entered behind him, evidently slower at racing over from the barn. Absorbing the situation, the two men exchanged a smile and shooed the cat out without his gift. Morten went over and hugged his horrified mother as Chuck

removed the suffering creature to outside. Needless to say, we all breathed a great sigh of relief to have the situation rectified. Fortunately, it jolted me from my previous state of maternal melancholy.

-39-

While I was sitting in the car waiting for Megan to emerge from the store, I caught a glimpse of myself in the rear-view mirror. I didn't like what I saw. Those grey hairs are really starting to accumulate amid my natural light brown colour. It is appalling how fast they seem to be multiplying. It's depressing. I'm so overwhelmed I can't work, the housework never stops, we're living in a dilapidated farm rental, and now I'm starting to look like an old hag.

I could dye it. I wonder if anyone would even notice? What if I just dyed the parts that were grey and left the rest natural? If there is a way to look younger, why not.

Unable to rid myself of the sobering realization, I eventually went to the drug store. I nonchalantly walked down the hair colour aisle, feigning I needed shampoo. I was careful not to be spotted by any book club members. I'm quickly learning that small town life involves bumping into acquaintances all over the place. There were endless selections from platinum blond, to dark black, pink, blue and green. It was an invitation to basically become anyone I want. Platinum blond seemed a little extreme but for $9.95 I could definitely come up with a medium brown that would blend quite nicely with who I am. I have never done this before, and it raised some important questions for me such as:

Do I want to be one of those people who strives to conceal their age? Why are a few grey hairs so offensive and frightening? Did Ida or Isabel ever dye their hair and if so, how? Would I look better with the pink?

Self-doubts and indecision aside, I quickly picked a box that looked closest to my shade and threw it in my cart (under some other items).

A few hours later, I was beginning to feel this was a mistake. This shade looked great on the twenty-five-year-old on the box but it's way too dark for me. Now the entire edge around my face looks completely bizarre. Undoubtedly, I should have been wearing my glasses when I applied the mixture because I could have sworn it said apply mixture to hair for 50 minutes but I've since learned that was a two not a five. Damn it, I look ridiculous. Now I'll have to do the whole head, so it matches. Luckily there was some dye leftover and now my hair is a very dark brunette. Since I emerged from the bathroom yesterday with my new look, everyone has been commenting on the change in my appearance. How mortifying. Just when I am trying to downplay my altered hair colour, it has suddenly become the topic of conversation. Matt says he feels like he's with another woman. "Is that a good thing or a bad thing?" I question, curious to hear his response.

"No worries Matt," I reassure him. "I notice they had hair dye for men too, in firefighter, contractor, lumber jack, ... "

In other news, Matt and I had a talk with the kids today. I explained that I'm not yet ready to return to work and Dr. Neal has extended my leave. We asked how they would feel if we were to stay on a few more months, and begin the school year here? There was mixed reaction. After the initial explosion by Megan, she began to digest that this meant more time with her new friend, Zach. It also meant starting high school away from her friends. Following some choice words, and a slammed door, she locked herself in her room to come to terms with this new possibility. Tyler, on the other hand, rather liked the idea. The internet wasn't too bad here and he kind of enjoyed the isolation and peacefulness he didn't get at home. Tyler, not being much of a socialite, wasn't too worried about where he began his term. Matt was delighted he could continue with his home office plan while enjoying cutting the grass on the sit-down mower. I felt a sense of peacefulness. Six more weeks of farm life before returning to the chaos of reality was an inviting idea!

Last night, the rectangle was talking about the changing climate. Don't people understand the earth is being poisoned and is slowly dying? How will they survive if nature does not? What will they eat and drink and breathe? I'm not very smart but I think they need to do something fast.

-40-

Matt's family is coming for dinner tonight. Once again, housecleaning is on the agenda: a thankless chore that causes no end of stress. Maybe I could ask the kids to help like in the 'old days'. After all, Isabel seemed to have her brood of seven well trained in that department.

It was Sunday afternoon; Matt was preparing chicken for the meal. Tyler and his new neighbourhood buddy Nick, were playing video games upstairs while guzzling large volumes of pop. I came in to deliver some laundry and went largely unnoticed, despite my very dark brown hair. They were glued to the game with familiar eagerness. When they got to a break in the action, I explained to Tyler that since we were expecting company, I needed some help with cleaning. I put him in charge of floors. I would like him to vacuum the living room and sweep the kitchen by 3:00 this afternoon. Nick looked at me like I was out of my mind and seemed to find my request somewhat comical. However, it was not completely foreign to Tyler to be asked to help.

"Ya, that's fine but I can't do it right now because I'm kicking Nick's butt at Grand Theft Auto." He continued punching at the controller while staring at the screen.

"Fair enough, when you are finished annihilating your friend... please turn on the vacuum." Nick laughed and they returned to the game.

Next was Megan. When I walked into her horrendously kept room, I could see that she was engrossed in a social media exchange on her computer. Megan tends to be more outspoken and resistant to helping around the house than her mildly co-operative, older brother. I knew I would have to put the concept out there gently or I would be met with a barrage of backlash. I carefully explained the situation and sensitively requested that Megan fold the next load of laundry and deliver it to people's rooms by 3:00 this afternoon... The response was staggering. "I DON'T HAVE TIME!! Why should I have to do this? What about Tyler, he's just playing video games and I'm reading a novel." Immediately her screen switched to a literary classic.

"Tyler has been assigned a job and Megan, if you would like your allowance this week, you are required to help out a little around the house. I think you can manage to fold and deliver some laundry given that most of it is yours."

"THAT IS NOT FAIR. TYLER SHOULD FOLD THE LAUNDRY... I HAVE TO DO EVERYTHING....." and on it went, an unreasonable response at full volume as I gently shut the door. Honestly, if we didn't control allowance, nothing would ever get done around this house.

I know I can get them to co-operate, but it requires a lot of energy and persistence on my part, withholding allowance, reminding, plugging my ears, unplugging Grand Theft Auto. I am usually exhausted by the end of enforcing it, making me question why I ever asked in the first place. The living room clock keeps ticking and I am wasting valuable time on this draining pursuit when I could just clean up the house and be done with it. This is why my kids are so poorly trained. I am always under a time pressure, so I usually take the path of least resistance.

Meanwhile, I got started on the bathroom. That is the job nobody will ever agree to do, even if there is substantial economic reward attached. While cleaning the mirror, I inadvertently knocked off a piece of the frame. When I removed the mirror to glue the frame, I noticed a cabinet door behind it. Curious, I pried it open. The cabinet was broken and empty except for one large bottle. The label was well worn with time so I couldn't make it out but there was a lot of liquid in it. I picked up the old, brown bottle and removed the lid to sniff. I was almost bowled over. Holy mackerel. That is one powerful shot of whiskey, and finely aged I might add. How could the inhabitants of the house have left this treasure behind? Didn't they all sign the Prohibition Pledge? Thankfully I didn't assign bathroom cleanup to the kids.

Matt agreed that this potent whiskey was likely stored in the cabinet for 'medicinal purposes or dental surgery'. Imagine having alcohol in your house that was never used. In 2120, I can't imagine there will be a bottle of something worth drinking leftover from my wine rack. We agreed to put it aside for a 'special occasion', i.e., sliver removal, a bee-sting or something.

The rectangle was saying some horrible things last night...something about a man going into a crowd with a big gun and shooting people. Apparently, it's happened before. That can't be true. Maybe it's that fake news they've been discussing. I don't know what to believe anymore. If people were getting automatic rifles and gunning down innocent people, I'm sure the leaders would stop that immediately. I can't imagine they'd put up with that. Daniel used to have a gun,

but that was to kill predators on the farm. He never pointed it at a person.

Sunday, June 24, 1900.

I sit here on the porch enjoying the lovely morning. The day of the picnic is upon us and there is great excitement in the air. Thankfully, we have a beautiful, warm day. After the service we'll gather in the pasture by the church, which is also handy to the creek for those who might like a swim. How I love this weather. You can smell the flowers. The birds are flitting about and there is a slight breeze. Oh heavens, I hear a hummingbird. It just dashes in out of nowhere, arrives at the feeder, flutters momentarily and is off. Those tiny wings are magnificent.

The girls are over at the barn as Chuck prepares the horses. We have a new horse and pony that Morten acquired recently. One of the farmers traded them, in exchange for some hay, a few quarts of maple syrup and some of Ida's jams. Morten felt the children needed some cheering up after so much sadness this past winter. There's nothing like a pony and a riding horse to create a happy distraction. It was such a fun surprise when he led them down the lane. Little Zoe was overjoyed. Morten has managed to both delight the girls and solve a recurring transportation dilemma. Now Zoe can ride the pony and Sadie and Carrie can double on the horse. I can hear them coming now on their lively mounts.

"Now girls, please ride carefully. Nothing silly and don't get sidetracked. The service starts in an hour, and I want you there clean and on time. Absolutely no racing." Despite assuring me they

would adhere to my sage advice, I'm not convinced they will pay those words any heed once they leave the laneway.

What a day it was. As usual, we had an uplifting service from Rev. Mactavish. He's such an inspiring, passionate preacher, one cannot help but be moved.

As smitten as James may be with Mary, it seems there is another girl who has her eye on him. When a young girl spies a potential husband, it gets competitive. The other young lady is Betty McAllister, and she attends the Presbyterian Church in Orillia. I've met her parents at their booth at the market. They seem like a nice family. James' mother Alice told me that Betty has been admiring James for some time. The McAllisters sit in the pew behind them each Sunday and she is frequently requesting James' assistance at the store. Alice has assured me that she hopes he continues to court Mary. Mary was serving at the sandwich table when she caught sight of James over by the elm tree with Betty. I could see Mary was upset, so I followed her gaze and quickly learned the source of her grief. As the two conversed, James appeared to be enjoying himself. Betty is a lovely looking girl with long, curly blond hair and flirtatious eyes, which he seemed aware of. Eventually, he freed himself from their conversation and made his way to where Mary was serving sandwiches. Mary tried to busy herself at the other end of the table so as not to catch his eye. The rose of love had a few thorns today.

Due to my condition, I was not able to participate in any of the picnic games, so remained with the older women in the shade of the big maple. As always there was the usual potato sack race and tug of war, but I was most interested when it came time for my senses game. What a hit it was. People lined the fences and children perched on the tree branches, as everyone looked on. We had many laughs during the blindfolded, 'identify your horse' segment of the game. The Coldwater team had arrived with a pair of Clydesdales, so they had a distinct advantage.

It seemed that Patrick was cajoled into attending the event after all. Unfortunately, he and a few of his pals had been drinking behind the shed while the games were underway. I know Rose was mortified. Imagine coming to a church picnic with illegal spirits and imbibing while a minister, ladies and children are present. Poor Rose. Rev. Mactavish finally told them to find their way home as this wasn't an event for alcohol. As they stumbled across the yard, Patrick suddenly stopped dead, and proceeded to relieve himself right there in front of everyone. There was a communal gasp of shock and the ladies turned away. Some of the children roared with laughter and a few men nearby promptly surrounded him and escorted him away. No doubt Rose was nervous what would follow once she arrived home.

Zoe was overjoyed to win the pony contest. She had the new pony's mane all braided with little ribbons, her tail so beautifully brushed, and she trotted around the ring like a perfect lady on her small mount. Everyone commented how much she was like her grandfather, who used to be the judge of this particular event. He certainly would have been proud of her today.

During the awards and speeches there was a tribute to Daniel for being an elder in our church for so many years, as well as memories of all those who have passed, including my sweet Nell. I tried to hold it together but was unable to contain my emotions from bubbling over. Ida weathered the storm more stoically. Morten held me close. It was hard for both of us.

Afterwards, Morten and I went down to the creek for some solitude. As we walked hand in hand along the path, taking in the warm afternoon breeze, we heard a giggle in the woods. Around the next bend, and off by a patch of bushes we could see Chuck's boots and Laura's hat resting on the ground by a tree. It seems they had chosen to 'picnic' down by the creek where there was a little more privacy. At first Morten was confused by the discovery and was tempted to intervene. I gently rested my hand on his arm and suggested he let it be. We walked a little further despite his agitation. I decided to inform him of the discovery Mary and I had made on the porch that night. Eventually he smiled. He confessed that despite his warm affection for Chuck, he was uneasy about his sister being with a farmhand who could barely read. How was his mother going to feel about this? Honestly, Morten cannot begin to understand how blue his sister has been. She needs to have her own family. It is not enough for her to stand by and witness us raise our brood or to hold her mother's hand as Ida grieves Daniel's death. Life needs to hold more than that. What else does she have? Chuck is kind, he makes her smile, he awakens some life in her, he is unattached and he's here. I know he's no scholar and he has few means to support her, but he's a good man and one she could count on. Morten will come to understand that in time. He likes Chuck, I know he does. I also know he and Ida have been concerned about Laura and her state of melancholy this past winter.

As we made our way back to the picnic, we walked around by the church yard to pay our respects to Nell and Daniel. We could see from a distance a patch of bright red atop the family stone. It was easy to pick out the Huntly stone even from a distance as it had a small lamb carved on the top. It seemed odd and we could make no sense of the colourful object from where we stood. The grass was just beginning to take root over the freshly dug graves. We both puzzled at what that could be. Perhaps it was a scarf or maybe a hat. It seemed so out of place waving in the breeze of the cemetery. Another twenty feet along the path, it soon became clear to both of us what the object was. There, by the head of the little lamb atop the stone, secured with a hair clip, was the first-place pony ribbon from the picnic. Clearly little Zoe had been out this way already and placed it where Daniel could be proud.

As the picnic grew to a close, the families gradually gravitated to the livery shed to collect their buggies.

It was quite a merry parade as everyone made their way along the laneway and out to the

concession. The Sunday School children stayed behind to help with cleanup and a few of the boys mucked out the shed and laid some fresh straw for next Sunday. Within an hour it was impossible to tell that anyone had been there that afternoon, except for a lone red ribbon waving from the Huntly family stone.

Monday, June 25th, 1900.

I could see that Mary had been crying. After supper, I suggested we take Lyle and Doug for a walk in the field so we could talk.

"Momma," she said, "He seemed so taken with me. How could he look at another girl....and Betty McAllister of all people."

"Honey, I know James seemed to be engaged in conversation with her, but you don't know how that began. Maybe it was Betty who approached him. He tried to talk to you later, at the sandwich table."

"Why are you crying Mary?" Doug asked, looking concerned.

"Mary's just sad Doug because her friend hurt her feelings," I explained.

"How do we fix that?" Doug asked innocently.

"We just let her know we love her and hold her when she cries," I offered.

Mary smiled a little as Doug hugged her leg. She reassured him with a tussle of his hair that she would be fine.

"Did you talk with him before leaving the picnic?" I asked.

"Yes. He asked how I was getting home. He wondered if I would like to ride in his family carriage?"

"How nice. What did you say?" I questioned.

"I said 'no thank you'."

"Oh honey, he was trying to show you he cared about you. Perhaps you should have taken the ride."

"Momma, he cannot court both of us at the same time. It's either me or her," she snapped.

"Well, I suppose that's true but maybe he doesn't have any interest in courting Betty. Maybe he was just being friendly. Between you and me, his mother told me that Betty has been pursuing him persistently. Remember he did end up at the sandwich table and he did offer you a ride home. It was you who turned him down .... Perhaps you should send him a note," I suggested.

"Mother," she snapped, "send him a note when he was seen flirting shamelessly with Betty right in front of me and everyone else at the picnic," she cried.

"Mary, he was hardly 'flirting shamelessly', he was just talking to her. If anyone was flirting it was Betty, and I hardly think anyone took any notice of it but you. Write to him dear," I insisted.

"I wouldn't know what to say," she pouted.

"How about,... Dear James, It was so nice to see you at the picnic. I'm sorry I was not able to accept your kind offer of a ride home with you and your family. Perhaps there will be another time. Hope you are keeping well. Kind regards. From Mary (and Mrs. Isabel Huntly)."

Mary was in no mood to jest.

"You know, as a matter of fact, I have to pick up some things at the store. Why don't you come along with me?" I suggested. She agreed to think about it.

-41-

Despite the semi-cleaned house and the disgruntled, 'overworked' children, the dinner with Matt's family was delightful. With twelve of us around the table, we had so much fun. After a glass of wine, I no longer cared how tidy the house was. How did Isabel ever entertain without alcohol? She had seven children and she lived with her in-laws. How did she do it? I'm exhausted preparing a 'home cooked' dinner for twelve and she did that three times a day. It took us all day to prepare the potatoes, beans, carrots and buns, and that was with Matt doing the chicken. Now to suggest it was fully 'home cooked' would be deceiving. The chicken was previously barbequed, and the applesauce came from a plastic jar. I didn't grow any of the vegetables, I just washed and cut them. Nor did I bake the bread or pick or skin the apples. When I say homemade, I mean that the chicken was heated in our oven and the beans and carrots weren't previously frozen and we ate it at our dining room table.

Leftover from this fine, 'home cooked' meal, were plastic applesauce containers, some Styrofoam packaging, a few pop bottles and a box from the frozen cake. Luckily for us, that wasn't part of the scene in 1900. Unfortunately, this seems to be the 'souvenir' we are leaving for the next generation.

The house smelled amazing, the table was full, and there was abundant life and noise in our tight, little rental farmhouse. I realize this farmhouse saw that daily, at every meal: at least twelve people seated around the table, to a truly home cooked dinner. There was life, there was co-operation and there was endless community, not to mention food. These seem to be all the elements we try so hard to replicate today, a few times a year, on special occasions like Thanksgiving or Christmas.

Every Monday I watch Matt and Tyler drag those big pails out to the end of the lane. I wonder where all that garbage goes?

-42-

Speaking of meals, we've been trying to establish a regular family dinner routine where we all sit at the table for at least ten minutes and communicate. Tonight, we had a rather disturbing dinner conversation. It started off with the run of the mill discussion about what everyone did today, which normally doesn't elicit gripping disclosures of monumental events. In fact, we are generally happy with any kind of response. However, tonight Tyler got talking about a new trick he figured out on the computer. He proudly announced that he had learned how to hack an email address. Everyone stopped cold and Matt's fork halted in mid air. Megan suddenly tuned into the dinner conversation (despite her secretive cell phone monitoring beneath the table). Meanwhile, I was envisioning a police investigation. According to Tyler, he was just 'playing around' and he hadn't actually breached anyone's email.

"Tyler, do you understand how serious that is?" Matt demanded.

"It is not just a harmless prank. I'm sure it is illegal. Don't ever do that again!" I emphasized.

When dinner was over the kids retreated to the television. As Matt and I were debriefing this worrisome turn of events, we heard a commotion from the living room indicating another sibling spat. Sure enough, there was some wrestling over the remote that ended in my daughter shrieking that her arm was seriously maimed.

I immediately intervened. Megan had a full emotional meltdown and claimed that Tyler had done lifelong damage to her arm. Tyler uttered some choice words to his sister and claimed she was at fault for hogging the remote when the baseball game was on. Suddenly I turned into my mom.

"That's it young man, go to your room and never twist your sister's arm again," I commanded.

We have a 'hands off' policy in our home. No matter how wrong or annoying someone might be, no one is allowed to manhandle the other to get their way. Tyler was quite fired up when I stepped into the fray and frustrated to be missing the game on TV. That is when he told me where to go. Unbelievable! I never swore at my parents, even as a teen. I might have thought it, but I would never have actually said it. Quickly things had reached a peak.

"Go to your room," I insisted infuriated. "No ball game for you for the next half hour." Tyler marched upstairs in an irritated huff.

After eventually calming down and the disturbance now passed, I turned on my computer. For some bizarre reason, my computer would not accept my password. That was odd. It's been the same cryptic password since I got it three years ago – dog's name + part of cell number. Neither had changed. I checked my cap locks, all good. I tried doing it slowly and carefully but that did nothing to remedy this puzzling problem. It drives me crazy when this kind of thing happens. I called Megan, who is handy with technology. She was stumped. I was growing extremely frustrated. It was then I heard a glib voice from upstairs.

"Having computer problems?"

Tyler is the family tech expert. Suddenly I needed him, but he was in lockdown.

"No, I'm fine. I'll sort it out. You take some time to think about what you would like to say to your sister and me," I firmly reminded him.

"I don't think you'll sort it out," he called out cryptically. It took me a minute to register.

"What are you getting at Tyler?" No answer. Surely Tyler couldn't have done anything to my computer from up in his room. I marched upstairs and barged into his room. His computer was open on his desk.

"Wilbur4023 not working for you Mom?" he asked sarcastically.

"Did you do something to my computer?" I demanded. A sly smile spread across his face.

"I might have. I could certainly undo it in exchange for being able to watch the ball game!"

This was dangerous territory. I struggled not to smile at the brilliance and deviousness of his plan. Bad parental move! What horrifying power he suddenly had in our family. Needless to say, I had him fix the problem, I confiscated his computer, and he missed a whole hour of the ball game rather than just thirty minutes. After all, this was a far worse crime than twisting your sister's arm and uttering a swear word at your mother. Sabotaging my computer so I can't use it - this is war! Suffice to say, we had a good talk that night, he apologized to both his sister and me. I changed my password; he promised not to do it again and all is resolved. Matt and I agreed to give him back his computer tomorrow but of course he won't be able to open it because it has a brand-new password! It's 'Ilovemysister'. He won't crack that one in a million years.

Tonight, the rectangle talked about many people being mistreated because of the colour of their skin. That is crazy. That's like saying only houses with red bricks are good and the ones with grey bricks are bad. That makes no sense. Even I know that it doesn't matter what colour your bricks are, we're all the same inside.

Tuesday, July 3, 1900

The house is quiet, and the moon is high. It's a warm July evening and I should be asleep, but I just can't seem to settle. Now in my final trimester, I recall all too well the discomfort it includes. I'm such a bloated cow no one could possibly find me attractive, but somehow Morten feels I'm beautiful.

It's comforting to have the windows open and feel the warm summer breeze. They must be having a campfire over at the Findlay's because there is a trace of smoke in the air or maybe it's just my imagination. Yes, I can hear singing. Why on earth would they be up so late, it's after 10:00 as I heard the clock gong moments ago. They will be very tired farmers tomorrow morning.

Money is so scarce these days. I noticed Morten was counting out the coins and dollars tonight before bed. He is such a thorough bookkeeper and trying to save a little extra money for the baby, not to mention put some aside for the winter months ahead. He has been talking about taking on extra employment this winter, perhaps cutting ice blocks on Bass Lake. Tomorrow he's going to the bank to make a deposit. Our first hay crop was very good, which was a relief. Perhaps I will have him take Mary and I to the store for some continued flirtation. I am worried about the bumpy ride in my condition. That's the only advantage to winter - the smoothness of the sleigh.

That Findlay celebration is growing louder. It must be a family event otherwise we would have been included. I wonder what the occasion is. I hope it doesn't wake the children. In fact, I think I'll close the shutters as the breeze is blowing their smoke in our direction. I'm going to have to lift my large, sleepy workable long-term plan. Neither unemployment nor retirement can be on the agenda for either of us. However, where is the wisdom in returning to an environment that requires medication to cope? Wouldn't it be simpler to just open a little piano bar in downtown Orillia? I wonder if I could make any money at that

-44-

Weeks have passed. Leaves are starting to fall, and the cool autumn air is beginning to arrive. In an attempt to keep my vitamin D levels up, I go for a walk with Wilbur and Megan. The three of us set off towards the lower field on this late September afternoon. We don't often walk here because it is out of the way and there is no set path. However, today for variety we took this route.

We sauntered along for some time as Megan caught me up on all the details of the drama happening with her friends back home. Sometimes I forget how traumatic it was to be a young teenager and how big and real those adolescent problems felt. Deep in conversation we trundled along, discussing the various dynamics and drama's of her clique. Wilbur dutifully watered each bush we passed, when suddenly he went uncharacteristically ballistic. Engrossed in who had stolen whose boyfriend, I hadn't really been paying much attention to Wilbur. However, when a 120 pound dog catches a whiff of something he urgently wants, you can imagine the toll it takes on one's shoulder. Without a second to think, I found myself ruthlessly dragged into the middle of a bush while a rabbit burrowed into the safety of a hole in the ground in indescribable panic. Wilbur, with his nose intensely shoved in the rabbit hole, was oblivious to my condition and was certainly not apologetic.

As Megan and I untangled the line, we discovered what looked like an old stone bench in the midst of this sprawling bush. How odd. The bench was overgrown with moss and the branches of the bush encircled it. The bench was so embedded in the bush it was no wonder we had never noticed it before. Upon closer inspection we found an engraving on it, 'Missing you always', Love Momma and Poppa. Did this signify a place to reflect, or a possible burial spot? Whatever its original purpose, it was a lovely, cobblestone bench. I realize there is history hidden all around us on this farm. Sometimes it is buried or concealed in overgrowth. In other cases, it is wallpapered or painted over. I must ask Matt to cut back this bush so we can sit on this bench. What a beautiful place to rest and ponder what its story might have been.

Last night, the rectangle showed crowds of people on either side of the street, carrying placards, and screaming at one another. It grew extremely hostile, and the police got involved. I was so nervous my shutters were shaking. Can't they find a way to resolve their differences before someone gets hurt? What do I know, I'm just an old farmhouse.

Wednesday, July 4, 1900

Heaven forbid. The family has let me sleep until the sun is high in the sky. The clock has just gone 10:00 a.m. and I'm a lazy slug again. Morten is not beside me. He was likely up hours ago even though he didn't return to bed until the wee hours of the morning. The horror of last night floods over me afresh. I can hear many voices downstairs, and I must get up and face the day. I brushed my hair in a daze and buttoned my dress over my ever-

expanding middle. I can scarcely bend over to tie my boots these days.

What a gathering in the kitchen. So many neighbours here to help. Planning was already underway for a barn raising. As soon as I appeared, Martha Findlay helped me to the table and poured me tea.

"Don't worry Issy. We are all here to assist and everything will be fine," she reassured.

"Is there anything left of it?" I asked nervously. I knew the answer by the silence that followed.

"Don't worry about that now dear. You must take care of yourself and the baby. The men are out assessing the damage and when they can re-build. They are erecting a lean-to in the field for some shelter for the surviving animals."

"Is Morten okay?" I asked warily.

Ida reached across and took my hand. "Yes dear, he's fine. It's a miracle no one was hurt."

How many cows are left?

"Enough that your family will have a steady supply of milk. You know we will all share what we have. Your family will not go hungry," Martha insisted.

We are blessed with wonderful neighbours. After finishing our tea, I was escorted outside and made comfortable by the little pear sapling that Morten had planted in the spring.

Ironically, it was a lovely day. Not a cloud in the sky but the smell of smoke hung in the air.

Morten returned from the remains of the smoldering barn and gave me a comforting hug. I could see the exhaustion and resignation in his eyes. I'm afraid there isn't much left but the foundation is still solid," he explained.

Many of the neighbours joined us for dinner on the lawn. Everyone had brought something, and much was left in the summer kitchen afterwards. We will be supplied well into the middle of September. They have all been so generous and I feel badly relying on the kindness of others. However, I know that I will return the favour tenfold when a crisis hits the next family.

Thursday, July 5, 1900.

A letter has just arrived from Rose. I thought it odd that she hadn't come by. In her note, she expressed her deep distress at hearing the news at the loss of our barn and she planned to visit soon. I have a bad feeling about this. Why, in heaven's name, would my best friend not come when my family has suffered a crisis? What has Patrick done now? I have a mind to go over there this afternoon. I know that isn't possible as we so badly need Chuck here with the state we are in. I suppose I could drive myself, but I don't think it's wise in my condition. I wonder if Tom Findlay might take me. Perhaps I'll take Doug and Lyle for a little walk in that direction, just to get away from this chaos for a few minutes.

The boys were eager to come along. I told Ida I was walking next door for a visit. I could barely keep up as Doug was dashing off in all directions and Lyle moves at a run.

Martha's farm is always so tidy. She's such a good housekeeper. I don't know how she does it except that she has three fewer children than I do. It must be so easy having only four. Her décor is lovely. The furniture is of the finest wood, and there is not a weed in her garden. It drives me mad. I must just get over these petty feelings, but I feel at such a low ebb, especially when I see their barn and am reminded of our own plight.

Martha spotted us walking down the lane and came to greet us. She said that of course Tom could drive me to Rose's later this afternoon when he returned from the fields. It was a warm day and I stayed for lemonade. She gave me some preserves to take home. Martha also showed me a lovely pram that she had and wondered if I might like to use it when the baby arrives. It had terrific big wheels and would be just right for the concession road in the fall.

Doug was growing tired and cranky, so I went directly home by way of the creek. As we came along the path, I heard someone crying. From where I stood, it sounded like a man. I motioned to the boys to hold their tongues so we might see who was around the bend. Miraculously, they did as I asked for once.

I was astonished to see Chuck buckled over as though in pain, crying shamelessly by the riverbank. From what I could see he was alone and certainly had no clue that there was anyone observing him. What on earth could be going on? I thought it best to leave him alone and make our way back along the road. Perhaps Morten would have some insight as to what's troubling him. I doubt it's about Laura as she seems smitten with him. The loss of the barn is more our crisis than his so it can't be that. No doubt there must be some reasonable explanation.

-45-

My friend Donna was up from Toronto. We had just gone for lunch when she told me all about her situation.

I remember when she and Paul got together, and they've since had two young children. About a year ago, he got a promotion which they both felt he should take. It pays better, but the position requires him to be on the road a lot. Her office job is stressful and with the added parenting functions at home, she's constantly exhausted. They return after work to all the usual household functions and it's survival just to make it to the end of the day. By the time dinner is cleaned up and everyone is in bed, it's 9:00. Neither have much energy left for the other. She tells me he zones out on his cell, and she turns to her computer. Weekends are really the only time they have as a family. However, he has been away a lot lately.

What did them in was the affair. She was enraged that he would betray her. Here she was holding the fort at home while he was on the road doing his job, as well as a number of other things and people. One day she happened to see a text and the evidence was self explanatory and stretched back several months.

Apparently, he didn't have much to say in response and was dismissive and minimizing. He explained that she was reading far too much into these messages, that Trixie is just a good friend from work and there was nothing going on. Yes, she said, 'she looks forward to our next trip together' and 'thanks for the back rub', but it isn't what it sounds. Honestly.

Donna was blindsided. Prior to this turn of events their marriage was in survival mode. Between the increased demands of work, her exhaustion and their ongoing arguing, it left little time for them to be together in some sort of meaningful way. She wasn't much interested in sex these days and frankly he felt quite rejected. When she wanted to talk, he was never there or if he was, he wasn't too interested in hearing about her beefs about him and the kids. They had reached an unwritten and unspoken agreement to just keep their distance, to bear their stress alone and find their own escapes. For her, it was her friends on social media. For him, it was his 'work'. The communication between them grew minimal. Sure, they talked about routine things, but gradually there wasn't the time or the inclination to share much beyond that. She grew to resent his work and how much time he spent away from home, leaving her with the bulk of the workload. He was tired of the cold shoulder, her 'lack of interest in bed' and her constant fatigue. She no longer seemed to be that fun person he married.

Over the last couple of years, they had grown apart; same tree, different branches. His world had developed in one direction and hers in another. The only apex at which they intersected was the kids. He found himself frequently on the road with 'colleagues' whom he had come to know better with each passing day. He found an attentive ear in one of them which soon grew to involve other parts of her body as well. There were no burdens or distractions. They could drink and relax and share a few jokes about the personalities in the office and the details of the workplace. It was so easy, and his wife seemed so tense these days. This woman wanted him, and his wife didn't seem to. There was a big bed in his hotel room, and no one would know (except his conscience). It would only be once. After a few drinks, their self-discipline swimming in alcohol, it seemed an increasingly good idea. Soon the die was cast. There was no turning back. A marriage of eleven years and two children was indelibly scarred.

Meanwhile, back at home, she was growing more frustrated and bitter by the minute. How come he gets to go away and stay in a nice hotel, no kids to feed and bathe, no never-ending housework to cope with? She tried his cell, no answer for the fourth time. That's when she resolved things are going to change.

Press replay about 500 times and before you know it, they are way out on different limbs of that tree with a lot of resentment burning in between. There was surprisingly little fighting, just an ever-increasing distance, tension and secrecy growing between them. Now the limb has broken off and come crashing to the ground. The trust has been broken.

Maybe it can be mended, but like a badly broken bone, it will never be as strong as it once was. This will leave a scar.

Often our lives grow apart in a million little ways, before we look over and realize there's a chasm between us. Maybe it starts with an unresolved argument, or a busy schedule, or too much stress, or an addiction. That space grows like an insidious weed that, in and of itself, may seem harmless. However, in countless number the weeds strangle the life out of a marriage and before you know it, you've reached that dangerous plateau of indifference. You are now looking out in different directions without much in common. The interest is lost, and the only glue is the children. In hindsight, they should have gone for help years ago when there was still a spark. Now they are just two lonely people under one roof.

I'm not going to let that happen to me and Matt.

-46-

When my kids are at home together, there is bound to be conflict. Some days it was a relief just to go to work. I remember one day last year when I was sitting in a meeting. My cell kept ringing and vibrating. I was sure there was some sort of emergency, so I reluctantly picked it up.

"MOM, TYLER HAS THE REMOTE AND HE WON'T SHARE IT," Megan screamed into the phone.

Then Tyler grabbed the phone from her, "SHE SAT ON ME AND CALLED ME A TWERP," he shouted back at full volume.

"GIVE ME THAT YOU STUPID JERK..0WW... LET GO OF MY HAIR...MOM HELP ME," "#$@$$3%%#, GET OFF ME!" Something crashed, then Wilbur started barking. The line went dead.

"Ok kids, thanks for calling. Glad you're having a good day," I said serenely in front of my colleagues around the meeting table at Ultra Luscious Relaxation Spa.

Hoping desperately that no one heard, I immediately hung up. My colleagues, who were talking amongst themselves, seemed oblivious to my crisis on the other end of the line. I smiled sweetly and apologized for the interruption, "where were we?" I continued.

When I arrived home that afternoon, I was ready to ream them out for their unconscionable behaviour earlier in the day. I stormed in the door only to find everything extremely quiet. This was a surprise. Perhaps they had killed each other. Instead, the crisis had passed, the storm had settled and each of them was now immersed in their own electronic device. There was a definite upside to electronics. Still infuriated, I found myself caught between wanting to take this on and wanting to enjoy the peacefulness. I plunged ahead.

"What the hell did you think you kids were doing?" The kids each looked up briefly and took in that I was home. I delivered my lecture about using their words to solve their problems. They both acknowledged my point, grunted some apologies and returned to their devices. My heart rate slowed a notch. I patted Wilbur, who was slobbering all over my leg in anticipation of my return home. Megan had returned to her cell and Tyler to his endless computer games. My electronic children. I should have called them Apple and Mac. The only time they get along is when there are separate screens in front of them. I realize now that they never resolved the TV channel issue, they just tuned out in favour of their own realities. They were not getting along; they were just co-existing in separate worlds - like Donna and Paul.

Letting your kids zone out is usually easier. It is easier to park them in front of a screen, even when they are little, just to get a few things done. How many parents relentlessly check their cell phones as their children play at the park? How many families watch television while they eat dinner? I realize, electronics divide us and pacify us. They also disconnect us from each other.

Isabel, and her family of seven kids, didn't have much. They didn't have their own bedrooms or even their own beds for that matter. They had to share toys, clothes, books, desks. They didn't have much, but they had each other. They had mealtimes that were bubbling with conversation and interaction. They had extended family. They were needed to contribute to the household chores for the family to survive. They had to play with one another and create their own entertainment through music, reading, cards, and games. They had to learn to get along. They had to spend the evenings in the same sitting room because there was insufficient heat and light in the rest of the house. These things added up to interaction. No doubt they had their disagreements, but they also had belonging. This is what often escapes us today, in both family and married life. Now it is so easy to isolate ourselves and focus on a screen rather than on the person beside us.

I remember Tyler's friend Jimmy, from years ago. They were around eleven at the time. Jimmy had a younger sister with special needs. She had many challenges which often meant the bulk of parental attention was directed towards her. It must be exhausting to have a child who needs constant assistance. These parents did a tremendous job supporting, advocating and coping with her challenges. All eyes and assistance were on her. Therein lay the problem. Jimmy had become accustomed to being overlooked, to being the easy, helpful and invisible one. And he was GOOD. He blended into the background, he excelled at everything he did, he was liked by friends and teachers and his schoolwork was excellent. However, he was profoundly lonely. Understandably, his parents didn't have much time or energy to notice him because he 'didn't need them' the same way his sister did. By the end of the day, between work and special needs, there wasn't much of anything left over for him. One night, when he was over for dinner, we got talking about dinnertime at his place, mainly that there wasn't one.

"No one eats together," he said. "I make myself a peanut butter sandwich when I'm hungry and I play on my computer. My sister eats in her room when my mom brings her food. She doesn't like to sit at a table or leave her room much. My mom eats later when she watches the news, and my dad usually comes home when I'm in bed. I guess he eats then."

This was the nightly custom. Not only did he eat in front of a screen, but no one ate together or even at the same time.

"I'm not a very good cook," he continued, "but I can make hot dogs, kraft dinner, peanut butter sandwiches, and french fries," he explained.

"You make your own meals?" I wondered if he was just leading me on, but Tyler confirmed it was true.

These were loving people who cared about their children, yet their eleven-year-old was not only malnourished, he was also extremely lonesome. He spent his time in front of a television and a computer, but his true wish was for some connection.

I asked him about his family and relatives. He explained that for the most part, they didn't live nearby so they rarely got together. However, he recalled a time when his parents hosted a family dinner. Jimmy was excited but when it came time for the meal, there wasn't enough room at the table. Instead, he sat at the children's table with his five- and six-year-old cousins. His sister remained in her room. He didn't feel included even when his family was present. How many of our children might describe elements of this experience in their own situation?

Friday, July 6, 1900

I wish I could just lie down in the hammock with a good book but there never seems to be time for that around here. Instead, I will work on this endless pile of sewing. Even though the children all do chores, the work is never done and that is with the help of a farmhand. Chuck's fee is a pittance, but I know Morten is trying desperately to cut corners. I sure hope he hasn't let Chuck go to save a few pennies.

Ida's age is starting to show. It's been hard on her losing Daniel. It must be profoundly lonely without him. She used to be so energetic with the children, teaching them piano, playing cards, and baking together so often. Now she seems to have lost her zest.

On the contrary, Laura is regaining hers. Her interest in life has rekindled and no doubt we have our farmhand to thank for that.

Finally, Tom arrived with his buggy. We had a nice ride together and he is a fine young lad. He told me all about helping his father around the farm and his thoughts for his future. He's keen to become a blacksmith and is planning an apprenticeship with Mr. Carr who has the shop in Prices Corners. It certainly would be handy to have another blacksmith nearby. He asked after our family, and you can be sure I went on for some time about Carrie and Sadie.

When we arrived at Rose's farm, all seemed eerily quiet. No one came out to greet us. Mind you I hadn't posted a letter to let her know I was coming. I didn't want to give Patrick a chance to say I wasn't welcome. No sign of Edward or Patrick in the field or the barnyard or anywhere that I could see. Tom helped me down and walked me to the porch. I suggested he wait in case there was no one around or I had chosen an inconvenient time. I rapped on the door and called through the screen. Nothing. Finally, I walked in. No one. Odd that the children weren't about. Then I recalled that Rose had mentioned in her letter something about them going to their grandparents for a few days over summer break. As I made my way through the empty house I was taken aback by the state of disarray. There were dirty glasses everywhere, dishes in the sink, a broken oil lamp, children's toys and clothes throughout. This wasn't like Rose. She normally kept a nice home. Something seemed off. I walked toward the parlour and called out but still no reply. Tom waited uneasily at the front door. The parlour door was closed. I knocked on it and called out Rose's name. Nothing. I was growing anxious that Patrick might show up. Slowly, I turned the door handle and peeked in cautiously. Oh my God. It was horrifying. I had no idea I could scream that loud. Tom was by my side in a flash. He took in the scene of Rose, sprawled on the floor, her dress torn, blood surrounding her head where she lay unconscious.

"Rose," I called out. In a panic, I shook her and hollered into her ear. "Rose, wake up, wake up. Please Rose wake up!" She moaned almost inaudibly.

Tom grabbed a blanket from the sofa and threw it over her. "Rose, what happened?" I screamed, "Can you hear me?"

Could this brute have done this to his wife? Surely not. Tom was infuriated but uneasy. He grabbed a woodstove poker in the event that he needed to defend us. He began looking around the room, in case Patrick was nearby. I stayed with Rose, shocked at the state she was in. How could he do such a thing? The man should be behind bars. Thankfully the children were away. Where was Edward through all this?

Gradually Rose started coming around. I held a cloth firmly on her forehead, in an attempt to stop the bleeding from the gash on her face. Eventually her eyes opened. Although disoriented, she was semi-conscious. Then suddenly terror shot into her eyes as if she suddenly remembered the altercation that had preceded her condition. When she saw that it was me holding her head, she relaxed somewhat but looked confused. In her agitated state she kept muttering, "Where's Eddy?"

"What's happened here Rose? Did Patrick do this to you?" I questioned. Her eyes were terrified as she shook her head.

"Rose, you can tell me. You're safe now." I insisted.

Eventually I was able to coax some of the story from her and it was as I assumed. Patrick had returned home from town in a drunken stupor. What I hadn't predicted, nor had she for that matter, was that Patrick might stumble upon she and Edward sharing a cup of tea and perhaps a little more. I reassured her that Tom had gone outside to keep a look out for Patrick's return. She was extremely fitful about that possibility as he had left only briefly to pursue Edward, but said he had every intention of returning to 'deal with her properly'.

Time was of the essence. We've got to get out of here. "Where are the children?" I demanded.

"... at my parents for the week," she mumbled.

"Can you get up?" I coaxed her.

"But where can we go? Patrick is furious and he'll definitely look for me at your house."

I was trying to think as I went. I have never had to flee a man in my life, and I must admit I wasn't terribly resourceful. I almost said, 'we will hide you in the barn'. Then I remembered my own plight.

"We'll come up with something. There are plenty of sympathetic neighbours on our concession."

"But what if someone told or it got back to Patrick somehow, he would really hurt me."

"Rose, he has already done that. As I find you lying here in a pool of blood, I don't need convincing as to what he's capable of. When he has a few drinks in him, he knows no bounds."

I cleaned up Rose's head and wrapped a makeshift bandage around it. I felt myself growing increasingly uneasy at how long it was taking to get her up. What if Patrick returned before we got out of there? There was no way I was leaving her here to be finished off by that inebriated brute.

Tom carefully carried Rose to the carriage and lay her down on the back seat while I quickly gathered a few clothes and belongings for Rose and the children. My heart was racing like a hummingbird and even the horse was getting skittish, sensing our anxiety. Moments later we were off, and Tom had his mare cantering down the laneway. I can't tell you how relieved I was to flee the situation.

Friday, July 6, 1900

Rose is now home and resting in our bed in a state of pain and confusion. If Patrick comes here, I doubt *he'd have the gall to barge into our home. I must think of a safer alternative. I have sworn Tom to secrecy, and he has assured me that he won't breathe a word to anyone as he understands Rose's safety is at stake. Morten was extremely alarmed at hearing the story and Chuck was recruited to carry Rose up to our bed for the time being. Neither man could believe what they saw, and both have agreed that Patrick will not pass the threshold of our home after leaving his wife in such condition. Dr. Moffat is on his way as Tom was asked to alert him of the situation. Meanwhile, Ida is cleaning up Rose's facial wounds.*

Rose is in a fitful state, simply beside herself and insisting we get the children at once. She's tossing and turning and going on and on about the children. She's terrified Patrick will head to Coldwater to fetch them. She pleaded with us to retrieve them at once and to warn her parents he may be coming.

"Morten has sent Chuck to get the children," I reassured. "Knowing your father Rose, he'll likely shoot Patrick if he poses any threat."

Between the commotion of the barn and Rose's ordeal, everyone has had quite a shaking up. My children were in a state of disbelief when they saw Rose and felt that Patrick ought to be imprisoned immediately. I couldn't agree more. What on earth could have possessed him to be so cruel to someone he loves and who is the mother of his children.

Rose's children have just arrived. According to Chuck, Rose's father was furious with Patrick and vowed to 'take care of him' if he showed up there.

Elizabeth was worried sick about her mother and went straight to her. Anna being timid, said little. She wept when I hugged her, and Zoe put her arm around her too. Robbie seemed sullen and angry and wanted to know "what had she done to anger father this time?" What an objectionable response for a nine-year-old. Little Harry was scared but stuck close to his big brother. Who knows what these children have seen. They were clearly more frightened than surprised.

We arranged beds in the parlour so their family could all be together in a comfortable, safe room. The girls gave them extra blankets and Zoe and Doug shared the stuffed bears from their beds. Rose and her family will be safe there. Butch will bark if anyone comes in the night. Chuck has agreed to stay on a cot near their door just to provide extra reassurance. It's odd to feel fearful of someone I know. Dr. Moffat has cleaned and bandaged Rose's lacerations and he fears she may have a cracked rib. It will take time for the pain to diminish. For now, we have left the issue of payment to another day as this came at us quite unexpectedly. Dr. Moffat would not agree to take any sum at all from us having just lost our barn. "We will work it out in time," he said, "Perhaps Patrick should pay the cost," he suggested, "as this was his doing."

I think it's Rose's pride that is most badly wounded. I'm not so sure that time will heal that without leaving a matching laceration in her soul.

Chuck is so preoccupied that he barely touched his supper. Perhaps it is the loss of the barn that is troubling him as it has devastated Morten. I told Morten about seeing Chuck reduced to tears down by the creek and he was somewhat perplexed as it really is our loss rather than Chuck's. I practically died when Doug said at supper tonight, "Are you still sad

Chuck?" Chuck was taken aback as he had no sense that he had been spotted earlier in the day. Luckily, he recovered himself quickly by saying, "we are all sad, Doug, to have lost so many animals so quickly." Then he returned to picking at his meal while Laura shot him a furtive glance.

After supper, some of the neighbourhood men arrived in the yard to plan the raising bee. We could expect anywhere from seventy-five to a hundred men, and their wives and children, so it is quite an event to plan, especially in my condition. However, I shouldn't complain. I think of poor Morten. The raising of a barn is a colossal task when one considers all the wood that needs to be felled and organized and cut to fit together. However, it must be done, and Morten is grateful for the help. He is going to a 'bee' this weekend on the 10th concession, and he will talk up ours and set the date. We will announce it in church as well to get the message out. Rev. Mactavish will pass the word to the other congregations when he does his circuit on Sunday.

Saturday, July 7, 1900

It's 3:00 a.m. and Butch has finally calmed down. My heart is still beating wildly. I've never seen Butch that upset. He was growling and snarling as though he was going to leap at someone's throat. He was reacting to the raucous outside on the lawn followed by some hollering and a barrage of foul language. Despite being clothed in his nightshirt, Morten was downstairs in a flash and Chuck was right beside him from the bottom of the stairs. The oil lamps were quickly lit. Rose and the children were terrified as they huddled inside the parlour with the shutters closed tightly. I peeked out the front window to the lawn below. Despite the dark, I could see a figure in the moonlight, staggering towards the porch and creating all the hoopla. There was Patrick, yelling and carrying on like the drunken fool he is, demanding that his wife come out. Morten and Chuck met him at the door, I could hear them talking in low voices which soon escalated into much louder ones.

"What's going on here Patrick? I don't know what you're talking about. Has your wife gone missing? Well, she isn't here. You are in no shape to be out and about in your condition." Talk of that nature went on for several minutes. Patrick responded with several threats that he would find his wife wherever she was. If he found out later that she was here, he would 'beat her within an inch of her life', he threatened in his slurred tongue.

Morten and Chuck were not intimidated, as there were two of them and Patrick was in a highly intoxicated state. They warned him that if he didn't leave, they would get the constable. He eventually retreated, mounted his horse with great difficulty and disappeared into the night. I wonder how he will remain in the saddle in his condition.

Rose was a wreck, as were the children. Robbie was the exception and berated his mother for making his father so mad in the first place. In my opinion, that little Robbie needs some immediate correction in his thinking. However, Rose was in no state to take a stand. I held her and reassured her. We reinforced all the doors and had Butch sleep in the room with them. That helped to settle her nerves. Now, if only I could return to sleep, but I no longer feel restful. I am all riled by that frightful man and I'm not even the target of his fury.

I mounted the stairs to find the girls anxiously gathered at their bedroom door. Zoe was beside herself with tears and the others looked terrified. A rush of fury swept over me at seeing my own children disturbed by this selfish and intimidating drunkard, and so close on the heels of all we've just been through. I hugged the girls. Sadie was livid that Morten let Patrick get away.

"Why didn't they just knock him out and drag him to the constable?" She demanded.

"It's not that simple honey. The law might feel Rose was to blame for leaving her husband. We want to help her, not complicate things," was all I could think to say. We sat together for a time discussing the injustice of it all. Finally, they returned to their beds.

Morten is lying beside me now and is much less rattled than I am. In fact, I hear the gentle rhythm of his snore as he enjoys the sleep that somehow escapes me. He must be exhausted after having so little sleep the other night. I can hear the clock ticking in the sitting room downstairs. I've been here so long that I'm starting to watch the sun creep over the horizon, awaking the first songbird before the day springs to life. Sure enough, there's Henry's call.

Wednesday, July 11, 1900

Days have gone by with no further disruption from Patrick. Life is gradually settling in. It is wonderful having Rose here and she is starting to return to herself, despite the bruising. The pain in her rib is subsiding a little.

Chuck and Morten have much work to do to prepare for the upcoming raising bee. One of the families from church has graciously postponed their *barn raising when they heard of our desperate plight. They have generously offered their prepared logs which we can replace later. That is such a Godsend as I don't know how we could ever come up with the required lumber all cut and organized so quickly.*

I believe I may have a window into Chuck's discomfort the other day. Laura was out in the drive shed while Chuck was doing the milking. We've taken to doing our milking there since we have no barn. While I was upstairs in search of some chicken wire, they were situated right beneath me. I could hear their entire conversation through the floorboards.

"But you didn't mean to Chuck. It wasn't your fault," Laura insisted.

"I should never have taken a lantern into the barn," Chuck replied.

"I am the one whose foot knocked it. The responsibility should be on my head," she explained.

"I feel wretched. Your family has always been so good to me. I've been here most of my life. How could I have been so stupid?" His voice was shaken as Laura comforted him. "I want to tell Morten but if I do, he might sack me for burning down his barn, not to mention taking his sister into the loft. Where would I go then? I would be homeless, and I certainly wouldn't get to see you anymore."

"We aren't telling anyone," she retorted. "They'll most certainly disapprove. My name would be mud. I know Morten is upset and it's going to cost our family dearly. He can't afford to do without you but if he knew the truth, he would be furious. We're not risking that," Laura insisted.

I was taken aback! I must say, I never suspected Laura and Chuck had been the cause of the fire. Still, I am more dismayed with Laura's response than Chuck's. Chuck's reaction is understandable especially since he could lose his position as farmhand. He has been on this farm for years, since he came over by ship as an orphan from England. Daniel had taken him in when he was thirteen, as they only had Morten to help around the farm. Morten was just a lad then himself. Chuck's family had been killed in a house fire and he had been abruptly left with no one. The world can be a cruel place when you are young and penniless. Eventually, he ended up at the orphanage when the hunger pains in his belly grew unbearable. He soon became one of the Home Children, shipped to Canada in hopes of some kind of life. He has been stuck in the menial role of farmhand ever since. At the time, he was delighted to have a roof over his head, food in his belly and inclusion in a kindly family, who treated him as their own son. He has been on this farm since then and counts himself lucky to have landed here. When I consider his history, I realize how deeply upsetting the fire would have been for him. Aside from losing our barn, it undoubtedly raised some very painful memories from his past. Imagine losing your loved ones in a fire and barely escaping with your own life. It's hard enough losing a few cows and pigs.

Laura, on the other hand, is choosing to conceal this information simply to protect her shameful behaviour. How dare she. She knows her brother is a compassionate man who is devastated by this loss which could have also meant the end of our family farm. It's only due to our neighbours that we will be able to continue. Should I tell Morten about their conversation? Should I address Laura and insist she tell him? Should I say nothing? I hate these kinds of decisions and I resent her for inadvertently putting me in this position.

Tuesday, July 24, 1900

Mary has asked me to deliver a letter to James when I'm at the general store today. Obviously, it's sealed with wax so there can be no prying eyes, but she did tell me what she wrote.

Initially, she updated him regarding our family. She thanked him for his kind offer of the ride home from the church picnic and that she was sorry she hadn't accepted. However, she had very much enjoyed their picnic together last month. She went on to say that the family would be hosting a raising bee, due to the loss of our barn. She was hoping that he and his family would be joining in as she looked forward to seeing him again. Apparently, she signed it 'Affectionately Yours', Mary.

Good for Mary. Sometimes you need to be a little bold and offer an invitation. If that doesn't initiate another meeting, hopefully the flirtatious "Affectionately Yours" will. I assured her I will deliver the letter right into his hands.

I had great difficulty sitting beside Laura in the carriage. I can scarcely look at her knowing what secret she harbours. How could she not tell Morten. I am trying to conceal my indignation but it's hard. Ida seemed to sense the tension and gracefully sat between us without so much as a question.

When we arrived in town, the store was buzzing with activity. We had a full list of needed supplies given the crowd coming on the weekend. Alice was helping in the store today and spotted Ida. I could see that she seemed brighter than when I last saw her and perhaps feeling a little more herself. She welcomed us with a hug and told us how sorry she was to hear about our barn. "What a tragedy to befall such a nice family. Of course, we'll all come to the bee," she responded.

Hearing the commotion, James rounded the corner, with Betty McAllister right behind him! I almost gasped and was so glad that Mary wasn't with us. I did grapple for a moment whether I would hand him the letter as promised. I know Mary would have tucked it in her purse, put on a brave smile, and said nothing. However, as her mother, who is both older and wiser, I thought differently.

"Nice to see you again James. My we enjoyed having you at the farm last month. I know you and Mary had such fun. Mary felt that you would be interested in our news and took it upon herself to write you a note." He smiled shyly but eagerly took it from my hand and put it in his pocket. I saw Ida smile at me. This poor boy has some thinking to do and neither Ida nor I will let him slip away easily.

"Hello Betty. Nice to see you again. I hope you have been well," and on the falsities went. I am sure she's a nice girl, but we all know that my Mary is far nicer. I know how taken Mary is with James and I hate to see a good prospect go to someone else just because she lives nearby.

It has been a long journey for a woman of seven months gestation. All that bumping is hard on me. I am so glad to finally be home and have my feet up.

Mary was keen to hear the news the moment I came through the door. She tried to act calm and somewhat disinterested in the results of my journey, but I know her well. Inside she was bubbling with curiosity. Knowing how sensitive she had been about spotting James with Betty at the picnic, I omitted that part of the story. I explained that I had indeed crossed paths with James, and we had a nice visit. He did ask after her and I did give him the letter which he did not read in my presence. I spoke to his mother about the raising bee and the MacNallys are planning to come, especially since Alice seemed to be feeling brighter.

"Did he seem pleased to see you mother? Did he ask about me? What did you say?" It sounded to me very much like a young lady with strong feelings. I do hope it blossoms into something. Mary is becoming quite grown up now and it would be nice for her to find someone to settle down with in the next few years. I know she wants to be a teacher but how long can a young lady really want that for? Before long she will want children of her own.

Morten and Chuck have been madly preparing the site for the new barn. Laura, Ida, the girls and I have been organizing the meals and getting the word out. The farms on the south side of the concession will be responsible for main course dishes and the farms on the north side will be responsible for snacks, buns and desserts. Luckily, we still have a good supply of flour on hand. We will provide the refreshments, as well as some pies. That is a lot of lemonade and baking between now and the weekend. None of which I feel up to doing. Mary has offered to plan some games for the children, such as red rover and hide and seek. I'm sure they will be able to entertain themselves quite nicely, but it is always better if there is something organized.

Men have been dragging down beams of wood all week while others have been cutting the notches so they will fit together snugly. I have never seen so many men sawing and cutting tree trunks in all my life. You would think they are erecting a village of barns. We have numerous trees and beams piled and I can hear Morten and Chuck out there day and night, sawing away... and this on top of their farm work! They spend so much time working together, it must be haunting Chuck's conscience to harbour a secret.

I hope Morten doesn't overdo it as he is not a young man anymore. I definitely don't want to be raising eight children without their father around to support us.

Rose has been lying low and of course didn't come to town with us, for fear of being seen. Word has it that Patrick has been everywhere looking for her. I haven't breathed a word to anyone that she and the children are at our farm. It's quite a challenge to conceal with so many dropping by to prepare for the bee. I fear he might return looking for her. I don't sleep well at night and awaken to any little noise about the place. You never realize how many sounds there are until you are nervous. It is so difficult to limit all the children to the back to play. It often spills out onto the front lawn where a passerby could spot them from the road if they glanced down the laneway. I am constantly reminding them to take their game of tag or tree climbing around to the back.

-47-

I try to get down to visit Mom as much as I can. I have been helping her with her bills lately because she has become a bit absent minded and slightly mixed up. It is so unlike her. All my life she meticulously balanced her books, recorded her spending, paid her bills promptly. However, she's had so much to deal with these last few months. Most importantly, she's lost Dad, her husband of 61 years. I can't imagine what that does to a person. Even if their relationship was not a blissfully happy one, they have been life partners for over half a century. There must be such a profound and indescribable emptiness.

In addition, she is no longer driving. We are all relieved she has voluntarily given it up. Who would have guessed. It had posed such a challenge for us to figure out how to wrestle the keys from her hands. Now the problem is solved because she seems to have forgotten she wanted to drive somewhere. Perfect.

Recently even her beloved cat has been ailing. Heaven forbid if anything happens to it. I realize without it she is totally alone. We have offered to have a live-in care giver to help her, but she is adamant she does not need that. Instead, she talks to Whiskers. The coddling he receives, while she ignores the rest of us, is shameful. Whiskers is even allowed in the living room. In fact, those plush red chairs that I was never allowed to sit in growing up have now become his scratching post. He even lies on the kitchen table. My Mom warms his food before they listen to music together in the evening. Sometimes I wonder if she prefers the cat to Dad.

Mom has caregivers several times a week to help with personal care, whether she likes it or not. Other than that, she is alone (except for Whiskers). She's never been much for hobbies or clubs and doesn't have many friends, hence her circle of people is small. I worry about her. I notice she's been calling two or three times a day just to chat. As annoying as that gets, I realize it is a symptom of loneliness. I'm trying to visit more often.

I arrived with the file of bills to go through, as well as my cell which is loaded with photos. Between these two things, that should give us plenty to talk about during our lunch. I must admit, the lunches are getting harder. Her mobility is growing increasingly limited, and I hover around her as though she's a breakable doll I don't want to slip from my grasp. The last place we went for lunch had a staircase that was out of this world. I've never seen stairs so steep and treacherous. I suggested an alternative restaurant, but Mom wouldn't have it. She liked the quiche at this particular establishment, and she didn't mind a challenge. So up she went, one painful step after another with me following right behind. It was all fine until another restaurant patron arrived on a limited lunch hour schedule. Fifteen minutes and a few impatient words later we were all at the top of the stairs.

However, what happened today was unexpected. When I arrived at Mom's, she greeted me as usual. We had a nice visit around the kitchen table. Eventually I pulled out her bill file and we went through the bills together as we sipped our coffee. When Mom signed the hydro cheque, I almost dropped my cup. It was an illegible scribble. You would not normally think this was a crisis, but Mom has always had immaculate penmanship. Initially, I thought she was joking but she didn't think anything was odd. That's when I knew something was wrong. I had her sign several times and the illegible scrawl repeated itself. She was not the least bit aware of anything out of the ordinary. Luckily, we had decided to have lunch at home today, partly due to the weather but mostly due to my dread of another stairway. After our visit, I called my siblings. My sister agreed that was odd and decided she'd follow-up with a doctor's appointment.

The doctor thought Mom may have had a mild stroke or TIA, which was the beginning of a slippery slope. When I saw her two days later, she was in the hospital, a shadow of her former self. I held her hand and found this sadly reminiscent of months earlier with Dad. It doesn't take long for life to change. Of the two foundations of my life, one had disappeared completely and the other was quickly crumbling before my eyes.

Mom is a feisty one. She was hospitalized for a week, and we all thought it was the end. We visited her daily and the grandchildren came from far and wide to say 'goodbye'. Then... she got better. You would think this is happy news and it should be. However, as we found with Dad, sometimes the state of recovery is not the same as the original, pre-illness condition. Mom was there in body only. Devastated, we watched her transition from her former determined, strong and adventurous self to a placid, dependent soul who mostly made no sense and slept a great percentage of the day. Maybe falling down the stairs on the way to a great lunch would have been a better ending.

The doctors had said there is no telling how long she might last. She has longevity in her genes. She was on medication to keep a recurring stroke at bay but there is no crystal ball when it comes to exact predictions on life expectancy. I wish for her a quick and painless exit. Perhaps there is a time when death becomes our friend.

Weeks passed. My mother deteriorated one cell at a time. I got the news this morning that she had finally let go. I was flooded with a mixture of relief and profound grief over the loss of my mother, who, for the past several months, had been my only remaining parent.

-48-

The hospital had contacted my sister to relay the sad news, as she was Power of Attorney. However, my sister happened to be out of town and her cell had accidentally been left on airplane mode. After a few unanswered calls, the hospital left a message on her home machine, to call the hospital immediately. Imagine my shock when I called the hospital several hours after her passing to ask how she was getting along today.

"She's dead," was the response and "why didn't you call us back?" the woman snapped, clearly annoyed with me. I was still back at "she's dead!"

"What?! She died? Oh my God, when did that happen?"

"We left you several messages. Why didn't you call us?"

Still stunned I replied, "You called me? Are you sure? I don't have any missed calls. Was anyone with her when she died?"

"We called and left several messages for you. Did you want to see her because the orderly is on the way up to take her to the morgue," the heartless voice insisted.

This was all happening so fast and why is this woman so insensitive? Shouldn't she be expressing some sympathy, was my thought. However, I was still stuck on, "she's dead." She's been my mother all my life so that takes a few moments to digest. You'd think they would know that, working in palliative!

Eventually I realized the woman on the other end thought she was addressing my sister. I quickly explained the situation and said, "yes, I would like to see her. I'm coming from out of town and if I leave in five minutes I could be there in an hour and a half."

"No, she's been here three hours already," came the heartfelt response.

"Won't she still be dead in one and half hours?" was my reply. "I will call my brother who lives nearby, he will be there in fifteen minutes."

"Fine, I'll try to reach the orderly, but I can't promise. Tell your brother to hurry," she stated without a trace of compassion in her response. Clearly nursing was not her calling.

It was a sad day. I wish I had been with her to hold her hand as she passed from this world. Suffice to say, Daniel had a nicer exit, relatively quick, painless and peaceful in his own bed, surrounded by family. Who could ask for more.

-49-

Today was Mom's service. She would have been very pleased with the event. The church looked beautiful, friends and family came from all over, and the pictures were outstanding. Each of my siblings, myself included, would be expected to say a few words in memory of Mom. I realize this is a very important point in a person's existence when their child must try to impart what their parent meant to them. This is the moment you find yourself looking back and reviewing your relationship with the person you are about to eulogize. It is a sobering reminder that our own children will likely do the same for us someday.

Normally you would think that a daughter would have countless good things to say about her mother, however I found myself coming up a bit short, as did my siblings. Although I loved Mom, we didn't have an emotionally close relationship. We got along better once I was beyond adolescence; however, the depth of connection was limited. Despite my 'friendship' and respect for her, we were not close. From ages 0 to 5, I depended on her, and she was very dependable. From ages 5 to 13, I was hypersensitive to and uneasy about her moods and her drinking, and she gave me reason to be. From ages 14 to 21, I was constantly enraged with her attempt to rule and control me, which she never did successfully because my respect had slipped a notch by this point. By 22, I had grown quite emotionally disconnected from her although we maintained a superficially pleasant relationship throughout my adult life. So, as I sat there with my pen, trying to draft a heartfelt speech, I was at a loss of what to say. At someone's 'Celebration of Life' one should highlight the positive things. Sometimes these services bear little resemblance to the person you remember as the stories are skewed in favour of a certain perspective. I realize that's why no one awful ever dies. You never hear people say about the deceased, "well to be honest, he was a real bastard."

Although she wasn't nurturing or affectionate, all my concrete needs were consistently met very efficiently. I am profoundly thankful to her for that. Throughout my childhood I never remember having any fun with her or her taking much of an interest in my daily life. She was there but she was somewhere else. She never read me stories or tucked me in, Dad and my siblings did all that and they were lots of fun. I remember trying to please Mom and I was able to do so, through polite behaviour and helping around the house. I remember her anger if I made a mess and the fights we had over my adolescent behaviour. It was her approach that was the problem. She didn't talk with me she talked at me. She didn't help me to make sensible decisions she told me what to do. Still not really eulogy material.

What could I talk about regarding Mom? As a young girl, Mom apparently loved camp. She also was a great diver in her day. (diver not driver). We had some wonderful lunches together at some nice restaurants once I was over the age of thirty. Mom was fair and organized. She reliably sent a thoughtful birthday and anniversary card on each occasion. She also was my biggest fan when I'd succeed. However, I sensed she might distance from me if I messed up, which I frequently did. Mom was charming, responsible, and dependable but she wasn't very loving and maternal. I can't forget those experiences and pretend they never happened. I know Mom did the best job she could with the emotional tools she had. I kept the eulogy on the reliable birthday cards, her love of camp and how much she enjoyed quiche. How will Megan and Tyler eulogize me and what would I like them to remember?

I don't see many barn swallows around these days. They used to swoop in and out of that barn in droves. There are only a handful of them now. What if they don't come back next year at all?

Friday, July 27, 1900

We are up early to prepare for the bee. I could hear Morten stirring while Henry was still snoring in the coop. Ida was in the kitchen stoking the woodstove.

For hours we made pies, the girls prepared tea and lemonade as well as setting up the tables. We opened the far field for people to park their rigs and turn out their horses.

Zoe and Sadie picked hollyhocks from the garden to beautify the tables. By the time people arrived the sun was just coming over the horizon. Laura and Mary served tea as carriages turned in the laneway. The men met to delegate jobs and discuss Morten's plan for the day. I know Mary was relieved when the MacNally's carriage arrived at last.

The day was filled with gruelling hard work, sweltering heat, annoying bugs, merriment and sociability. The children had a wonderful time running about, swinging from tree ropes, playing hide and seek, and taking turns on the neighbour's penny farthing bicycle. Mary had some games planned so it kept them busy when they weren't doing errands to help. I have never seen men work so hard in all my life. Ida and I counted sixty-four men and older boys who were involved in the construction. They had it organized into sections. The site had been cleared of debris, so they were able to focus on constructing the walls. They began by building the frame of the north wall. Chuck, Morten, and some of the other men had arranged a well-honed pulley system involving horses, wheels and giant ropes. The heat was overwhelming. We went through so much lemonade I thought we might run dry. Old man Cliff

Stoles from down the road had brought his fiddle. At breaks we all clapped and sang along before returning to the project. Poor Rose, I could see her peeking out the window gazing at the activity outside. There she was with her children, shut up in our farmhouse on a beautiful day, hidden away from everyone. There had been no sign of Patrick attending this event but then again, one never knows. He's not the type of man to lend a helping hand. The local tavern regulars are not known for their selfless participation in community events. Nevertheless, you can be sure that if Patrick's barn burned down, the whole community would arrive to rebuild it. No family can survive the winter without a barn. In order to have cows to milk, pigs to eat, chickens to lay, horses to pull the plough and carriage, a loft to store hay and straw, one needs a solid barn!

By the time the sun was beginning to descend in the western sky, it must have been 9:00. The bugs

had grown unbearable at dusk, but the barn frame was taking shape. It must be completed by tomorrow evening as the next day is the sabbath so no one will work then.

Many of the family members had come and gone throughout the day to maintain their own farms. That is the problem with farming, it never stops. It doesn't matter whether your barn burns down, or someone is sick with the plague, the farm chores continue. I can't even conceive of all the constant needs of the fields and all that requires. If I had a choice, I wouldn't choose this life.

These days many people are moving to the bigger towns to work in factories or shops. Farm life is all Morten knows. As the only male in his family, he knew he didn't have a choice. Sometimes I do dream of something easier. Perhaps to be a minister's or a doctor's wife might be better. Then again, I don't envy poor Margaret having to get up with her husband at ungodly hours in response to someone's deteriorating condition. Imagine the countless funerals and house calls of a minister's wife. I don't know what we are suited for, but I do know that poor Morten will be exhausted tonight and there is still a barn party to follow tomorrow evening.

Friday, July 27, 1900. (Continued)

We all heard him scream as he fell to the ground with a tremendous thud. The men raced to his aid knowing full well that falling from a high beam can be deadly. Cam was knocked out cold but was finally roused to consciousness. He was extremely disoriented. His shoulder was clearly injured and his back hurt as he wailed in pain. It seemed an eternity before the ambulance rounded the corner at top speed pulled by two sleek thoroughbreds. Two men jumped out and addressed Cam, who responded incoherently. Soon they had carefully placed him on a stretcher in the back of the covered wagon. His screams of pain were unforgettable. They gave him a whiff of ether that seemed to temporarily calm his discomfort. Seeing the sight of the ambulance, pulled by two galloping horses, is bound to create much attention around the countryside. It wasn't long before word got out of the terrible accident. Perhaps it was this turn of events that perked Patrick's inebriated attention to our farmyard. Not long after the departure of the ambulance, Patrick appeared in the barnyard.

"Where is she?" He demanded.

Morten stepped forward, with a host of men behind him. "Patty we've been through this before. I'm sorry to hear about your wife and kids but I don't know where she is," he lied again, trying to avoid a scene.

Many of the men looked genuinely confused. They all quite honestly attested that no one had seen any sign of his wife or children here. The women appeared visibly uneasy and distanced themselves from the conflict, they gathered together away from the commotion. The children sensing tension, also kept away. My eye glanced to the farmhouse where I could see the curtain had drawn closed. There was no trace of Rose at the window.

The situation ended without incident. One of the men shouted that she likely ran off due to his drinking and poor temperament, which did not go down well and almost started a fight. However, a few men escorted Patrick down the lane and out to the carriageway. Nevertheless, it has left us all on edge, particularly Rose and the children. Obviously, I couldn't go to her right away as I didn't want to give away her presence. It wasn't until later when I feigned I needed to rest that I was able to go inside.

After such horrendous events, the work on the barn did resume but with far more solemnity than before.

The dinner was wonderful with a collection of delicious dishes from around the neighbourhood. Evelyn Barclay contributed some delectable spareribs, as they had just butchered one of their pigs. She's such a marvellous cook and I certainly am not. All I did was make tea and a few pies.

Mary and James appear to be back on track. James, of course, has been helping with the building but Mary is constantly bringing him lemonade and cheering him on. I was quite beside myself when I had lost sight of them and wondered where on earth they could be. Mary is a well-mannered young lady and knows not to disappear with a suitor. Eventually I spotted them seated in James' carriage, within full sight of the gathering.

Chuck and Laura seem to be under great duress. Clearly, she's on him to conceal the truth. My sense is that he wants to confess to Morten the true reason we are all brought to this situation.

When I came inside Rose was a mess. She was shaking like a leaf. "The children.... Issy I shouldn't be here. I am putting you and your family in danger. This isn't right."

"I see. Where do you suppose you would go Rose?"

She looked at me with a hopeless expression and we both knew there were no alternatives.

"Perhaps he is now satisfied that you are elsewhere and that will be the end of his search," I suggested.

"And what if you're wrong?"

"What if I'm wrong?" I responded. "There is nothing to be done. If I call the constable your

husband will get his knuckles rapped with a stern warning and you and the children will be sent home in disgrace. I won't have it Rose. His brutality is too much for any woman to bear," I insisted.

"Perhaps I was wrong to challenge him about his drinking. He only does it occasionally and I could bear it if I just keep to myself," she concluded.

"Have you lost your mind? Surely you are not thinking of returning to him. The next time he might kill you." I was dumbfounded.

"I don't believe he would do that. The longer I stay away the more irate he will grow. Oh Issy, what should I do? I do still love him. I don't know why."
"I don't know why either!" I could not believe what I was hearing. What has happened to my friend that her judgement has become as impaired as her husband's self-control. I could talk no sense into her. I do worry what has come over her. I know the children are missing their home. It's difficult living out of a valise, but to return to a home which is rampant with disrespect and abuse is beyond my understanding. Perhaps she's just confused, and the morning light will bring a clear perspective.

I discussed it with Morten, and he was equally amazed at her thoughts of returning. Nevertheless, his advice to me was to stay out of it and not to meddle in their matrimonial affairs. How could he say such a thing? She's my best friend. Ida simply shook her head and said she had seen this sort of thing before and quoted the bible saying, "what God has joined together let no man put asunder." Ida is so old fashioned. "Surely God would not have my friend and her vulnerable children exposed to a husband and father who beats her brutally. Surely God saw the state of poor Rose when we scraped her off the parlour floor and whisked her away in a galloping cart. What about Patrick being held to account and thrown in the county jail for a time. What would God think of that plan?" I shouted at Morten. His response was that my escalated mood is related to the baby but truly I am furious. I am amazed at everyone. Is there no one who has any moral conscience in this household?

Rose's boys are infuriating. Little Robbie is a chip off the old block and so disrespectful to his mother. If that were my boy, I would give him a good scolding and send him upstairs, but Rose just sits there meekly and absorbs his insults. I have a mind to give that boy a talking to.

Each night, I cannot wait until supper is done and the dishes are finished so we can just sit on the porch. It is nice to enjoy the evenings singing with the piano or playing a hand of cards or listening to Mary read aloud.

The new barn is close to completion. What a weight off our minds. The men can finish the stalls and pens throughout the week. Morten boasted that this structure will last a lifetime, provided there are no more fires. I didn't say a word about the cause of the fire, but I was tempted. The nerve of that Laura, deceiving her own family so shamelessly.

"We have so little money left." Morten grumbled as he counted it out last night. "We'll pray for a long growing season and a short winter."

Fortunately, he's a rigorous bookkeeper. Years ago, he and Daniel had set aside an emergency fund. Decades of saving wiped out in one night. What would have become of us if not for the coins he tucked away so meticulously?

Despite the tedious labour of the men and the dangerous mishap of the day with poor Cam, it was a cheery event to have the neighbours gathered. The evening ended with such fun and high spirits. It's our remaining animals who are happiest of all to be back underneath a proper shelter and finally out of the heat and bugs. How did our grandparents ever cope? I couldn't imagine settling this land. It is hard enough when you already have cleared fields, and a well-built home. Imagine starting with acres of trees to clear. It is daunting to think of.

Saturday, July 28, 1900.

Hallelujah, the project is finally complete. The roof has been set in place and all the beams are secure. A monumental achievement. It's a wonder what sixty-four men can do when they all pull together. We gathered to admire the fine construction and workmanship before the dancing began. The men went around slapping each other on the back and generally congratulating one another. Morten gave a heartfelt speech of thanks to all who had come and so generously contributed in our hour of need. There was whooping and laughing and a large round of applause. The men often get a little carried away once their work is behind them. I won't be kicking up my feet but rather will find a comfortable pile of straw to settle into for the evening. Nevertheless, it will be great fun to watch everyone enjoy themselves on a summer's night. Our fiddler Cliff has rounded up a few of his friends and they will be entertainment for the evening. He has agreed to do it in exchange for a healthy supply of Ida's raspberry preserves, which he favours. I could see James and Mary chatting together and Betty McAllister was noticeably absent from the event. Once Cliff brought out his fiddle, the square dancing began. Even the children were allowed to stay up late to join in the celebrations.

That barn dance was such a fun celebration. I remember it well. We had some good times back then.

-50-

Aside from missing my parents, one of the hardest things is that soon our childhood family home will be sold, and that history will be demolished forever. My parents are now gone and by the end of the year, their home will be too. Disposable homes and neighbourhoods, a new trend in this new millennium. The large purchase price was not for the substantial building that could easily house a family of six. No, the ridiculous price tag was for several square feet of land in a now sought-after Toronto location. Apparently, to prospective buyers the house was just 'in the way'. The home of my childhood will soon be destroyed by a wrecking ball. Years of family history will be cleared away to make way for a faceless, pricey, oversized home that will abut the boundaries of the property line. The obscenely high price tag on this modern newcomer will undoubtedly mark the end of my family's tie with this neighbourhood forever.

What was once a middle class, family area, where kids played ball hockey on the street and we referred to our parents' friends as Mr. and Mrs., is now disappearing. As I stroll down the old familiar block, I lose my sense of orientation as to where I am, nothing looking even vaguely familiar. Even the names of long-established families are only a distant memory. The medium sized family homes on regular sized lots are now a thing of the past as most of the neighbourhood families have cashed in their asset and long since dispersed. Their homes have been unceremoniously leveled and replaced with mini mansions complete with three car garages, filled with pricey cars. Who is this new breed of upwardly mobile, exceedingly wealthy professionals? My parents, who bought in this neighbourhood fifty years ago, could not afford to set foot in it today.

I remember as a child, we'd walk to the local variety store to buy a chocolate bar or a comic book. Now, the variety stores have been replaced with upscale restaurants, fancy boutiques, expensive art stores, and some swish looking offices housing lawyers and real estate agents. Where can I get some licorice and an Archie? It all feels so foreign.

It's not just the buildings that have changed but the whole feel of the area. The history does not feel buried it feels demolished, as though it never existed at all. No story will ever emerge from the walls of my family home or be discovered buried in the dirt of my backyard. In keeping with our culture, it has simply been replaced, not necessarily for better but certainly for bigger, newer and more expensive. Our western culture doesn't often build on the past, retaining the beauty and character of what came before us. Instead, we destroy it and start brand new. Where is our history? What shall become of our rootedness? In time, how will we know who we are?

-51-

Today an era has ended for me. In some ways nothing monumental has happened, in other ways my whole world has shifted. My family home officially sold today. In a month, it will close and change hands forever. Thirty days from now, a few papers will cross the desk in some lawyer's office, and the money and keys will be transferred.

We are now at a point of cleaning out the old place. Countless are the memories I have of this family home. Aside from several arguments I shouldn't have overheard, it was a fairly happy upbringing. It will present some emotional hurdles to take it apart, room by room, drawer by drawer.

Mom had a number of rules, most of which were ridiculous. These included, children come in the back door, all shoes are taken off and placed on the mat, no one under twenty is allowed in the living room and dinner is at six, don't be late. Thankfully Dad was a fairly easy-going guy who didn't bother much with rules (you can imagine where they ran into marital difficulties). However, his relaxed approach made life more bearable for the kids and my mother's organization made the whole thing functional. My parents argued constantly and despite all that, three out of four of us grew up somewhat okay.

So here I am, all these years later, dismantling every memory of childhood I ever had. I minimized the power of this, and I thought I was together about the whole thing. My parents were both very elderly when they died. Both had lived good, healthy and long lives. They died happy and it was clear their time had come. Therefore, closure should come relatively easily, or so I thought.

My very beginning was at this address. It was the setting for my life. My siblings recalled stories of following my parents' car on their bikes as it turned onto our street with Mom and the new baby. I remember opening Christmas stockings by the fireplace at five a.m. on Christmas morning. I recall dinners around the table, watching countless comedy sitcoms on the couch with my sibs, having sleepover parties in the study, listening to records in the basement with my high school friends. I remember family barbeques in the back yard, our kids' clubhouse in the tool shed, and my messy little bedroom where I hid all my securely locked diaries under the bed. I remember the neighbourhood kids, playing ball hockey when drunk old Mr. Smith took his garbage out completely naked!

The sale of our childhood home was a process rather than an event. It started when Mom died and ended the day the deal closed. It seemed such an overwhelming task to clean out a home which was filled to the brim with a combination of memories, furniture, clothes and copious personal remnants. Where does one begin?

I guess you begin with your own room. There's a trip down memory lane and a daunting challenge. My cupboard seemed a reasonable place to start until I realized it had not been cleaned out in a while. I pulled down a single box from the shelf and opened it up. There on the top was my old ponytail from Grade 7, still in its elastic. "Matt... look at this and look... here are all my old hair ribbons.... And here's my box of letters from camp- oh you've got to read this, and ... Oh my goodness, my high school year book from grade nine. "Matt, you'll find this funny...." Four hours later, my knees were killing me from pouring over the contents of my early life and I only went through half a box. Most of it I wanted to keep. This isn't good. This could take forever. I am going to have to pick up the pace. At the rate I'm going, the house will change hands with all the family baggage still in it.

By now I am overwhelmed and drained. Luckily, most of our family house cleaning events end in a dinner out where we commiserate over the contents of our cleaning and what lies ahead. I am seeing more of my siblings now than I have in the past twenty years put together.

Gradually, with every trip back to our rental farm, I come to terms a little bit more with the fact that my parents are never returning. As obvious as that seems, it does take some time to digest. As I sort through my mother's clothes, another layer of permanence takes root. All Mom's beautiful clothes that she took such meticulous care of in life, will end up donated to the thrift store. Eventually, our sorting was reduced to three basic piles, Garbage, Give Away and Keep. The garbage pile was overloaded, the giveaway pile was close behind and the keep pile was quite small. I soon realized that the more I kept the more I'd be leaving for my own children to sort through some day.

The living room was next. How many meaningless trinkets can one use in a lifetime? Here was a room I wasn't even allowed into as a child and now I found myself wandering through it with a garbage bag, ruthlessly deciding the fate of things.... garbage, give away, garbage, garbage, keep... All my life these items were considered so important, and now, not only was I allowed to touch them, I was actually in charge of their destiny. I had always been under the impression they were priceless and suddenly I found myself questioning, do they really even matter? When I die, will Megan and Tyler walk through our living room with a big garbage bag feeling empowered?

Then there were the photographs. These seemed of much greater value. However, I need to put that in perspective too because there were thousands of photographs. Don't think the guilt wasn't gnawing at me as I placed many of them in the 'garbage' pile. Obviously, we kept all the photos of our childhood and family life. Then came the boxes of jumbo size photographs of my father in his late 20's, numerous enlarged photos of my parents wedding, immense pictures of my grandmother as a child. How many of these do we need? There were numerous shoe boxes full of tiny pictures of my grandparents on both sides of the family. I couldn't do it. I just had to hang on to all of these. I suppose I could rent a storage unit and hang poster size photos of my parents' wedding from the ceiling and have a gallery of postage stamp size photographs of my mother's childhood. Then there were boxes upon boxes of pictures of my parents with their friends, most of whom were now dead. I did feel very badly as I ruthlessly pitched the latter into a dumpster, but those memories were not mine.

During the week prior to closing, my siblings and I made tremendous headway, both with the clean out and emotional closure. On our final night, we had a farewell celebration by the fireplace in the living room. With most furniture gone, we sat on lawn chairs with our feet up on the last remaining coffee table. As my sister passed me a plastic veggie tray, I accidentally spilled some dip on the carpet. Frantically, I bent to clean it up. Then I realized the futility of the exercise as the fate of the carpet stain was the same as that of the entire house. Life had come full circle. We raised a glass of champagne in a good-bye toast to our old homestead that would likely be leveled by the end of the week, carpet stain and all.

Monday, July 30, 1900

Rose is no wiser this morning. She is talking nonsense about missing Patrick and returning to her farm. It seems as the bruises heal, her memory fogs. For the life of me, I don't understand. I wonder if her son Robbie, with his constant blaming and his chatter of missing his father, is wearing Rose down?

Mary is sparkling after the bee. Nevertheless, she's still wary of Betty McAllister and her mother, who so dearly want a marriageable prospect and future store owner in their web. Men have no idea of the scheming that goes on beneath the surface.

A letter came in the afternoon post to inform us that Mary was accepted at the normal school in Toronto. She was ecstatic although Zoe was quite emotional at the thought of her big sister leaving home for a time. According to the letter, the school offers some names and addresses to write to enquire regarding lodging. How remarkable, my first-born, ready to leave home to attend normal school while I am expecting yet another child. Who will help me take care of Doug and Lyle?

Rose is beginning to feel herself again as I hear her at the piano quite regularly now. Her healing tonic is to lose herself in a moving rhapsody. In the summer, with all the shutters open you can hear it into the valley, over by the barn and down by the pond. It is truly delightful. Even those passing in their buggies will sometimes comment on the lovely music exuding from our laneway. They all comment how much Laura's playing has improved.

-52-

Megan's room is in a constant state of chaos. I don't know how she functions. How can she think straight with her room in such disarray? I've asked her nicely to clean it up, I've offered to help, I've hidden 'decluttering books' under her pillow, I've bribed her with shopping outings, I've threatened her with cessation of allowance or confiscation of her almighty cell phone. None of these approaches have worked and most have produced a barrage of backlash. What I am really hoping is that she will discover the joy of 'being organized' and the lesson will spill over into her daily life. Despite my wishful thinking, there are clothes piled everywhere, clean and dirty laundry mixed together in a lump, the bed is unmade, purses and scarves are scattered haphazardly throughout. Her walls are littered with a combo of her girlhood passion for horses and her emerging hormonal drive for handsome movie stars. I've been instructed by Matt to just close the door.

Today I couldn't take it anymore. It was the laundry mixed with the clean clothes that was the tipping point. 'I'll just separate these into two piles, was my innocent thought. In the process however, I tripped on some f$#%^^%$ing thing. What the hell was that? I fumed as I collapsed onto the unmade bed. Somewhere buried under the rubble in Megan's room was her coin collection carefully sorted in a metal coin box. As I bent over to pick it up, I couldn't help but be impressed at how well organized her coins were (in contrast to the rest of her room), neatly rolled packs of dimes and quarters. Obviously, my children's comments about insufficient allowance were coming home to roost. Megan had amassed an impressive collection of pennies as well, despite them being obsolete. Maybe the entire coin collection will face the same fate soon.

Someday we probably won't even have cash even though it's helpful to be able to count out tangible pieces of a dollar. It makes it more real. Why is everything tangible disappearing? I realize I like 'tangible', whether it's a coin, a book, a calendar or a clock. It helps to understand things in greater depth than just a digital number symbolizing the concept on a screen. As babies and toddlers, we learn about our world through tactile exploration. We touch, taste, smell, see, hear things to understand them more fully. As we gradually eliminate objects and replace them with digitized representations, how will we understand our world and the objects in it? How will children understand a hundred '1's (or pennies) equals a dollar? Understanding fragments of time are becoming more about digits on a screen than fractions of an hour. We are starting to think differently. Will babies put cell phones in their mouths to explore and learn about their world? Perhaps we won't need to bother with senses at all. Back to the coin collection though, if we get rid of cash in favour of plastic cards, how will we protect our privacy? All spending will be traceable. It's an advertiser's dream. We will become little market commodities with never ending spam emails soliciting our business. So much progress, so little questioning. We are being catapulted into a new world before considering the costs. However, if everything were digitized, Megan's room might be tidier, and my foot wouldn't hurt so much.

-53-

Today I rummaged through that box we found in the attic at the farm. The photos were fascinating. The first was of a man in overalls standing beside a cow and a little boy holding a pail. That must be Chuck, with Tulip the cow who kept the Huntlys in milk. Wasn't Doug's job to help Chuck with the milking? Yes... he had to carry the pail and give Tulip an apple. Today, I just toss a plastic bag of milk into the grocery cart from some nameless agribusiness, where I highly doubt the cows have a name let alone a human being to milk them or feed them an apple.

The next picture was of an elderly woman beside a woodstove. There was an iron face-down on the stove and a big heap of clothes in a basket. Surely not. Don't tell me that old gal is going to spend her entire day applying that iron to that basket full of clothes. No wonder she looks worn out. She's probably 30.

There was also a photo of a large family on their way somewhere. They were all dressed up, some were holding a book, and they were standing near a horse carriage. Likely, they were on their way to church.

The last picture was taken by a garden. That was some garden, about twenty times bigger than mine and bordered with beautiful hollyhocks. There were two little children sitting in the dirt with a basket between them, probably doing the weeding. A thankless job. I don't envy them with all those rows of vegetables. I see a woodshed behind the house that is filled to overflowing with cut and stacked wood. No wonder Chuck had such a great body. I'm sure that wasn't lost on Laura. Imagine developing a physique like that without even a gym nearby.

There was one other picture - a little baby in a big, old pram. A woman stood beside the pram and Chuck had his arm around her and his other hand on the carriage. Maple leaves were scattered over the yard and a huge pumpkin sat on the porch.

It is hard to believe these people from yesteryear lived their lives right here in this house.

I also found a letter in the attic box.

"My dearest Mary: How have you been getting along? I miss you so much and every day I think of you. Our town has not felt the same since you left, at least not for me. Although I have been busy between my grandparent's farm and the store, it has felt empty without our frequent walks and your cheery laugh. Father and I have been busy with the haying which is a lot of heavy work. Dad has been trying to help since my uncle died but it really isn't his passion either. It certainly isn't mine. The more work I do around the farm, the less I like it. I realize I am much more suited to commerce and still see taking over the store as my main direction in life. Mother doesn't like to hear of it so I don't talk about this with her yet, however sooner or later I must. Dad understands my struggle and has said he is very impressed with the work I am doing at the store. He has given me more responsibilities and raised my wage as well.

I am almost twenty now and you are eighteen. Perhaps someday soon I will be able to make good on that promise ring I gave you. As soon as I have enough money saved to support a wife, you will be the first to know! You know the saying, 'I will make the living and you will make the living worthwhile'. I look forward to that day arriving. I think it would cheer mother up to see us wed and settled.

I hope you are well and enjoying the excitement of the big city. How is school? I imagine it is a lot of work, but you will be a great teacher. Maybe I'll go back to school and sit in your class and keep the older boys from flirting with you!

Take care my sweetheart.

Yours always,
James

Wow, those are some sexist comments, 'I'll make the living and you make the living worthwhile'. Glad some things have changed. My goodness, 20 and 18. I'll be delighted if my kids even have a summer job by then or have started college or university or at least have an inkling to move out of the house. Marriage, I don't think so. This mother would not be as delighted.

Tuesday, July 31, 1900

I have been relegated to hanging out the wash. In my condition, that is about all I'm able to do and even that can be a struggle. However, it's peaceful work and it is much less rigorous than working the tub and ringer. The line hung out, I rested briefly under the big maple to drink in the warm summer breezes and the surrounding nature. The children, having finished their chores are out playing in the new loft. Morten and Chuck are down at the pond putting up a rope swing so the children can leap in from a ridiculous height. I can hear Rose's music drifting from the window. A pair of Baltimore orioles are zipping about the yard and singing their distinct love song to one another. Such a restful lull-a-bye for a summer afternoon. We are overrun with blue birds again this summer as they return yearly to those same boxes that Daniel put out years ago. I do admire the barn swallows. They are my favourites because they can make even a new barn feel so alive. They've been homeless recently so are overjoyed with our new barn and have been immediately busy rebuilding their nests. It doesn't take nature long to make itself at home. They swoop in and out at a tremendous clip.

Oh darn, whose carriage is that turning in our lane? Can't a lady just put up her feet for a few minutes without expecting company to come and spoil the peacefulness.

My contemplative rest in the shade soon turned from peace to panic. I recognized the horse right away – the one with the distinctive blaze down the front and the white socks on each leg. Patrick! My heart immediately began racing. None of the men were nearby, not even the children were about. It was one of those rare, precious moments I had to myself yet the only time I don't want to find myself alone. This nervousness is not good for the baby. The music previously seeping from the farmhouse had abruptly stopped. I froze. I didn't know what to do. There I was, exposed, in the middle of the lawn. Eventually, I regained some semblance of composure. Should I approach him in a friendly manner, or should I keep my distance and leave my friend and her children at his mercy? I must confess my ire was quickly coming to the fore and I thought 'the nerve of this man, coming onto our property!' Why should I feel uncomfortable on our own land. Nevertheless, I must not do anything that endangers the baby. My terror and my resolve intertwined somewhere up in my chest, as I waddled cautiously over in the direction of the carriage. I approached his horse, not knowing what to say or do next. To my great relief, Patrick was neither drunk nor impolite. Despite his demeanor, I kept a safe distance. He pulled up his rig and tipped his hat to me as though he were some kind of perfect gentleman, who had never so much as scared a bird let alone terrorized his wife and children. However, we both knew the truth and this charade was pointless.

"I know she's here Isabel. There is no need denying it any longer. I have heard the piano from the concession, and I have come to collect my family."

I had no further power and we both knew it. He called out and Rose obediently appeared in the window.

"Get your things. I will have no fuss. Collect up the children," he commanded in a benevolent tone as though nothing had ever gone amiss. I didn't know what to do.

Rose came around to the door. She looked timid and pale as she stepped onto the porch but resigned to do as she was told.

From her own mouth, I heard "I'm sorry Patrick, I truly am," as she convulsed in tears. I could not believe what I was hearing and seeing. I was stunned. Could this really be happening after all we've been through? It was ludicrous.

It was then it dawned on me. Had Rose been banging out those melodies near the open window, in hopes of giving away her location to Patrick, somewhat like the orioles in the field?

Laura was dispatched to fetch the children (and the men) as Rose set about collecting her belongings. I excused myself from the laneway and told Patrick I was going to assist her.

"No funny business now," he warned. "...because I will catch up with her."

I entered the house, "Rose, what are you doing? Have you lost your senses?"

She appeared numb and her eyes looked vacant and resigned. "I must go Issy. I have been thinking about it for a while. What options do I have? My father would not hear of me leaving my husband despite his shortcomings and he could certainly identify with being firm with one's wife. I would be constantly on the run, looking over my shoulder. How could I make a living? I would be looked upon with scorn and disapproval wherever I went. What kind of life would that be for the children? Their life would be haunted by shame and poverty. Robbie talks about nothing else but his father and perhaps he's right. Maybe I did aggravate Patrick. Sometimes I can be tiresome. He's a hard worker and is a good provider for us. You've been so kind, and I thank you from the bottom of my heart. You're a true friend."

I could see it was no use trying to reason with her. He had worn her down over the years and now her son was picking up the torch where his father left off. She wasn't seeing things straight but rather through a blurred prism that somehow portrayed Patrick as the wronged soul.

"What about your girls Rose? Is this the married life you want them to emulate some day? Will they be safe back home?" I demanded.

With this she stopped, looked me in the eye with a determination I have never seen in her, and said, "I'm returning for the children. What kind of life would they have Issy, growing up with only a mother who has no money and no relations to support her. It would indeed be selfish to leave. I can bear a few bruises if that is what it must take to give my children a future and a family."

Stunned by her confused rationale, I relented and gave her a hug. "We're here for you always and we hold no judgement over you but rather over your brutal husband who mistreats such a kind woman," I whispered in her ear.

The tears flowed down her cheeks. By this point, the children had gathered in the front yard. Robbie was madly hugging his father, but the girls seemed wary. I stayed at the window as Rose made her way out to the carriage with her valise. As Patrick gently helped her into the carriage, Morten and Chuck rounded the corner with a sense of urgency.

"What's going on Patrick?" Morten called out. I could see the men gathered on the front lawn in discussion as Rose and the children waited in the rig. Clearly Morten was giving him quite a talking to about treatment of a family.

"I sure hope it never comes to this again Patrick. Your family is counting on you to keep your drinking and your temper in check and be a better man. You know we would always welcome you at the church if you chose to come," Morten reminded him.

Patrick gave him a dismissive look and he mounted the carriage and took the reins. He turned the conveyance about, and they were off down the lane to who knows what. Poor Rose. Not only has he abused her but worse still he has stolen her ability to believe in herself. He has changed her. I wish her the best but am doubtful of a happy outcome.

Morten held me for a long time afterwards as I wept in frustration at the injustice of the whole thing. I am thankful to have such a kind man as a husband.

"Issy," he said, "I have something to tell you."

Wednesday, August 1st, 1900

I am beside myself. Chuck and Morten had a long talk yesterday and Chuck apparently divulged his feelings for Laura. In fact, Chuck has asked Morten for Laura's hand in marriage. With Daniel gone, it seemed that the only reasonable thing to do was to ask Morten's permission. Poor Morten was unprepared although any woman would have seen it coming a mile off. After all, he had caught a glimpse of them together at the church picnic. While Morten and Chuck were down at the pond affixing the swing, Chuck didn't seem to be concentrating on the task at hand. Finally, Morten could stand his preoccupation no longer and asked why he was so distracted. Chuck confessed that he did, in fact, have something big on his mind. Now that they were alone, man to man, he wondered if he might ask Morten something. Morten said that he looked nervous, and he was worried Chuck might be leaving. When he instead asked for Laura's hand in marriage, Morten was relieved, but amazed.

"I had no idea you felt strongly about my sister Chuck. Does she know how you feel? Is she expecting this? When did this courtship begin?" A million questions were spilling from his tongue. Chuck eventually revealed how their relationship had been developing for some time. It seems however, that he omitted a small detail about the origin of the barn fire.

"Of course, I give my blessing Chuck. You know I have always felt you are a man of fine character. I would be happy to have you as a brother-in-law provided you would continue to work here and continue to accept an income," to which Chuck happily agreed. This critical detail finalized, they shook hands and Morten said that he hoped Laura would accept his hand in marriage.

Their conversation was abruptly interrupted when Laura rounded the corner in a state of emergency, breathlessly explaining something about

Patrick arriving in the yard. The subject was instantly dropped as the men made a dash for the house.

Now I don't know what to do. 'A man of fine character', yes, I had always felt that myself. Nevertheless, I did feel Chuck left out an important detail in that he and Laura were responsible for the fire. The nerve of asking for Laura's hand while not disclosing the true state of affairs. Although they didn't intend to burn down the barn, they ought to accept responsibility.

I see the plan. They marry. The true reason for the fire is eventually revealed with a profuse apology, and what more recourse can be taken? By then they are brothers-in-law. Chuck has secured his position for life. Shall I tell Morten the truth? If I do tell him, he might let Chuck go. How would Chuck get another job without a recommendation from his previous employer? He would certainly lose any chance of Laura's hand in marriage, especially after their disgraceful behaviour in the barn. Ida would be mortified, and Laura would have to decline his proposal. This could be awful for Chuck and Laura. However, if I say nothing, I allow Morten's blessing to stand knowing full well there is an omission. I am thoroughly torn. I do value Laura's happiness having myself witnessed her tortuous grief since her husband's death. How could I cheat her out of a future partnership? I highly doubt at her age that another offer would be forthcoming.

What will Ida make of this being a lifelong match? Chuck has been like a son to her. Imagine, grandchildren by the farmhand. It's almost too incredible to think of. I will sleep on it and decide in the morning.

Tonight, my mind is with Rose. I wonder how she is getting on. Those poor children caught in the midst of all that. As her friend, I must respect her wishes and try to stand by her as best I can.

-54-

As the calendar approaches the end of its pages and the sun sets earlier and earlier, the farmhouse is developing a distinct draft. It seems surprising with so many newspapers sandwiched between the crevices of the outer bricks and the remaining stylish panelling and layers of flowery wallpaper. Clearly, placing a furnace with all its pipes and venting in this home, was an afterthought. This century home was created for woodstoves and peat fireplaces although that is pretty labour intensive in this day and age. The heat venting system looks like elephant trunks running along the cellar ceiling with floor vents the size of an extra-large pizza in the hallway, covered by an iron grate. It's fun to admire on a summer afternoon but not so amusing as the temperatures start to dip and you need to rely on it to stay warm.

The kids have made a surprisingly smooth transition to the new school here. Who would have ever guessed that would go well. I am greatly indebted to Zach who has taken the edge off starting high school north of the big city. Tyler has offered few complaints. He's made a new friend and taken up an interest in music.

Tonight is his band practice. Our home is filled with the sound of badly played, competing trumpets trying to practice intro to band tunes. Megan and Tyler have both selected the same instrument so you can imagine the sibling rivalry when it comes to performance. Tyler asked if he could have his friend over to practice. "Of course," I hear myself saying half-heartedly, really wishing the barn was heated for this sort of occasion. However, last week when they practiced out there the horses promptly filed out of the building. It is tough to find an appreciative audience. It seems even Wilbur's musical appreciation is limited.

Of course, the real highlight to playing the trumpet is its tremendous capacity to torment your sibling during early morning wake up. The high school bus comes by our driveway at 7:20 a.m. so early morning wakeup is a challenge. Generally, Megan and Tyler roll out of bed around 7:10, stumble downstairs for a quick shower, fly into their clothes, grab a granola bar, and their knapsack and sprint to the end of the driveway to arrive by 7:19.45. No birds catching worms in this household. Weekday mornings are rarely, if ever, relaxing or organized in our home. Sure, we have made resolutions to do things differently, but let's face it, mornings are generally difficult. The last-minute dash to the bus is often accompanied by shouts of 'hurry up' (and other, more objectionable words) by harried parents and children. By no means do these sorts of mornings result in pleasant goodbyes. In our race to get out the door, typically numerous things get left behind, such as, homework and lunches. Recently, part of my morning routine has become swooping by the school to deliver the forgotten item(s). The school secretary and I are now on a first name basis, and she is not amused by my frequent deliveries. She is a rather humourless gal. I have begun to bring her coffee with each delivery which has gradually warmed her up a little. Now, when I go to the drive-thru it is not just a 'medium coffee with milk', but also a 'medium coffee double cream'. It's a true sign that your children are too rushed in the morning when you know the secretary's coffee order.

I realize that I spend way too much time and money in drive-thrus. Jim is the guy at the coffee drive-thru and he now knows my order by heart and calls me by name. Yesterday, when I pulled up to the order microphone and requested my usual, he responded, "Hi Amy, do you also want a medium with double cream?" Matt looked confused as that's not his order. I had to explain about the secretary because I think he wondered if I was seeing someone on the side.

With the long coffee line ups, I have a lot of time to think. I figure normally, I spend about fifteen minutes twice a day in coffee line ups (and that's conservative). That's at least thirty minutes a day. That's approximately three and a half hours a week which is one hundred and eighty-two hours a year. What could I do with one hundred and eighty-two extra hours a year?! I could write a book or get to the gym more. On the days I don't buy the school secretary a coffee, I am spending about five dollars a day on my daily coffee fix. My habit is costing me roughly $1,825 a year! That's a trip to Mexico for two (in the off season).

I'm such an inadequate mother compared to Isabel. I can't even imagine getting up with the rising sun to collect eggs and put a full course breakfast on the stove. I'm just trying to survive in the morning.

Sam has been on my case again. He's been calling me almost daily with concerns about 'Relaxation Spa'. He really wants me back there now, but I just can't bear the thought of returning to the office. All that pressure, those deadlines, the traffic. I'm hyperventilating just thinking of it. Plus, it would mean less time with the kids. I'm finally starting to breathe and take in the world around me. Ultra Luscious Relaxation Spa is just losing its magnetism for me. Mind you, our money is getting tight and maybe it's selfish of me to think so much about my own needs. Our debt load is climbing. We really need my full income, not just a fraction of it. I know it makes no sense, but deep down I wish I could just start that little piano bar on the main street of town. That would be so inspiring. My anxiety has never been better. Do I want to return to a lifestyle I have to medicate myself to cope with? I'm starting to enjoy the simple life. If only it paid better.

Thursday, August 2, 1900

Last night was a restless one, especially in the summer heat when I am so large and cumbersome. I tossed and turned all night trying to decide whether to tell Morten the truth. Should I be a dutiful wife or compassionate towards a fellow woman and sister-in-law? Somewhere in the night, I concluded I must be honest with Morten. He might never forgive me if I hadn't, and I really do not want to bear the brunt of Chuck and Laura's indiscretion in my own marriage.

When Henry crowed, Morten was downstairs. By the time I made it to the kitchen to assist with the breakfast, there wasn't a private moment to be found. The children sauntered in after gathering eggs. Doug and Chuck arrived from the barn with a pail of Tulip's milk. Before I knew it, everyone had taken their seats around the table. Chuck and Laura were seated beside each other but I knew immediately from the look on Laura's face that he had asked her. She was alight with excitement, and they were holding hands under the table. I should have told Morten last night, but I guess I was so preoccupied with Rose and Patrick. It was then that Chuck rose at the table, and said he had something he wanted to announce while all were gathered. He went on to reveal that he and Laura were soon to be married. Well, you should have heard the gasps and seen the general looks of amazement. As the news gradually seeped in, the family began to talk excitedly, and the disbelief melted away. The girls began reaching over to hug Laura and to shake Chuck's hand. There was general merriment and orange juice toasts and even a round of applause. And so, the die is cast, Chuck will become an official member of the family.

Perhaps if I had arisen an hour earlier, I might have informed Morten beforehand. Maybe it is the best of both worlds…I can feel proud that I had every intention of telling Morten, but my best efforts were superseded by their haste.

The talk soon turned to wedding plans and dates and where they would make their home. I must say I'm delighted to see a happier Laura. It's so nice to have some optimistic news for a change.

It's mind boggling to think that Laura and Chuck will be joined in marriage. What in heaven's name do they have in common? He doesn't play an instrument or enjoy a novel and he has no family or property to speak of. Nevertheless, he is a kind and gentle man. His wife would need to be content to limit her conversation to topics connected to the barn, the livestock and haying season. He's a man of very few means. Laura does not bring any substantial dowry to the union, except the promise of permanent work on the family farm. Which, until the very recent turn of events, was already a given for Chuck.

Ida wants nothing more than for her daughter to be happy again. She knows that Laura's future is limited indeed if she doesn't find a husband. There still could be time for a child, although it is unlikely. At least, though, there will be ongoing companionship and independence from her brother and mother. No wonder Morten was so agreeable. He won't have to look after his sister for the rest of her life.

A letter has arrived from Rose in the afternoon mail. I can tell it is not authentic and that it had to pass Patrick's perusal prior to being posted. It contained nothing but meaningless niceties that "she was delighted to be home again. She cannot believe she left their marriage even temporarily and please excuse her indiscretion." It sounds like Patrick wrote it himself and she copied it down in her hand. I don't believe a word of it. I know she's miserable and cannot do a thing about it. I know she returned for the children and felt she had no alternative. I just wish we had had a chance to talk further. I'm sure Patrick is reading whatever I send. No doubt she is missing Edward and I wonder what has happened to him. I worry how she will survive there without his companionship. Patrick will likely shoot him if he comes around. I do know that Rose will not be permitted to visit here for some time. Thankfully, she has the solace of her piano.

Saturday, August 4th, 1900

The house is abuzz with wedding talk. Laura continues to float on air and Chuck wanders around with a permanent smile on his face. They have decided upon a late August wedding which doesn't permit a lot of time to get things in place. There has still been no discussion of the reason behind the fire. I have decided not to interfere with their happiness and let them disclose it themselves when they feel ready.

As my body expands my thoughts turn to the baby's arrival. Given this is number eight, I am hoping for a quick delivery.

Mary has been wonderful. Sensing my constant state of fatigue, she and Zoe have taken Doug and Lyle under their wing - forever entertaining them. They have had them play in the sand, wade in the creek, catch frogs, jump in the straw, let them sit on Gaby's back, pick wildflowers, and every other childhood distraction to keep two little boys occupied during long summer days. Carrie and Sadie have been at each other constantly since school let out. Clearly, they are spending too much time together. One minute they are inseparable friends, and the next they are feuding over who will wear what dress or whose turn it is to weed the garden. Those two squabble as sisters do. I remember when Agnes and I were growing up. She was so unpleasant with me at times and then at other times she was my closest friend. It's difficult with her living far away, with at least a half day's journey between us. I knew when she and her husband settled in Brechin that we would only see them on special occasions. Although we exchange letters frequently, it is not the same as having her here.

I'll get Zoe to help me with the flowers for the wedding. We can pick gladioli from the garden as well as wild roses from near the church. The hall always looks transformed when it's decorated in wedding garb. Reverend Mactavish will announce the banns of marriage in church this Sunday and the next. By the time it's officially declared it will be old news anyway, but it must be done according to tradition.

Laura still has the lovely dress she wore for her previous wedding. It must be changed as she does not want it to appear as it did in the photograph of her first marriage. Ida and I will change the buttons, sew on a bow, add some more frills and some colour. This is a second marriage, so she won't want a white dress on her wedding day. I have my wedding shoes from years ago and given we wear the same size this will save her the added expense of a cobbler. Ida has a necklace and brooch of her mother's so that will go nicely. The ladies at the church will organize tea for after the ceremony. Evelyn Barclay has agreed to bake the wedding cake as she's perfect with pastry as with everything else. Morten will arrange for the man from the studio to come and take a photograph. All is in order.

-55-

It's impossible to get 'me time'. Recently Sam has been calling frequently for advice on how to handle this situation or that problem. I feel the 'not so subtle' pressure to return to the office as soon as humanly possible. I thought there was some rule in HR that employers aren't allowed to call their employees at home when they're on sick leave. Sam never did give a damn about rules.

I've recently found this fantastic café in downtown Orillia. There's an old plaque on the front that reads, 'Will and Son's General Store–1900'. Amazing. Today it's a great place, where I can slip away for a few minutes with a good book. As I savour this great cup of coffee and eat this horribly fattening peanut butter cookie, I try to get my mind away from returning to the office. My mind wanders from my book, and I find myself reflecting on a baby shower I attended a few weeks ago.

My cousin's daughter lives just outside the city in a beautiful home twice the size of our barn. It is situated in a new development that, not long ago, was a farmer's field. There are other monstrous homes around her that are springing up in the 'neighbourhood'. They are quite a hike apart and with the gated fences and all, they are not particularly inviting. She's 30. Her husband works for an advertising firm and likely can afford a home of this magnitude. They are expecting their first baby in about six weeks, and they are understandably elated and excited. This is going to be one lucky child, materially anyway. There were about thirty-five people at the shower, and they were all bearing gifts more costly than my entire bank balance. Many of her friends and family had gathered for the occasion.

Noticeably absent was the young, expectant mother's own mom (my cousin), who was away on business. The new father's family lives on the West Coast, except for an aunt in Saskatchewan.

I soon realized that I was one of the few family members who was able to attend and no doubt, she was obliged to invite. If the relatives can't even attend the shower, who will be available to help this young couple when the baby arrives? Who will they turn to when they require a much-needed break or to catch a few hours sleep? Who will hold the baby, or impart some wise baby tips when the couple are at their wits' end? Perhaps some of the other 30 somethings who are on the brink of going through the same thing. Where are the grandmothers, aunts and godmothers who have all been down this road several times before? At least Isabel had substantial back up. Today's child seems to be born into a nuclear family that may not have much support beyond that. I don't know my cousin's daughter very well, but I know all too well what she is about to experience, especially in those first few months. I hope her husband reduces those crazy work hours and late nights at the office. It could begin to feel pretty lonesome in that big house with a crying newborn.

The presents were astonishing. There were pricey monitors that enable the mother to roam throughout her large dwelling while remaining always within earshot of her little one. There were tiny designer outfits with impressive labels, all of which would be outgrown within about a week, not to mention soiled at both ends. As the gifts were passed around, I could not help but notice that one label said, 'dry clean only'. That's handy. What new mother doesn't have ample time to take her newborn's fine clothes to the dry cleaner? There was a hardcover copy of the latest bestseller in case she has time to read between nursing, laundry, diapering, cleaning, sleeping among other tasks she'll be doing mostly on her own. There were computerized toys, stuffed bears the size of Wilbur and everything a newborn could possibly need (except some extended family involvement). It seemed that this young relative of mine was about to embark on the age-old journey of child rearing in an extremely well housed, emotional vacuum. I fear the journey ahead for this couple could be paved with isolation.

Wednesday, August 8, 1900.

I've recruited Zoe to return my diary (the 'Pickling Book') back behind the pickles on the cellar shelf when I'm done with it for the day. I've explained to her the necessity of replacing it there so that the instructions and recipes are easy to find when required. She has been so helpful to me in this regard as I can no longer manage the cellar stairs. I must rest frequently, and Ida is always fetching me lemonade for fear I might faint. When I had Mary, I was only twenty-one. I don't recall it slowing me down much and that was even after I had already lost one. That was eighteen years ago. She's quite a young lady now and I know she's smitten with James. She tries to conceal it, but I sense he's never far from her thoughts. I also know she's disappointed she can't be here when the baby arrives. She helped with Lyle's delivery, which I believe was enough to make her steer clear of nursing and midwifery. I will invite Carrie, Sadie and Zoe to assist, as this will be their last chance to help a sibling arrive.

We have planned a birthday dinner for Mary, and she can invite two guests for the celebration. Of course, her first choice was James and her second was her good friend Carolyn. Carrie suggested she invite Betty McAllister as her second choice just to make things interesting, which Mary did not appreciate.

Ida has knit a beautiful blanket for Mary's bed which she can take with her to Toronto. She will need something to keep her warm as she won't have a room full of sisters there. I hope it won't be lonesome for her. In September, she will travel to Toronto where she will board with a family near the school. I'm so proud of her. Imagine my oldest baby leaving home and on her own. It seems like just yesterday when I was rocking her in the cradle. Life zips by so fast, despite that clock ticking out the seconds so evenly and calmly. Time feels like sand slipping through my fingers. Next thing you know she'll be offered a position in a schoolhouse. While I do hope for her advancement, I also wish she'll be able to get an appointment near home. I know she's worried what will become of her romance with James. There are so many things for a young woman to consider these days. It was easier when I was a girl. It never crossed my mind to teach. I married Morten at twenty, just two years older than Mary.

Morten and I are getting her a valise for her eighteenth birthday. The one I had when I first moved here is old and worn and we're due for a new one.

I'm not surprised Mary was accepted to normal school. She'll be a wonderful teacher. She was always a good student and so it was no difficulty providing evidence of her superior skills in reading, writing and arithmetic. Her former teacher, Miss Walker wrote a glowing letter of reference and Reverend Mactavish spoke so highly of her exceptional moral character and the fine family she comes from. She will soon be eighteen which is an advantage over the sixteen-year-olds who are applying in droves. They need so many teachers these days. The pay is not good, so few men are interested. I doubt Mary will be in it for long as I imagine she wants a family.

I heard a rap at the screen door. It was James coming to call. Mary and James joined us on the porch for iced tea where we passed a lovely afternoon. Martha Findlay dropped by for a visit. We marvelled at our resident hummingbird who seems taken with the flowers beside the porch. Imagine being able to fly. How amazing it must be to see the world from above. After tea, we did our sewing outside and peeled the potatoes for supper. We began making adjustments to Laura's wedding dress by attaching a ribbon around the waist and some decorative buttons on the back of the gown. Laura has chosen to dye the dress a mint green shade, which unfortunately won't be noticeable in the photograph.

It's been a few days since I've received a letter from Rose, and I am growing nervous. Evelyn Barclay told me the other day that Patrick was spotted emerging from the tavern again. For the life of me, I never understand why people consume alcohol. It only leads to intoxication. I wish everyone would sign the Temperance Pledge, but I know there are some who have not, even in our own church.

It has clouded over quickly, and I just felt a few drops of rain. As I write this, I can see Mary and James turning around at the end of the lane and racing back under the ominous sky. The heavens have suddenly opened and we're getting a heavy downpour. We've all moved inside, and Mary and James are sprinting towards the house. By the time we were settled in the sitting room, it had become a veritable deluge as we listened to the rain pounding against the tin roof. James gave Mary his vest as they darted for the cover of the porch. They were absolutely drenched.

Monday, August 13, 1900

James has presented Mary with a 'promise ring'. It's now official that they intend to continue together. No wonder James seemed so distracted on the porch and put four sugar cubes in his tea earlier that afternoon. We all thought he was quite comical and 'far off'. Apparently, he had bigger things on his mind.

According to Mary, this means they are 'reserved' for each other and that they will 'continue where they left off' when she returns. That is a nice sentiment, but sometimes life doesn't obey the rules, especially at eighteen. In my opinion, they need a little more time to get to know each other before making a commitment. After what Rose has been through, I've told all the girls that who they marry is the single most important decision in their life. If they are not sure, don't do it because once you are joined together, there's no turning back. Unlike most mothers, I've encouraged them to take their time. It is better to be late to marry than be on schedule with the wrong man. But girls are often so impatient to be settled. I can understand their pressure, but they are too young to understand all the implications of a hasty decision.

I like James. He seems like a nice young man, and he comes from a good family. His parents are wonderful people who've done a lot for our community. They always extend credit to those in need. They've had their own struggles with Alice's melancholy. Alice's family has been through so much when her brother Don died suddenly and there was no one to continue the family farm. Will has the store, and the plan has always been for James to take over some day. Alice and Will have been trying for another son since Don died, but it's most likely too late for them. Before he took sick, Don and his wife managed his parents' farm and planned to take it over eventually. His unexpected death dashed those hopes. No doubt this has put young James in a terrible bind. His heart was set on running his father's store rather than farming his maternal grandparents' homestead, which I'm sure contributes to Alice's melancholy. Life is never easy, and I can only guess that young James has some big decisions to make.

Wednesday, August 15, 1900

We had a terrific birthday celebration for Mary. Morten gave a little speech at the end of the meal as to what a charming young lady Mary has become. Ida, Laura and I followed with a welcoming to 'womanhood', to which her sisters giggled hysterically as Mary blushed. She loved Ida's knitted blanket as well as the valise we gave her. No doubt her favourite gift was the bouquet of wildflowers from James.

I assume Chuck and Laura have no plan to tell Morten the truth. The wedding draws closer and so does my impatience with them. Nevertheless, our new barn is a very fitting replacement to the old one with its tremendous loft with built in ladders on each side. There's even a pulley system on the ceiling which can move the hay and straw around as needed. It will make life so much easier.

Our second crop of hay has been stooked in the field and is ready to be collected and stored for winter. It was devastating to watch our last crop go up in smoke. Luckily, there are many young lads around to help with the haying in exchange for a meal or two. It always smartens Carrie and Sadie up when there's a young man joining us for dinner. Finally, there's an 'upside' to haying season.

-56-

I managed to extend my leave until mid January, but Dr. Neal said this is the final extension. In the meantime, I was settling into Christmas season at the farm, until the call came in. I should have let it go to voicemail. However, I could see it was Sam and my guilt got to me. In my knee jerk reaction to please, which seems hardwired into my brain, I picked up.

"Hi Sam, what's going on?" I asked without really wanting to know.

"Amy, are you sitting down? I have something very big to ask you." He sounded serious.

"Are you okay Sam? What is it?" Now my curiosity was perked.

"How would you like a $50,000 raise?" he chuckled. Silence. "Amy, are you still there?"

"What are you talking about Sam? Are you high? Is this some kind of joke?" I responded somewhat annoyed.

"No, I'm completely serious. Cindy resigned today. She's leaving at the end of January. She's tired of the travel and wants to be close to home. I want to promote you to National Manager and that comes with some enticing perks... $50,000 extra on your paycheque to start with. What do you say? I could really use you back here. We're drowning!"

I almost dropped the phone. This was the break I had been waiting for all my life. I would be General Manager of a National Spa! A raise of $50,000, Matt would be ecstatic! This was unbelievable. That would solve all our financial stress.

"Wow, I don't know what to say. What's involved in the job?" I asked cautiously, my heart beating like a drum.

"Well, it is National Manager, so it would involve some travel across the country to monitor how all the branches are operating and there would be some weekend meetings. You'd essentially be running Ultra Luscious Relaxation Spas nation-wide, but the pay and the benefits would make it worth your while. I really want you for this position Amy. You're the one who knows 'Relaxation' the best. What do you say?" He pleaded excitedly.

"Sam, this is amazing, but you must be devastated to lose Cindy."

"Not really," he replied, "I've had you in mind for this position for a while. It was just a matter of time. Will you take it? You'd be perfect," he coaxed.

"Sam, I'm so excited I can barely speak. Thank you so much for this offer! I have to talk to Matt. Let me sleep on it. I'll call you back tomorrow."

"Of course," he laughed, "Take all the time you need. You can let me know after the holidays if you like. This is your dream job Amy. I'd love you to run the place. Think on it."

I was in a state of shock as I hung up the phone. Is this for real? That is the most incredible job offer I've ever had. Those don't come along every day.

My brain was moving a million miles an hour. My mind kept gravitating back to the $50,000 raise. That is like winning the lottery every year. I was already figuring how we would spend it....pay down our growing debt, replace my old car, an overdue vacation for Matt and me, etc... However, it does mean more responsibility, cross country travel, being away from Matt and the kids, and stress.... Plenty of that! I've been planning to go back in January anyway. On the other hand, this lifestyle has really been good for me. I really needed a rest from the craziness. My health feels much better, I'm getting reconnected with Megan and Tyler, Matt and I have finally had some time together and the family tension has practically disappeared. What will being National Manager do to all that?

Hello indecision. How will I ever sleep tonight?

-57-

As I anticipated, Matt was overjoyed at the prospect of this sudden spike in my salary. However, he was far more reserved when he heard the emotional price tag attached.

"Amy, think of the stress. It would be back to the grind except this time you'd be hopping from one plane to the next as you oversee the entire country for Ultra Luscious Relaxation. It's a huge responsibility," he pointed out.

"Yes, but Matt...maybe if I were in charge, it wouldn't be so bad. Half of my stress was being in middle management," I argued.

"Amy... six months ago you could barely get out of bed," he countered, "I never want you to feel that way again. Without a doubt the extra cash would be a life saver, but the job might kill you."

"That's a little extreme Matt, but I get your point."

"Let's keep thinking about it. The one thing Sam never has is a timetable. Let's get through Christmas and then we can have some time to reflect." Matt concluded. I was just about to add another thought when Matt's cell rang.

"Oh yes, hi Steve. How are you doing? Yes, the place has worked out nicely. We've really enjoyed the experience. What's up?"

.... Silence... "Oh really. When did that happen? That is interesting. How much is she wanting for the place? I see. The animals too. Well, that is certainly an interesting proposition, but we weren't really planning on staying beyond mid January. That is very kind of the family. When would you need to know? I'm glad you called, and I'll talk to my wife. Okay. I'll get back to you after the holidays. Take care." He hung up the phone and stared at me.

"You're not going to believe this Amy. That was the realtor. The owner has decided to stay in the retirement home, and she would like to offer her farm to us first. She really wants the animals to continue to have a home here. She wondered if we'd be interested in purchasing! If they sell it to someone else, they'd likely have to rehome or euthanize the horses and the elderly lady really doesn't want that. But it's not cheap. There's no way we could afford to buy this place without selling our home in the city."

"How much is she asking?" I asked, not believing what I was saying. Five minutes ago, I was considering ramping my career into overdrive and returning to Toronto. Now I'm tempted to cash in the entire package, be unemployed and buy an old farmhouse with some rapidly aging animals. Have I no rudder? "I could open that piano bar in town," I offered whimsically.

We were both disoriented. "It's one or the other," Matt reiterated.

Time for some serious reflection on our priorities. What's important to us? What will our kids want? What if those two things are different? ... And I thought Christmas would be relaxing.

Thursday, August 16, 1900

More mail from Rose today with the same old edited material. Patrick might as well write the letters himself. Who does he think he's kidding. I have a mind to pay them another surprise visit. I'd take Chuck with me just to be safe. I don't know that Morten would allow it but maybe I won't tell Morten. I will ask Chuck to drive me to the church to arrange some things for the wedding and then drive over to Rose's afterwards. Likely Chuck would resist. I'm worried about Rose and her children. It was absolutely chilling the way she came out the front door and 'apologized' to him. How infuriating. He should be the one on bended knee apologizing to her and releasing her from their marriage vows due to his mistreatment. Instead, he's out carousing at the pub and editing her letters. I wonder if I should ask Rev. Mactavish about this without mentioning names. I know Rose wouldn't want that but I'm nervous for her safety. I don't know how to help her. Where is Edward? He's likely fled the township and abandoned Rose and the children to that beast of a husband.

Friday, August 17, 1900

Our hardy little pear tree is thriving. Morten planted it in the spring in hopes of some pears in years to come. I've been watering it diligently and keeping the goats away from it. It's the least I can do given I'm useless to help these days. Those goats can be such a nuisance, particularly the billy. He can get downright fierce when whisked away from a food source. Yesterday he got into the garden and was inhaling our lettuce, efficiently reducing the rows to almost nothing. Ida was furious when she saw him from the kitchen window. She tore out with the broom. He lowered his head to ram her with his horns. She smashed him in the head repeatedly. She's a feisty old gal. That goat took off for the barn and we all laughed so hard as I recounted the story at dinner.

Saturday, August 18, 1900

After meeting with Reverend Mactavish at the church regarding arrangements for Laura's wedding, I explained to Chuck that we had to stop by Rose's and drop off some belongings.

"Is that wise Isabel?" he questioned. Patrick has put us through a lot. "Could it wait until another day? Morten has asked me to get back directly as he wants to get the remaining hay up before it rains."

I reassured him I would be brief and that it was important. He expressed concern about visiting the Reilly farm, but eventually agreed.

When the cart pulled up, Rose was sitting on the porch minding the children. They were playing in the yard and Elizabeth was hanging out the laundry.

"Issy, what a pleasant surprise!" She ran out to give me a hug as I climbed from the cart. She seemed genuinely delighted to see me. There were no nervous glances over her shoulder so I knew that Patrick must be out. "You look so well, perhaps it's twins," she teased.

"Oh, be quiet. If it is, I'll give you one," I joked.

Chuck led the horse over to the trough for a drink but did not tie up as we were only there briefly. I followed Rose to the porch and joined her for some lemonade. I could see a bruise on the side of her neck, just barely hidden by the collar of her dress.

"How are you getting on?" I asked sincerely.

"It's okay Issy. It has been quite liveable since I returned. I've learned just to agree with him and stay away from him as much as possible especially when he's been drinking."

I didn't believe her. What kind of a life is that? I felt for her. What other option does she have? I will visit her whenever I please and if that Patrick lays a hand on me, I'll smash him in the head, just like Ida did to that goat.

My heart was heavy as Chuck and I made our way out along the tree lined drive to the carriageway. Chuck, his fists clenched on the reins, said that if Patrick had shown up and given us any trouble, he was ready to take him down. How sweet of Chuck. I have no doubt an inebriated Patrick would have proved no match for a strong, sober labourer like Chuck. The entire way home Chuck expressed his profound disgust for a man like Patrick, who would use his strength against a woman, let alone his own wife. He could not begin to understand how a grown man could be so cowardly and cruel as to raise a fist against someone he loved and who bore his children. Inwardly, I was quite impressed with Chuck's sense of justice. Perhaps I have underestimated what a fine catch of a man Laura has secured for herself. In fact, now I truly am happy for her. If only Rose could have found such a husband.

-58-

How did they stay warm in these houses before hydro, when the thermometer was well below zero. We have the furnace up to maximum, heaters everywhere, sweaters on and still the house has a chill.

We've agreed to put our decision making on hold until after Christmas, but that is easier said than done. It permeates all our waking hours and most of our sleep as well.

As is customary on December 25th, we started the day early. It used to be that the kids were up first. Now they sleep in, even on Christmas - clearly a benefit of adolescence. By 11:00, we all sat naround in our pyjamas, sipping coffee in front of the warm glow of the electric fireplace. The kids were delighted with the treasures they found in their stockings. Megan loved her teen fashion magazine. It appeared filled throughout with scantily clad adolescents and articles about improving your love life. Matt and I had wondered if it really was suitable for a girl in Grade 9. However, it was starred several times on her Christmas list, so we gave in. Tyler was overjoyed with the single bottle of imported beer. There was only one and it was not to be opened until after 6:00 p.m. on Boxing Day and sipped slowly throughout the evening. There were a jumble of other trinkets and edibles, enough to keep them busy while Matt and I put the turkey on. Matt's mother and sister and her family will be joining us later in the day for the big Christmas feast. It felt odd not having Mom and Dad with us.

A few months ago, my life was proceeding fairly predictably, despite my crippling anxiety. Now a cloud of confusion has descended. 'National Manager', that sounds as impressive as the salary enhancement that goes with it. Unemployed and budgeting, living in a rundown farmhouse, hours from the city, ... not so impressive. However, surprisingly enjoyable. Which is my destiny? The question continues to haunt me. Two enticing choices. Here I am at a crossroads in my mid 40's, trying to decide who I want to be.

It was an unwrapping frenzy for an hour. Weeks of shopping and wrapping consumed with such efficient speed. However, the big present this year was yet to be unwrapped. Matt and I had decided to splurge and surprise the kids with a family trip, kind of a final celebration of our time at the farm.

We're off to Mexico! The kids were ecstatic, and Megan immediately texted all her friends with the big news. However, I think I am the most excited. Imagine a week of heat, sand and reading. That is what I want for Christmas, a destination where the thermometer is consistently in the high 20's and I don't have to do a damn thing for seven days.

When our relatives arrived, it was time to break out the eggnog. Much to our horror, my sister-in-law realized she forgot the rum which she was to bring. Such a painful oversight. She even considered driving the two hours back home to retrieve it. Despite my insisting differently, I secretly wished she would. It was then I remembered the 'medicinal treasure' I had found in the cabinet a few months earlier. This could be considered an 'emergency', a kind of Yuletide crisis. We both agreed that would be a wise plan and gingerly mixed it into the eggnog. What a memorable beverage it was. Before long we were all feeling the 'medicinal effects' of the 'well aged tonic'. Who would have guessed the strength of that small, forgotten item in the cabinet. However, if you had to have a tooth pulled or the doctor was going to perform emergency surgery on the dining room table, it's nice to know it works.

Sunday, August 19, 1900

There were about thirty at Laura's wedding shower. The gifts were remarkable, with no end of household items: tea pots, dish towels, woodstove pokers, a scrub board, sewing materials, and several other useful things that any woman would want when getting married. If you had seen Laura months ago, you would not have recognized her this afternoon. Chuck has transformed her from a disenchanting, unmotivated widow to an optimistic, charming woman of contentment. I'm finally beginning to see her resemblance to Ida.

Zoe was delighted to be included. She was such a help too, passing the cakes, pouring tea and generally being available to assist. All my girls were there, dressed in their Sunday outfits and looking like fine young ladies. Before you know it, the bridal showers will be for them. Most of the ladies were impressed with Mary's plans to become a teacher and marvelled at the boldness of this next generation. There are always a few who don't approve of progress and women's rights, but I won't even waste my ink telling about their limited perspective. Mary handled it so gracefully and just smiled and acknowledged that it is hard to comprehend all the changes that seem to be happening in our world. I was so proud of her. Of course, they were all interested to know about her plans with James and her humble promise ring soon became the main focus.

I have become a huge round ball with legs. My first plan after I deliver is to regain my shape. It won't take long once I'm back to laundry, weeding, nursing, and all the rest. So many neighbours and friends have offered to help with baby minding as well as with Doug and Lyle. There are never any shortages of helpers when there is a newborn in the vicinity. Nevertheless, there was an emptiness without my Nell here today. However, when I divert my mind to little 'Daniel Jr.' or 'Danielle', my spirits brighten.

Friday, August 24, 1900

Tomorrow is Laura's wedding, and the house is buzzing with excitement. Laura's sister Florence will be her only attendant as I'm unable to be on my feet for that long a period. Zoe will be a flower girl and Doug a ring bearer. Is he ready for a job that requires focus and responsibility? Carrie and Sadie will each read a scripture, Ida is Mother-of-the-Bride and of course Morten will walk her down the aisle on behalf of Daniel. I will be containing little Lyle and praying that he does not break free of my grasp during the service.

Tomorrow morning Ida and Zoe will fill the vases around the church with flowers. The Ladies Aid has the reception hall ready for cake and tea following the ceremony. Evelyn Barclay will bake the cake. Of course, none of these details matter much, as long as the couple are happy with each other.

After the ceremony, they will have their photo taken. They plan to honeymoon at the Coldwater Inn. Chuck has arranged for an extravagant two-night stay, so is quite pleased with himself. Morten, Ida and I are treating for an additional night as a wedding gift for the couple. Poor Morten is fretting about how he will spare Chuck around the farm for so long near the end of summer.

What Laura doesn't know is that Chuck has procured a very humble, little 'farmhouse' on the next concession that backs onto our acreage. Although it has been abandoned for many years and is not much to look at, they will no doubt have great joy fixing it up and making it their own. She is under the impression they will continue to reside in the Huntly home until Chuck can save some money. Thankfully, the farmer who sold the lot and cabin to Chuck didn't want much as there's no acreage and only a very small yard. This is a relief to Morten as it shows that Chuck has every intention of continuing on the Huntly farm rather than trying his hand at his own.

As I write this, James and Mary are in the yard sitting near the pear sapling. Mary tells me that James is concerned about his mother and quite torn about whether he should take over his maternal grandparents' farm. It's not the life he wants but then what will become of it if he doesn't take it on? His heart has always been set on continuing his father's store. I can see James as a merchant as he has a good way with people. What a difficult dilemma it must be for him. If they do eventually end up together, I would much prefer to see Mary set up in town, the wife of a store merchant rather than chained to the daily drudgery of farm work. I would never admit this to Morten as I know it would crush him. Farming is an endless circle of work with undependable and fluctuating compensation. There are no promises whether the harvest will be good as that changes yearly, depending on the weather.

However, if Mary is the wife of a merchant, her workload would be lighter, and her husband's pocket would be consistently full. There is no dry or rainy season to consider and perhaps they might even get a holiday away occasionally, having no animals that require daily attention. I know Mary would love to go to Niagara Falls someday. It's a long train ride from Toronto, but what an exciting journey that could be for them eventually.

Saturday, August 25, 1900

Laura and Chuck have a beautiful day for their wedding. It reminds me of the day Morten and I married, right here at the house. It seems so odd to think of us without any children. All that idle time just to be with each other. Those were the days when we could go for long walks or take meandering carriage rides and talk endlessly about all the things that lay ahead. Morten's mind was filled with dreams about what crops he would plant, and which room would be ours. When I think back on our wedding in 1880, we were so young. I remember our wedding night and how nervous I was. Rose had given me some idea of what to expect as she had already married Patrick by that point. We giggled for hours as she related the tales from their first night. I couldn't imagine what it would be like to share a bed with a man, but I must confess that I was shamefully eager to share one with Morten. I recall Morten's eagerness, yet he was patient with my shyness. He reassured me that no one would frown upon it now that we had exchanged vows. It seemed so odd that it was condoned. I will never forget the warmth of feeling his body against me for the first time and how close it all felt. I had never anticipated how arousing it was even though we had certainly exchanged some increasingly passionate embraces in the weeks leading up to the wedding. How shy I felt at disrobing in front of him for the first time and how beautiful he made me feel with his admiring eyes. When he began to caress me, a shiver went up my spine and there was no turning back from that point on. It was a beautiful night together exploring each other's bodies. In fact, we hardly slept at all. However, it wasn't until the next morning that we consummated our marriage. I am ashamed to admit that I was too scared the night before. I had never done anything like that in my life. When I think back on those days of innocence and discovery, it seems so long ago. I realize Laura knows what lies ahead as she has been married before. I do hope their marriage together will be a happy one.

...The church was alive with excitement as we listened to the carriage enter the laneway, the clip clop of the hooves delivering the bride to the chapel. As Morten helped his sister down from the shiny rig,

a hush fell over the sanctuary. Laura glowed as Morten escorted her down the aisle to meet the strapping, well turned-out Chuck. I must say, we all marvelled at how dashing Chuck looked in his well-tailored jacket, which was one of Daniel's from days gone by. He sported a high collared shirt, a handsome cravat, Morten's pocket watch and, after the ceremony, a Derby hat! He looked quite the gentleman and amazed us all as we were not accustomed to seeing him in such elegant attire. When I think of Chuck, I envision him in his plaid shirt, overalls, barn boots and smelling like a horse. However today, he looked downright dashing and I dare say this did not go unnoticed by the ladies in the congregation. I cast a glance at Rose, who met my gaze with a slight smile of understanding, but beyond the comprehension of Patrick who sat awkwardly beside her in the church pew. As the organ music began to play the 'Wedding March', Zoe led the procession with a bouquet of wild roses while little Doug stood dead still at the front beside Chuck, looking like a deer caught in the clearing. I held my breath, as the ring perched precariously close to the edge of the cushion which Doug held on a definite slant. I tried to catch his eye to correct the mistake but to no avail. He was uncharacteristically focussed on the procession. Luckily, Lyle was mesmerized by the music and remained still. However, as the wedding party gathered at the front, he stood on the pew and hollered at full volume, "Aunt Aura and 'Uck'. With that distraction, the ring hit the floor as I feared but Morten quickly retrieved it. We all breathed a sigh of relief when the couple finally exchanged vows and left the church amid much fanfare and excitement.

Once the couple was thoroughly congratulated, we celebrated with a lovely afternoon of music, square dancing and singing. Eventually, the carriage was brought around, and the number of shoes and boots tied to the back of it was astonishing. The girls had braided Barney's mane and even placed some wildflowers in the front of his bridle. What a fitting way to travel for the new couple. We waved goodbye as they set off on their new life together. We are all hoping this union will bring a child, especially for Laura's sake. I know that is what Laura wants more than ever. Perhaps there is still time.

-59-

Tyler had wanted a hamster for awhile. It seemed like a smart idea at the time. It was a cute, hairy little thing and it would be good company for him. What a great way to disconnect from the computer. Tyler was delighted to receive Marvin for Christmas. It was a highlight of the holidays as we watched Marvin run through ceramic toy boots with holes in them. Here's the thing the pet store doesn't tell you about hamsters. They're NOCTURNAL. That means they stay up all night running on that annoying little wheel they have in their cage. Just as the household has finally descended into a nice deep sleep, little Marvin decides it's time for his workout. Why is our family up half the night with a pet rodent while just last week we had sprinkled warfarin in the cellar for his relatives? It's a fine line. I considered putting Marvin and his workout equipment in the cellar but then I was too freaked out to go down there at night. I suppose I could just let Brutus take care of the situation.

Marvin is driving me crazy and now I can't sleep. Placing him in the basement is getting more tempting as the night wears on. However, I'm still recovering from that time in August when I spent a night alone in this farmhouse. Matt and the kids were away camping overnight. I had opted to stay behind to have a rare night to myself. I guess Matt had been in the basement earlier that day and had forgotten to turn off the light bulb by the basement stairs. When I turned off the hallway light that night, I noticed the cellar light through a chink in the floor. Horrified, I bravely re-assured myself that it had just been an oversight and that Matt just forgot to switch it off. Cautiously, I lifted the floorboard door to the cellar, descended halfway down the wooden staircase and gingerly turned out the light. I immediately felt better with that behind me and went up to bed to read. Naturally, being alone in the house, I heard countless creaks and sounds that I wouldn't normally notice. Eventually I drifted off to sleep (that was pre-Marvin). About four in the morning, I woke up. As I made my way toward the bathroom, my eye was magnetically drawn to the same crack in the downstairs hallway. I noticed a tiny light seeping through the crack in the floorboard. Why is that on? I had turned it off. Feeling extremely rattled, I switched on every light in the house, the tv, and the radio. I tried to call Matt but he was out of cell range. Wilbur, who isn't generally allowed upstairs, was immediately summoned to my bedroom. He was overjoyed and seemed undaunted by any activity in the cellar. He had a delightful sleep drooling on my pillow while I monitored the hallway shadows from my bed throughout the remainder of the night. When Matt eventually arrived home with the kids the following day, he investigated the unsettling situation. It turns out there was a loose electrical connection in the switch, causing it to flick on and off sporadically. That was the last time I was in the basement so lucky Marvin can remain upstairs for the time being.

-60-

Soon we leave for Mexico and the packing mayhem begins. I'm not big on winter. The snow, the ice, the bone chilling cold, the boots, the mitts, the cars that won't start, the barren looking trees, the road conditions, need I go on. It is discouraging just to think of it. My distaste for winter is the single reason we are dropping $6,000 on a trip that takes us hours in a southbound direction. I have been pouring over computer ads and brochures of glossy white sandy beaches with bikini clad women and hot looking men holding hands while sipping exotic cocktails. I realize it's time to locate our summer clothes and my bathing suit. Heaven forbid. The one drawback to heading south is the horrendous thought of wearing my bathing suit in a public place. I'm counting on not seeing anyone I know.

Who knows where we stored those summer clothes back in September. The garage is a disorganized mess. After moving the summer tires, several rakes and multiple tools, I came across the boxes marked 'summer' in big black marker. Did I mention that the garage is detached and therefore freezing cold in the middle of winter? I found myself rifling through shorts and sandals while swear words and frost poured from my mouth. After grabbing a handful of bathing suits, I headed back inside.

How depressing climbing into a bikini the day after Christmas dinner. Meanwhile, everyone was busy packing their bags as tomorrow we leave ridiculously early in the morning. Megan is the first to have her suitcase ready. It consists of 75% bathing suits, 24% teen fashion magazines and 1% books. Mine is the exact opposite, 75% books, 24% sunblock and 1% bathing suit (and a conservative looking one at that). I want to lie on a beach and sort out my life direction in comfort. On a sunny day, I can be found in the shade, but my kids prefer maximum sun exposure. It worries me constantly so the one agreement we have is they must wear a hat and sunblock. I don't care if they hang out at the swim up bar, or if they stay up too late, or if they never go to the exercise room. I'm happy, provided they slather plenty of sunblock over them and keep their heads covered.

We leave on our trip tomorrow. Today I experience the Christmas financial hangover. We don't usually splurge at Christmas. It's just fun to be together, have a few gifts and a couple of eggnogs laced with 120-year-old painkiller. We're never able to afford the big-ticket items. Nevertheless, as I look at my post Christmas bank balance, I wonder if we did the right thing sinking all our savings into this Red Tag Event. The problem is I want to live a little now while we are all young enough and well enough to enjoy a week in Mexico. I want to enjoy our kids and have some family time together while they are still agreeable to be around us.

I know all too well the weight of debt, the constant snowball that gets bigger and bigger as it is rolled from one year to the next. The trick is never to let the snowball form in the first place but that is incredibly hard to do. As we lie on a beach for a week, the bills don't stop. In fact, they keep automatically withdrawing from the account. I once read about a man who was found dead in his home, propped up in an armchair with the television on. Apparently, he had been that way for some time. No one realized he had died. No creditors came knocking on his door. His pension was deposited electronically, and his bills were automatically withdrawn, so financially everything worked without him having to do a thing. Suffice to say, if I didn't have a paycheque, they'd find my dead body within about six hours.

That's what scares me. I know we must make a financially dependable plan going forward. If I take the position with 'Relaxation Spa', we're automatically $50,000 ahead each year. What an influx of cash that we so badly need! However, it means significantly less time with Matt and the kids and a lot of increased stress. Could I cope with all that and do I want to? If we sell our place in Toronto, and buy this farmhouse, we need to do some badly needed renos and upgrades to make this home liveable year-round. While we would come out ahead on the sale/purchase equation, the renovations required would add up. Also, we'd need some savings to fall back on until I have an income. Could I really open that piano bar I dream about, or would that just dig us deeper into debt? It's risky. I have grown to enjoy this lifestyle, but could we really leave the city permanently? How would the kids feel about this? We'll get a chance to talk it over with them when we're away. Both options are tempting for very different reasons. We have a week to sort out our priorities. I've promised Sam an answer when we return.

Sunday, August 26, 1900

Rose and I were reduced to exchanging pleasantries at the wedding as Patrick would not leave us to our own devices for even a moment. Obviously, he does not trust me one bit and the feeling is mutual. I was secretly inspecting Rose for bruises but how would I know with her long gown, high collar and lace sleeves. We would almost have to be in swimming costumes to spot a bruise. I can feel the tension when I am with them. Rose is usually so free spirited, but I find this quality greatly stifled when Patrick is around. I was about to ask after the children when Morten cut in with some lively conversation about the square dance. I could tell Patrick was eager to cut the discussion short, probably wanting to get to the tavern and away from civilized company.

As August comes to a close, Mary's thoughts have turned to normal school. A letter arrived a few weeks ago from the family she will be lodging with. From their correspondence, they sound like nice people and have been approved by the school. They have two daughters and a son still at home. The girls are close in age to Mary, so she's delighted at the thought of establishing some new friendships. They attend the Presbyterian Church, and the husband is a milliner. James is so supportive but eagerly awaits her return. Once she is a certified teacher, she can likely get hired at one of the local schoolhouses as they are always needing teachers.

Being Sunday, our family has gone to the service and Ida has stayed behind with me. She says she doesn't like to leave me alone when I'm so far along. I'm grateful to have a day to put my swollen feet up. We rarely miss church, so it feels odd to be here on a Sunday morning with the house so uncharacteristically quiet.

We passed a relaxing morning. The family seems to be thinning out with Daniel, Nell and now Laura and Chuck, no longer in the mix, and Mary leaving soon too. How will I cope with a newborn and the children without Laura and Mary to help!

Monday, August 27, 1900

The barn swallows have completed their flying lessons from the beam above Gaby's stall. It's always so entertaining to watch. The mother had all four of them lined up. She would go first, swoop out of the barn at a tremendous clip, circle the barnyard and whiz back to her offspring. Then the next little fellow would be expected to model her behaviour, which he did with some clumsiness while the others waited patiently on the log beam for their turn. It's a show I've seen repeated many times over the years. These are the flight lessons in preparation for the long journey south, which will, sadly, not be long off. I'm not fond of winter and dread the biting cold wind that is an inevitable part of those dark months. I dread those signs that summer is drawing to a close – birds beginning to form V s in the sky, geese landing in our lower field. I loathe the migration as it symbolizes what comes next. I've watched these little barn swallows through all stages of their lives. I've witnessed their mother gather materials to nest in our new barn. Within weeks, we've enjoyed being greeted by tiny little beaks peeking above the nest in search of food. Every time we milk a cow or harness a horse, we hear them squabbling and filling the barn with a newfound life. The barn becomes an ecosystem within itself.

Our goats have formed quite an attachment to Gaby and follow her everywhere. They graze beside her in the field and huddle near her in the barn. Occasionally they butt her with their horns, but she takes it all in stride like a big maternal grandmother with the patience of Job. Similarly, Gaby can instantly become a fierce warrior if she feels one of her flock are threatened. Then Gaby's grandmotherly type personality instantly evaporates, and she turns into a mean-spirited hyena ready to fatally kick the intruder. It is unnerving how this gentle creature can turn from a wise, old sage with oversized, rabbit-like ears into a malicious weapon, in mere seconds.

As everyone knows, the highlight of every barn animal's day is feeding time. The goats receive their cracked corn in their pen. The horses had begun lingering nearby following their feeding. Undoubtedly, they were waiting to consume the goats' feed. Initially, Morten thought Gaby was heading into the pen to do the same. Instead, she would park herself defiantly at the door so that no horse could enter to steal the goat food. Only when the goats had completed their meal, would Gaby move her large, stubborn body from the entrance. I hardly think Morten and Chuck will be able to remove those goats for butchering if Gaby has anything to say in the matter.

However, there is an appalling side to those goats that I had a tough time explaining to little Doug. We were in the barn to milk Tulip and the goats were romping about, generally being a nuisance and butting their horns into each other. Morten had purchased the mother goat and her one remaining son. The little fellow started off small and quite adorable. However, with all the cracked corn that Gaby is enabling them to finish, he has grown to quite a size, certainly bigger than his mother. Despite being fixed when he was young, he seems to have retained his drive to reproduce. Unfortunately, the only other goat in the barn is his mother, which does not seem to present any deterrent to his insatiable impulses. This was very upsetting for Doug who could not grasp why the goat was pursuing his mother aggressively around the barn and then climbing on top of her when clearly, she did not appreciate it. Luckily, Doug has a short attention span and can get easily sidetracked by other distractions without much effort. I must bring this up with Morten to get some additional goats to fill out our herd.

Tuesday, August 28, 1900

Chuck and Laura had a wonderful honeymoon. Laura loved the new 'homestead' and was delighted when Chuck carried her over the threshold. Although it's humble, it will meet their needs for now. The girls worked hard at cleaning it out and washing down the old furniture in preparation for their return. They planted a flower garden, washed the windows, and swept the floor and apparently it looked much more presentable upon completion. The newlyweds joined us for our evening supper, and we heard all the highlights of their exciting stay in Coldwater. They spent much of their time swimming and row boating on the river. It's so nice to see Laura shine again.

Everyone is eagerly awaiting the arrival of our new little one. There is growing excitement about the upcoming birth. I do hope little Daniel or Danielle doesn't keep me waiting too long past my due date as the heat of the summer has been draining.

The neighbourhood is preparing for the corn roast. I've seen many posters up around Jarratt Corners, in the general store and posted on several fences around the concessions. It's the event of the season.

-61-

We have arrived in our tropical paradise. It is hard to imagine a week with no obligations. No cooking or cleaning, no calls from Sam in crisis, just a week to lie around with a good book on a white sand beach and stew about my future. The thought is heavenly. Strolling along a warm expanse of beach while wading through turquoise water is simply unbeatable. Regardless of the paradise around me, the internal turmoil regarding our future direction looms large.

Over dinner last night, we dropped the bombshell to the kids regarding the monumental decision we were facing. They were understandably blindsided, and the shock was followed by colourful discussion. In a nutshell, Tyler is keen to stay, and Megan is adamant she is returning home. Either way, we upset someone. It's a no win. To be honest, I'm most surprised at Tyler's response. We have seen him come to life on the farm in a way that was unanticipated. He loves the animals and has spent more time outside in this past six months than he has in the past five years put together. Megan misses her friends, but she has made some new friends, not to mention the blossoming relationship with Zach. However, I suspected the possibility of staying would not go down well with her.

It's almost New Years and who knows what the coming year will hold for us. I've made my resolutions, ... lose weight, enjoy life more and spend more time with my kids, whether they like it or not. I find New Year's kind of a silly celebration. No doubt there will be noise makers and revelers dressed in party hats who have consumed far too much alcohol. There will be a buffet, dancing, unlimited punch and by midnight the champagne corks will be popping. As far as I can see, the only up-side to the overindulgence of New Years is that I might actually get a lawn chair tomorrow morning. Something tells me there won't be many heading to the pool at 8:00 a.m..

Wednesday, August 29, 1900

Ida, Carrie, Sadie and Zoe will be with me for the delivery. Unfortunately, Mary will be away. She was such a help when Lyle was born. Ida will prepare the girls, as Sadie and Zoe have never been present at a delivery before. Each will be given a job to do during the event so as to keep them busy and useful. Ida, of course, is an old hand at this as she's helped in countless deliveries, as have I. I will never forget the year Martha had such a trying time with little David. That delivery went on almost twenty-four hours and the midwife had to be called. We were all frightened we might lose both mother and child. Then there was the time Grace Gillies lost her wee one when the cord was wrapped around his neck. It was a tragedy and Grace has never really gotten over it. I have been mostly lucky with pregnancy as I have only lost one. I'm always anxious before delivery, but Morten reassures me I have the right hips for childbearing. He's such a flirt. I'm always relieved when the whole painful experience is over with. There's no point worrying as there is nothing that can be done to avoid the situation. If all goes as it should, I still have a few weeks before the arrival.

Saturday September 1, 1900.

It was a terrific corn roast. We had well over a hundred from all over these parts and the corn was plentiful and sweet. I knew Rose was coming but I'm always relieved when she actually shows up. Patrick would never let her help with my delivery.

Mary and James are becoming quite a pair. I see them walking everywhere together and this evening I noticed James was holding her hand. I know Morten was a little uneasy with that and felt that she should be properly chaperoned. Then again, a little hand holding is bound to happen especially given that they will be parting soon. Morten forgets what a romantic young fellow he was when we were courting. The only other one who's uncomfortable with their affection is Betty McAllister. I do feel badly for Betty, but I think Mary and James make such a happy pair so she might as well set her sights elsewhere. He is smitten with Mary. They only have another day together before she is off to normal school. Mary tells me that James is leaning towards taking over his father's store as he had originally *planned. He has not yet told his mother as he fears she will have a setback with her melancholia. Nevertheless, his heart is not in farming.*

The children enjoyed the wagon rides and consumed so much corn I worried they might be sick. By the time the fiddles started up for the barn dance, the little ones were exhausted and many of the adults left to take them home to bed. The younger people headed to the barn for some celebrating which would no doubt go on half the night.

Sunday, September 2, 1900

Mary has been busy packing her belongings into her valise and finishing her good-bye letter to James. Tomorrow morning she will board the train to Toronto. From there, her host family, the McGregors, will meet her at Union Station. Mary is such a confident girl and is excited to begin her adventure, but is a little uneasy leaving James. Ida and I have reassured her that if James truly loves her, he will be waiting for her upon her return. Also, she can write to him as much as she likes and the same for him. Often 'distance makes the heart grow fonder', we reminded her. Ida gave her a beautiful stationery travel set for her journey. It comes complete with a portable ink well, ink, a pen, paper and envelopes, all in a genuine leather binder bound with a ribbon. Mary has always been very close to Ida as she is the oldest grandchild at the farm, and they spent so much time together. Ida went well beyond her means when she purchased this lovely writing kit from the store, but I imagine Will gave her a discount knowing it was for Mary. It's Ida's way of encouraging her to write home regularly. If she doesn't use all the ink on

James, I'm sure she will drop us a note occasionally. She'll be keen to hear of the baby and be eager to receive mail from home as well. I told her to expect a telegraph on the big day. She's beside herself that she cannot be here for the birth, but life must go on.

Monday, September 3, 1900

I heard Mary up early when I was up to use the chamber pot. The clock had gonged five and I noticed the oil lamp on in the girls' room. Morten had planned to leave around 7:30 to drive her to the station in Carley. Mary emerged from the bedroom in her travelling dress, boots, and hat, with her valise ready to go. She peeked her head around our door. I lit the taper and we talked for some time. She was quite weepy, and I think the reality of leaving home was settling in.

"Momma, do you think I'm doing the right thing? What if I come back and James is no longer interested in me?" She asked anxiously.

"Don't be silly dear. He seems to care for you a great deal. Before you know it, it will be Christmas and you will be boarding the steam train for home to meet your new little sibling. I've no doubt that James will be there to meet you at the station. If he isn't, he has a fickle heart that could not be counted on in the long run anyway. Perhaps it's a good test."

"What if I don't like the family I'm living with?" The worries were starting to bubble to the surface.

"Mary dear, I'm sure they'll be fine people, but if they prove otherwise, we will arrange for a change. It is good that they have people your age who can help you get adjusted there." I reminded her.

"What if normal school is too hard?" and on it went for the better part of an hour. Little did she know, I too was filled with worry regarding the situation. I have never left home for an education as she is doing. The only time I left home was to marry Morten, whom I had known for years. What help was I in this progressive world of 1900.

By the time the morning gong struck, others were rousing. With the rising of the sun, the shadows of doubt receded as they often do in the light of day. Her nervous thoughts gradually evaporated as the sun rose over the horizon. As we prepared for the day and busied ourselves with chores, Mary had regained her happy spirits. We all gathered at the door as her valise was placed in the boot and she climbed aboard the buggy beside her father. We gave her a cheery yet weepy send off. James would be meeting them at the Carley station to wish her a final farewell.

It's exciting to think of my young daughter training to become a teacher. Imagine leaving home all by herself and boarding the train to the big city. I do hope she will be safe. I will eagerly await her first letter home so that I know she has arrived and is happily lodged with a kind family. You can be sure I've mentioned to Evelyn Barclay several times that my Mary will be attending normal school in Toronto and will come back a teacher!

I'm beginning to identify with that mother barn swallow. You teach them to fly, but in doing so it means they will soon fly away. It's an edgy joy to watch them take flight. By the time she returns at Christmas, I'll have delivered the baby and life can settle into some normalcy at last.

-62-

The clock is ticking. Vacation time is running out. What will it be? A life of impressive career accomplishment, material comfort and chronic stress or creative fulfillment, a relaxed pace, family time on an extremely tight, shoestring budget. Only one child will be talking to us regardless of what we choose. I feel my anxiety percolating. Decisions are tormenting. Let's face it, a $50,000 a year salary increase is very hard to walk away from. I'd be a fool, and irresponsible too. Although as Matt points out, the cost of living in the city is astronomical and you never get to relive these years. Who knows how much time we have left. Why not enjoy life while we can? My mind swings back and forth like a pendulum, unsure where to stop.

It was a restless night last night. Matt and I tossed and turned all night. I was relieved to see he was as torn as I was. However, I think deep down, we both knew what we had to do. I just hoped that what he felt we had to do and what I felt we had to do, were the same thing. What if it wasn't? The year ahead was starting off with a worrisome cloud. We agreed that we would each make up our own mind, sleep on it and go for an early morning walk on the beach and make our final decision together.

Before I knew it, Matt was rousing me.

"Amy, the sun is rising. Time to decide."

Groggily, I rolled out of bed and put on some shorts and a t-shirt. We headed to the beach without discussing what the other was thinking. It was like one of those renovation shows on television except with a lot more at stake. It wasn't about which house to choose but rather about which path to take through life and with the kids along for the ride.

As the sun appeared over the ocean, and the occasional early morning jogger passed us on the beach, Matt and I walked along and hashed out our choice. Difficult as it was, the decision was made. I'm just relieved we had both reached the same conclusion.

-63-

Only one of the kids took it well but Matt and I were happy with our choice. The first thing I had to do when I got home was call Sam.

"Hi Sam, we're back. Thank you for being so patient. How was your holiday?" I asked.

"Yes, we had unbelievable weather," I said.

"Well actually, I can't start." "...I'm not kidding." "... I know it's a lot of money." "... You have been extremely generous," I heard myself saying.

"I know you need me Sam, but I'm replaceable," I insisted.

"No I have not lost my mind. I've found my soul. The truth is, I don't want to return to the grind. I have grown to like this new pace." I closed my eyes and stuck to my script, trying hard not to waiver.

"Yes, I have thought about it. I don't need anymore time. I know, it is hard to believe."

"No, I can't afford to turn down an extra $50,000 a year, but I can't afford to take it either. The stress was too much, and it was destroying my life. I'd hardly see Matt and the kids. Some things are even more important than money. Ultra Luscious Relaxation is going to have to cope without me." I kept thinking about the kids, my health, my marriage and just how good I've felt this last little while.

It was one of the hardest calls I've ever made. At the time, I was a nervous wreck. It's hard to listen to my heart and not just my head. That has been part of my problem. I always make my decisions mainly with my head. What pays the most? What has the most status? What looks good? What would please others? What is the most responsible? What makes the most sense? I rarely ask myself, 'what do I really 'want' to do?' That is generally the last thing to consider. This decision required both my mind and my heart. No more commuting, no more competitive stress, no more sleepless nights, no more striving and worrying about things that don't really matter. Instead, I'll have time for the things that do matter, myself, Matt, my kids, my health, my friends, life. I'm going to take care of myself, exercise, eat right, rest. I'm going to create a lifestyle that doesn't require medication to cope. Instead, I'm going to do something creative that I will genuinely enjoy, like start that piano bar. This is a whole new path for me and it's terrifying. It may be the first time I ever actually achieve one of my new year's resolutions.

It takes tremendous courage to follow your heart, Amy. I think you will be very happy here. Welcome home!

Friday, September 7, 1900

Several days have passed since I last wrote, and we have just now received a long letter from Mary. What joy to see her handwriting upon the envelope. Morten rushed in after fetching the letters from the mailbox and we all gathered in the sitting room to hear her news.

"Dear Momma, Poppa, Grandma, Laura, Chuck and all my dear siblings... I wanted to write as soon

as I arrived to let you all know that I am safely in Toronto. The city is such a sight to see. There are horses and carriages everywhere and the streetcars are really something. They whiz along so quickly almost like a small train with antenna attached to a track above their head. It is part of the way of life in the hustle and bustle of the city. There are countless shops and grocers, and the people are all so finely dressed. It's difficult to imagine that such a hub of commerce exists only a day's train trip from our sleepy farmhouse. The train ride was so exciting. The conductor came and took my ticket as you said. I sat with some lovely people, and we shared the sandwiches you packed. The McGregors were there to meet me at the station. They seem like very nice people. Mr. McGregor is quite a bit older than the Mrs. He is tall and slim and stern looking with a long beard and she is almost the opposite... short, with plenty of smiles and laughter and very warm and kindly. They have three children who were all there to greet me as well. William is the oldest, a handsome young man of twenty, Rebecca is nineteen and looks very much like her mother. Charlotte is seventeen and very shy and reminds me so much of Nell. They are all so pleasant and welcoming. This evening William, Rebecca and Charlotte are going to show me around Toronto and introduce me to some of their friends. I hope you are all well and Momma do take care of yourself. Please give my regards to James and his family. I will write again tomorrow once I am settled in.
Love to all, Mary."

These darn cramps are back again – three weeks before my time. They are mild and no doubt they'll subside as they did before.

Thursday, September 13, 1900

It's the middle of the night now and the pains are getting worse and growing fiercer. They are still sporadic and have not yet gained that rhythmic momentum that is unmistakable. However, I fear the baby may soon be on the way. I have been pacing around the room for the better part of an hour and I can feel the familiar contraction, perhaps in its beginning phase. I will wait to rouse others as the household is asleep. Morten is snoring away like a locomotive, so exhausted from his days in the field. I hate to waken him if it's unnecessary as he needs his rest so badly. Oh heavens. There it is again. No one dares speak of the horrors of childbirth, but the searing pain and unrelenting contractions is something even the most devout mother could not overlook. How I wish for a cloth of ether at my nose in times like this. This speaks nothing of the risk that every expectant woman knows lies ahead of her but dares not discuss.

The pain is growing as overwhelming as my fears. Now is the time to wake Ida and Morten. Oh God, spare me this unrelenting pain....

Ida was by the bed instantly. The water was boiled, and the girls aligned themselves as planned. In the early hours of the morning, Isabel's screams of pain were heard throughout the farmhouse. It even started Gaby braying and the cattle mooing in edgy chorus. The screaming intensified as the sun rose and

continued throughout the day. Some of the neighbourhood women began to arrive to offer their support and a break for Ida and the girls. The delivery was getting dangerously long, the age-old sign of a difficult birth. The screaming went on well into the evening. Morten was beside himself with worry and Doug and Lyle cried, wanting to see their mother. They had great difficulty settling that night and remained up for much of it, until finally their eyes closed as they stretched out on the sitting room couch with an impromptu blanket tossed over them. Morten remained there with them, trying to stay alert throughout the night. Isabel's cries and moans continued well into the night when abruptly, around 3:00 a.m., everything fell suddenly silent. There was a nerve-racking, long-drawn-out pause, when not a sound was heard coming from the room. Then finally, another scream, a smaller more subdued, comforting scream of a little one, trying to catch her first breath. Morten awoke with a start from his drowsy state and semi exhaled and waited for more - his wife his first concern. Nothing came. Then the door opened. Out darted Zoe weary but wide eyed to announce the birth of her little sister Danielle and her mother's safe arrival through the draining journey. Morten wept. He grabbed Zoe in his arms and hugged her tightly. He was unspeakably relieved. He was terrified of losing Isabel and he feared it had come perilously close. Normally her deliveries were within a few hours. It was puzzling why it would be so different this time, but then these things are unpredictable. All he cared about was that all were safe and thriving. Morten smiled with relief and made his way to the room where his wife lay in a state of relieved exhaustion. He held her hand and kissed her forehead and little Danielle's as well. Isabel, delirious and drained, smiled weakly and held the baby to her breast. Soon afterwards, she

slipped into a deep sleep while she was cleaned up, the baby washed and swaddled and passed around the room to meet the women in her family. With the rising sun, little Danielle would meet her big brothers. It was a bittersweet arrival.

Friday, September 21, 1900

It has been at least a week since I have written but I have a good excuse. My little Danielle is here with me now and certainly a delight to have around. She is pink and plump and thankfully, she sleeps constantly. Lyle was such a restless little one and has now grown into a rambunctious toddler. Danielle, on the other hand, appears to want nothing more than to cuddle in next to me and continue to eat and rest, a girl after my own heart.

What a horrible ordeal that was. Thankfully, it is over, and my family is now complete. My job is done! Morten will not have another son to help but I did what I could. Lyle is rather unhappy having a baby sister, as older siblings often are. No one wants to feel the threat of replacement and Danielle, being such a cuddly little bundle, has stolen the heart of all who hold her.

Mary, having heard the news via telegram, has sent one back.

"Momma, Poppa, Little Danielle and All - Stop - Such happy news -Stop- Welcome to my baby sister Danielle - Stop -Can't wait to meet her -Stop- So glad all are well – Stop - Love and kisses Mary

The telegram was soon followed by a letter.

"Hi Momma and Poppa: I'm so excited and relieved to hear of the safe arrival of my newest sibling. Please give her a big kiss for me. I can't wait to see her at Christmas. Momma do take care of yourself and remember to rest a little.

I'm having a wonderful time here in Toronto. The McGregor family has been very welcoming, and Rebecca and I are becoming fast friends. William often tags along with us as he enjoys long walks and sightseeing. His lady friend, Lillian, is also attending normal school so no doubt I will meet her soon. This evening we are going to a sing along at the neighbours.

I have had several nice notes from James, and he tells me his mother is faring better.

Please remember to have a photograph taken of young Danielle and send it along so I can see who she looks like. Much love to all, Mary

-64-

Since arriving back from holidays, life has begun to feel different. Although my thoughts have returned to the mundane tasks of mid January, i.e. shovelling snow, scraping ice off the car and doing laundry, there's an undoubtable lightness I feel.

The one exciting thing in our immediate future, is Matt's 50th birthday. It's fast approaching at the end of the month and of course there will have to be a celebration. I will never forget last year, trying to make small talk with Dad as he lay on his back in the living room. There he was in bed, in his early nineties and nearing the end of his life, immobilized and being fed through a tube. I had told him about Matt's impending birthday crisis re: turning the big **5–0** in the coming year. "Ah to be 50 again," he said wistfully with a tear in his eye.

While planning for the big event, I remembered that collection of recipes from yesteryear that we found in the attic this past summer. Then I got the idea of making Matt a 'turn of the century' meal for his 'turn of the half century birthday'. I recruited Megan as she loves to cook and I figured it would be a great mother/daughter bonding afternoon, in which we could rebuild our sometimes tumultuous relationship. Megan and I poured through the old recipes and came across some fascinating choices. We both agreed we would like to start with a nice soup. I'm not much of a cook, but how hard could it be? You just follow the instructions. We were to begin with melting 2 tablespoons of salt pork into a skillet. Oh oh, we were stumped. What is salt pork? Then it said, cook until translucent. What does that mean? Megan looked it up on her phone. Add 3 tablespoons of shallots. I think a shallot is some kind of onion. Do we have any of those in the fridge? Megan and I were starting to get overwhelmed, and we were only on the fourth instruction. Then... 1 quart of hot stock from a country cured ham. How much is a quart in litres, and do I need to buy a cured ham so I can drain some hot stock from it? Do they sell those at the corner store? My goodness, by this point we were only partly through the first recipe, and we were starting to feel impatient. Add 3 well beaten egg yolks (do they come apart?), 2 tablespoons finely chopped parsley, 1 cup sautéed, coarsely chopped mushrooms... Now I'm starting to get annoyed. Look, I don't have all day. Maybe we should just dump in a tin of minestrone soup and move on to the next dish. We agreed. Let's pick something easier.

We had decided on something from the 'game section', thinking maybe a nice chicken breast. We were shocked and appalled to find this cookbook, dating back to the early

1800's, had recipes for bear and raccoon. At that point, Megan suggested we just order in. NO, I insisted. We can do this. If they did this back then on a woodstove with cast iron skillets surely we can do it today with an electric oven and stove and fine, stainless steel cookware. How about this chicken dish? We flipped past some of the horrific diagrams of how to behead, pluck, cut up, stuff and truss a bird... and went directly to the recipe. 'Simmer the chicken about 15 minutes and remove scum'. That doesn't sound good as we convulsed in laughter. Next. 'Continue to simmer uncovered until the chicken is tender, two hours or more'.

"Get out. That's insane. Do you think we could throw it in the microwave?" I asked exasperated.

"Let's order takeout." Megan suggested looking at the clock on the stove.

The remainder of the page required intense dicing and multiple herbs, most of which I had never heard of and certainly didn't grow in my garden. 'When the butter reaches the point of fragrance, add the floured chicken.'

"Is that a joke?" Megan was getting restless. Her cell phone was continuing to vibrate incessantly.

It was hard to stay focussed on this intense project. Perhaps this was a bad idea.

"Do you want to just bake him the cookie recipe?" I suggested.

For once we both agreed, and we immediately turned to the oatmeal cookie page.

1 cup butter, 1 cup brown sugar, ½ tsp salt, ½ tsp vanilla, 1 tsp soda dissolved in ¼ cup of warm water, 1 ¾ cups of each flour and rolled oats. Roll these into balls, press with a fork and bake.

We could do that. They turned out to be unbelievable. We consumed most of them before they made it to the cookie tin. Immediately, we made another batch and renamed them 'Turn of the Century Oatmeal Cookies'. That is the full end product of our day in the kitchen, aside from a great deal of mess and a sink full of dirty pots. Matt will love them.

Friday, September 28, 1900

At only two weeks, Danielle is a robust, contented little baby and has lovely green eyes like her father. I, however, seem to be having a little challenge finding my energy and the pain in my lower abdomen is unusually stubborn. Ida reassures me it's not uncommon post-delivery although she suggested we have the midwife come in case of infection. I'm supposed to get plenty of rest. How do you do that with eight children and a husband?

We've had several letters from Mary, and she is enthralled with normal school and her adventures in Toronto. Apparently, Rebecca, William and herself make quite a trio. She is not taken with William's lady friend, Lillian and believes she will be far too strict a teacher. Mary can't seem to say enough nice things about the McGregors. Apparently, Mrs. McGregor is a wonderful cook, and the chores are much lighter as they only have three children. Mary and Rebecca frequently walk along King St. to see all the shops. I suppose our lumber town of Orillia does not hold the same fascination for young people today. When I was a girl, not many in Jarratt Corners could afford to board a steam engine to go to the big city on the Northern Railway. I have been to Toronto once.

Apparently, Toronto has grown into quite a sizeable city since then.

Fall fair season is upon us. Chuck has the most tremendous size pumpkin. We all believe he will win a ribbon. Zoe insists on taking Gaby, although I can't imagine any ribbon is in store there except maybe 'most stubborn' or 'biggest ears' or 'most lovable' animal. Morten will be entering a few chickens that he feels are impressive and Ida has been baking pies. No doubt, she will win. Morten's best pig was lost in the fire. The girls will enter some baking contributions and Carrie will submit a shawl she knit. They are all encouraging me to put Danielle in the baby competition, but I feel she is too young to attend a fair, even though she looks adorable in her little pink dress and bonnet that Rose made her.

Oh my, the pain is ruthless when it strikes, and I seem to have developed a little chill. I really look forward to putting this behind me. I would like to take Danielle down the road in Martha Findlay's pram and show her off to the neighbours. However, I'm not up to it yet. In the meantime, we have had many visitors to see her.

Sunday, October 7, 1900

A whole week has passed. Morten is threatening to call the doctor, but I feel that is quite unnecessary and a wasted expense. This will pass. I attended church this morning and Reverend Mactavish offered a prayer of thanksgiving for bringing both Danielle and me safely through the journey. I'm glad the christening is a few weeks off as it will give me time to regain my strength. I haven't been totally forthright with Morten about the pain. It doesn't *seem to be subsiding. In fact, I fear it's growing worse. I'm starting to feel uneasy about this. I sleep far too much, I am drained of energy, I have a constant pain in my side and I feel warm. Something isn't right. Perhaps I should be seen by the doctor. I hate to add that expense to Morten's burden, especially after losing the barn in the summer, so I try to take my mind off it.*

Mary has been writing frequently. She is thoroughly enjoying normal school and talks constantly of Rebecca and William. Rebecca and Mary have apparently been a support to him when Lillian speaks to him in an abrupt tone.

Rose came for a visit today. Patrick insisted he wait in the carriage. Rose expressed great concern that my colour doesn't look good. When we were alone and she was holding Danielle, I confessed to her the pain has been excruciating. She insisted it was time to call Dr. Moffat. I begged her to leave it another day and promised if it didn't improve, I would let Morten know. She agreed but was adamant it could not go beyond that, or she would tell Morten herself. She would check on me daily from now on, regardless of what Patrick said. I don't want her putting herself at risk for this annoying situation. I pray it will subside in the next day as the degree of pain is reminiscent of childbirth.

While we took our tea on the porch today, Laura and Chuck confessed to Morten the cause of the barn fire. Morten was dumbfounded to hear his sister disclose the truth. He didn't say much but I know he felt hurt by their omission. Laura wept as she told him. Chuck confessed his shame but explained he worried Morten might deny him Laura's hand in marriage if the truth were known. I hope this doesn't change things. I must never tell Morten that I knew of it. Sometimes men don't understand how important it is for a woman to find a husband and have a family and that they aren't prepared to let much come between that. I'm sorry Morten is feeling hurt, but I'm glad the two have wed despite it. I do hope they will not be too late to have a family.

Tuesday, October 9, 1900

When I awoke, Rose was sitting beside me holding my hand. I gave a start and asked what time it was? Had the clock gonged six? Had I missed Henry's wake up call? Why was she here at this early hour? Was she okay? Had Morten gone to the fair with the girls?

Relax Issy, she told me. It is almost three p.m. and you have greatly overslept. Morten is very worried about you and has sent for the doctor. I am just trying to keep your fever down.

She put another cold cloth on my head and told me to lie back. It was going to be all right. Then Ida walked into the room and started mumbling to her. I think it was Ida, I couldn't really see. My God, the pain has become unspeakable. Dr. Moffat appeared, looking concerned and placed a cloth over my face. That is all I remember.

I woke up screaming for Morten and then I realized he was right beside me weeping. "What is going on? Where am I?" I could hear the baby crying but I couldn't get to her. Is this a dream? "What is happening?" I demanded with a fraction of my voice.

It was a terrible night. The worst in my whole life. Worse even than the delivery. For a moment, I thought I was having another baby, but it felt different. Dr. Moffat was there, Morten, Ida and Rose. I woke, slept, woke, slept, and screamed. The *cloth was applied, and I don't remember what happened next.*

That was two days ago. Dr. Moffat explained that I have quite a nasty infection that he is trying to control. He has treated it with a salve that should help but I am to try to rest.

What about Danielle? Where is she? Who is taking care of her?

"Laura and Chuck have moved into Chuck's old room and Laura is tending to Danielle's needs until you feel stronger," Dr. Moffat explained. "You need your rest, Isabel. Danielle is in good hands. It is good practice for them anyway," he said reassuringly. Morten appeared as if from nowhere and leaned over the bed.

"Issy, the main thing is that you get better. Danielle is doing just fine with Laura and Zoe is helping."

"What about the pickling? I must help Ida with the pickling," I insisted weakly.

"Don't be silly. The girls can help with that." I could hear Lyle and Doug crying and arguing to get into the room to see me. They were permitted but with strict orders not to climb on the bed. Doug let out quite a start when he saw me and refused to come near me. I must look a sight. Perhaps I am very gaunt and pale as only a four-year-old's expression can tell me so honestly.

When he finally came to me, he was convulsing in tears. I reassured him I would be okay and that soon we would go for a walk and pick some pumpkins. However, my body ached, and I wondered how I would ever get out of this bed. What is going on? Could it be that I may never get up? Even the doctor has not reassured me I will recover. I am really getting scared now.

Thursday, 1900

I am propped up in bed but feeling extremely weak. In fact, I don't think I will be able to hold this pen for long today. It is taking everything in me to write this. Rose has just brought Danielle in and she helped me to hold her. It felt so good to feel her little warm body snuggle into me and root around for her mother. I was so profoundly sad that I couldn't produce any milk. Maybe I will never be able to provide for her needs. Am I going to die? Oh, I must stop all this weeping. Perhaps it is just my troubled thoughts getting the better of me.

Rose read me a letter from Mary:

"Momma, I have recently learned how sick you have become after Danielle's arrival. Poppa tells me you are quite out of sorts. I have spoken with the principal here and requested some time away to come and see you. He has been very understanding and assured me that I may do whatever I think best without repercussions to my schooling. Mr. McGregor has inquired about the train schedule, and I am planning to leave on the next one going north. I eagerly await word of your progress. Rebecca has been so helpful during this trying time and William has been such a supportive ear. He too feels I should return to you in your hour of need.

I have had many lengthy letters from James. He has diligently kept me posted on the news from home. He will bring his carriage to meet me at the train.

I hope you are feeling better mother, and that little Danielle is holding up well too. I hear Laura and Chuck have become a doting aunt and uncle and are taking the best care of her until you are better.

I cannot wait to see you and hug you. Until then, Your loving Mary. Xo

Oh, I do not want this illness to jeopardize her time away at school. What terrible timing. I must get better. How did this happen? I must rest now.

1900

I have no idea what time it is or what day it is even. The room is bright so it must be daytime. I can see a blur of orange and red leaves on the branch outside my window. It must be autumn. I feel weaker and weaker each time I open my eyes. Zoe is sitting with me and saying something to me. I can't quite hear her, but I manage a smile. She holds my hand and I notice her tears as she sings to me. How sweet. My sweet Zoe. Why isn't she at school? No, it's not Zoe, I think it is Mary……

I sat up in bed again today but only briefly. Mary has gone to fetch me tea. It takes so much out of me just to write in this little diary. I must write how much I love them in case I don't come through this. I hear the family coming up the stairs now towards me and I will lay down my pen and rest. I love it when they surround me. Tomorrow I will write about how much I love them all.

-65-

That was the last entry. I searched the back pages of the journal... nothing. Surely, she didn't die. How could she die? Why am I such a wreck, it was almost 120 years ago. Poor

Morten! And all those children. How will they ever cope? What will happen to cuddly, little Danielle without her mother? The whole thing just seems so unfair. She never wanted an eighth child to begin with.

The tears trickled down my cheeks. Then it dawned on me, some of Isabel's descendants might still live nearby. Why hadn't I thought of this before? Maybe I could look them up and return the diary to her family. I ran the idea by Matt, and he thought it sounded like a viable plan. But how would I find them? They might go by a different last name by this point in the family line.

I talked to the kids about my idea. To my surprise, they were quite intrigued. Tyler immediately flipped on his computer and began tracing her ancestry on-line. It wasn't long before we were able to find the daughter of cuddly little Danielle Huntly. According to her family tree, her name was Sarah Fairmount. She was still living and almost 93 years old. When he looked her up on Canada 411 we were astounded when it listed our farmhouse as her address. How weird. Despite the initial moments of confusion, some clarity eventually set in. Of course, the elderly woman we rent from, who has moved to the retirement home is Isabel's granddaughter. I hadn't thought of that before since her last name wasn't Huntly.

Now I was determined to get the diary to her. Afterall, it belonged to the house and therefore to her. It was her grandmother's diary. I could call the retirement home and see if she would be willing to meet with us, especially since we are living in her old house.

A day later, I got a call back from the home. She would definitely like us to come and see her.

The day came and the whole family was in the car on route to meet Sarah Fairmount. They were in various states of interest and disinterest. Megan needed a ride to town so tagged along, prior to meeting her new friends at the local mall. Tyler being a bit of a historian, was actually rather interested to meet Isabel's granddaughter, given how I had given them all daily updates from her diary. Matt was very keen.

-66-

I chewed my fingernails as we arrived at the retirement home. A staff member buzzed Sarah's room to let her know we had arrived. We crowded into the elevator with all our historical remnants in tow: the diary, the portrait, the bibles.

Eager with anticipation, we arrived at Sarah's door. It was slightly ajar, and we could see an elderly woman seated in a chair. She was fixated on a sparrow picking seeds off a birdfeeder outside her window. Slowly she turned as we knocked. She looked surprisingly spry for 93. Her warm smile welcomed us in. Immediately I felt like I knew this woman, although we had never met. I knew intimate details about her mother's birth, her grandmother's death shortly afterward, and the childhood of her aunts and uncles. I knew every room of her family home and have found multiple treasures that really belong to her. Her eyes twinkled as she took my hand in hers and told me how glad she was to meet us. After all this time reading the diary, I couldn't believe I was actually meeting Isabel's granddaughter. I wondered if she knew the story of her mother's infancy and what her grandmother's feelings were about having her mother in the first place.

I'm so pleased you will continue living in the old family homestead. That is just wonderful that someone will keep it on," she said.

"It's a great old home and we are so pleased to be there. This is my husband Matt and these are our children Tyler and Megan." The kids smiled politely and said hello. It is astonishing how well they clean up when you least expect it. Matt commented on her bird feeder and asked her all about the various birds it attracted. This struck an endearing chord for her as she talked all about her chickadees, nuthatches and sparrows.

She seemed very kindly, much as I would have imagined Isabel herself. We talked at length of birds and several mutual topics of interest. Then we got down to the reason for our visit. I wondered if she might be a little angry at me for reading her grandmother's diary, but she wasn't. In fact, she appeared excited to hear of the discoveries about her family history and happy to have visitors as well.

"Tell me about what you've found," she implored. "I never met my grandmother, nor did my mother for that matter. She died when Mother was just an infant. My mother, Danielle, was raised by her Aunt Laura and Uncle Chuck, because her own father was so busy with the farm and had just lost his wife. Laura and Chuck were like grandparents to me. Grandpa Chuck was such a wonderful man. Grandma Laura died when I was only eight, so I do not remember her well. All I remember is that she used to play the piano and we would all sing along. She was rather quiet, but she loved to bake and of course my little sister and I loved to eat. I remember playing at Grandpa Morten's farm as a child. My mother was very close with him, and we spent a lot of time there. It wasn't until Chuck died, that my husband and I moved in there."

It was mesmerizing to hear about these people from a different vantage point.

"I grew up just behind their farm, in a small house on the next concession. I was over at the farm all the time as my 'grandmother' Laura had grown up there as a child herself. The old place holds a lot of memories for me. I'm so glad that a nice family like yourselves have moved into it."

I told her how I had found Isabel's diary in the cellar behind a forgotten jar of pickles. She laughed and said she couldn't believe it had been there all these years.

I explained that during this past year, I read the diary. I explained that I had not done it to pry but because it told a fascinating story that helped me better appreciate the setting where I lived. It brought the old farmhouse to life in a way I never dreamt possible. It connected me with a history and a way of life that might otherwise dissolve into the past. She was fascinated as I described her grandparents, aunts and uncles living in such compact quarters, stories she had no doubt heard before. I asked her about her relatives, few of whom she could remember well. She did however remember her Uncle Lyle who was a farmer all his life right there where we lived. She recalled his beautiful, sprawling gardens, his calm ways with the cattle and the twinkle in his eye when you made him laugh. He was a wonderful man, so kind-hearted and easy going and he had a great sense of humour. She remembered Aunt Zoe well too. Aunt Zoe was her mother's closest sister, almost like a second mother to her own mother Danielle. Aunt Zoe and her husband lived in the town of Jarratt Corners. The big family joke was that being the second youngest of six girls, the only dowry Aunt Zoe had when she married was an old donkey named Gaby, whom she loved dearly and took with her to the marriage. That suited Aunt Zoe well because she loved horses and animals of all kinds. Sarah explained that she never knew her Uncle Doug as he was killed in the First World War, before she was born.

She had memories stretching back over 90 years of her family, the house and the barn. It was a memorable afternoon with Sarah. She appreciated our visit a great deal. She loved the family portrait and identified some of the relatives she could remember. She was very taken with the family bibles and the inscriptions in the front. At the end of our visit, I placed Isabel's diary in her hands. I felt that Isabel would want it to be passed along to her granddaughter and to stay in the family, especially given that so much of it was about Isabel's pregnancy with Sarah's mother Danielle. Sarah was very moved to receive the diary, even though she had to wait

93 long years to learn of its details. She held it a long time as though cradling a treasure. Her eyes were moist and wistful while she listened to the stories. She felt badly that she wasn't able to answer so many of my questions about her long-deceased relatives but suggested we take a look in the churchyard as all the dates and names would be on the stones.

Of course. The churchyard. Why hadn't I thought of that? We assured her we would do that. She thanked us profusely for the diary, the bibles, the family portrait and all the other memorabilia we had left for her. We each gave her a hug and told her how nice it was to finally meet her. Matt refilled her birdfeeder with seeds before we departed and promised to visit again. It was a fascinating afternoon.

-67-

Following our visit, we decided to take a drive to the cemetery by the old Presbyterian Church, only a few kilometers up the road from where we now live. Mossy Stonecrop Trail had sadly since been paved and was now easily passable by SUV. There was no sign of wild roses anywhere however, there were a number of hydro poles and a cell tower. As we pulled up to the little, ivy- covered church we couldn't detect any indication of a horse shed ever having been there. The church was clearly still being used as there was a sign announcing the time of the service on Sunday and the Reverend who would be presiding. Sadly, it was not Rev. Mactavish. We parked the car and walked past the fellowship room jutting out the side. This must have been where Laura and Chuck married, and where the receptions for Daniel and Nell's funerals took place, many years ago. We made our way to the churchyard on this beautiful May afternoon. There was clearly someone keeping the grounds as the grass was nicely cut and there were flowers on a few of the graves. We let ourselves in through the black metal gate and began examining the stones. There was a mixture of newer stones in amidst the well-aged ones. On some, the engraving had become just a fuzzy indent, almost impossible to make out what it once said years ago. We walked along reading the names but didn't see much we recognized. Then suddenly Tyler hollered from several metres away.

"Here's something, 'Moffat'," he bellowed excitedly! "Wasn't there a Dr. Moffat?"

"Really?" I called, racing over excitedly.

There was a big grey stone with 'Moffat' carved on top. It listed countless Moffats in order of age. Among them we found Dr. Andrew Moffat, born 1861 – died 1912 and his wife Margaret, born 1864 - died 1913 along with their infant daughter Margaret Jr., died 1889 at 2 days old. I found myself taken aback. I never knew they had lost a child. How hard it must have been to attend to the aftermath of difficult deliveries like Isabel's. They had never mentioned that.

It wasn't long before Megan came across the Findlay stone. "Look Mom isn't this the stone of the 'handsome', Tom Findlay," she joked.

She was absolutely right. Again, there were many names to sift through, but there was Martha Findlay. Wow, she lived to a ripe old age of 96 but I see her husband died years before. And look, Tom Findlay, blacksmith and his wife Zoe Huntly Findlay. So little Zoe snagged the cute guy from down the road. I can't imagine Sadie and Carrie were pleased with that turn of events. According to the stone, Zoe and Tom had four children, only one of whom died in childhood.

Oh my goodness, "Barclay", here lies Evelyn Barclay and her husband Robert. It appears her oldest son never married, as he is buried here as well, age 42, a bachelor. The rest was too faded to read.

We wandered on. Next, we found the Reilly Stone. Rose Sinclair Reilly died suddenly on March 18, 1902 – in her 41st year. Also buried here are Elizabeth and her husband Michael, Robert and his wife Patricia and three of their seven children. Patrick D. Reilly born 1863 and died 1936. His second wife of only two years Ruth (1887), predeceased him in her 34th year (1921). That cradle robber. He was 24 years older than her. Clearly old enough to be her father. However, more importantly how did Rose die suddenly? Did he do something to her? How is it that two of his wives died in the prime of their lives? I never liked that guy and I like him even less now.

Eventually, I stumbled upon the MacNally stone, recalling that James' grandparents' farm was out this way. I scanned down, looking for familiar names. Excitedly, Matt pointed out Alice MacNally born 1867 died suddenly of an accident in 1901. Matt inquired, "wasn't she the one who was so depressed all the time?" I wondered to myself if she took her own life in the end.

Matt exclaimed, "Look here is her son James MacNally died 1915 (due to injuries sustained from the Great War) and his wife Betty McAllister MacNally died 1943 and 4 children listed, one having died in early infancy, and one being born in 1915 shortly after James' death. So Betty got him in the end. Whatever happened to the promise ring he gave Mary Huntly?"

As we wandered along in pensive moods, getting some unexpected answers to how their lives turned out, we finally found it: the Huntly stone. There it was, on the far side of the churchyard, underneath a big, stately maple tree as though it had been patiently waiting to be discovered. It was dark grey in colour and had a little lamb carved into the top of it. I half expected to find a red ribbon still blowing in the breeze. I stood there in awe as though discovering a lost treasure. Here they were! All the names I had read about in Isabel's diary over this past year ... right beneath my feet. There was Daniel and Nell, Ida, Morten, Laura & Chuck, Carrie, Sadie, Doug, Lyle and Mary. Mary and her husband ... William McGregor of Toronto.

Last, but not least, was Isabel Huntly, born 1861 - died 1900, from complications of childbirth. Mother of 8 children. That is all it said. It seemed so limited to sum up her rich life.

As I leave the cemetery with my husband and kids, I realize that I finally learned the ending that Isabel was never able to finish. They all died. I realize that the old clock is the only one still ticking, but the ending doesn't change. In the end, we all die. There is lots of variation about when and how, but no one can stop the clock from ticking. Things are always changing, some for the better some for the worse. That is life. We can't always choose whether things change but sometimes we can choose how we change.

Maybe I will start a diary of my own and hide it behind our wine rack for some unsuspecting new homeowner to find in years to come. Maybe I will plant some memorial trees to mark our lives and remind future generations that we were once here.

Now is our time. I am glad we moved to this old farmhouse. I have felt fully alive here and I have learned something about history and life. As we passed over the graves on our way to the gate, I found myself filled with a fresh appreciation to be on this side of the sod. ("Ah to be 46 again!") In the scheme of things, we're not here for very long. It makes me wonder what we want to leave the generations that follow us, and how we want to be remembered. Afterall, the clock keeps ticking even though we don't. We are only a brief link in a long and hopefully continuing chain.

THE END.

Acknowledgements

A heartfelt thanks to my late grandmother. She was the inspiration for this novel. It was always fascinating visiting her in her homestead and hearing what life was like when she was a girl.

My deep gratitude to my most faithful editors -Fred, Lois, Jay, Jennie and Murray, Olivia Podmore, Log McQuaig, Jane Christmas and many others who read, and re-read this book too many times to count.

In particular, an enormous thank you to my husband Fred whose support and confidence in me has been boundless. How many late dinners and quiet evenings he endured as I was overly engrossed in writing my novel. My son Jay produced no end of creative ideas and was a tremendous role model as an author himself. Jennie, daughter, tech support and social media guide, was always at my side when I started swearing at my computer because it wouldn't behave as expected. My youngest son Murray was wonderful with his keen eye for editing and diplomatically telling me what had to go. Olivia Podmore was an invaluable magnifying glass when it came to detecting even the smallest errors. Thanks also to Timber and Millie for their constant patience. I will finally take you for a walk now.

I am indebted to the Orillia Public Library Local History Room (Orilliana Collection), the Orillia Museum of Art and History, the Coldwater Canadiana Heritage Museum and the Simcoe County Museum. I have spent many hours over the years, pouring through your incredible collections.

Thanks also to Cathy Johnston Walton, Author of Vanishing Barns (2019), for the pictures of barn construction on pages 278 & 279, as well as the photo of the horse and buggy on page 233 (photo courtesy of Dorothy C. Giffen).

The picture of the woman reading in a lawn chair on the front cover, was purchased from Alamy Limited Stock Photography Company.

The other photographs throughout this book are random pictures I have been given over the years from various relatives and friends.

This book is not intended to be a factual account of Orillia and area in 1900. Much imagination was used regarding the history of the area. Unfortunately, no diary was every found in the cellar.

And....

Many thanks to you for reading Behind the Pickle Jar. I hope you enjoyed it!